the
'idiot spy'
(the series)
book twelve

all about the trillions

c. benjamin lattimore

all about the trillions
Published: December 2025
Printed in the United States of America
ISBN: 979-8-9889509-2-9

DISCLAIMER: This is a work of fiction. Names, characters, businesses,
places, events, and incidents are either the products of the author's
imagination or used in a fictitious manner. Any resemblance to actual
people, living or dead, or actual events is purely coincidental.

a lattidreamer™ publication
© C. Benjamin Lattimore, 2025

to Marisa, my number 1 everything!
Thanks again for your dedication to all my
endeavors. I appreciate all that you do!

ACKNOWLEDGEMENTS

to my children, Christopher, Monica, and Courtney—my grandchildren, Isaiah, and Desmond. A heartfelt expression of love to my younger brother, Darryl Andre, and my nieces and nephews. Yet again, again, and again, esteem regards to my devoted friends, Maurice E. Cheeks and Reginald W. Wilkes.

lots of love ethereally to the Lattimore clan, Walthro Male, Mary Alice, Barbara Ann, Walter Eugene, and Mary Elizabeth, my newest guardian angel. To my friends, Gordon Gant, Joseph Bongiavanni II, Monique Gorham, Rahsaan Stevens, Mrs. Marjorie C. Cheeks, and Richard 'Dickie' Hood.

CHAPTER ONE

The Beckmire clan spent the last 18 months in their individual homes in Alabama after returning from Switzerland with a bundle of joy. Those who didn't have a place to live were provided space among the group and commissioned the construction of a home for themselves and their families. No announced or unannounced termination attempts were made against the group and everyone enjoyed being in one place and not always having to look over their shoulders for the next threat.

Neither Courtney nor the Sarge had heard anything related to proof of life or a request for funds from their wayward child and they reluctantly believed that he had met his demise as a result of attempting to play the unscrupulous and unnatural game of assassinating his parents and everyone else that made up their clan. Marcelus, the Sarge, and Courtney's new son/grandson was growing and maturing well. Rarely did he cry, smiling seemed to be his passion.

Courtney said to Monica on one occasion, "Do you remember when you asked me if I was too old to go down that road? Anyway, it's the best damn thing that could have happened to me and Ben. I mean my son tried to kill us, all while asking me for money. He fathered Marcelus but prior to, told the mother to get rid of his seed. Little could he have imagined that his seed is now my son/grandson, and he alone stands to inherit a shit load of money with the proviso that not one red cent will go to the benefit of my adult son, his father, if he is still alive."

Monica asked, "Why are you focusing on negative stuff? I thought you had moved on from wondering about your son who tried to kill us all. After all, from what I heard, it appears as though he got more than he bargained for. I'm happy for you and Ben and I must admit I was initially concerned about the impetuousness of the decision to adopt, but after seeing the glow and enthusiasm from you guys, I am 100 percent convinced that you guys are doing the right thing."

Courtney hugged Monica and said, "Girl, I'm still tired at the end of the day because he requires a lot of attention, or perhaps I overindulge him. Not sure which one is at play at this moment and that Ben Beckmire just won't put him down. He is always hugging, kissing, playing, and laughing with the child. Marcelus is a God send. Ben and I are extremely happy and lucky. Anyway, what's going on with you guys? Oh, and whose turn is it to provide dinner on Friday and Saturday?"

Monica indicated that she would have to check.

# # #

Months later, kicking and screaming on the way to the hospital, Ayesha signed to all who were in attendance, "I will not have this child unless I am married."

Michael vehemently signed, "I asked you to make the arrangements and to let me know when things were going to happen. I even suggested a date, time, place, and I spoke to Clyde and asked him if he would perform the ceremony. I think sometimes what you sign, and my replies are completely misinterpreted. Do you incorporate slang in your signing?"

Courtney interrupted their signing and signed time out. She then signed, "People, get your shit together!"

To Ayesha, she signed, "You don't control nature and how things occur."

She then turned to Michael and signed, "Get your mess in order and be prepared to become a father, one of the most important roles you will every play in life."

After everyone had calmed down, Ayesha began to cry and signed, "I don't want to be like my mother, having babies and barely in a relationship."

Michael hugged her and replied, "I don't know your mother, but I can assure you that we will be married as soon as possible. I'm praying that there is a person of the cloth at the hospital that will perform the ceremony unofficially until we can stand at the altar and swear our allegiance to each other. Listen, I love you more than life and our baby is going to have his father right there watching every step that he or she takes. By the way, do you know the gender?"

Ayesha began to cry harder and signed, "This is the first time you asked me about our baby's gender."

Michael exclaimed, "Time out! I really don't care about gender. I just want to be a father. I've been reading about being a parent and it's a job that I'm prepared to handle."

Courtney continued to stroke Ayesha's head and eventually she stopped crying. She signed, "I thought you weren't interested in me or our child. You seemed so aloof lately."

Michael looked at her, then at Courtney and signed, "Everyone depends on me, whether they know it or not. Listen, after you've had the baby, I'm going to show you how much I am prepared to help. I've read books, seen an actual birth online and I've studied the possible mood swings after delivery. Baby, I am here for you and our child. You'll see and I'll show you the materials I have secretly been reading to prepare to be a father."

Ayesha asked, "Why secretly?"

Michaels signed, "Because when I get in, you're asleep and I don't want to wake you up. Nothing more than that. Ayesha, I love you. Once again, more than life. Do you remember when the Carbon Factor was detonated, I came back to that house because of you and those children. Lady, whether you like it or not, I am here for the duration."

Jilkes said to John Lee, "I'm having a lot of pain in my right knee. I can barely walk sometimes. Today it's hurting like hell."

John Lee replied, "You need to ask the Doc to prescribe you some of that Embrel or that Humira drug. I be thinking you done got bit by that rheumatoid bug?"

"What the hell is that bug you're talking about and how come your country ass knows so much about those drugs?" Jilkes asked.

"I be taking a shot once a month to help me with my joint pain. Sometimes it be like being stung by a thousand bees at the same time in different places. My misses can't touch me, and the children know to give Daddy his space when I be having that problem."

Jilkes asked, "How come I didn't know about that issue?"

"Mr. Jilkes, you don't need to know when I have to pass gas and a few other things that I do. I be loving you, but sometimes I just don't like sharing things about what hurts me. You know we've been shot, and Lord knows what kind of germs we done picked up over there in that jungle. Shit just be happening to me and I know it's from all of the mess we be doing."

"Listen my brother from another mother and I'm only going to say this once, if you keep secrets, then so will I and then before you know it, we'll be addressing each other in a formal manner. I have cut leeches from your ass, burned spiders, ticks, lice off your back, picked shit out of your head that I didn't know what it was, and I have held you in my arms like a baby. Don't fuck around with me on this one. We are getting to the point where we will die naturally, or someone will kill us off. Am I clear?"

John Lee, crying his eyes out, said, "I just sometimes think that you don't be wanting to hear drama from me and therefore, I just bury my issues in my pocket because I don't want to bother you with my problems."

"Stop this shit right now!" Jilkes exclaimed. "I have a few other issues that I haven't shared with you, but I'm saying that we can't get this far in life, and I mean at the threshold and begin to not involve each other in our independent issues. I love you as much as I love my wife, of course in a different manner and ever since we had that defining fight in basecamp, my life has centered around you. Now, I've said it, and I won't repeat it. You are me and I am you, and we must never build false channels between us as a result of some health issue. Damn it, we are getting to that point of no return. Between being shot, stabbed, gassed, and bad choices, we are lucky to be around to make sure that the rest of our group survives. It's you and me that makes this ship right. You and me!"

CHAPTER TWO

Deep in the shadows of an alternate world, malevolent forces were congregating and conversing about the reinstatement, control of and the final push to obliterate the Beckmire clan, seize it's fortune, eliminate all of the parasites that wield power in the most powerful institution in the world, and restore its rightful and anointed potentate. The events to occur, the mayhem that would materialize, the carnage that would be left, all signaled Armageddon!

From the bowels of hell, it seemed as though a new liaison was spurned by all that was evil and vengeful. The missing pontiff, who was never found, somehow was resurrected from the bottomless pit that he commanded and was now prepared to do battle with all who stood against his principles, missions and his undeniable need to capture, convert and mentally seduce the only person that could provide him with pure love, unmitigated power, and control of all that is mankind.

Notwithstanding the unnatural obsessions of the ex-pontiff with Ms. Beatrice, when Sister Mary saw a look-a-like in a Mexico City bar, she was certain that the woman was the key to solving her own problems. Sister Mary began to fast track the development of the plan for the eventual reemergence of the ex-pope and to be by his side. His desire and her schemes and the importance of Ms. Beatrice to their grand plan were seemingly flawless.

Ms. Beatrice was a developing sorceress whose powers only the citizens from Hades, the ex-pope, Sister Mary, and Ms. Viola were aware of. Her current status was between good and evil, with evil having the most despicable minds working to corrupt and capture her unproven abilities. Ms. Viola knew that her great grandbaby had special talents, but she could never fathom that she was to become a high priestess. Ms. Beatrice was surrounded by love, family, faith, commitment, community and sometimes violence and death. The mistake that some would make is that all who considered her a powerful witch because of her environment, were presented with false impressions and images. The fact of the matter was that Ms. Beatrice was maturing into a dominant and living Angel.

Nothing had really changed from the first attempt to conscript Ms. Beatrice. A ruse was established, a medium was identified, and the target or the conscription attempt was obvious. The ex-pope's concubine, Jelani's, and Ben Jr.'s mother, was allegedly killed by the ex-pope's stealthy hit team. She was shot with counterfeit bullets that displayed blood splatter and false wounds. To ensure that she was dead, Zanthius shot her twice in the head. Her body-double/look-a-like was one in a million, in that she looked like Helga, acted like her, and was provided key words that only Helga would have known to use with 'the idiot spy'."

The underground pope was adamant about the permanent disappearance of his concubine, Helga Spengatsenburg/Sister Mary, because of her childbearing, known fornication with others and obvious involvement in all kinds of mayhem at his direction. Her ex-employer often stated, "Your footprint is too visible to the world. Therefore, I am mandating that in order to continue in your role, a complete and bloody vision of your demise has to be implemented and executed with all involved believing that it is your death."

Without hesitation, Helga knew that the only person she had to convince was 'the idiot spy'."

During a trip to Mexico City, on a mission sanctioned by the ex-pope, Helga sat at the bar in a restaurant and watched what appeared to be a spitting image of herself from head to toe. She was so fascinated with the woman that she interrupted her initial liaison with a man and asked the woman if she would like to make a quick thousand dollars by just having a drink with her. The woman, who spoke perfect English, responded, "You look so much like me, and I look like you that I'm afraid any conversation with you would be to my disadvantage."

Helga responded, "Nonsense, I'll give you two thousand dollars right now and another five thousand if you agree to meet my ex-lover in St. Thomas and repeat a scripted message to him. There will be no violence involved, no sex, or anything else that should concern you. I'm offering you seven thousand dollars to just get the motherfucker off my back. He is a gorgeous man. He's sexy, persuasive, in control and will do almost anything except commit violence to get me back into his fold."

The woman thought about the financial aspects of the offer and decided that there were too many missing links to fly off to St. Thomas and feign a relationship that she knew nothing about. She said to Helga, "Although I need the money and we look like twins, I can't just fly off to another country and act like I am someone else's lover and convince them of the same.

Helga said, "You won't have to act or do anything. The fucking guy gave me a STD and all I want him to do is get over his guilt and leave me the fuck alone."

Helga began to cry, and the woman asked, "How important is this matter to you? Wait, before you answer. How much is this deed really worth to you? I think that there is more involved and that you're lowballing me on the payment. Listen, my man is going to go ballistic if I don't go over and let him know what is going on. Now, he is the violent type, and I don't want to have my ribs bruised or broken because he thinks I'm trying to fuck another woman without him. I wish I could leave his ass permanently, but he'll send people looking for me and when I'm found, he will personally remind me that I am his for life. I'm not married to him, but I live in his house, eat his food and he does whatever he wants to me and around me. I don't know how to unchain myself from him and his forced drug nights."

Helga paused, stared at her look-a-like, and then at her man and said, "If you do this for me, I will pay you $10k and make sure that your man never bothers you again."

The woman looked over at her man as he was smiling at a newcomer to the scene, then at Helga and said, "You know I'm tired of being slapped, humiliated, and forced into menage a trois relationships with women I don't know. If you can handle my problem, then I will for sure learn your mannerism and consider doing this thing for you in St. Thomas."

Helga slipped her card with her cellphone number to the lady, returned to the bar, and told the gentleman she was talking to that she would be back in an hour. Of course she would never see him again.

#

After expressing her plan to the underground pope while in the midst of providing him with stimulation, she knew that the bigger of the two brains would prevail and that is when he said, "I will send an elite eradication squad to handle the ruse. By the way, who is this look-a-like and what is she to you?"

"When I was in Mexico City, I watched this stunning woman enter the bar who was controlled by a buffoon who held her in bondage, apparently often beating her. The woman looked exactly like me and made me wonder if I had a twin. Anyway, after a late-night conversation with her, I told her that I would take care of her man, if she would handle my lover in St. Thomas. We came to an agreement, and the event was slated to occur when 'the idiot spy' and his clan are scheduled to be there. I had my people canvased a booking agency and it looks as though that is where the group will be in two weeks. I'll request a meeting with his father and I'm sure he will want to bring his son along. Now, that is when your elite squad will waltz in and orchestrate the termination of my-look-alike with fake ammunition, in front of both Beckmires and their security team," Helga stated.

After a few more strokes and sounds of pleasure, the underground pontiff was relaxed and amenable to the proposal. He said, "Give me the final details by Friday and then let's calculate the success quotient of this undertaking. I want to make sure that no Beckmire dies at that meeting and that they are astonished by the precision and stealth of my people. I only want them to know that we can make trouble happen no matter where. Well, almost anywhere. There's that Outback. In that place both good and evil have schematics for operating that boggles my mind."

The ex-pope continued, "As if time stood still, and I was the only one able to move, I mean everyone else appeared to be frozen at that moment. I saw this huge anomaly that looked like a crocodile, fling a bag onto the shore that landed at my feet, and I was to present it to Mr. Beckmire. In the bag was a diamond ring. Now how in the heck can a crocodile know that I'm there in the Outback, fling a pouch that lands at my feet that I have to give to Mr. Beckmire. No, no! We will never take our matters to that place again, for we would certainly lose because of things that dominate that place. Go forth, give me an executable plan, and make it happen."

# # #

Helga and her look-a-like, whose name was Seagalie, conversed on many occasions about the St. Thomas matter. Seagalie knew that her phone conversations were being recorded and therefore, the quid pro quo notion of the relationship was never mentioned. On one occasion Seagalie mentioned to Helga, "He slapped me again because he thinks that I'm trying to have an illicit relationship with you. I know my phone conversations are recorded but he just likes hitting me and I have nowhere to go or hide." Seagalie broke down and began to cry.

Helga asked, "Is he a God-fearing man?"

Seagalie responded, "He has statues of the Virgin Mary and other religious- looking artifacts in his place. Why do you ask?"

Helga responded, "A man that hits a woman is not a man, but he is a coward. Conquering a person and then abusing them are not the traits of a true man. A true man never hits his woman, but finds ways to negotiate a terminating set of circumstances when all is not right. Anyway, are you comfortable with my mannerisms, speech and the key words that will describe my previous relationship with my nemesis? Remember, when he asks you why you're here, your reply should be, "Not to play Marco, Marco, Polo". That will ease any tensions he might have. More importantly, your next statement should be about our bambino. Remember those lines and there will be no problems."

Seagalie asked, "What if he wants to have a drink and discuss parenting?"

Helga responded, "Trust me, he and his father won't want to spend a lot of time there, because they are going to be apprehensive about being there with me in the first place and there is no trust between them and me. It is especially important that you wear dark glasses at all times. Avoid eye contact with my ex-lover as much as possible and pay more attention to his father, Benjamin Beckmire. I will have a date of arrival in the morning, a ticket and half of the agreed-upon payment. You will get the final amount upon your leaving the meeting place. Thinking about where you should meet, I'm going to suggest the other side of the island. Just study the notes I gave you and positions you should assume while talking to 'the idiot spy' and the other part of the deal will be attended to before you leave. As a matter of fact, I'm kind of bored. Perhaps I'll take care of it tonight, but if I do that then you become the number one attention-getter. I'm expecting a call later that will indicate when I need you to take that trip. Listen, first class flight accommodations, a suite at the Four Seasons Hotel and room-charging capability beyond belief. Do you have any questions?"

Seagalie asked, "Suppose my man wants to come along?"

Helga responded, "I hadn't thought about that. However, if he so desires to make the trip then by all means include him in the equation. As a matter of fact, I'm going to include another $5k just in case that is a reality. He won't be in first class, but he'll be on the same plane if all else fails."

Reading into the hidden message, Seagalie replied, "Sounds good. I'll see if he wants to come and if so, we'll make it happen. Nice to hear from you. I'm sore from where he hit me."

Helga announced, "You may not know it, but I can make sure that abuse never happens again. All you have to do is tell me that you are finished with being a punching bag and I will make the puncher vanish immediately."

Seagalie paused and said, "Talk to you later."

#

After arriving in St. Thomas, Seagalie was met by the hotel's limo driver. Seagalie pretended to be preoccupied by a document in her hand in order to avoid trivial conversation with the driver. After he asked how was her trip, she gently shrugged her shoulders and smiled.

After checking in at the hotel, Seagalie entered the restaurant to scout it out. She saw a table with low lighting in a corner that would give her the least amount of exposure. She knew she would be wearing sunglasses and a provocative outfit that would be the center of attention. She hoped her true essence would be overlooked.

Once in her room, Seagalie made contact with Ben Beckmire as instructed and invited him and his son to dinner at the Four Seasons Hotel. At first Ben Beckmire was hesitant to meet the ever-shape-shifting Helga Spengatsenburg or Sister Mary because she had been intricately involved in many attempted terminations of the Beckmire clan. However, he knew that this woman was the mother of Jelani and little Ben and that Zanthius would want to hear her demands for the cessation of hostilities.

# # #

Later that evening at the Four Seasons Hotel, sitting in a darkened corner quietly, there was a person that looked like, smelled like, and acted like Helga Spengatsenburg or Sister Mary. When the Sarge saw her, his first thought was, "Damn she be fine!" The woman rose from her seat and greeted Ben Beckmire with a firm handshake. She embraced Zanthius with a close and feel this thing kind of hug. Zanthius backed away and said, "We are not hungry, but we are interested in hearing why you're here on the island and as Helga Spengatsenburg?"

The woman, on point, responded, "So much for small talk. How is our child? How is he developing? You were always to the point, lover boy!"

The Sarge said, "I'm not interested in any of the things I've heard so far. Why did you invite us to dinner?"

"Shall we at least have a drink before we enter the world of demons, weapons, betrayals and demands?" the woman asked.

"Water is fine for me. We don't plan on being here that long. What is your purpose? Has the Holy Father been located?" Ben Beckmire inquired.

"Mr. Beckmire, what Holy Father are you referring to? Are you considering the person from hell, or the one who paraded around as the Pope and the Holy Father? You people have no idea who you're dealing with. You've been manipulated at every turn, and you still don't understand the game that's being played on you, around you and with you as major players. I'm the key to your salvation and longevity. However, I don't come cheap," the woman announced.

Zanthius asked, "What is it you want?"

"What is it that you think I want? I certainly don't want to play Marco Polo with you—that wasn't very lasting," the woman stated.

Beckmire said, "Okay, enough jousting. Exactly what are you seeking, Ms. Spengatsenburg?"

"I am seeking righteousness. That's the only thing on earth worth having, righteousness. Can you provide me with that, Mr. Beckmire?" the woman asked.

"I'm only going to ask you this one more time and then we're out of here. What is it you seek?" Ben Beckmire demanded.

"I seek that which was stolen from me, Mr. Beckmire," the woman lamented.

The Sarge looked at Zanthius in a perplexed manner and Zanthius aggressively asked, "What the fuck was stolen from you, Helga?"

"My heart and soul," the woman announced.

"What in the hell are you talking about?" Zanthius asked.

"I want that child, my child that was purchased by you from those crooked ass nuns in that monastery in Valencia. I want that child, my child, who I entrusted to a bunch of money-hungry nuns to care for and who sold him to the highest bidder. I want a life with that child, my child and that Mr. Beckmire, is how I become righteous."

Zanthius moved aggressively towards the woman but was restrained by his father, who responded, "Lady, that just ain't going to happen. There is no way in heaven or hell you'll get that baby. Legally, the die has been cast. Oh, and don't try that storm trooper shit and go out and hire a bunch of mercenaries, because we'll provide them with a quick trip to hell, to join the thousands of people who are awaiting our arrival. Lady, you should go back as Sister Mary because Helga Spengatsenburg is out of her fucking mind."

The woman proclaimed, "Zanthius, give me my child by noon tomorrow or watch your entire tribe be destroyed by people from hell. Every place that you call home is rigged, your plane is rigged, your so-called Sanctuary is rigged, and you don't even know how. Do you want me to tell you how?"

The Sarge looked at the woman and said, "Give it your best shot. I hope you don't hold your breath until noon. There will be no transfer of any child to a nut case. Have a wonderful evening."

The Sarge looked at Zanthius who had a look on his face that his father had seen before and he firmly commanded, "Don't you fucking think about doing anything crazy. Don't you dare!"

As soon as they turned around to leave the table in the dark corner, 12 well-armed and attired mercs quietly entered the restaurant from all available doors and caught everyone off guard. Laser lights moved methodically around Zanthius and the Sarge's bodies, as well as their protection team, through the windows. The Sarge thought that they had been set up and silently cursed himself for not adding more security.

There was no talking, just a perfect execution of commandeering a place without firing a shot. The leader, with a weapon in his hand, walked over to the woman, bent down, whispered something in her ear, and smiled at her. The woman smiled back at the merc. The leader rose from the bending position, smiled again at the woman and descended to ear level again. The person whispered something in her ear, rose from the bending position, and smiled once again at the woman. Unexpectedly, the leader fired two fake rounds into her heart and one into her head. The leader turned, walked towards the door of the restaurant, and twirled a finger in the air indicating that they were out of there. At no point did they pay attention to the Sarge, Zanthius, or their security team.

Zanthius walked over to where the look-alike person lay, grabbed a pillow off the chair and placed two additional rounds into her head. His father screamed, "Now you've implicated us in this matter. What were you thinking?"

# # #

Helga Spengatsenburg was not the person in attendance in the restaurant at the Four Seasons Hotel when an elite squad of pristine combatants surrounded the venue and placed everyone in harm's way. No, it was her sacrificial lamb in the guise of Helga that received more than she had bargained for, and everything was sanctioned by Helga. Helga knew what the ultimate outcome would be and outsourced her demise to a look-a-like that was innocent and naïve. Yes, Helga Spengatsenburg's true colors and nefarious nature came to the forefront, when she befriended a gullible young lady and unknowingly, sentenced her to death, so that she could continue her reprehensible relationship with a demon.

It was clear, Helga Spengatsenburg had supremely pissed someone off, so it seemed. They sought and assumed they got their revenge. Unfortunately, a person seeking freedom from abuse, who believed in a stranger, was sacrificed and few would care.

CHAPTER THREE

The underground pontiff, although still excited by Sister Mary's company, and her seemingly unnatural and natural proclivity to bring things to an epic conclusion, knew that at some point he had to officially excommunicate Sister Mary from his life. More importantly, he knew that she was the sole monitor of his illicit gains and accounts and the mother of his child. He also knew she had special talents and over time had protected him from suitors, would-be leaders of the church and more importantly, nuns who were looking for a closer view of the mortal selected to lead the Catholic Church. Yes, Sister Mary was behind the scenes and times, as AI was providing more modern approaches to capturing millions of minions who were in search of a higher purpose. He knew that the key to his salvation, and return to the Papacy was Ms. Beatrice, and her hopefully demonic powers.

In Mexico City, his chosen place of hiding, he often wandered the streets seeking a closer understanding of those who live in abject poverty. Although it saddened him to see his forgotten flock struggle to meet basic living considerations, he would take his walks in different directions hoping to find that poverty was not universal. As Pope, he rarely ventured into the neighborhoods and felt that those who came to pray in St. Peter's Square represented the conditions of his flock universally. He had conflicting thoughts about who showed up in St. Peter's Square, and who he was actually living with.

The ex-pontiff and his group boarded a plane for what was considered to be a working vacation to Ixtapa Zihuatanejo. On his agenda was a scheduled meeting with a person who allegedly was the go between to the individual who was from the loins of Ben Beckmire. Sister Mary discounted the meeting and expressed the fact that the real son of Ben Beckmire had been fed to the fish by those who he allegedly tried to hoodwink. She went as far as to indicate that his known DNA was registered with a hospital in Switzerland where he fathered a child and where she had a contact. It was agreed that the meeting would be held just to see if there was new information that was being offered. The only important item that the ex-pontiff was concerned with, was how to conduct his conscription and bring a true sorceress into his camp. Any information coming to him on that matter was important and he did not want to miss an opportunity to emerge from the bowels of hell and into his perceived legitimate seat at the head of the Catholic Church and to be in control of the entire world.

On their first evening in Ixtapa Zihuatanejo, the ex-pope was once again deceived by who he thought was his flock. As he watched people swim, drink, flirt, and partake in food, he assumed that this is how his flock lived, not like the pictures in his mind of the residents in Mexico City. Sister Mary would interrupt his moments of disillusionment and remind him that this was not his flock or their living conditions that should matter, but that his passion should be about the control and servitude of his congregation to him. She would often remind her master that his desire for world domination would primarily include those in poverty, his largest contingency, those afflicted, those corrupted and those in need of a guiding light—his reemergence to his rightful throne. It was only in moments like those when Sister Mary inflicted her vision onto his that he would see why caring for the few was not to the advantage of the many. Often, he would hear Sister Mary's words over and over in his head as if she were managing his thoughts. Unlike others, Sister Mary was a survivor and often considered whether this ex-pontiff was the person to carry out her long-term mission. After all, she came from a long line of brujas, a thing that her master didn't consider, know about, or even think was possible. It would only come to him that she was more than just a nun when and if he decided to cross the line in the sand and declare her useless.

#

Sister Mary's mother was more than a seer. Wajickee knew it but couldn't define it. She was an interloper between heaven and hell and could transverse each one. She knew her daughter had the fire in her when she was born and knew that her grandsons would bargain between the good and the bad. Her vision of Ms. Beatrice was not precise, because Ms. Viola was more clairvoyant than an actual bruja and, therefore, her great-grand-daughter remained an anomaly—undecided.

Sister Mary was aware of all of the dynamics in play and was only concerned that Ms. Beatrice might be in conflict with her and her vision for the ex-pontiff. She discounted the possibility that her own bloodline could come between her and her vision.

CHAPTER FOUR

The Beckmire clan began to slow their rollers, enjoy the lazy afternoons, evening drinks, food, and then sleep long into the next day. The children were under the watchful eyes of their peers, security, and intruder alarm systems. The group felt so secure that they would in pairs go to town and shop as if they were not some of the most wanted people on the planet Earth.

On a Thursday, Gladstone and Whitmore decided to drive into town to purchase a few personal items. They stopped at the same Starbucks where people had unsuccessfully attempted to dispose of members of their group, years ago. The group had been back to this place a hundred times and had placed the past episodes behind them.

On this day, a mentally unstable and sexually unsatisfied person, decided that he was going to kill the person of his fantasy, who did not know that he existed except as a customer. He never invited her to a movie, dinner, concert, or for a walk, but felt that she should have responded to his non-verbal cues.

Customers lounged around the expanded Starbucks and talked, did business, made acquaintances, and enjoyed their coffee and tea. No one realized that a demented person was preparing for an assault on an unsuspecting worker and innocent people enjoying their day.

Gladstone and Whitmore placed their order and that would be the last order that they would ever submit. In a blaze of gunfire and malice, they and other innocent customers were cut down by bursts of bullets from an automatic rifle. The Starbucks was sprayed with bullets from one side to the other and at the end of a clip, the assailant pulled out a handgun and began to methodically murder people.

The source of his affection was frozen in time, watched as he slid a clip into his automatic rifle and began to spray her body with bullets until the clip was empty. He then pulled out a clip, slid it into his pistol, and concluded his life.

The two men, Gladstone and Whitmore had been in many battles from Vietnam to Florida, to Rome, Spain, Hong Kong, to the Outback, Virginia to DC, St. Johns to London and many other places. To have their lives ended by bad timing and by being in the wrong place at the wrong time, would be hard for the group to understand. Two warriors, along with many innocent people murdered by a person who wanted another human being but did not know how to introduce himself, or attract and date her. Their deaths as well as the others were sad, unfitting, cowardly and unfortunate.

When the news reached their community, only tears and sorrow were obvious. The Sarge and Mallory, accompanied by the two sisters and their husbands, ventured to town to claim their brethren. The Sarge introduced himself to the Chief of Police and told him that Whitmore and Gladstone were two of his boys. The Chief indicated to the Sarge that it was a crime scene and that he would personally see to it that his boys and everyone else who lost their life in this tragic arena were treated with the utmost respect.

#

It would be three days before the bodies were released to the Sarge. The local mortician, a friend of John Lee's, was commissioned to prepare the bodies for burial. He suggested to the Sarge that a closed casket funeral would be fitting because of the damage that was done from the rounds that entered their heads and face. The Sarge shook his head violently and said, "I want you to perform a miracle and bring those boys to me for burial looking as if they were asleep."

The Mortician said, "We will work to restore their essence as best as possible."

#

The Sarge was distraught, incoherent, and delusional. He hardly slept, ate, or bathed. Courtney realizing that her man was on the brink of collapsing, decided to spike his water with 5 mg of a sleep-inducing drug. It would be 14 hours before the Sarge would awaken. The first thing he asked his wife, was, "Did you slip a mickey into my drink?"

Courtney laughing replied, "Honey, the only thing I will slip into your drink is some Cialis or Viagra." They both laughed for a few moments and then the Sarge transitioned from laughing to crying his heart out.

#

Clyde and the Minnesota group boarded their plane for the flight to Virginia where a portion of the farm had been designated as a burial plot for the group and family members. At the ranch, Clyde, Bertha, and other members of their community waited to send their friends off to the next dimension. It was such a solemn affair that even the horses realized that there was sorrow in the air and made their way slowly to the burial area.

Clyde gave a masterful eulogy! Everyone was in tears throughout the entire service. He specifically said of the two men, "They were warriors, they loved a lot and meant so much to many people. Their deaths were unnecessary, cowardly and on any given day could happen to any of us because that is the way of the world, we now live in. We will honor them as the troopers that we knew them to be. God be with them and may God bless us all as we reach the point in life when all that is dear to us, is in line to follow these brave men."

Montomie read a delightful poem to honor the two men and McArthur hobbled through a tearful farewell.

Later at the repasts, there were stories of heroism and mischief, for male ears only and stories of their search for the perfect mates. By the pool, their buddies gathered and talked about the Nam, the Outback, and various other skirmishes the team had engaged in. Mallory rose to offer a toast but was interrupted by Jong, who said, "I love my departed friends, I love you guys and what's important is that those of us who are alive, make sure we find a way and a reason to stay alive and announce our commitment of love for each other. Untypically, I will say that I love John Lee Jones, even though he is a bully and a pain in my ass. I will also say that I love Jilkes, even though he thinks he's the brains of this operation and never sanctions John Lee. The rest of you know how I feel, but those two, were always fence hangers."

Hearing that, John Lee stood up and said, "Listen, Hyshime, tonight and forever more, whenever I see you, I would like to receive a hug, a handshake, or some expression of friendship. I used to think that we were invincible. The same fucking place we went for coffee a while back and had a gunfight, where them there nuts tried to kill us and now today we buried two of our own who were assassinated in the same fucking place. We all done shared each other's blood, spit, shit and here we be, many years later, alive. So many people have tried to kill us for reasons my little brain can't fathom and to have our leader's son leading the pack to gain our resources, well, I be done heard it all. I will, moving forward, be more diligent in loving and protecting every member of this here clan. I used to think we would live forever, but now I am sure that death awaits us all and we know not when."

Jong crying his eyes out yelled, "I didn't know you knew my fucking first name. How long have you known my given name?"

John Lee Jones looked intently at Jong and said, "From the day we entered base camp, and you witnessed me beat the shit out of Reginald Jilkes. I just thought that people liked being called by their last names, unheard of where I be from. Anyway, I know each and everyone's last and first names. We survived, we ended the lives of people we didn't know, in the name of the country that hired people to conclude our existence. Now that be some ironic shit. They send us to kill people, and when we return, they send people to kill us."

Jilkes responded, "How eloquently my country ass friend has expressed himself about our moving forward. Our fallen comrades were the epitome of soldiers, friends, family, and confidants. We each have a story and fortunately, only we can tell it about each other. No wives, no friends, no families, no preachers, or anyone else can tell the real story about each of us. I remember I saw Gladstone and Whitmore in a bad place in the Nam, and I knew it was a setup, because I had been in their exact same shoes with the same two women who were the draw and once in the room, you were beaten and robbed. During my encounter, however, I beat those guys worse than I beat the former racist."

John Lee loudly exclaimed, "I be supposing you be mixing my politics up with racism. You always go there and frankly, I be getting a little tired of you thinking that because my grandparents were in certain groups and my parents were flag-toting members of the clan, you be thinking that I inherited that there gene. It be time that you forget about all that and look at how many times I be done saved your black ass from all kinds of craziness."

Jilkes smiled at first and then broke into a crying frenzy. John Lee yelled, "Don't you be doing that there crying shit and think that I'm going to fall for it."

Jilkes looked at him, and then began to walk away. John Lee yelled, "Now you be trying that reverse philosophy on me and I ain't going to fall for none of your shit today."

Jong announced, "I think you mean reverse psychology. I know you didn't mean philosophy."

John Lee looked at him and said, "Why you always be joining his camp? Anyway, let me go and make up with his black ass and find out how long him not going to be speaking to me. You should stop being that follower."

CHAPTER FIVE

As with most young girls, eventually they become of age when the messy times in their lives begin. Ms. Beatrice was not exempt from this voyage. In addition to certain mannerisms, she began to make adult statements, suggestions and even decisions. Ms. Viola, who watched her like a hawk, knew that her granddaughter was approaching adolescence. Ms. Beatrice's disengagement from her normal routines, her admonishment of the other children for acting childish and her disconnection from associating with everyone, was very obvious to her grandmother. Yes, Ms. Viola was aware of the impending events and knew that she would play an important role in transitioning her great-grand-daughter into puberty as well as into the living angel or the satanic priestess she was destined to become. Her mindset and questionable actions/reactions seemed to multiply overnight, creating a sense of disharmony within her immediate family unit. Ms. Viola knew what was happening and felt that the timing was beneficial for the evil overlord, knowing full well that Whitmore and Gladstone, as well as all the members of the group were destined to spend an eternity in Hades. The number of deaths that each man and woman was responsible for, was unpardonable, reprehensible and a direct route to hell. All that was evil was aware, and their awareness created a feeding frenzy as well as a distraction for the conscription of Ms. Beatrice.

# # #

At breakfast, several months later, Chakes asked, "How is my most beautiful and intelligent little girl?"

In front of all who were in attendance, Ms. Beatrice stridently responded, "First of all, I am not related to you in any sense. Second, my mom married you and I was just a part of the package. Therefore, this jig is up. She made her choice, my grandma invited you in and now I just don't want you thinking that you can tell me what to do. This jig is over!"

Chakes looked long at Ms. Beatrice as his eyes began to water. He asked, "Honey, did I offend or say something that upset you?"

"Mr. Chakes, I am done playing this childish game. I want to find and be with my real father. I appreciate all that you have done, but I no longer need to hear war stories, your stories of friendship and family or your ancient manner of parenting. I think that I can manage on my own without you as an over-lord."

Luana, witnessing the exchange asked, "Have you lost your mind? What on earth has gotten into you?"

Ms. Viola, who is never far away from her family broke into tears and screamed, "That there ex-holy father is summoning that child from the depths of hell. I know this, I feel this and that wizard fella cautioned me on it. Please, let me have a go at this child and see if I can see how far she is from deciding which path she is going to take—Godly or malevolent. I need to get this child back to the Outback where evil has a hard time conscripting the righteous. So much we don't know or understand, but I can tell you, this child is in the decision-making mode that will impact us, the world and possibly help restore evil at the head of the Catholic Church if we're not careful."

With bruised feelings, Chakes placed his napkin on the table, looked at Ms. Beatrice, and said, "Regardless of what you think of me, I will love and cherish you for as long as I live." He turned and walked out of the room followed by his wife, who was also deeply hurt. Her child had just castigated the man she loved, the man who protected their daughter, cuddled her, and loved her unconditionally.

Everyone was visibly upset and concerned as Ms. Beatrice said to her great-grandmother, "Are you going to have breakfast with me, or are you going act like everyone else in this place?"

Ms. Viola looked at Ms. Beatrice, touched her arm, and whispered, "Tell your demons to back down and let you make up your own destiny, or I will summon the angels that walk amongst men." Ms. Beatrice's body shuddered for a moment, and she burst into tears suddenly.

She said, "Grandma, I feel like someone else is controlling everything I say and all that I think. I need to see Wajickee because there is something happening to me and I have no control over it."

# # #

On the long solemn ride to the Outback, Marcelus slept little, played and ate a lot. Courtney asked Ben, "Do you think this is an inopportune time to ask Ms. Viola for assistance?"

The Sarge replied, "When Mr. Sleepy hits him, he's going to be out for a long time. Naw, Courtney, let Ms. Viola and her family be for now. Ms. Beatrice turned on a dime and overnight. Something or someone is hunting that child and depending upon who gets to her first, will determine our collective fates. I always knew she was special and now she has come of age in so many ways. I'm hoping that whatever or whoever is seeking her, we beat them to the punch, hopefully with the help of Wajickee."

Once the plane was halfway to the Outback, a crying and deeply sorry Ms. Beatrice woke Chakes and her mother up and beckoned them to the belly of the plane. Ms. Viola was already there waiting for the group.

Once they all were there, Ms. Beatrice walked over to Chakes and said, "I know I hurt you with my words earlier and I am begging you to forget that I ever said them. Between this new thing called menstruating and someone filling my head with evil thoughts, I just don't know what is going on. I do know that if you ever turn your back on me, it will be the end of days for me, for I will find a way to end all of this torment that keeps me from sleeping. I need you more than anyone if I am going to win this battle that I am fighting. You are the only father that I know and recognize. It is your love for me, my brother, sister, my mother, and my contentious granny that keeps me going. I am haunted by all kinds of things that I didn't know existed. I see things, I hear and understand languages that I have never heard before. I'm in trouble and only you can free me from the demons and the thoughts that I have. I love you so much and I could never turn my back on you. Please forgive me and say that you'll help me get through this female mess that has appeared suddenly and all the demons that keep sniffing and attacking me and telling me that I am their new leader and that all will worship me."

Chakes, crying his heart out, as was everyone else, said, "I told you once before, I am here for the long haul. Of course, the words spoken were hurtful, but I have faith, and my faith knew that my little girl was tripping and being manipulated by demons. Listen, I know that you're special and that you'll have to make the biggest decision that you will ever make in your life. I'm just hoping that no matter which one you make, you'll always remember that I love you, your sister, your brother, your mother, and your provocative granny. Naw, baby girl, those words just made me realize that I have to work harder and make sure your path is righteous and meaningful. We will fight those demons together. However, on that female stuff, check with your mother and your antagonistic granny."

#

As the plane began its descent into Sydney, Ms. Beatrice began to curse her mother in an obvious tone and demeanor that was not hers. Her grandmother grabbed her wrist and watched as she passed out. Ms. Viola yelled, "Them there other people are beginning to get scared because of where we be going. She'll be alright, don't y'all fret, she'll be fine."

Chakes came back to Ms. Viola's seat with cold compresses and said, "Let me begin my work now. Let me sit with her, soothe her, and attempt to learn the nature of the forces we're dealing with. I will die before I let any mental or physical harm come to my child."

"Ms. Viola said, "I always knew there was a reason for you trying to pick me up them many years ago, scoundrel."

Chakes sat with Ms. Beatrice, placed the cold compresses on her forehead, and told her how much he loved her and how proud he was of her. He recalled several instances when she demonstrated leadership skills and compassion. He reminded her of when they first met, and he asked her what is your name and you responded that your mother told you never to tell strangers your name. Chakes said, "I knew right then and there we were going to be a family. As a family, I will protect you until there is no life remaining in me. I will die trying to defeat things that I don't understand in the only way I know how. I love you so very much, my darling. Please give me the chance to show you that I'm not about words only. I can and I will fight this battle with you and for you."

Moments later, Ms. Beatrice and Chakes were fast asleep. Chakes drooled a little and it was attended to by his lovely wife, Luana. As she lightly patted his lip, she cried because her daughter was in trauma, but she knew the man she loved, was a God send.

Ms. Viola noticing her granddaughter crying, grabbed her hand and said, "It all seems troublesome right now, but deep in my heart I know it's going to be alright. Don't you worry about that interaction earlier. That there scoundrel is going to figure this thing out with the help of that wizard."

#

The plane landed and was refueled within a couple of hours. Ben Beckmire saw Chakes and asked, "How is Ms. Beatrice?"

"Sarge, something or someone influential and powerful is tormenting my child and I don't know how to begin to help her."

The Sarge replied, "Chakes, that's your first mistake. You ain't in this mess alone. We have a family to help us in making heads or tails of this issue. No, sir, we got your back, and we certainly have Ms. Beatrice's back as well. My only concern is why now. I mean we have been on easy street, meaning no known threats were out there trying to kill us. Why now?"

Chakes paused for a moment and whispered to the Sarge, "The child began menstruating and it's flowing by the bucket full."

The Sarge looked long and hard at Chakes and announced, "Someone or some force is trying to capture her purity. Why else would all of this start to happen now? You know the ex-pontiff took an illicit liking towards Ms. Beatrice and even tried to conscript her. Shortly thereafter, he went missing, Sister Mary was assassinated, and now your daughter is under attack. When we see Wajickee, I'm sure he's going to have an opinion and point us in the right direction. Again, your family is in this fight with you. Use us as you please!"

#

Once in the Northern Territory, the group felt secure and happy. As expected, Wajickee met the bus when it entered the village and greeted each person exiting it. He shook everyone's hand and when he reached out for Ms. Beatrice's hand, he felt the burden that she was carrying. To Wajickee, it was simply a choice—good or evil!

Ms. Beatrice hugged him and Wajickee said, "So those things that challenge you will make you strong. Only you can choose the directions your mind and body will travel. Your family will make you comfortable, but the choice will be yours. You, by now, understand the nature of good and evil. The choosing of your destiny will feel like torture because at each end of the spectrum, there are demands, there are requirements and there are commitments. You may not chose one and sample it. No, Ms. Beatrice, your initial choice is your permanent one. There is glamor, trappings, pleasure, bounty and meaning at each end of the continuum. All that is good may not be good in your eyes, just like all that is evil may be appetizing to you. Your family is here to help you, but they can't force a direction from you. I am here to help you as well and I too, can't influence a direction. However, I will be your aide no matter which one you choose."

Ms. Beatrice quietly said, "I don't want to have to decide on either one. I just want to be with my family and most of all, repair the damage I did to my father."

# # #

In the Outback it appears as though one could reach out and gather a shooting star. On this night, the sky was filled with stars majestically flitting to and from unknown parts of the universe.

The Sarge sat by the billabong that housed the Great Saltie, contemplating the anguish his man was feeling. The Sarge knew that Chakes was as committed to Ms. Beatrice as he was to his other two children born from his seed. Wajickee knowing and seeing all in the Outback, eased up beside the Sarge and said, "My friend, I know exactly what you're feeling but I also know that no one can influence the direction Ms. Beatrice will take. Her dad, your friend, is consumed with false failure, and thoughts of suicide have entered his mind more than once. I suggest that you and your people surround him with real love, earnest conversation, and genuine acts of fellowship. I fear that he has become so fragile from memories of all those dastardly things that you people committed and that admonishment from Ms. Beatrice, well, in my opinion, has placed him over the edge."

As the two men continued to discuss Chakes, the Great Saltie briefly appeared and thrashed his tail repeatedly. Unbeknownst to the Sarge, its actions were a message to Wajickee. Wajickee rose from the seated position and told the Sarge that there was trouble in the village.

When the two men arrived in the center of the village, they witnessed a gutted and stretched out dingo nailed to a makeshift cross. The Sarge started to enter aggressively and was cautioned by Wajickee to learn the meaning of the event before barging in and making an inquiry.

As the Sarge slowed his pace, Ms. Viola screamed, "Evil is not welcome in this place of harmony. We are family, we are loyal, we are believers in the righteousness of mankind, except when contrary beliefs are directed against us. This is my doing. I slayed that beast that would feast upon any of us. I made that cross and I nailed that predator to it. I know some of you think that I have lost my mind, however, it is not my mind or my soul that is in question but that of my great-granddaughter, affectionately known as Ms. Beatrice. I know many have accused me of being a bruja. My own granddaughter, Luana, often calls me a witch. Tonight, my friends I am announcing that I am a witch and that any cultist that seeks to commune with my great-granddaughter will face the wrath of the witches of the water, the earth, and the sun. He who thinks he is the rightful head of that empire in Italy will be profoundly abused, banished, and destroyed if he or any of his disciples attempt to sway the decision of my great-granddaughter. Here and now, I do decree these actions against all foes good and evil. The decision must be hers and hers alone and without any influence or cajoling from either camp. Be mindful all, this I declare and this I will enforce."

Wajickee ever mindful of Ms. Viola's resolve, announced, "Let us all pray that the decision made by Ms. Beatrice will be the one that joins us, not the one that separates us forever. With that I proclaim that this event is over and goodnight!

# # #

In the morning, as the camp came to life, the smell of bacon aroused the senses of everyone in the camp. The menu was clear, eggs, ham, and bacon. No one asked, but everyone deduced that the previously nailed to a cross dingo, was the object of the delicious smell.

After the wonderful breakfast, Chakes made his way to the billabong where the Great Saltie resided. His reasons for going there were obvious. He felt that he had failed Ms. Beatrice as a parent and that his war history and the faces of those he had personally executed were prevalent in his mind. He looked back on his ventures with the group and recognized that they too were filled with disdain and pain, and he decided to offer his body and soul to the crocs in the billabong.

Chakes took his clothes off and proceeded into the billabong. He smiled as he witnessed the residents of the billabong approach him. Chakes closed his eyes and expected to feel massive jaws rip his body to pieces, but instead he felt the gentle hand of Luana who said, "Scoundrel, if this is the way you want to go, then I too will go with you." Surrounded by crocs, Chakes began to cry as Luana hugged him. She said, "Honey, we have three children but my love for you is so strong that I will not survive without you. So, if this is your choice, then it is mine as well. So be it. Kiss me one last time."

The Sarge entered the water and announced, "The entire village is concerned about you people. Listen, no one can influence Ms. Beatrice's mind except her. Chakes, I know it's tough and I can say that I have been there and done that with my son however, this act that you're attempting to commit only makes me and the rest of the team new parents. We will all face this event together and relate to whoever she becomes. Besides, my people don't do suicide, so get your arses out of that billabong."

CHAPTER SIX

The following morning, Wajickee was seen having a heated discussion with Ms. Viola, who allowed him to rant and rave until he made a conclusive statement. As the Sarge appeared on the scene, the two lowered their voices but continued the discussion.

The Sarge asked, "Do you two wizards need some intervention? I mean it is obvious that the entire camp is in disarray over the direction our young seer may take, but I don't think it helps when the two of you are apparently in battle. Is it possible to share with me what this negative discord is about?"

Wajickee started to speak, but was rudely interrupted by Ms. Viola who announced, "Our Lord on high chastised me for killing a dingo."

"Ms. Viola, the dingo, and all animals are sacred and cherished by Wajickee. I must admit when I saw that animal on a cross, I too knew it was going to be the source of a heated conversation."

"Hold up a minute, General. What's up with you men? Why not ask me how that all came to be?"

The Sarge knew he was jousting with a champion and decided to ask, "Can you please explain to us how that dingo came to be nailed on the cross?"

"Mr. Sarge, I like your humor and I'm going to ignore the slights. That dingo came to me and died in front of me. It wanted me to make a statement and that was the essence of how it came to be."

Wajickee asked, "Why didn't you just say that?"

Ms. Viola responded, "I like when you appear annoyed. It's so very sexy!"

The Sarge cleared his throat and said, "I must see to Marcelus. Have a great day."

# # #

That following afternoon, Jong asked John Lee if he could have a serious conversation with him about all the drama that was being manifested. John Lee responded, "Jong, I don't be understanding a lot of things, but I can tell you one thing and that is I believe that there Ms. Beatrice is different than any of the other children. That there ex-holy father's interest in her has always been a source of discontent with me and mine. Just think about it, that there person oversaw that big Catholic Church. I mean, I do believe that although him be mighty and important, him still be a human. Now, you add a damn dingo nailed to a cross and Ms. Viola swearing and declaring things that I don't know about, well, I just believe that there might be some yeast in this here story. We done seen a lot of strange things, especially when we be here. That there beast in the billabong, animals attacking our enemies, spiders and snakes that obey commands, I mean that there is enough to make a simpleton like me scared."

"That's why I am asking you about all this. You usually see through the smoke and spell out the answer in your own inimitable way," Jong stated.

"What's that big fancy word mean?" John Lee asked.

"It simply means that you don't get scared easily and you have an answer for everything. Let me say this to you and please do not spread it. My wife has been having horrible nightmares about Sister Mary and Ms. Beatrice. They both portray half human and half animal bodies in her dreams. At first, I thought she was being dramatic, but she has been having the same dream since we've been back here in the Outback. Who should I talk to? I mean, I have doubted the wizard because I don't believe he is as old as he says he is."

John Lee looked hard and long at Jong and said, "I don't be talking bad about the wizard because too many things have happened at his command. You be needing to go up to him and tell him how you feel and what's going on in your tent. Him the only one with the answer. He is powerful, Jong. Don't play with fire use it to get the answers you need."

"Will you come with me?" Jong asked.

John Lee responded, "It's about your missus, he would be suspect seeing me with you asking about your lady. No, I think this be a Jong and Wajickee moment."

As though expecting Jong, Wajickee made himself conveniently visible to Jong as he concluded his interlude with John Lee.

Wajickee asked, "Mr. Jong, do you have a minute?"

Jong hesitantly replied, "Absolutely."

Wajickee suggested that they take a walk down to the billabong. Jong asked, "I ain't in trouble with the monster, am I?"

"Do you mean the Great Saltie? Of course not. I want to talk to you about the dreams your missus be having concerning Ms. Beatrice and Sister Mary. In the Outback, I know about most things that are going on that are troublesome for the individual or the village at large. Listen, I know you have doubts about my age, my mission, my abilities, and my resolve. Why don't we ignore all of that for the moment and talk as you did with John Lee—you know, man to man."

Jong said, "If you know what's going on, then why are you playing games with me?"

"Mr. Jong, I am a wizard and as such, I can get the outcome I want in any fashion that I want. I know you're skeptical of all that is imagined of me, so, let's do this thing without any bravado. It's troubling you and eventually it will have a negative impact upon your children. Her dreams have been forecasted. Her nightmares are about half-humans and half-animals. I have seen them, and I know what they mean. My concern is, do you?" Wajickee asked.

Jong studied Wajickee's facial expressions and blurted out, "I don't believe in magic. I don't believe in wizards, and I don't believe in you."

"Now we're communicating," Wajickee announced. "I know you believe that those animals that defended us way back when, just happened to be there. Jong, I can summon them if you like or even invite the Great Saltie to our meeting. Mr. Jong, look behind you and you will see twelve rather large crocs. I'm going to walk into the water and if they eat me, then you'll know that I was full of dung."

Wajickee walked into the water and the crocs moved stealthily towards him. He yelled, "Mr. Jong, please join me."

Jong replied, "I see your point, and I guess I have to rethink all that I have seen and could not comprehend. Please, please, come out of the water." During his egress, Wajickee patted two crocs on their heads. Once Wajickee was out of the water, Jong noticed that he was dry as if he had never entered the water and said, "Here again is when I think I need help. You just came out of the water, yet you're as dry as I am. Please explain that to me."

Wajickee smiled and said, "If you will come in the water with me, then I will explain all that there is."

Jong headed towards the water first, and Wajickee yelled, "Unless you're trying to commit suicide, I wouldn't take another step towards the water."

Jong paused, looked at him with contempt, and continued towards the water. Surprisingly, the crocs swam away as if they were afraid of Jong. He turned to Wajickee and said, "Hey make-believe wizard, the caper is up."

Wajickee lowered his head, fell to his knees as if he were praying and said, "No, Mr. Jong, you have just forfeited your life. Behold, the Great Saltie!"

Jong defiantly announced, "That's going to be my next mission and that is to make sure everyone knows that there is no such thing that lives in this billabong."

Wajickee smiled and said, "You will be remembered as the fool who willingly walked into the jaws of the Great Saltie. Once again, behold the Great Saltie!"

Jong with a scowl on his face said, "When are you going to stop this nonsense?"

Wajickee replied, "After you have become a snack for the Great Saltie." Jong heard splashing behind him slowly turned around and saw the anomaly called the Great Saltie. That would be the last thing that he would see on that day, but the memory would make him a convert.

Needless to mention, from that point forward, Jong, when he encountered Wajickee, or when he was questioned about his sudden turn-about concerning what was fact or fiction, a wizard and the Great Saltie, Jong would indicate that he had seen the light. Wajickee somewhat punished Jong for seven days by making him constantly reflect upon what he saw and how he was saved by the very person that he didn't believe in—Wajickee. However, Wajickee was still annoyed by the arrogance of Jong.

Mary Alice was a basket case who required the help of Courtney, Monica, Ms. Viola, and the wizard. The wizard was still a little pissed at Jong for challenging him but showed compassion when it came to Mary Alice. He minimized the occurrence of the fauns and satyrs in Mary Alice's dream state, however, he knew that this was a distraction. He never let Ms. Beatrice or Ms. Viola out of his sight. Some demon thought that by violating Mary Alice, the road to Ms. Beatrice would be clear and easy.

Wajickee entered Jong's hut and realized that he and others had tracked all kinds of demon matter into it. He asked, "When is the last time you've been out in the sunlight?"

Mary Alice blankly stared at Wajickee and asked, "Are you a doctor?"

Wajickee knew from that inquiry, that she had been chosen as the distraction. He suggested, "Come, walk with me to the billabong and get some fresh air."

Mary Alice shot back, "I can't go outside. Those things with their horns, tails, horse bodies, and instruments will hurt me."

Wajickee called out for Jong to join him. When entering his hut, Jong saw that his wife was pale, withdrawn, and incoherent. Wajickee said to Jong, "You're familiar with the distraction while the real subject is being targeted. Anyway, I need you and your wife to join me at the billabong where you and I had our come to Jesus meeting."

Jong replied, "Immediately. Let us all go together."

As the trio headed towards the billabong, the Sarge showed up and said, "You are just the people that I was looking for. May I join you on your walk?"

Wajickee replied, "It would be a great gathering if in fact you were to come with us, my liege. There are a lot of distractions in the camp, and I think we all should be at the fire tonight to keep them from impacting another like they have Mary Alice. Yes sir, by all means, please join us."

Prior to arriving at the billabong, strange sounds could be heard, and the Sarge slowed his pace but was encouraged by Wajickee to walk as if he were the king of this land.

Wajickee said, "By the way, if a king was the highest rank in the land, then it would be you. Your people stopped the ghastly things that were being done to the Aborigine. Without monuments or accolades, this land rightfully belongs to you, Ben Beckmire, for if your family had not been as bold as they were to stop the horrendous slaughter of our people, there would be no Outback. It makes me sad to think about your forefathers, for they were mighty, determined, faithful and dedicated to making sure our people were not obliterated by foreigners."

A solemn Ben Beckmire announced that he was humbled every time his feet were on this great continent. He said, "I heard so many stories about Andy Beckmire and how he became the Great Saltie. Of course, I didn't believe them because humans don't naturally transform into other life forms such as saltwater crocs, after they die. Not only that but the largest saltwater croc known to mankind. Each time I have the pleasure of seeing him, I marvel at what's before me and realize that some hearsay has truth to it. Andy Beckmire, my-great-great-great-great-grandfather, from what I am told mainly by you, was an incredibly determined lad but became who he was when his wife was murdered during a raid on his village and now he reigns supreme."

As they approached the billabong, Mary Alice screamed, "You people are trying to feed me to the beast in the billabong. I don't want to be eaten by a croc. I want my children, let me go back to them." Jong tried to ease her fears, but she continued to resist going near the billabong.

Wajickee said, "Mary Alice, you are in the company of your husband, his leader and me. We all have one goal and that is to rid you of those fauns and satyrs images that visit you while you're trying to sleep." Wajickee looked at the billabong and knew that all was not right. He said to Ben Beckmire and Jong, "Mary Alice is too upset to go near the water. Let's try some natural herbs that will relax her."

As the group headed back to the village, Wajickee excused himself, saying, "I have some other local business to attend to. I will catch you blokes later."

Back at the billabong, Wajickee noticed that the normal predators were absent. He walked around and searched for any signs of tampering and decided that there had been no foul play. As he slowly turned to leave, he heard a large flapping sound coming from the water. It was the Great Saltie anxiously moving backward and forward to the shoreline. A small croc slid up beside the Great Saltie, and he showed it compassion. It left and a large croc came up to him, and he made an extremely aggressive move towards the beast and it hastily fled. Wajickee stood in place for a moment, looked around, considered what he had just seen and deduced that the show of compassion to the younger croc and the hostile reaction to the larger croc was a sign. He knew he had failed in getting Mary Alice in the billabong but had not tried to bring Ms. Beatrice to the site. He uttered his conclusions to the Great Saltie, and it slowly swam away.

Once back in the village, with his mind racing a million miles per minute, he sought out Ms. Viola. He realized that the entire Chakes family had been missing from most meals, as the focus was trying to keep evil away from Ms. Beatrice. As he approached their hut, he heard Ms. Beatrice announce that the false prophet was at the door. Wajickee, having experienced evil of epic proportions in his time as a wizard, knew that Ms. Beatrice was no match for him no matter who her mentors were, especially in his backyard.

He calmly said, "I am no prophet, and I only want to see and speak with my friend, Ms. Viola." There was no reaction for as many as thirty seconds. Wajickee knew that the entire Chakes family was under duress. He said, "I guess you blokes are busy, I will try again tomorrow to see my friend."

After leaving the Chakes' hut, Wajickee made his way to the Beckmire's shelter. Approaching it, he saw Ben and Marcelus playing. He asked, "My friend, is it possible for your lovely wife to monitor Marcelus for a spot? I have a few major issues that I need to address with you." Ben looked at him and knew that there was something major afoot and yelled for Courtney to come and get Marcelus.

When Countney came outside, she looked at Wajickee and asked, "Are you alright? You look pinkish. I don't know how to treat a wizard but if you need my help, I am available for you." Wajickee bowed and thanked Courtney.

Wajickee asked Ben to escort him to the billabong. Once there, he said, "I came down here with Jong, Mary Alice, and you earlier. I was astonished by what I saw and when I returned, I was given clear indications from the Great Saltie that all is not right with the Chakes family. Prior to my arriving at their hut, Ms. Beatrice announced that the false prophet was about to enter their hut. I denounced the prophet nonsense and stated that I wanted to see my friend, Ms. Viola. For close to a full minute, there was no response. My other skill set kicked in, and I realized that Ms. Beatrice is holding them hostage. Although her behavior is erratic, she has not fully been converted. I was convinced of all of this by the theatrics of the Great Saltie, using a little croc to show compassion and a large one to illustrate aggression. Please do not ask me to explain each episode, just realize that I am with great certainty that some vile thing has temporarily captured Ms. Beatrice. We can't go busting in there like gangbusters."

"My liege, without clear information, I can't participate in a questionable course of action. Precisely, what is it you want me to do?" The Sarge inquired.

"Ah, my friend, I want you to command a village dinner, where everyone is mandated to attend. I have already begun the preparations insofar as the menu is concerned. Everyone likes John Dory, and therefore, that is the main course tonight.

The key to uncovering the weak link will be in their recall ability. Ms. Beatrice will be on the spot and therefore we have to look for another ruse. Mary Alice would be a poor choice because we have exposed her. It would be too obvious to utilize anyone from the Chakes's camp. I'm leaning more towards Monica or Ayesha."

"Why those two, Wajickee?"

"Because they are rational and unlikely to believe that their behavior has changed suddenly. However, that doesn't mean that there aren't others, and I may be totally wrong."

Beckmire mumbled under his breath, "How many times have that happened in the last 100 years?"

Wajickee announced, "I heard what you said, Ben Beckmire."

# # #

At dinner Luana kept making excuses for Ms. Beatrice. Wajickee and Ben Beckmire gathered Ms. Viola and Wajickee asked, "Are you afraid of the sunlight?"

Ben Beckmire was clueless and looked at Wajickee as if he had lost his mind." Ms. Viola responded, "I see both night and day, those coming and going, those who are making the offerings and those who are the receivers. Within the hut, there exists an everlasting somber mood. My family is sad, but they don't know why, and they are unaware of the shenanigans being played on them as well as attempted on Ms. Beatrice. I act as if I am normal because it is best to know your adversary rather than to let him sneak in before your very eyes. I am aware although I have not indicated any knowledge of anything that is happening. At one point, one of the purveyors tried to summon my aura but was unable to. I have only seen the dark side petition her services. That which is good and pure, has not appeared."

"That which is good and pure does not barter for allegiances," Wajickee indicated.

Chakes came over to Wajickee, Ben Beckmire and Ms. Viola and asked, "Is there anything that I can do to help my child?"

Wajickee responded, "There is, and that is to never stop referring to her as your child. No matter the blowback, keep acknowledging that she is your little girl and will always be until the day you die."

Ms. Viola asked, "Are you aware of anything abnormal happening in your hut?"

"The only weird thing is once I enter it, all I want to do is sleep. Why do you ask?"

"I'm just gathering information before I make assumptions and predictions," Ms. Viola stated.

Wajickee smiled at her and asked, "Maybe later we can take a stroll, and behold all that is Australia pure?"

Ms. Viola smiled and replied, "That would be magnificent."

Ben Beckmire in the meantime checked out Chakes and asked, "That rash on your neck, is that from that mess we encountered in the jungle?"

"Sarge, I don't know what it is. It sometimes itches but other than that, I pay it no never mind," Chakes responded.

"Nevertheless, please see my wife, and let her examine it."

# # #

That night, while the rest of the camp slept, Ms. Beatrice made her way to the billabong unknown by most except Wajickee. As she sat with her feet in the water, the inhabitants of the billabong came suspiciously close to her. In the background there was a massive thrashing of the water, and they hastily disappeared. In their place was the largest saltwater croc in the entire universe. Ms. Beatrice neither fretted nor made an attempt to retreat. She sat there as if she wanted the Great Saltie to feast upon her confused body and soul. Wajickee eased next to her and said, "The Great Saltie has accepted you as an ally. He wants to know in what dimension will you exist?"

Ms. Beatrice looked at Wajickee and smiled. After a few seconds, she stated, "I like what the other side is portraying; the glitz, the power and my association with the holy father who is in disrepair. These are the things that I want. However, these are the very things that I should not be considering. Truthfully, I was hoping that the landlord of this place would consume all that is me. I am so conflicted that it tires me when all that is possible is thrown before me. I don't want to be a goddess, an empress, or any other such thing. I want to be no more and that is why I am here. He knows what is right and he also has decided that my time on this earth has come to an end. I don't want to disappoint the Holy Father, and I want to make him as happy as the chronicles indicate I can do. On the other hand, I have hurt the only person that genuinely loves me for me. My dad is in conflict because of those creatures that make me say mean and awful things. My dad ignores me and that is the most hurtful thing that I have ever felt. He saved my mom, granny, and me. He is all that matters, and I let something manipulate my true feelings and I lambasted him, breaking his heart. I don't want to be on either side of the proposed equations. I want the Great Saltie to consume all that there is of me."

Wajickee looked long and hard at Ms. Beatrice and said, "Your wish is my command. I will leave you here with the landlord, as you call him, and may your journey be swift and painless. I will say this to you Ms. Beatrice before we part, I have seen many souls make decisions that are advantageous to their existence, however, I've not met any who reneged on the option for everlasting life. You are special my friend and I will never forget you."

Ms. Beatrice asked, "Can I depend upon you to care for this rag-tag-tribe? Can I count on you to make sure that my mom, brother, sister, and granny, most of all my dad, know that I am in a good place and that my decision was the only one that would please all parties?"

Wajickee arched his back and said, "Yours is not to please, yours is to command and help." There was an extremely long pause while Wajickee cogitated about the future. He said, "You, my friend, will not be going anywhere other than back to your hut. Your choice was not a negotiation session, it was a choice between good and evil. Somewhere and somehow, something distorted the meaning of your purpose and provided you with a compromise situation— either/or!"

# # #

Hood with Dempsey in tow, saw the Sarge playing with Marcelus and approached him with a sense of urgency. Hood said, "Sarge, I hate to bother you"—The Sarge cut him off and replied, "Then don't."

The Sarge looked at Marcelus and asked, "Can you excuse me for a minute? I am not going far. I just have to listen to these two people." The Sarge looked at Hood and asked, "What is so important that you two have to interrupt my playtime with my son?"

Hood replied, "Sarge, I guess I should have taken this up with Ms. Monica first and then came to you with a solution. Anyway, we're here and we might as well bring you up to date."

The Sarge asked, "You two couldn't deal with whatever it is that's bothering you?"

Dempsey replied, "Absolutely not! It's about Marcelus."

The two remained quiet until the Sarge asked, "What about Marcelus?"

Hood replied, "Nurse Matthews called a few days ago and left a message that Marcelus's Swiss grandparents filed a police report that he had been kidnapped by you with help from Nurse Mattews and Joan Nuehergun and you people forced him and his wife to sign a termination of parental rights decrees."

After considering the information, the Sarge asked, "What do you think they want?"

Hood blurted out, "Really?! Money of course."

"How would they pursue that course. We never flaunted things while there," the Sarge stated.

"Sarge, remember foreigners invested heavily in the new home for children. I think they got wind of it, realized that the timing was the same as the disappearance of their unwanted grandchild and they began to develop a love for the kid that only money can cure. I'm sorry, Sarge, I'm being crass, but when we were there they wanted no part of a biracial baby. Now, all of a sudden, they want to file police reports. Listen, I know we left Nurse Mattews and Joan Nuehergun financially well off. One of the things that I think should happen immediately is that we send a text telling them to listen but not to act. If you yield to this extortion, then the next time it will be for an even greater sum," Hood stated.

"What else do you think we should do?" the Sarge asked.

Dempsey chimed in and said, "Our two ladies are packing as we speak."

The Sarge looked at him and smiled. He picked Marcelus up, hugged him and said, "If I must obliterate all who would barter for your unwanted soul, then so be it. Find Larry for me, I may want him involved in this matter."

Later that afternoon, Larry showed up at the Sarge's hut and announced himself. The Sarge yelled, "Come on in, I'm changing a diaper with a motherload from Marcelus."

Larry replied, "Been there and done that. I'll just wait outside until you're finished."

The Sarge came out and said, "Whew!"

Marcelus walked over to Larry and gave him a fist bump.

Larry asked, "How are you doing?"

Marcelus mumbled something inaudible.

The Sarge said, "I seem to be involved in a kidnapping. Is there any way you can accompany Hood, Dempsey, and their mates to Switzerland to clean up the concern?"

"Dad, if that's your call, then count me in."

"Thanks, son. I don't ever want to be in a position where my people can be hurt as a result of a lack of coverage."

"What's the timetable, Dad?"

"It's immediate. I have been charged with kidnapping, with support from Joan Nuehergun and Nurse Mattews. I'll get back to you after dinner."

# # #

That night would be filled with spiritual jubilation. After the group feasted on John Dory, Ben Beckmire indicated that he had a couple of announcements to make. Everyone grunted and made other barely audible sounds. Beckmire said, "Listen the longer you people ignore me, the later we will be here." Beckmire then announced that he was being accused of kidnapping Marcelus and that Nurse Mattews and Joan Nuehergun were named accomplices. He then stated, "I have asked Hood, Dempsey, their brides and Larry to attend to this matter for me."

Courtney stood up and said, "Oh, no, Ben Beckmire. This requires a root canal. If you don't clean it completely out, it's going to come a calling again. I think we all could use a trip away from paradise."

Monica yelled, "I'm with my sister." Then there was a rousing amount of noise from the rest of the female attendees.

Ben Beckmire said, "I like your commitments, however, if we all go, that means the children will have to go as well. I don't want to create any tension or separation issues if we take Marcelus and find out that our adversary is connected, and Marcelus is taken from us at the airport. No, my friends, we need a contingent to stay here with the children and protect them." The vociferous group calmed down after hearing Beckmire's rationale.

Courtney said, "That is why I love this man and have loved him ever since he begged me to have dinner with him when he was a cop. Lucky him."

# # #

Ms. Beatrice, who had tears flowing down her face as if she were a faucet of some kind, said to Wajickee, "I no longer want to be of this world. The only man who genuinely loves me is now in despair from the remarks that I made. My dad, Mr. Chakes, is a clever and adorable human being. Of late, all he does is sleep. I think he is taking some kind of native drug to induce sleep so that he can avoid any further humiliation from me. I love my dad, and he is the most important person on earth to me. I mean granny and my mom are really cool, but my dad, well he told me when I was little that he would love me until the earth reversed its course and time was no more. Every time I visualize him saying that to me, I lose all respect for myself. I can't face him and therefore, I don't want to live any longer."

Wajickee watched, with his arms folded as Ms. Beatrice made a quick and unexpected dash into the billabong. The Great Saltie slowly pushed her to shore with its tale. It then swam off and disappeared into the night. Watching her cry, Wajickee said, "Ms. Beatrice, when you're finished with your theatrics, let's go and get Mr. Chakes and have a sit down with him. What about that?"

Approximately an hour later, Chakes was summoned to the billabong by Wajickee and once there, he saw Ms. Beatrice. He said, "Baby, are you alright? What are you doing down here by yourself?"

Ms. Beatrice responded, "Dad, I'm not alone. Wajickee is somewhere near."

"Don't you think you're a little too close to the water's edge?"

Ms. Beatrice looked behind her and said, "The landlord has no need for me. I offered myself to him earlier and he pushed me back to land."

"Okay baby, what's going on?"

"Dad, I tried to end my life, because I disrespected and admonished you in front of everyone and in the harshest of terms. I offered myself to the Great Saltie, but Wajickee and he just ignored my childish attempt. I can't take those hateful words back, but I can say with all my heart that I didn't mean them, and I want you to still consider me as your child."

Ms. Beatrice, with tears flowing at a level that could fill a billabong, was gently embraced by her dad. Chakes said, "Girl, I know you love me, and I love you. Throughout our existence, we have seen strange and beautiful things that no one can explain like the Great Saltie. I am smart enough to know that possession is a mighty thing. This group is made of iron, not plastic. Shit happens and then we address it. I'm just pissed because I didn't have the opportunity to confront whoever or whatever took control of your mind. Baby, do you remember what I told you when you were a little girl?"

"I do, Dad. You said that you would love me until the earth reversed its course, and time was no more!"

A smiling Wajickee loudly noted, "All is well in the Outback, and the Outback is where all are fortunate!"

CHAPTER SEVEN

As the group gathered their belongings, two SUVs pulled up to baggage claim. The group was studying the vehicles when Joan Nuehergun stepped out of one and Nurse Mattews out of the other and Joan said, "Pile in people. My brother loaned me this thing to pick you guys up. There is much to talk about, and I know that you're tired. Some of you get in Nurse Mattew's vehicle."

Dempsey said, "I want to go to the suddenly loving grandparents' place and have a look see. I want to study them before they realize that we're here. These people wanted nothing to do with a biracial child and consequently, that decision led to the suicide death of their daughter. It's all about money and I don't want to waste time talking about bullshit."

Nurse Mattews exhaled and exclaimed, "Wow! So much for small talk."

Larry butted in and announced, "People, I am senior here and these are my goals and objectives. I want Dempsey and Nurse Mattews to ascertain the legal aspects of this issue. I want Hood and Angel to be my enforcers and find out how this unwanted child turned into a desirable bounty for the grandparents. Who leaked who we are? Anel, you will work with me to check out the status of the grandparents, you know, any criminal records, bank accounts, infidelity, and anything else we can find on them. They don't want that child, but they want to be paid. We can pay them or make them go away permanently. I want to be as transparent as possible in these matters, but I also want to make sure that people know we be from both heaven and hell!"

The following morning, Nurse Mattews and Dempsey visited the grandparents at their home and realized that the place was in disrepair. The grandfather stated, "I tried to contact the people who are in possession of Marcus."

The wife said, "Marcus is our only spiritual and emotional connection to our daughter, who committed suicide because that black man raped and impregnated her. That is all we have of our daughter, and we want that child in our home to raise, nurture and guide."

Nurse Mattews asked, "Wasn't your initial response to the fact that your daughter had a biracial child, disappointing?"

The husband responded, "The press always gets it wrong. We have always said that we wanted that child here with us to raise and to care for. We have no idea where those comments about us being racist started. There was never a moment when we didn't want Marcus in our home to live and to care for."

Nurse Mattews asked, "Have you ever seen the child? Did you visit him in the hospital? Did you see him while he was in the orphanage? Did you make any connections with the child after it was confirmed that he was bi-racial?"

The husband said, "We called the hospital, but they wouldn't give us any information about Marcus until we showed up. Well, the misses had that Covid 15 thing and we didn't want to expose the child to that terrible virus."

Nurse Mattews asked, "Did you get the vaccine for Covid and when did you come down with it? Why did you file a report of a child being kidnapped, over a year after the fact?"

The husband stumbled over his words and replied, "Well, well, we tried to gather information about his status, but they kept putting us on hold at that welfare place. We didn't want welfare we just tried to find out what was happening with our grandson, Marcus."

Nurse Mattews said, "The grandparents from the African American side of the equation want to make a deal. They're suggesting that you keep the child during the winter months, and they keep him during the summer, on a rotational basis each year."

The wife was about to speak when Dempsey said, "You guys do know that the adoption is final, legal and that the child has become attached and dependent on his other grandparents. Why didn't you contest the adoption when you had the chance? Did someone tell you that Marcus was adopted by a wealthy family?"

The husband said, "Now, wait a minute. These questions aren't necessary, because we believe we were hoodwinked into signing that termination of parental rights agreement under duress, at that. We were told about your group's history during and after Vietnam. You people bullied us."

Dempsey replied, "We never saw you, talked to you, or even cared about you. You were so concerned about your image and the fact that the little human being was a throwaway. Now you want to share in his care, sounds like and smells like crap."

Nurse Mattews said, "Let's try to reason this matter out. As you stated, you were forced into signing a termination of parental rights agreement. Can you tell me who brought this matter to you?"

There was a pause, then the man said, "The woman from the adoption office. She said important people were interested in adopting our grandbaby and that they will give us $1,000 Swiss francs as soon as it happened."

"Did you receive the money?" Nurse Mattews inquired.

"As a matter of fact, we did, but we think it's worth more than that, but we were afraid of you people because of your history of violence."

Dempsey pardoned himself and called Hood. When Hood answered the phone, Dempsey asked, "What was the amount of money we gave to that adoption lady for her help in securing Marcelus?"

"We gave her $50,000 Swiss francs. Why?" Hood asked.

"I'll get back to you. I think the adoption lady pulled a fast one. I'll call you back." In the meantime, Dempsey placed a listening device behind a picture and another one behind a coat rack.

Dempsey returned to the meeting and asked Nurse Mattews if he could speak to her in private. The two stepped out of the house and Demspey said, "I think the lady in the adoption office pulled a fast one by distorting our history, scaring these people and making off with $49,000 Swiss francs."

Nurse Mattews said, "Well, she did resign her job and leave the country right after you guys left."

Dempsey shook his head and said, "Well, I hope she puts it to good use."

Back inside, Dempsey said to the husband, "You did say that you received $1,000 Swiss francs, is that correct?" The man shook his head in a manner affirming that statement. Dempsey then said, "I want everyone to be transparent here." He looked around the house and said, "Do you think you can take care of another human being in your house. I mean, it doesn't appear that you people are living high on the hog, but more like low on the ground. I'm not casting any aspersions, but I don't think your home is conducive to raising a small child. Now tell me the truth. Do you think you can faithfully keep a child six months out of the year?"

The husband said, "I don't know what kind of fancy place you have, but our home is our home."

Dempsey shot back, "Automation took over your job. You're about to forfeit your home to that thieving ass bank and you're hiding your truck because it too is in foreclosure. What will it take for us to never hear from you again? Before you answer that question, I want you to remember what the crooked adoption lady told you about our history. We're only going to do this dance once and if you attempt to extort us again, there will be a heavy price to pay. Am I making myself clear? This is not a bribe, this is not a negotiation, this is a transparent statement of what it takes for you to continue to exist. This kind of thing will never come across our table again. So, what will it take to end this charade forever?"

The husband replied, "You can't bully me. I'm going to call the police."

Dempsey said, "That is the last thing you want to do. We'll buy this place from under you, buy your hidden truck, and watch you try to get welfare but are denied because of incorrect and fraudulent information provided."

The man's wife screamed, "Stop this craziness right now. Harold, we won't have a pot to piss in, after next week. Give the man a reasonable number and let it be. We don't want the police involved in this matter."

Harold, in tears, hugged his wife and said, "Mr. we won't bother you ever again, but it's going to take $10,000 Swiss francs.

Dempsey pulled out two stacks of Francs and placed them on the table. He said, "I think we're done here. Remember, never again, never again!" He helped Nurse Mattews out of her chair and said, "Goodbye."

Once in the car, Nurse Mattews asked, "How much money did you leave, if I may ask?"

Dempsey smiled and said, "$80,000 francs and a note correcting their understanding of the child's name. It simply stated, "There is no child named Marcus. There is a child named Marcelus!"

#

After meeting with Nurse Mattews and Joan Nuehergun about the status of the rebuilding of the orphanage building, the group went out to dinner. Dempsey allowed Nurse Mattews to tell the story of the meeting with the grandparents of Marcelus. Those in attendance agreed that there was no coercion, cajoling, or manipulating the result that they wanted. Those people were on their last leg and thought that there was a happy ending in using the kidnapping proposition. She said, "Initially, I thought it was not going to go well, especially since Mr. Dempsey called them out by embarrassing them and their environment. It always seems to boil down to the notion of money. It was money in Joan's case, it was money that almost tempted me, and it was an insignificant amount requested for a baby. Money, money, money; it rules humanity."

The following morning, the group assembled in the hotel lobby for their ride to the airport. Joan Nuehergun said, "I am still in disbelief about your group's intentions. You helped me, Nurse Mattews, those children, and we don't have a legal document in place."

Larry said, "I'd like to tell a story about a member of our team who we adopted. If Michael were here, he would say, "That is the same thing my dad said to those pirates when they offered to gut his dilapidated hotel and make it a five-star resort. My father knew that there was a hustle somewhere in the middle of it, but he didn't live long enough to find it. What he did find was a group of people who care about humanity and not the almighty dollar. Listen, I have been with them for a long time, and this is what we do. We don't buy fancy cars, boats, or mansions; we help people help themselves."

## CHAPTER EIGHT

Back in the Outback, the group planned its annual financial meeting. Jong, with his inimitable self, concluded that the group was so rich that it was hard to keep books on the assets, currency on hand, bullion deposits, stocks, bonds, and bearer bonds that were in their care. Jong said, "As an example, we purchased 100,000 shares of Nvidia at a cost of $295 per share or $29,500,000. It is now selling at $1,450 per share and the value of the group's holding is $145,000,000, a profit of $115,500,000. We have bullion that is worth $125,000,000 and uncut diamonds worth billions. Now, my nephew knows that if a single dollar is unaccounted for, his entire family will be decapitated while he watches. I say that to say, our money is in good hands, and he has said that our portfolio and holdings have topped one trillion dollars." Everyone screamed and gave each other high fives and hugs.

Zanthius asked, "Is there any possible scenario in which those funds can be embezzled?"

Jong made a guttural sound and said, "He is our bookkeeper. Him, no handle our funds. He gets reports from all of those brokerage houses and places a summary in a binder, a binder that each one of you will have after this meeting. Other than the new guys, those who started this adventure in the beginning, are billionaires."

Zanthius said, "I'm not making an accusation. I want to know how my other brother and his brigands were going to take over our assets. It's a question that has bothered me for a long time, even after we believe that he exists no more. How was he going to become the rightful inheritor of our funds?"

Jong turned to the Sarge and said, "This son makes a valid point and one that I have considered myself. Is there a forfeiture clause that directs all of our assets to you?"

The Sarge screamed, "Don't be ridiculous. I could give a shit about money. I prefer to take my new son home and live in peace without the past rearing its ugly head on occasion."

Zanthius said, "Hold on Dad. No one is accusing anyone. We're just trying to figure out if things had gone your other son's way, how was he going to be able to capture all that we have. It's a question, Dad. It is not an accusation."

The Sarge stood up and said, "I never accepted it as an accusation, not from people who I have bled with, slept in ditches with and killed a shitload of enemy with, both foreign and domestic. Now all of you Johnnie-come-lately types, well that's a different kind of analysis, I think."

John Lee asked, "Since we all be thinking about that question, why don't we have a conversation tomorrow about any holes in our armor. I be meaning where we be vulnerable, where someone can slip in on us legally. I think Ms. Monica be the right person to chair such a meeting and since that other boy of yours, *'the idiot spy'* asked the question, make him co-chairperson."

Jilkes stood up and said, "Once again, my country bumpkin makes sense and I second his motion. I mean really, how was your boy, or any of the other groups, going to take advantage of our assets? He and they must have had a plan and a method to make it happen. I mean he did attend that military school and studied finance I think."

The Sarge replied, "People, I apologize if it seems as though I was trying to defend any action against us, including that of my son. My problem is that it is a hurtful subject and one that makes me and my wife sad."

The Sarge and Courtney started to walk away, but he turned around and said, John Lee Jones, I like your thoughts. People, please pursue all avenues that leaves us vulnerable but more importantly, investigate how my son was going to benefit from our holdings.

# # #

No one had seen Wajickee in days. However, he could see everyone from his viewpoint high on a mountain range. He watched the comings and goings of the group and knew that his time as Sheppard was coming to an end. He also knew what act he had committed that accentuated his end point.

During an episode with a demon that was pursuing Ms. Beatrice's soul, Wajickee summoned the elders to intervene. The act was forbidden, because Ms. Beatrice was of clear mind, a position that allowed her to fend for herself. The elders knew what was happening and allowed Wajickee to do this final act with the tribe. He knew that at the next full moon, which was scheduled on the next day, he would have to, without ceremony, end his relationship with the tribe, Ben Beckmire and the Great Saltie, an affiliation that he had shared for centuries.

That evening would be his last amongst the group and he wanted to go out with a bang. The menu was phenomenal; it consisted of native plants, nuts, fruits, and, of course, John Dory. Wajickee appeared in a regal costume that everyone admired. Ben Beckmire asked, "What's the occasion, my liege?"

Wajickee smiled and replied, "I'm just celebrating my input with this rag-tag tribe. It has been the most rewarding adventure that this old man has been a part of. I was just thinking about how people came to burn down the town hall to destroy the only records of ownership in this area. They came for diamonds, they came for gold, they came to take this land from its rightful owners. They brought thousands of souls who will never be heard from again. Their base DNA resides in the dingoes, wombats, saltwater crocs, and other animals indigenous to this land. This tribe, with my help and guidance, thwarted every effort to seize this land by force. We developed a new prototype for tribes all across Australia. Never again will people be able to waltz up in here and plant their flags because we don't look like them, eat like them, worship the same deity and dress like them. No, my friend, what we have been able to establish here today will last forever. Look at all of the babies that have been born here in this wonderful land. God and the Spirits embrace and enjoy all that we do, even if it means to take another's life. We have been blessed, despite the efforts of your own seed who tried to manipulate and destroy us. However, look at what happened; he planted a seed, suggested that it be thrown away, and you and that wonderful doctor lady have become parents all over again. Now, that is a blessing from heaven and the spirit world. My friend, this day, this evening, shall live in infamy."

The Sarge looked long and hard at Wajickee and realized that he had just given him a farewell sermon. After a few moments, he astutely asked, "What have you done to be summoned and to never return? Don't give me noise, give me facts."

Wajickee asked, "What on earth are you talking about, Ben Beckmire? Because I recall our great triumphs to free our people and to make sure foreigners can't come up in here and in all of Australia and rape us of what is ours. That makes you think that I have committed some violation of my tenure and I'm being called away?"

Ben Beckmire said, "Once again, it sounds like a bunch of malarkeys. Tell me the truth, which you are obligated to do when asked by me. Tell me what you have done to be summoned?"

There was an extremely long pause before Wajickee softly stated, "I interfered with Ms. Beatrice's decision. I called on the elders to help me thwart an attempt by a ranking demon."

Ben Beckmire announced, "I know you can speak louder than that. I only got half of what you said. Please repeat."

"I played around in a venue that I should not have. I interfered with Ms. Beatrice's decision. I coerced some of the elders into helping me direct her decision-making process by feigning the existence of a super-demon. The funny thing is, I could see myself doing it again, if the matter presented itself to me. I know right from wrong and the other side, well, they were playing with crooked dice, as some of your people would articulate."

Beckmire, with tears in his eyes, asked, "So, my friend, you, for the sake of that child, decided to bring about your own kind of magic. I'm sorry that your actions will create a void in our existence, for you more than any other know the ways of the Beckmires. However, you were warned about involving yourself in mortal affairs, but come to think of it, everything that you do gets you closer to human nature. Had I known, I would have forbidden any such actions. When will you transition?"

"At midnight. I will move to the other side and watch over you from afar, but not too far. My son, I will be with you until the earth stops rotating and humanity, as we know it, is no more. Please, let me spend my remaining time in laughter and joy, and not in sorrow," Wajickee stated.

Ben Beckmire asked, "May I hug you?"

"Of course you can," Wajickee responded.

# # #

The following day, Ms. Beatrice received a text message from an unknown number. She paid it no matter until it kept repeating itself every few minute. Opening the text message, she read, "Your decision does not hurt our relationship, it only makes it more adaptable. Signed, your friend and mentor!"

Ms. Beatrice initially thought that the message wasn't for her. As if someone was reading her mind, a second text message signal buzzed, that read, "Guess who?" She did not respond and just thought about the message. Again, as if someone were clairvoyant, a third text message buzzed that read. Some have said that I am ecclesiastically oriented."

At that point, she dropped the phone and screamed at the top of her lungs. Seemingly, the entire village came to her side. Ms. Viola asked, "Child, what on earth has gotten into you?"

Ms. Beatrice pointed to the phone and announced, "He is not dead. He is alive."

Ms. Viola asked, "Who is not dead? Who is alive?"

"The Holy Father!" Ms. Beatrice stated.

Zanthius picked up the phone, examined it, showed it to Chakes, and whispered, "The phone is not on."

Chakes checked the phone and agreed that it was not on. He then asked Ms. Beatrice, "Honey, did you get a call or a message?" To which Ms. Beatrice responded, "I received three text messages."

Chakes asked, "Baby, can you put your password in so that I can see the substance of the messages?" He handed Ms. Beatrice the phone and watched her turn it on. At which point Chakes asked, "Baby, did you turn the phone off after you received the messages?"

Ms. Beatrice looked at him and said, "I dropped the phone after realizing who was texting me."

Chakes hugged her and said, "Let's get you back to the hut."

In their hut, Luana put in her password and saw that there were no new messages and that the last message was dated a week ago. She whispered to Ms. Viola, "I think they're now trying to play mind games with my child. Where is the wizard?"

Ben Beckmire dropped his head and replied, "He has been given another assignment."

No sooner had he finished his sentence, Wajickee appeared at the entrance to the hut and announced, "I am sorry to be late. And indeed, although there are no messages of late on Ms. Beatrice's phone, she clearly received messages from that demon. They will stop at nothing to achieve their mission and bring her into the depths of hell. Please forgive my absence, but other matters of state have been shoved into my path. Please leave me and Ms. Beatrice alone for a few moments, so that we can see what path is needed to be taken."

Less than an hour later, Wajickee and a smiling Ms. Beatrice exited the hut. Ms. Beatrice announced, "Since I have been the victim of games that I don't understand, I now believe it is time for me to play a few of my own. To express the nature of my actions would be to forewarn my adversaries. With the help of my family, especially my dad, along with guidance from Mr. Wajickee, I think we might be able to see the end of these adverse efforts to sway me to a particular mindset. It is my firm belief that the Holy Father has returned from his hiatus and will make an all-out attempt to gather my feelings and get me to be at his side. My only response at this time is that only men can anoint men to powerful roles and therefore, I will only be a follower of our Lord Jesus Christ."

Dempsey and Hood were wading in the billabong reflecting about their fortunate alignment with the group. Hood said, "Did you ever think that we would be in the position that we're in today? I mean, look at us. We're rich, great wives, children, friends and a totally accepting new family." Dempsey was about to respond when his Apple Watch began to buzz. He looked at it and proceeded to get out of the water. Hood asked, "Is everything okay?"

Dempsey not responding, picked up his phone and read a message that was forwarded to him from listening devices that he planted in the grandparents' house in Switzerland. As he listened to the distorted message, he said, "I think we need to see the boss. This sounds like a tornado coming our way."

Ten or so minutes later, Hood and Dempsey saw the Sarge, and Dempsey said, "Boss, we need to talk. When we were in Switzerland, I placed two high-end listening devices in the grandparents' house. Although slow in relaying its content, they work quite well out here."

The Sarge asked, "Are we going to talk about devices or circumstances?"

"Sorry boss, but I think you need to hear a conversation that happened three days ago." Dempsey gave the Sarge his headset and told him to listen closely. After four minutes, the Sarge exclaimed, "I can't fucking believe this. Are you sure about this?"

"Sarge, we are only the messengers on this one. If the information or sounds are correct, it appears that your boy is alive, or someone is playing his part and is consorting with our adversaries."

The Sarge stared into space and finally said, "Not a word of this to anyone, until we can be absodamnlutely sure. Not a single word guys. I need you to come back to me with a strategy as to how we check this thing out. Why would he go back to those people, if it was him, they hate everything about him including that he is the cause of their daughter's demise? I just don't get it."

As the Sarge was talking, Dempsey's watch and phone began to buzz. It was another message. He retrieved his earphones from the Sarge and listened to another transmission, which wasn't a message at all, but sounded like three shots being fired from a weapon of some kind. He slowly and somberly handed the headset to the Sarge. The Sarge listened to the sounds and stated, "That was gunfire. Can we get confirmation from the two ladies over there?"

In the meantime, Hood made a call to Nurse Mattews. Once she answered the phone, Hood asked, "Is everything okay there?"

Nurse Mattews responded, "And good day to you as well, Mr. Hood. Oh, yes, I am fine, the construction is going well and the kids, Joan Nuehergun and I just returned from that marvelous farm that you people have in Virginia. The kids had no idea that there was so much open space and freedom to roam. Now, back to your question. It appears the wife found out that her husband was supporting another woman and that is why they were about to lose their house and truck. It is alleged that she shot him twice and then turned the gun on herself. It also appears that there have been people asking about a mixed-race baby. No one came to us because I guess we were away. However, I feel this situation is all too convenient. Someone is house cleaning, and I think it all has to do with that child."

Hood replied, "You know we placed two listening devices in that house. It would be great if you could somehow obtain those devices. They are incredibly special in that they record, filter, and forward every sound made within a 10-foot radius."

"Mr. Hood, are you suggesting that I break the law and enter a crime scene?"

Hood remained silent for a minute and then said, "That is exactly what I am asking. I also understand that this is not your forte. However, it might lead to a better understanding of what happened and whether a tenacious enemy is still amongst the living." There was quiet on the other end of the phone to the degree that Hood asked, "Are you still there?"

"Oh yes, I'm just thinking about how to pull this caper off. Better still, I will just go there and pretend that there is information that I need about their daughter."

"Nurse Mattews, I wouldn't dare ask you to do anything like that. However, once I send you a file that you'll need to open, I will ask that you inconspicuously walk past the house and hold the reset button on the login notification for fifteen seconds. If that fails, it will alert you by buzzing your phone. I prefer you make this attempt during the night. That way, hopefully, no one will be able to identify you," Hood indicated.

Nurse Mattews replied, "I was looking forward to breaking the law and becoming a criminal. This AI stuff takes the fun out of everything. When will you send me the file?"

"As soon as we complete this conversation. Give it five or so minutes to load. Just place your phone on a table and leave it be for that amount of time. It will make a clicking noise once it has successfully downloaded. If it fails, it will give you a message that indicates you are an unauthorized user of this file, and it will lock and subsequently delete the file. In any event, it will not compromise your phone," Hood stated.

Nurse Mattews stated, "I am looking forward to this caper. Once I get the file, I will call you for direct instructions. I appreciate the fact that you trust me to do such a stealthy task. I will speak with you shortly."

Nurse Mattews began her evening by dressing in a black outfit and completed her look with a black baseball cap. She donned sunglasses but realized that she couldn't see with them on. She made the drive to where the grandparents of Marcelus resided, parked her truck two blocks away, walked down the road on the opposite side of the street, passed the house, and then crossed the street. She began to sweat profusely and for a minute thought that she looked like a crook. She paused once she crossed the street, pulled out her phone, pretended to make a call, and began her arduous journey that would take her past the house where two people died. The writing on the tape stated, "police activity, do not enter." She pulled up the file that Hood sent her, followed his instructions, paused for approximately twenty seconds and when both devices uploaded to her phone, she sent the file to Hood.

As she entered her car, she breathed a sigh of relief. She dialed Hood's phone and waited for him to pick up. Hood answered and said, "You're a natural crook. You did this with ease, and the recordings, photos and sounds are immaculately clear. Thanks, Nurse Mattews, you saved me a long trip. Go home, have a drink, and realize that you are a part of solving a crime of murder."

Nurse Mattews replied, "You Yanks are so full of "bs". However, I wouldn't have it any other way. I must admit, I was scared to death but decided to woman-up and get the job done. I feel really good about how I handled the situation, and I'm going to go out, and get laid. Goodnight, Mr. Hood."

CHAPTER NINE

On the other side of the world, Helga Spengatsenburg searched high and low for any information about the detached Beckmire son. Although keeping his last name on official documents, he changed his getaway name to Vincent Lassiter, after the real person moved back to South Africa. She started her search at the Naval Academy, in Annapolis, Maryland. And, seemingly, the only official picture of him was destroyed in a suspicious fire at the Academy. He and his friends rarely posed for pictures, knowing full well that their missions in life were not honorable ones. However, his class picture showed him with two significant scars on his face and with one eye nearly naturally shut.

Helga, after adding all of the pieces together—poor parents turned to rich parents, no contact with them until money is an issue and the blatant disrespect of those who gave birth to him. She found herself in a restaurant watching people break and eat that most disgusting of bottom feeders—the crab! She watched with fascination how people would open them, clean out a substance, and then eat all of the meat inside. She said to the barkeep, "I'm told that if a person has ever been in this place, you would remember them."

The barkeep looked Ms. Spengatsenburg up and down and stated, "I can't imagine anyone that you know, leaving you."

Helga smiled, thanked him for the compliment, showed him a photo, and said, "I'm looking for someone, this someone who was allegedly murdered and his body parts thrown into the water for fish food."

The barkeep's eyes opened wide, and he said, "Lady, that is not a conversation you want to broach with people. That is still a messy investigation because nothing was ever found that could identify the person.

Helga pulled out a stack of $100 bills and said, "Maybe today is your lucky day." She placed a napkin over the money. "Can you direct me to any of his old friends?"

The guy looked around the room and realized that everyone was fascinated with this well-dressed, good-looking woman who was talking to him. He quietly asked, "How much is in that stack?" Helga smiled and softly replied, "Five thousand."

The barkeep said, "Let me pour you a drink and act as if this is a romantic issue and then we can continue with this conversation.

Helga searched the bar offerings and to her amazement, there it was, a bottle of Cruzan Rum. She asked, "Do you sell much Cruzan Rum?"

"It keeps up with the other rums in terms of sales," the barkeep replied.

"I'll have a rum and coke, please. Did the person of interest come here a lot?" Helga asked.

"During the summer, probably twice a month. He wasn't a big crab eater, but his buddies were addicted. I mean they would spend $1,000 on crabs and beer, leave $300 to $400 in tips and they always paid with cash. Every time they would come in, one of the guys would hand me $100 bill and say, "keep the beer flowing". The strange thing about them is that they would have beers and talk amongst themselves in low tones, but with serious looks on their faces. This would last until the crabs came and then they would lighten up and begin their feast."

Helga asked, "Any way you can direct me to any of those buddies of his?"

The barkeep looked at the stack and stated, "This is some scary stuff, way over my head, but I certainly can use the money."

Helga slid the napkin and its contents to the barkeep and told him to put it in his pocket. She then pulled out another stack of hundred-dollar bills and said, "The better the information is in the next three minutes, the larger that stack becomes."

The barkeep announced, "I don't want to keep playing this game and I don't want to get greedy. I'm happy with what you have given me. When I go to the other end of the bar to take the orders of those folks, why don't you go to the restroom and look at the guy looking at you who has on a shirt with a picture of a pirate on it."

Like clockwork, the barkeep went to take the orders of a couple and Helga went to the restroom. As she passed the table where the guy with the pirate shirt was sitting, she never glanced his way, but his eyes never left her body. Entering the restroom, she was appalled at the conditions and decided not to touch anything. On her way out, she passed the guy again and never looked his way. Once back at the bar, she placed another stack of money discreetly under a napkin, slid it to the barkeep and said, "The next time I am in town, I'll stop by to see you. Take care!"

Once across the street, Helga winked at her two henchmen. As expected, she had company in a matter of minutes. As she browsed in windows, the guy in the pirate shirt showed up behind her. He apologized for disturbing her, but confessed that he was entranced by her looks, her aura, and her attire. He admitted that he rarely saw anyone dressed as impeccably as she was and that everything about her looked, reflected, and articulated pure class.

Helga smiled faintly and asked, "Have we met before? You look like someone I know and that's not a pick-up line. You really remind me of an old friend."

The guy in the pirate shirt responded, "I sincerely wish to all that is heavenly that I was that old friend of yours."

Helga smiled and said, "If that's your pick-up line, then I don't want to hear your seduction line."

The guy in the pirate shirt announced, "I am Frank, Frank McClellan. May I ask your name?"

Helga looked at Frank and said, "I'm not accustomed to meeting strangers on the street and offering my name or any other information about me."

Frank immediately stated, "Listen, I am a Naval Academy mid-shipmen and we pride ourselves on being gentlemen first and naval officers second. I know I don't look like an officer, or even smell like one, but I am one."

They both laughed and Helga replied, "I am Helga and for now, that is all you get, pirate." They both laughed again.

Frank asked, "Would it be too uncomfortable for you to have a cup of tea or a drink with me in an outdoor establishment?"

Helga knew she had her man, looked at him in a serious manner, and asked, "How do I know that you're not a reject or a serial whatever?"

Frank smiled and replied, "How do I know that you're not a friend of that Bobbit lady?" They both laughed again, and Helga sternly stated, "Any act of ungentlemanly behavior will have me walking away and without you following or harassing me. Is that a deal?"

Frank responded, "In Annapolis, an officer who insults any human being, is subject to being kicked out of the Academy. We do not take advantage of or denigrate anyone, and besides, I am enamored with your beauty, smile, style, aroma, and sophistication. I just realized that I may make mistakes in talking to you because I have never talked with anyone as beautiful as you are."

"I think I'm a little older than you and I don't normally date younger men." Frank saw an opening and quickly said, "At least you think of being with me as being on a date, if it were to happen."

Helga smiled and asked, "Where is this public place where I can be watched by the world to make sure that you're not a certified nutcase?"

After a five-minute walk up Main Street, Frank stated, "This place has outdoor dining. Would you like to have a drink or a cup of coffee here?" Helga began to survey her surroundings and said, "I guess this is as good as any place."

Frank asked, "What would you like to drink?"

Helga responded, "I would love to have a Cruzan Rum and coke. Do you think this place sells it?"

"Is that what you were drinking at the crab house?" Frank asked.

"My goodness, aren't you attentive and inquisitive? For conversation's sake, I must admit that I was drinking rum and coke. What are you going to have?"

"If I may be so bold. What is the bartender to you?"

"Oh, my! You barely know me and now you want to quiz me on my drink proclivities and my relationships? How long do you think I am going to be here answering questions that are, frankly, none of your fucking business?"

Frank realized that he had crossed the line in the sand and reported, "I am with Naval Intelligence, and it is my job to notice, decipher and question to the void any situations that plays in my mind. In your case, your beauty has me multiplying this day by the hundreds. Listen, I am in awe of you, your charm, style, sensuousness, and that marvelous aroma. Before you leave me if this becomes too annoying for you, will you tell me the name of that fragrance? I feel as though I want to touch it, fondle it, kiss it, caress it, and love it to the beyond. Inquiring is a natural function of mine by training, but I promise not to ask any more questions other than those related to you and me. Is that fair enough?"

Helga smiled faintly and said, "Silly boy, at least let me sit down and have a drink before you cross-examine me. Remember, I was minding my business when you came up to me and began to ask me questions and comment about my looks. Somewhere I read that the past is prologue and as a Navy man, you must understand what that means."

#

Despite her resolve to find Beckmire's son, as the evening progressed, Frank became an admirer and a potential suitor. Helga left the small table they were sitting at, called her two associates, told them that she had the situation under control and that they could take off.

The lead guy said, "You know the rules, Ms. Spengatsenburg, we have to stay on task, regardless of any contrary demands from you."

Helga, annoyed at the audacity of an underling to question and countermand her decision, politely stated, "Motherfucker, if I turn around and see you, then you're both dead men. Get the fuck out of here because I'm going to make a night of it."

When Helga returned to the table, she asked Frank, "What kind of car do you have?" Frank, feeling a little embarrassed responded, "I have a long-wheel-base Range Rover?"

Helga fired back, "Why didn't you just say that you have the biggest Range Rover made, instead of all that wheelbase shit?"

"I didn't want to seem pretentious, because the truck is exactly that."

Helga replied, "Do you have enough gasoline to take me to some place that is not pretentious, where I can crawl into the back seat and show you all that you want while you're driving?"

A startled Frank stammered and said, "Why can't we go to my condo?"

"Because I am well known and so is my husband, who is soon to be my ex. And besides, I didn't say I was going to have sex you. I said I was going to show you exactly what you want, while you drive. I like you, Frank, but you're not going to have sex with me tonight. You can look and watch me take care of my own needs and desires, but you mustn't stop the vehicle at any time and attempt to come in the back seat with me. Is that something you can agree to Frank?" Helga asked,

"A bewildered and excited Frank, responded, "I just want to be your lap dog, I'll do anything you say. I just want to be with you. I want to watch you do your thing and maybe, just maybe, in the future, if I get the chance to participate, I will remember how you did it to yourself and I guarantee you that I'll do it better, longer, and gratify you exponentially beyond your wildest undertaking. I'm not bragging, I just know that you are what I want and need. Make me yours and show me how to satisfy you. Falling in love with you is going to be fast and furious, because you tantalize me and make all of my senses erupt, and I want to learn how to love you."

"Frank, you barely know me. However, I feel so attracted to you and I want to cautiously give you my essence, but not tonight. I just want you to watch me make love to me and when and if we ever do that dance, you had better be more creative than I could ever be to myself."

Frank drove slowly and at every opportunity stared at Helga having a go at herself in the dimly lit back seat of his Range Rover. Frank stopped at a red light, gawked at the pleasure Helga was having without his involvement and slowly but methodically asked, "Is there any part of my anatomy that could possibly help you reach nirvana?"

As if at any moment she was going to reach that pinnacle of pleasure, Helga in an almost demonic voice announced, "I want to feel your tongue deep within the confines of my body."

Frank proceeded through a red light, pulled into an empty lot, left the engine running, exited the driver's seat, opened the rear door, entered the vehicle and without hesitation began to explore, ready the prize, connect to the zone, and work it, feverishly. That would be last thing he would consider. As he dove into her zone of craziness, her hypodermic needle pierced his neck, and the orgasm of the needle would leave him unconscious.

#

Six hours later, Frank's Range Rover would be found abandoned in a seedy part of town, with the radio and other valuable items removed from it. In real time, Frank woke up in a chair with a hood covering his head and his hands and feet bound. He repeatedly asked, "Where am I? What is going on? Why are you doing this to me?"

Minutes later, a familiar voice asked, "Did you like my show? Did you like touching my essence? Frank, not that it matters, but I really enjoyed our short time together. However, it is time to do some big things, like give me truthful answers to the questions my people are going to ask you, or they will inflict pain to your body. Now that the ground rules have been articulated, Frank, do you have any questions?"

Frank could hear a cacophony of muffled sounds that caused him to panic.

Helga said, "Oh, Frank, don't be alarmed by the noise, it's just my people sharpening their blades. Please, when my people ask you a question, answer it honestly. A lot of information has been gathered and therefore, some of the answers are known. Please don't get caught in that paradox of lying. Frank be honest and I will set you free."

After a moment of silence, a male voice asked, "Are you familiar with someone named Beckmire?"

Frank yelled, "Is that who this is about? That son-of-a-bitch baited and switched the conversation about a small fortune from us to him. His old man was allegedly in charge of billions from a third-world country and it has been purported that they ripped the government off for billions of dollars. Why have you kidnapped me to ask me about that traitorous bastard?"

The male voice asked, "Were you a part of the group that used him for chum?"

There was a long pause, and the question was repeated. Finally, Frank said, "I was not a part of his demise, or the plan for his demise and I don't know anything about it."

The man speaking said to his comrade, "This fucking guy thinks that we're idiots. Let him feel the heat and then perhaps he'll fess up."

After a few minutes of rattling metals and turning on machines, one of the men said, "We told you that there was a penalty for not telling the truth. We have confirmation that it was your plan, you oversaw it, and you made the first cut. Now we have that validation from one of your partners. You rich boys think that you can make your own rules, don't you? Any further untruths will leave you with significant amputations. That noise that you heard was a laser contraption warming up. Here's what's going to happen next. You tell a lie and the volume on the stereo will be turned up to mask your screaming because your fucking foot is being amputated. Do I have you undivided attention?"

Frank began to panic. He started sweating profusely and asked, "Can I please have some water?" The men began to laugh.

One of them said, "After burning your foot off, we were going to waterboard your ass. That's why we're laughing. I guess you don't find that funny, do you? Okay, it doesn't matter, back to the questioning. Was the demise of the Beckmire person your plan?"

"Absolutely!" Frank exhorted. He played us out of millions and couldn't deliver a fucking penny. Yes, I planned his demise. My only fuck-up is that I am not sure we killed the right guy. One of my less than mentally capable associates blasted who we thought was Beckmire in the face with both barrels of a shotgun. Sort of an over-kill if I must say so myself."

One of the men asked, "Why aren't you sure who you killed?"

"It was dark, and this person went into Beckmire's condo and within minutes, came out with the same outfit on and my man shot him in the face. I can't really say we killed the right guy. I began to be concerned a few months ago when both of the people assigned to terminate him met with suspicious deaths," Frank stated.

Helga asked, "If you had to rank it from 0 to 100 and 100 being absolutely certain, what number would you give it?"

Without hesitation, Frank said, "I would probably assign a ranking of 80 percent. The person killed that night looked like him, wore that same stinky cologne, had Nikes on and one of his fancy-ass belts. Other than that, from his chest up to the top of his head, was it was gone. I frankly couldn't look at the body. It was savage what we did to him or someone he hired to look like him. I stand by my 80 percent and perhaps lower and I keep looking behind me everywhere I go.

Helga said, "Not sure you heard about this but one of your frat brothers was found hanging by the neck at his condo. We thought he was the weakest link and targeted him instead of you. We went to his place and found the police surrounding it. I asked a neighbor what happened and was told that the guy in 3-B was found hanging from his balcony."

Frank remorsefully said, "I talked to him yesterday and he indicated that he thought he was being followed. I asked him if he had been smoking that shit again and he said, yes, and that it gave him clarity for his environment."

Helga looked long and hard at Frank and summoned her two compatriots to another part of the facility. She asked, "Do you think we can use this guy, or should we conclude this matter right now?"

One of the men shrugged his shoulders while the other said, "You know we are down by two. Let's give him a simple task and see if he can deliver. Also, if you express your connections to the church, your awareness of the Beckmire clan and the fact that the long game is looking at trillions of dollars, he might want to join your organization."

Helga looked at him and said, "The Holy Father will probably want him for himself which may turn out to be a source of friction. Naw, we need to save us from looking over his shoulders. Put one in his heart and another in his head, clean the place thoroughly and then get out of dodge. I need to find that Beckmire boy soon, or the Holy Father is going to rid himself of all of us."

When the group approached Frank, he stated, "I know you're going to kill me, and I don't want to die. I can be useful to you in many ways. I am loyal and besides, do you even know what Beckmire looks like if he's still alive?"

There was a silence in the room when Helga said, "Your 80 percent sticks in my head. Why aren't you, say 90 percent sure that it was Beckmire?"

Frank smiled and said, "Because he was crafty, shifty, and full of surprises. If you're looking at old photos of him and using those as your guide, well, good luck with that process. He is like a human chameleon, always shifting from one form to another."

Helga stared at Frank for over a minute. She touched him on his shoulder and said, "Any sign of betrayal will leave your entire lineage dead. I work for the Holy Father who went missing a few years back. He is up and running again and I'm his emissary. You fuck around with this one and you will be eating your own balls. Untie him and give him the 411."

# # #

Young Beckmire unofficially changed his name again to Vincent Lassiter and was not without resources or surveillance capacity. He had clear pictures of Frank, Helga and her two companions. It was not accidental that he would take their pictures because Frank was next on his hit list. As he floated Helga's picture on the dark web, conceivable matches came back for his view. After scanning about a dozen photos, he said, "I thought this bitch was dead. She must have nine fucking lives. I heard she was the main man's toy. She is also the mother of my stepbrother's son, and I must stay close but not too close to her.

Helga exited the building looking as fresh as she did when she went in. Young Vincent rationalized, "Looks as though she didn't do Frank and I guess he is dead. I really had something scientifically special in mind for that asshole."

Vincent, being extremely calculating, knew that Helga was not driving and would probably hire an Uber. As if he were clairvoyant, Helga stopped at the bottom of the steps and called an Uber that was less than three minutes away. The Uber driver would be the one and only Vincent Lassiter. As he pulled up to the pickup point, he mused to himself, "More beautiful in person".

Helga entered the car and noticed that the driver was a handsome lad. She had entered the no-conversation protocol on the order but decided to find out who this person was. She asked, "Are you a local?"

Vincent looked into the mirror and responded, "Yes Ma'am."

Helga responded, "Do I look that old that you're saying yes ma'am to me?"

Vincent smiled and replied, "To the contrary. Your presence is regal, your scent is intoxicating and your beauty stimulating. I have never picked up a fare or seen many women who could stand near or next to you."

Helga smiled and said, "Oh, my! How enchanting you sound. Do you do anything else besides drive people around all day?"

"Actually, this is my part-time job. I am a graduate of the Naval Academy."

"How impressive," Helga responded. After a few minutes of quiet, Helga asked, "How about you take the rest of the day off, spend it driving me around and perhaps even have dinner with me?"

Vincent replied, "We have certain rules that we have to follow. I would first of all have to take you to your initial appointed destination and then call off for the balance of the day."

Helga responded, "That doesn't seem that complicated. Are you married, or do you have a possessive woman monitoring your whereabouts?"

"None of the above. Listen, you are who every man would like to have in his company. I am petrified by your beauty and you're simply above my pay grade."

Helga looking a bit disappointed, responded, "Then it is time for you to get a raise." She reached into her purse, pulled out a wad of $100 bills, and gently leaned forward and placed them on the seat next to Vincent. She then said, "I want to hire you to escort me around Annapolis and to dine with me. I am reversing the roles; I am propositioning you."

Vincent looked at the money and said, "I would gladly escort, drive and dine with you at my own expense. I really can't accept money for doing something I would absolutely enjoy and be proud to do."

Helga looked out of the window for a few moments, smiled, and said, "I hope you're not a bullshitter. I like what you have said, and I just need a breath of fresh air and a conversation about basically nothing. Listen, pull over at that light. I'm going to get out and you're going to call in stating that you're off the clock. How about that? By the way, what is your name? I am Helga Spengatsenburg."

"I am Vincent Lassiter. Great to meet you."

Vincent knew he had gotten her attention and now was the time to offer his playbook.

# # #

After that first glass of vino, Vincent and Helga began to relax, touch innocently, smile flirtatiously and enjoy each other's company.   After the second glass of vino, the conversation turned to religion, beliefs, idolizations and the need, or lack thereof, of a person to rule the universe. By the third glass of wine and two Halibut dinners, Helga decided that this Naval Academy graduate was going to make her momentarily happy.

Helga yawned and announced, "It's getting late and I'm getting a little sleepy after a long day. I don't want to end this evening by falling asleep at dinner. I would rather fall asleep after a wonderful expression of passion with you."

Vincent looked at her and asked, "Why me? You're as beautiful as the setting sun. You could have anyone you want. Why me?"

Helga first looked away and then back at Vincent and finally, said, "I would like to go somewhere and tell you exactly who I am and what I do. Perhaps a change in scenery will give my mind clarity and I can look beyond the physical."

As she walked towards the restroom, she summoned the waiter and gave him $500, and said, "Don't say anything to my guest."

In the meantime, Vincent summoned the waiter and asked for the check. The waiter said, "Give me a moment and I will return with it. How was everything?"

Vincent smiled and said, "Your halibut, was excellent."

Helga returned to the table and said, "I can't believe you tried to pay for our meal. I asked you to turn off your work clock and join me for the day, because I have heard a lot of bullshit but none with the flavor of yours. My treat young man. Shall we go?"

Once outside, Vincent asked, "Would you like to walk down to the water, or shall I take you to your hotel and bid you goodnight?"

"Silly boy, I don't want this night to end yet. I enjoy your company, I love your manners, and I admire the fact that you are a graduate of that expensive academy, and you work to earn a living. I like simple things, not necessarily simple people, but I like those who are not pretentious but who are genuine and smart. In other words, I like you and I want to get to know you better." There was a moment of quiet, after which Helga said, "I told you that I hoped you weren't a bullshitter. Well, I am bullshitting because in essence, I want to spend the night with you. Can you make that happen?"

Vincent smiled, scratched his forehead, and said, "Helga, I am tantalized by you. Please don't make light of my visible feelings."

"Vincent, you amaze me. I'm not making light of your emotions. I sincerely want to experience, enjoy, and seduce you all at the same time. Is that too much to ask of you?"

Vincent replied, "Helga, if all you say is true, then that would be a dream come to fruition. You got in my car and all I could think about was how beautiful you are. I'm no Romeo, but damn, my heart sank into the middle part of my body and my mind started fantasizing about a liaison."

Vincent started to say something when Helga placed a single finger on his lips. On Main Street, Helga slowly placed her body within inches of Vincent's, and said, "I want to walk, talk, kiss, hold hands, laugh and be happy for once in my life. I have lived a life of servitude, and I have never felt love, just desire and abuse. Before I die, I hope to experience love, just once."

# # #

Vincent was caught between two scenarios as he calculated his next moves. He has without a doubt committed to a relationship of sorts with Helga for this night, but his endgame was to conquer, mentally seduce and terminate her after finding out her need to know about him. However, on this night, his entire mindset would change forever.

Helga and Vincent walked down the hill on Main Street in Annapolis, Maryland holding hands and smiling. At a dimly lit intersection, he gently gathered her close to his body, leaned forward, and kissed her on the cheek. He announced, "This is a fantasy that is becoming, stimulating, and exciting. I feel like a little boy out on his first date."

Helga responded, "I don't know if it's the three glasses of vino that we had, but I too am feeling as carefree as I have ever been. I don't know what spell you've cast on me, but I am enjoying every moment."

Vincent looked hard at Helga, moved his left hand to the base of her neck, and gently maneuvered his lips close to hers. He softly asked, as he stared intently at her lips, "May I have the pleasure of touching your lips with mine?"

Helga, who was breathing heavily, said, "Please, please kiss me, but act as if you're in love with me. I've never felt love, just lust, abuse, and defilement. Please kiss me as if you love me."

Five minutes later, the two concluded their marathon kissing session in the midst of people passing by. Helga, feeling weak and shaky, stated, "I want to make love to you, even though I don't know you. I want to feel your essence in and around every aspect of my body. In return I will try to give you all that I am free to give."

Vincent feeling the need for this interaction said, "Helga, I feel the same as you, except I thought I loved a woman, but she was in love with another. Sad, to say, I don't know if I have ever felt what I feel currently. I don't know you, but I am either so horny or so enamored by your presence that I want nothing more than to be all about you."

# # #

In the lobby of her hotel stood her two companions. She saw them but gave no acknowledgement. They knew that if she didn't look towards them, then, they were not to approach or to continue to look at her.

In her modestly appointed room, she said to Vincent, "There are condiments and booze in that little fridge. I wouldn't mind having a martini. Olives are in there as well."

Vincent announced, "I would love to have the same." He looked at Helga, smiled, approached her, and stated, "I would love to shower with you. Am I being too bold?"

Helga laughed and said, "Let me help undress you!"

There were no theatrics, breaking of shirt buttons, pulling of hair and or forceful kissing and fondling. No, this became a monumental, precise, and expert seduction. She unbuttoned his shirt, and he undid her blouse. She placed her hand over his heart and said, "No matter the outcome, tonight I want to be loved and not fucked. Can you promise me that?"

An over-stimulated Vincent responded, "We have already begun to make love! From the moment we left the restaurant and kissed and then really kissed without concern of people passing by. That was epic. I avoided placing my body too close to yours, because you would have felt the embarrassment I was going through with a stiff member. I've been hard most of the night just thinking about the possibility of an encounter with you."

Helga looked down at his crotch and said, "Do I look that obtuse to you? I saw and felt your body's reaction; I visualized my becoming extremely familiar with it and then having it enter the confines of mine. I want to be loved, Vincent, not fucked, just be my lover for a single night and give me a lifetime memory."

After an invigorating shower and the visualization of each other's bodies, the two patted and dried each other off. Helga asked for a moment of privacy to relieve herself. Meanwhile, all Vincent's goals and objectives were thrown out of the window because he never took a moment to realize the importance of another human being. His desire for Helga and his want for a tremendous completion, left him vulnerable to any task or tasks that were presented to him.

When Helga arrived at the bed, Vincent was sitting with his back against the headboard but had respectfully covered his other brain. Helga smiled and asked, "What are you hiding under the cover? Is it something that I want to see? Is it something that I want to touch? Is it something that I want to have in my mouth? And is it something that I want inserted into who I am?"

Vincent responded, "Let me first of all state that all that you have asked, is appropriate and correct. Under this tent is a brainless object that is anxious to meet, greet, extend, and protrude into the very fiber of your being. Do you have any other questions or concerns, or would you like to dim the lights and the two of us explore the sensuality of each other?"

In the dimly lit room, Helga began to kiss the lips of Vincent, who began to fondle her authentic and magnificent breasts. Vincent said, with a deepened bedroom voice, "I would like to freely and without limits explore and investigate your anatomy. In doing so, if you feel the need to investigate any aspect of my body, then, by all means, don't hesitate.

The two explored, sampled, tasted, sucked, and consumed each other's essence. At the mutual culmination of their exploratory event, they both lay exhausted, bewildered, excited and confident that they had met their match. Helga announced, "You touched, caressed, and kissed every aspect of my anatomy. You with your tongue and member entered every orifice that I have. You left no chasm untouched. I enjoyed every moment and every sensation."

Vincent breathing heavily stated, "Ditto! If I am to ever enjoy your magnificence again, I had better get in better shape. Your body is curvaceous, firm, soft and a thing of beauty to look at and touch. I don't know your age, but in my travels, I've never had the pleasure of making love to anyone as fine as you are. And, when I use the phrase making love, that is exactly what I felt was happening at every thrust, kiss, sigh, and those seemingly nuclear orgasms that we both shared.

Helga, I truly hope this is the beginning of something special, lasting, and honest."

Helga asked, "Why do you emphasize honesty? Are you accustomed to less than faithful partners?"

Vincent looked at Helga and replied, "There is so much we don't know about each other and yes, I have had some less-than-honest relationships. To some I was the charlatan and to others, well, they were brujas. Today is not the day I want to spend my time talking about prologue. I want to talk about the future and my first question regarding that is when will I see you again, if ever?"

Helga stared intently at Vincent and replied, "I am often on-call, and I spend an enormous amount of time in Italy, where I work. Listen, my job is sensitive, and one might consider it secretive as well. I don't want to get into what I do, because it will only sadden this precious moment and these feelings that I am confused about."

Vincent asked, "What feelings are confusing?" Helga stepped into the bathroom and exclaimed, "I'll be out in a minute.

While Helga was in the bathroom, Vincent was considering his next move. He happily admitted to himself that he had no idea that Helga would be a prize, a beauty, and the most sensuous woman that he had ever met. He fantasized about a lasting relationship with her and was startled when she appeared nude behind him. He looked, he conquered, he savored, and he lusted after every inch of her body, again.

Twenty minutes later, the two lay side by side, breathing deeply and holding hands. Helga rolled over to Vincent's side and began to play with his nipples, which were at the height of sensitivity. He said, "That feels good and funny at the same time." He started to laugh and the two ended up kissing deeply with their tongues.

An hour or so later, Helga announced, "I must run some errands and try to find an old colleague of mine. Are you free for dinner tonight, or do you have to work?"

Vincent smiled and said, "I'll go and make a few fares now, so that I can pay for dinner later. What time do you have in mind?"

"How about six?" Helga asked.

"Perfect! He walked over to Helga and stated, "You are the most exceptional woman that I have ever met. We met, broke bread, had vino together, walked, talked, and then made unparalleled love. Not once did we screw or have sex. We began to enjoy the core of each other immediately, while we discovered, learned, and became intoxicated with the fruits that we tasted. If it weren't such a cliché and used frequently without meaning or understanding, I would actually say, I love you."

As he turned to walk away, Helga grabbed his arm, pulled him intentionally close to her, and began to cry. She whispered, "I feel the same as you do. In my life, people screwed me, never loved me, and just used me for my looks. You confess to a higher level of connection, and I want to experience this until you say to me, 'I'm moving on.' Vincent, I feel as though I love you as well."

"Do you think we should exchange phone numbers?" Vincent asked.

After the exchange of numbers, the two stood in place, swaying their bodies to un-played music.

## CHAPTER TEN

Frank met Helga and her companions at the appointed time and place and the first thing out of his mouth was, "You're so beautiful and I'm happy you didn't terminate me."

Helga thanked him for the compliment and asked, "Have you been able to find out anything on young Mr. Beckmire?"

Frank stated, "I didn't want to put out feelers because if he is still alive, that would put him in the disappearance mode. I asked a few reliable people who work for our esteemed government to do me a few favors quietly." Helga gave him an astonished look, and Frank said, "Don't worry, they owe me big time. They dare not botch this event because they were in on the disposal of our alleged Mr. Beckmire."

Helga asked, "Did you happen to meet a guy by the name of Vincent Lassiter while you were at the Academy?" Helga covertly took a picture of Vincent but neglected to share it with Frank.

"Vincent Lassiter was a square. We used to call him Titmoma. Why do you ask?" Frank inquired.

"No stone is to be unturned in this investigation, no stone or lead," Helga emphasized.

Frank replied, "I don't expect to hear back from my people until next week. Are you planning on being around that long and if so, do you think we could have dinner without my being drugged and kidnapped?" Frank smiled and announced, "I really find you delectable. I want to consume as much of you as possible."

Helga smiled and proclaimed, "I love another and I'm trying to figure it out for the first time in my life."

"Are you telling me that you're interested in that Lassiter person?" Frank asked.

"I'm not telling you anything. Those are your words, not mine," Helga replied.

Frank responded, "It seems as though your entire team is more mellow than when I first encountered you people. If I'm not mistaken, it's only by the grace of God that I am still alive."

Helga quickly stated, "God ain't got nothing to do with your ability to breathe air. If I find out that you and your crew killed the Beckmire boy, I might relieve you of that misconception and cut your fucking head off."

#

Later in the day, Helga called Vincent and asked, "Where are you?"

"I'm in DC," Vincent replied. A momentarily disappointed Helga asked, "What's going on in DC?"

"Just taking care of some old business. Why don't you hop into an uber and meet me down at the Wharf?" Vincent inquired.

Helga paused before answering, and when she did, she said, "If I thought you were serious I would do just that. I must admit, you've been on my mind most of the day. I kept looking at my phone and wondering if you were going to text me or call. I resigned myself to be disillusioned when I heard nothing nor saw anything from you."

Vincent chuckled and softly said, "I didn't want to disturb you, and I kept looking at my phone and I didn't see anything from you. I don't want to appear that I'm stalking you or anything, but I am really feeling giddy about you. I guess I'm trying not to overplay my hand. You know, I'm trying to be cool just in case this goes sideways."

"Where do you want me to meet you?" Helga asked.

"At the Hyatt House, 725 Wharf Street, in Southwest. I'll be in the bar looking lost and lonely." There was a click on the other end of the phone.

Vincent thought that he had said something wrong but eventually shrugged his shoulders and said to himself, "We shall see, we shall see."

#

Sitting at the bar in the Hyatt House, forty-five minutes later, while having a ginger ale, Vincent heard a voice say, "You've started drinking without me?"

Vincent turned around, saw Helga, stood up, and embraced her tightly. At the end of the embrace, he kissed her passionately for over a minute.

At the end of the kiss, Helga stated, "What a welcome. That was a straight to the bed kind of kiss, with no pun intended. Oh, my goodness, you never kissed me like that the other night or morning."

"I didn't know that I could miss someone as much as I have missed you in that short period of time. When you hung up, I thought I had said something that was taken the wrong way. Anyway, I am happy you're here. What can I get you to drink? Oh, are you hungry?"

"How about one drink and then let's take a stroll around the harbor and look at those expensive yachts and this renovated area?" Helga asked. After a leisurely walk around the Wharf area, Helga announced, "I'm beginning to get hungry. How about you?"

"I could do with a bite to eat, but more pressing is whether we are staying here, if I may be so bold and presumptuous or are we heading back to Annapolis?"

Helga smiled faintly and said, "I brought a toothbrush and a change of undies. I also made a hotel reservation at the Hyatt House. I guess I was being presumptuous as well. I'm not suggesting anything, but I do want to spend the night with you and look at the river every so often."

Vincent laughed lightly, hugged Helga and said, "I have reservations at the Hyatt House. Not sure the room is overlooking the Potomac River, more likely the room is facing the HVAC unit."

Helga laughed and said, "I don't care what it overlooks, as long as you're looking down at me and I'm looking up at you and vice versa."

At the hotel Vincent said, "I would like to pay for our living accommodations for the night. It probably won't have a spectacular view but the only view I want to see is you. Will that be alright with you?"

Helga pulled him seductively close to her and said, "I could care less about the damn room. I just want to be with you, my lover."

#

After dinner, when Vincent and Helga entered Room 903, Helga responded, "Oh my goodness, this room is astonishing. You are such a storyteller. You knew what you had reserved, but what impresses me the most is that you wanted to make me feel secure and surround me with an elegant atmosphere. I will never forget this night, or last night for that matter, and I will always hold a special place in my heart for you, Vincent." She kissed him and said, "I so desperately want to shower with you. Will you please wash my back and let me wash yours?"

In the shower, the two performed all kinds of foreplay. Helga started by giving Vincent a most thought-provoking kiss, arousing all matter that allegedly have a brain. She then began to suck his breast while watching his reactions to her motivational efforts. She finally descended to her knees and began to perform mouth to member resurrection. She created a monstrous response from Vincent, as witnessed by his strong and aggressive thrusts of his member into her mouth.

As she began to rise from that kneeling position, Vincent began to literally go down on Helga in the most aggressive fashion making sure that each orifice knew he had been there.

In the center bay window of Room 903 and supported by the frames that held it in place, Vincent and Helga began to provide the outside world with a portrait of lovemaking in a frame. Because of the unnatural footing, Vincent, between the deep moaning sounds of ecstasy, whispered, "I'm getting dizzy from this activity and this height. Can we relocate?"

After calming down from her high, Helga responded, "That was the most intense set of feelings that I have ever had. Each thrust was as if I were flying. I became discombobulated as well. Let's take a break, have some water, maybe a little drink and if you like, I would like to start all over again. I have had three magnificent orgasms, but who's counting?"

Vincent, caught between this new and amazing set of feelings and his ultimate goal, asked, "Can you lie and just relax close to me? Somehow looking down on the water from that height I became lightheaded." Vincent then loudly said, "Come here my love. I have more of me to give to you if you're willing to accept me."

Unaware that she was doing so, Helga stood in the center frame of the bay window with the light of the full moon accentuating her silhouette.

Vincent screamed, "Please don't move. Please!" He then said, "I would like to take a picture of you right now. I can take it with your phone and therefore, you can control whether you want to share it. However, this is a fleeting moment. Tell me that I can capture your essence."

Helga started to turn around, and Vincent said, "Please don't move. Do I have your permission to capture my Mona Lisa?"

Skeptical of the analogy, Helga cautiously asked, "Will I ever have to regret anything that I have done with you, by allowing you to take a picture of me in the nude?"

Vincent dropped his head and said, "I know exactly where you're coming from. Just forget it, my love. It is a moment in time that will never repeat itself."

Helga yelled, "Take the fucking picture." Vincent grabbed his phone and said, "Say nothing, do nothing and think about nothing." After those comments, he snapped the picture. He then said, "You should have this picture in your collection." He handed Helga her phone, she unlocked it, and Vincent took the picture.

When Helga saw the results, she said, "Oh, Vincent. Oh, my God, at this moment in time, you are the most important person in the world to me." As they both viewed the picture, Helga stated, "It is as if I am posing on the moon. This is an incredible shot. You are a mind-boggling person. At this moment Vincent, I love you."

Vincent stared at Helga and as his mind conjured up all of the evil things he was involved in, a tear began to flow from his eyes and he said, "Helga, I know I love you."

Vincent and Helga both cried because they were both evil people. Helga said, "I don't want to visit the past. I want to enjoy today and our being together. No more reflections, let's just enjoy each other to the max."

After another hour of intimate interactions, Helga and Vincent fell asleep in each other's arms. At 3:00 a.m., Helga's phone rang. Half asleep she looked at the screen and saw that it was her employer. She jumped out of bed and ran into the bathroom. Once the door was closed, she said, "Good morning. Is there a problem?"

The person on the other end asked, "When will you be back? I'm sick of these neophytes who are unable to give me the clarity and satisfaction that I need. I want you on the first thing flying in the morning. I want you here to do your job. Is that clear?"

Helga took a deep breath, and as she thought about the stranger in the other room, she had mixed emotions about what was being discussed. As a tear fell from her eye and as she recalled the idea of love, passion, and honest emotions that she experienced with a stranger, she said, "Your holiness, I am not a whore, and I will not be on the first thing leaving to provide you with a fucking thing. I am done being used without feelings. I demand more from this life than just to satisfy the anointed holy penis. Good night."

Clearly hearing Helga's side of the conversation, Vincent sat up in bed and waited for her to return. Upon her arrival, he said, "You didn't try to hide your emotions, did you? I mean I heard you clearly articulate what you were not going to do. Were you using the term holiness as a euphemism?"

Helga began to cry and walked out of the room. Vincent retrieved robes from the closet and put one on. As she sat staring out of the window and crying, Vincent placed the robe around her shoulders and kissed her on the back of her neck. He then said, "I meant what I said earlier. At this moment in time, you are the most important person to me on earth. I have a lot to confess, but I'm not going to spoil the most romantic and satisfying event that I have ever had in my life. I have had relations, I have had feelings, but I have never had both in the same person. These past few days have been tumultuous for me and my heart. When you entered my Uber, I knew that you were way above my pay grade and the only thing I would be good for was to transport you from one destination to another."

Helga quickly placed a finger on Vincent's lips. She said, "I only want to feel wanted and respected, as you have shown me from the beginning. I will eventually tell you about my employer, but right now I just want you to hold me, until night turns into day."

Vincent whispered, "I wish we could run away from our past and live and learn to love each other without agendas."

Helga crying, said, "I know this guy is going to come after me. I mean, he himself is not going to come, but he's going to send people after me." She looked at Vincent and said, "It will not be safe for you to be with me. I just told one of the most powerful people in the world, to go fuck off. I know his account numbers, and I control them. I know his secrets, his ambitions, and his crimes. He will definitely send people to terminate me."

Vincent, not appearing to be upset or scared, asked, "Those things you said to me, you know, that at this point in time you love me. Are they true, or just lustful thoughts?"

Helga turned around, looked deep into Vincent's eyes, and said, "Let me repeat myself, I just told one of the most powerful people in the world to go and fuck off. I don't have a death wish, but I do like the feelings that I get when I am around you. I told you once, people don't respect me, they use me, they abuse me, they take advantage of me, they never even pretend to love me. You, my friend, out of nowhere, pick me up for a ride, convince me to have a drink, begged me to have dinner with you and then you seduced me with mixtures that you added to my drink and my food. Now, the question is, should I trust you or those that I know who will do whatever is needed to get what they want?"

A laughing Vincent responded, "That's not quite how I remember the interaction, but if it gives you leverage, then so be it. Here's a serious question and it's one that I asked you before.   Is it possible to run away from this impending assault?"

Helga looked at him and responded, "It's an international event, meaning no place is off limits from his reach."

Knowing full well who Helga was talking about, Vincent asked, "Who is this person or institution, the US government, the Pope, or the Russians?"

"It is the missing former Holy Father of the Catholic Church. The one and only. He has made a covenant with the dark side and is dependent upon the corruption of a child to fulfill his demented destiny. Also, there is another person that I have been looking for to help him fund this event. Although it was reported that there were billions in bearer bonds taken from a certain dictator, the actual amount of those bonds is nearly a trillion."

Vincent slowly and deliberately asked, "Are you sure of that number? I mean, that's an awful lot of money. What is the importance of the other person that you are looking for?"

"His father, Ben Beckmire and his group are in control of the bonds but do not know their true value. It is alleged that the son has been trying to gain control of the bonds for a while by trying to eradicate the entire clan. The son, a former graduate of that place you came from, the Naval Academy, hired mercs and other assassins to kill everyone connected to the clan, including his parents." Helga dropped her head, and began to cry.

Vincent inquired, "That announcement caused you a lot of grief, why so?"

Helga replied, "This person has tried to kill and wants to kill his own parents for those bonds. What kind of person even thinks of a reprehensible event like that?"

Continuing, Helga, yelled, "Also because my sons are members of their tribe. I met a dashing young man that I was supposed to kill in Switzerland and momentarily let my guard down. He impregnated me and later he and his family retrieved my son from a crooked monastery in Valencia. So, this whole thing comes down to me wanting to feel human and not like a droid and trying to find out if the Beckmire boy is dead or alive. If alive, he unknowingly has a lot to offer the ex-pontiff. A few years back, rumor has it, his father's wife was alleged to be on her last leg, meaning that she was not expected to survive several hits to the head and a fall. Once she recovered, she secretly went to the records office in the Outback and purchased 500 acres of land for her son. What she didn't know and for that matter, no one knew, is that the land is home to probably the largest diamond mine in the world."

Vincent said, "Wait a minute. How do you know if that information is correct?"

Helga smiled and then began to laugh. When she finished an almost record-breaking laughing session, she said, "You know how those billionaires keep trying to outdo each other and get to the moon and beyond, and return safely? Well, secretly, the ex-pontiff provided a couple of them, for a generous donation, with information from the experts. I mean DaVinci, Copernicus, Galileo, Newton, Herschel, and others. In addition, specialized equipment sanctioned by the ex-pontiff was a part of the process. You see, Vincent, only money buys innovation. The historical assumptions that guide modern-day achievements were a function of the experts. The ex-pontiff, being an evil anomaly, is involved in all kinds of businesses from interstellar navigation and missile deployment to GPS to locating precious minerals around the world."

Vincent said, "I'll ask you once again, can we run away? Before you answer that question, are you saying that Beckmire's son is the sole owner of the largest diamond mine on earth? And if so, is there a bounty on finding him alive?"

"Silly boy, I am told that he is dead and that he was chopped up and fed to the fish," Helga stated.

"What kind of enterprise are you in? You speak of killings and death as a function of doing business. Why was the Beckmire boy killed?" Vincent inquired.

"Because he couldn't deliver the easy money that he sold his compatriots on. It became impossible because his father and his crew have proven to be formidable," Helga announced.

"That is a powerful word, Helga," Vincent stated.

"Vincent, rumor has it that they are responsible for more than 2,000 souls floating around in hell who are waiting their arrival."

"If nothing else, I have been able to take your mind off that negative conversation." Vincent approached Helga, untied her robe, fell to his knees, and began to give her the benefits of momentary pleasure.

"Why are you toying with me?" Helga between sighs inquired.

"I am not playing with you. I never want this interlude to conclude. I once again state that I have never felt this way about a woman. I have never recklessly dropped to my knees and attempted to imitate actions that I have seen in porn movies," Vincent said.

"Is this an example of your YouTube education? If it is, then I must commend your instructor, because he or she has directed you to the very place where the mind leaves the body and the rush of a tingling sensation takes control over your entire being."

Helga rubbed his head tenderly and began to walk away as she once again began to cry. Vincent reached out for her hand as he stood up, and after retrieving it, he began to kiss her hand. He slowly made his way back to the floor and began to provide Helga with immeasurable pleasure.

Helga responded, "I'm there Vincent! Oh, Vincent please love me. Don't pretend, don't abuse me, and—Oh shit, right there, right there." As she approached her epicenter of pleasure, she loudly exclaimed, "Right there Vincent!"

The next sounds and motions demonstrated gratification, as Helga heaved and maneuvered her incredibly special place to Vincent's tongue and lips. She quietly gasped, but finally yelled, "I have never experienced a conclusion like this. Oh, my goodness, Vincent, please hold me and never abuse me. If you must do anything negative, then leave me here and now."

## CHAPTER ELEVEN

It was a sad day in the Outback as the group prepared to attend the transitional services for Ms. Viola. Her death was unanticipated, sudden and in the company of the wizard. Wajickee sat with Ms. Viola at the billabong where the Great Saltie resided and knew that his friend, his wannabe lover, was at the end of her time on earth.

Ms. Viola asked Wajickee, "Will it hurt?"

He smiled at her and said, "Look at those big eyes looking at you. Now, if he was to get a hold of you, then pain would be swift and traumatic, but there would be a sense of finality as well."

"Why is he just hanging out there?" Ms. Viola asked.

"He is saddened by the fact that you will no longer be available to entice me to human temptations. I think he's showing both sides of his torso. You are lucky you managed your issues well and without a lot of fanfare, meaning people were not running up to you every moment and asking how are you doing. No, my friend, he feels my pain and angst, for he also knows that no one will ever be able to replace you and your wisdom. He also is making sure that I don't consider abandoning my station in order to die a human death to be with you, my friend."

"Mr. Wizard, why on earth would you want to go where I am heading? That is a good group of people that you oversee. They help people help themselves. Even before they ran into all of that money, they never had a mission of being rich and arrogant, no, their mission was to embody the spirit of others and make the world a better place. And besides, I might get to where I am going and find a younger model that may just catch my fancy." They both laughed. Ms. Viola said, "I am ready to go, but I wish I could touch you in that human form one more time before I move on."

"Ms. Viola, I have been assuming this uncomfortable form since we have been sitting here."

Ms. Viola, with failing eyes, used her hands to search out the truth. When she accidentally touched and caressed an arm, she said, "Wizard, why didn't you tell me that you were out of uniform?"

There was a long pause before Wajickee announced, "I have known many, but none like you, my love. Goodnight and goodbye, Ms. Viola." Wajickee touched the back of her neck and Ms. Viola exhaled her last breath."

# # #

Clyde and his crew flew in to perform the last rites. During the ceremony, he said, "People, I have to go off script for a moment, and I apologize to the family and friends of Ms. Viola. Most of you know that when you are here, there be some amazing things happening around you. I know ya'll be thinking that I'm about to go off, but there be some real "*effing*" bizarre stuff going on here. If you don't believe me, go to the wrong billabong and if you survive, you be one lucky you know what. I know what I've seen, I know what I've heard, I know the sounds of people being shredded and consumed strategically by dog like animals. Come on now, you can't get this kind of show in St. Thomas, Virginia, the Mid-west, or anywhere else in the world. When we get here, the toilets appear to run in the opposite way and people are black as coal with blonde hair and blue eyes. The snakes and spiders are particular about who they bite. This is the world of Ms. Viola and Mr. Wajickee. I ain't going to go there because if I offend him, he might turn me into a dingo or something. My first time here, my faith and that of my wife were challenged by what we saw. Once we agreed that we never smoked weed or took any other hallucinogenic mushrooms at our age, we realized that God has many creatures and servants. And, as such I am happy that this group of pirates came to our little ranch that was about to be consumed by the avarice of people who were used to just taking what they wanted no matter the cost in dollars or human lives."

Clyde paused for a few moments as he hydrated and wiped the tears from his eyes. He then said, "People, Ms. Viola was some kind of special and now the forces of good and evil are bargaining for the soul of her great grandbaby. This cannot happen because even though the forces of evil are gathering strength by the minute, Ms. Beatrice is incredibly special and Lord knows, our future and that of the world are dependent upon decisions that she will innocently make. People, we're at war once again but this time the foes are not hiding, they are walking amongst us and trying all of the old games to divide and conquer us. Ms. Viola knew this and worked tirelessly to make sure that Ms. Beatrice was given the right foundation to make the necessary decision for self-determination.

Listen, I'm sorry for going off script, but the fact remains that, if we don't stand up against evil, evil will be our standard of living and at that point, all that you people have accomplished will be at the end of a firing range with you all fighting against each other. Ms. Viola shared this vision with me once as we rode around the ranch. I thought she was a little off, until I crossed the waters and landed in this place. God is simply amazing, and all of his good creatures shall inherit the earth. Your grandmother, your great grandmother, our friend, and life coach shall always be with us. In silence, please pray for her soul, the souls in this clan and people throughout the world. God bless us all!"

Later at the repass, Wajickee eased away from the celebration of life for Ms. Viola and headed towards the billabong where the Great Saltie rested. On his way, he heard a rustling in the bushes and it was Ms. Beatrice. He asked, "Why are you hiding in the bushes?"

"I wasn't hiding in them; I was resting until you got here. One of the things that has become clear to me is that I can sometimes read the minds of others. It was hard at first but after concentrating on you, your mind became easy to conquer. I also know that my granny and you had a special kind of relationship. She used to whisper, 'Oh, that wizard fellow, him be special."

Wajickee smiled at Ms. Beatrice and said, "Ms. Viola was easy on the heart. Her soul was pure and even I could find solace when in her company. She also used to tell me how special you were, not that I didn't know it, but when you sassed your dad, I knew I had to tamper with the laws that govern our kind and turn your head towards the heavens. When you were a little girl, we used to speak to each other without saying a word. I tried hard to correct that behavior of yours, but you are a stubborn person at times. Doesn't mean we don't love you, but you were testy at times."

"Do you think I am a bad person?" Ms. Beatrice asked.

"Absolutely not. Why would you ask me a thing such as that?" Wajickee inquired.

"I think everyone remembers my words with my dad, you know exclaiming that he was not my dad and all." There was silence and no further words were spoken until they reached the billabong," Ms. Beatrice stated.

At the billabong, Wajickee said, "You're on a self-directed mission. I am not allowed nor anyone else to provide you with guidance. Ms. Viola told me a lot about your family, including how your mom's mother was drugged and seduced by a famous actor and that seduction resulted in the birth of your mother. Ms. Viola also told me about your dad and how he was a challenge and not the right fit for you and your mom. I know a lot about you my dear, your dreams, nightmares, images, and most of all your love for Mr. Chakes. You acted out because you thought that he was going to leave you, your mom, your brother, and sister because of a somewhat loud argument you heard between your parents. Listen, the person formally known as the pope was ambitious, greedy, and determined to operate on both sides of life as we know it— good and evil. Your presence alongside him would make the world a not-so good place to live if you were one of his conscripts. His need for purity was discovered on that visit you had to the Vatican. He touched you with pure evil and found out that you were simply pure, not tainted, not coerced, but free and kind. The combination is tantamount to extreme power, a power he would have used to seduce the world into following his leadership. He truly is a megalomaniac," Wajickee stated.

"He was kind and good to me. How could he be that evil?" Ms. Beatrice inquired.

"His kindness was equivalent to persuasion. He would do anything to have you under him. That everything included killing your family and the clan back there at the village. He was and is an evil person with tentacles that reach into the bowels of hell. Your righteous choice is what the world needs and the good things that you'll be able to do with that power will only benefit mankind. Your choice is godly, and your mission is humanity, helping people help themselves."

CHAPTER TWELVE

On the other side of the world Vincent was driving Helga back to Annapolis. Helga seemed pensive and jittery after her comments to her ex-employer. She knew that he was not going to settle for any loose ends and that she was probably a target of the very two men whom she employed to commit violence. Vincent lightly touched her leg and Helga jumped in her seat.

He asked, "Helga, what's going on? Why are you so jumpy?"

Helga didn't immediately respond but after unyielding questioning by Vincent, she exclaimed, "I am sorry I got you in this mess! My ex-employer has probably placed a hit order on me. I'm really thinking it's more of a capture-and- detain order, because he knows I am the key to his riches."

Naively, Vincent asked, "Why on earth would he do that?"

Helga looked at him and thought how obtuse the question was. She then said, "I told the ex-pope to literally go fuck off. Do you think he's going to let me walk away freely, knowing all that I know about him and his finances? No, sir, that guy is going to have me apprehended and detained and if you're anywhere near, you're on that list as well. I would be absolutely distraught if anything were to happen to you as a result of you just being kind and loving to me. Instead of Annapolis, can you drop me off at the train station in Baltimore?"

Vincent thought about the request and did not like it one bit. He vehemently stated, "I am not going to drop you anywhere unless I am accompanying you. I told you on several occasions that at this moment in time, I love you Helga. If you get on a train, then I'm getting on it as well."

After a pause in the conversation, Helga said, "You don't know the kind of work my associates and I do. We hurt people and have killed a few here and there, as well as sent a few to act as our intermediaries knowing full well that they were going to be terminated. I am an unbelievably bad person who has fallen for a guy that I know little about, but I am willing to trust my life in his hands."

Vincent made an erratic move from three lanes over to the shoulder, put the emergency flashers on, faced Helga, and said, "I love you. I don't want to be away from you."

Helga began to cry as Vincent kissed her and said, "This is all new to me, but you are on my mind every second of the day and besides, I'm no angel. I've participated in some pretty bad stuff that I won't disclose at this time. I just know that if I put you on the train, I'll never see you again and if something were to happen to you, I would feel that I could've intervened. No, Helga, where you go, I go unless you feel that I am a burden and no longer a useful toy."

Helga rolled her eyes and shouted, "I am in love for the first time in my life. I mean my thoughts are pure, my goals are long term, and you make me whole. I am accustomed to being used and abused. Your touch, your kisses are so intoxicating that I want to lip lock yours to mine and never let go. I need you but on this journey we won't survive."

"How do you know we won't? Are you clairvoyant or something? Listen, I'm willing to go the distance with you on your separation from your ex-employer. Now, that means I will take my resources to find a way for us to leave on a slow boat to China and beyond. I have untraceable accounts that will allow us to move about without anyone being able to track where we are. I have a wonderful friend who is an expert make-up artist. Listen, I am not new to the game that I think you're playing in. However, no matter any of that, I am willing to, if you will have me, trust our faith in each other and try to manage our disappearance," Vincent stated.

Helga looked intently at Vincent and then out of the window. As Vincent was about to get back into traffic, Helga asked, "Can you wait a minute before you start driving again? I want to ask you a few questions. If we start this adventure, will you stay with me until it is completed and will you promise never to lie to me, abuse me, or be unfaithful?"

"Damn, Helga, that's a tall order. In the scheme of things, life sometimes is full of small untruths that negate elongated discussions about bullshit. You know, if you ask me how was my day, be it shitty or not, I am going to say it was okay, for the sake of not having to rehash shit that happened at the office if I were an office type. The other two, well, they're easy. I could never be unfaithful to you because I have never experienced the kinds of emotions that I have with you. I mean, I've had sex with women, but I never made love to them because I didn't know them or how to make love. With you, I learned the real meaning of feeling loved, scared, sacred and special. Naw, if you'll have me, then I am here for the long run."

"Vincent, you talk a lot. I'm just hoping that your words have substance. I have to change the subject. Do you have any idea how we can disappear?" Helga asked.

"I really do, however, what are our assets? Now, this is when we have to start to trust each other to the max. Listen, I'm an Uber driver, but I have somehow managed to place approximately $9 million in secret accounts. How about you? Do you have any accounts that we can access while we're on the lam?"

Helga looked long and hard at Vincent and said, "Vincent, no matter the feelings I have for you at this moment, if you try to fuck over me, I will execute you in public. I'm placing my life, faith, and my resources in your care. Please don't scorn me. If you treat me like I am your queen, with love and respect, then I will have your back at every turn. Insofar as disappearing funds, I probably have between $60 and $80 that we can use," Helga announced.

Vincent replied, "That's good, $60 to $80 thousand gives us additional leverage."

Helga whispered, "More like $60 to $80 million. Vincent looked at her, and she commanded, "Drive, James and I'll tell you where we're heading. I need to go to Annapolis to retrieve documents from the safe in the room adjoining mine. I rented a connecting room under an assumed name just so that I could move out in a hurry if I had to. My only current problem is trying to guess whether my former lord and master has ordered a hit or better still detainment order on me. He knows I know where all the bodies are buried, the little boys and girls that he has had interludes with and more importantly, the numbers to his accounts. If we get to them first, $80 goes to $300 plus million."

"How on earth can you clean out $300 million without drawing attention?" Vincent asked.

Helga responded, "The idea is not to take the money but to change the passwords and codes and therefore, lock it forever if something were to happen to me."

Vincent, shaking his head said, "I'm afraid this is going to be over my pay grade."

Helga looking out of the window, asked, "Are you having second and third thoughts about this plan?"

"Not at all. I'm just trying to figure out who you are and what the limits of your information are, as well as if I will ever have to look over my shoulder if I disagree with you on procedures," Vincent noted.

"I'm going to try this one more time my friend. The only thing my beauty and my body have gotten me over my lifetime is being fucked, abused, humiliated, and being on call for the ex-pope to satisfy his human needs. No, no, my friend, people have lusted for me, taken what they wanted from me and left me in the back seat of a stolen car. Other than my mother, I don't recall anyone telling me sincerely that they loved me, even if it was for a moment in time. You, Vincent, have uttered the words more times than anyone I have known. You also showed me affection, attention, humility, and you treat me like you respect me, not like I was supposed to do everything that you wanted because someone else ordered it. Tell me now if you're having second thoughts and if you won't be able to secure my back if we decide to go on the lam. Tell me, Vincent, can I count on you to pull the trigger, if necessary to save me?"

Vincent moved into the center lane, then into the right lane, engaged the hazard warning lights again and pulled safely off to the side of the road. After looking in both mirrors to make sure they were safe, he turned to Helga and said, "In my lifetime, I used women for sex only. Some I knew, some I used regularly for a fee. I have never felt this way about anyone. I have never freely gone down on a woman to make sure she received the maximum pleasures from my actions. I have never told a woman that I loved her, including my mother. Therefore, I will watch your back, as long as we have an open and honest relationship and we enjoy each other for the sake of each other and not the enjoyment of the act. This is our third day together. I want to have 300 million more days with you, if possible."

# # #

Once in Annapolis, Helga showed Vincent a picture of her two associates, who he was familiar with. She asked him to take a stroll toward the hotel to see if they were hanging around. "I would ask you to go to my room and retrieve my documents from the adjoining room, but that might cause a little problem especially if they are in my room waiting for me. I assure you that if the ex-pope gave the terminate or detain order, those two buffoons are going to stop me on sight and beat me into submission," Helga stated.

"Let me take a stroll and see what the outside looks like. If I see them, then I will let you know. I'll call you and give you their location and once you enter the building we can either dance there or take them somewhere else and dispose of their asses," Vincent announced.

"I don't want to cause any problems at the hotel. I gave them bogus identification, but that camera behind the desk captured my very essence. I have a better idea. I'm going to call them and tell them that I am stuck on Route 50 at exit 301. I'll tell them to come and fetch me. What do you think?" Helga asked.

"Sounds plausible. Once they leave, you can waltz into the hotel, gather your belongings and off we go. My question is simple; how will you know that they're supposed to terminate or detain you? You won't, now, will you? Suppose the order hasn't reached them yet?" Vincent asked.

Helga replied, "Would you kill the person that has the combination to your fortune? Of course you wouldn't, however, to gain that information, I would cut your first born into pieces in front of you until you gave me what I needed."

"You have a weapon with you?" Helga asked.

"I do, and it's legal," Vincent replied.

Helga asked, "What does that mean? Anyway, my question is the same one; will you abuse me and sex me, or love me and protect my back?"

Vincent approached Helga and kissed her tenderly. He said, "Listen, what I shared with you was never shared with another. You have captivated me, and I am here for the duration. I want to get away, leave everything behind, and begin a new journey with my newfound lover. In other words, I got your back, your front, and every other angle. I feel weak around you, I feel protected, and I feel loved. Real or imaginary, I'm on this train until it reaches its destination and then I want to see if I'm invited to continue."

"Silly boy, I gave up a significant amount of power when I told the ex-pope to kiss off. I think you know the difference between making love and having sex; well, I'm done pleasing people because that is what they expect. I want feelings, I want emotions, I just don't want to please someone and at the end of the session, they say something lame like, thanks, I needed that. I want to be held, kissed, loved, and made love to. No more screwing Helga. That's Old Testament."

Vincent said, "When you get to the hotel if they are still there and they demonstrate any sign of being in control, flash two fingers on your right hand and I will do the rest but not in public unless, unless there are no other options. I will not let anyone touch or harm you. You're my new mission and I love it and you."

She and Vincent arrived at the hotel at 10:20 a.m. On entry into the hotel, her two companions were not visible. Vincent entered the elevator first, and acted oblivious to Helga's presence. He hit the appropriate floor and heard a voice say, "Hold the elevator please."

Helga made her way to her room without incident and began to hurriedly pack her belongings. She opened the door to her adjoining room, entered the safe and retrieved documents, cash, credit cards and two weapons. There was an unexpected knock at her door. She froze, retrieved a weapon, clicked the safety off, and yelled, "Just a minute". Helga stood to the side of the door and asked, "May I help you?"

Vincent responded, "I sure as hell hope so." She opened the door, and he saw the Smith & Wesson 13+1 weapon in her hand.

He asked, "Is it safe to enter?"

Helga replied, "I thought you were going to wait by the elevator."

Vincent replied, "I rode the elevator down to the lobby and saw your associates looking a little aggressive when they entered the hotel."

Her once companions, now with a detainment order, knocked on her room's door. There was no answer, and the second set of knocks were more definite and aggressive.

Helga handed Vincent a weapon and a silencer. They both carefully screwed the noise reduction units onto their respective weapons and waited for an uncertain event. One of the men asked loudly, "Ms. Spengatsenburg, are you in there?" When there was no answer, the two men looked at each other and one of them decided to kick the door in, a mistake on many levels. Two maids heard the commotion, saw the broken door, and called the front desk, who in turn called the police.

After seeing that the room was empty and some of her belongings were still in place, the two men hurriedly exited room, hurried down the stairs and out of a door in the rear of the hotel. Once in the alleyway they split up and headed in different directions.

#

Helga and Vincent exited the adjoining room and Helga said to the maid, "What kind of people do you allow in this place? That is just incredible that people would kick in a door to a guest's room to rob them."

As the police began to arrive on the scene, Helga waited for Vincent in the lobby with a view of the front of the hotel. Once he arrived, Helga waltzed through the doors and into the car. Vincent said, "You looked regal exiting that place.

Anyway, we need to get rid of this ride. I have a close friend who is renting a car for us as we speak."

Helga looked at Vincent and stated, "You shouldn't trust anyone."

Vincent looked over at her and said, "And how do you suppose we're going to get out of town with this vehicle that's on everyone's radar screen?"

Helga smiled and whispered, "I'm trusting you, and that's all that matters."

Vincent pulled out a map and said, "Look for Hanover Street."

Helga replied, "This is ancient technology. Just use the GPS."

Vincent smiled and said, "That would leave our footprint and a way for people to begin trying to track us."

Helga smiled, looked out of the window, and said, "That Navy education wasn't wasted, was it?" Vincent didn't bother to respond.

Fifteen minutes later, Vincent and Helga turned on to Hanover Street. It was in a quaint and suburban area. As he drove up the street he saw the Ford Jeep that his friend had rented and disconnected the tracking device. Vincent said, "I'm going to need you to get in that Jeep and move it and I when I ready, follow me to a garage that is 5 or 6 blocks down the street where I will leave this car."

Helga pulled the Jeep out of the parking spot and Vincent opened the trunk and placed their bags into the new vehicle.

Helga said, "It's been a long time since I have driven a vehicle."

Vincent replied, "Please follow me slowly for the next 5 or 6 blocks.

Arriving near where the garage was, Vincent got out of the old vehicle and walked back to Helga and said, "I need you to wait here. I'm going to take that vehicle and leave it in that garage."

After leaving the car and walking back to Helga, Vincent said, "Please move over and let me navigate out of this place."

Helga asked, "How do you know you can trust this person?"

Vincent laughed and said, "I have an active contract on his ass. I bailed his parents out of foreclosure on their house. He followed the wrong crowd, and they tried to pit him against me and my crew." Vincent realized that he was opening up a can of worms and decided to leave that issue alone.

Helga asked, "What did you and your crew do and how can you have an active contract on someone?"

Vincent knew that he had just blown the lid off his pot and needed to figure out how to retrieve it. He said, "At some point in time, I will tell you about that. At the Academy, beyond academics, we also had several different schemes in play that would build a network for us, provide us with additional income, and give us the ability to hold people for ransom and earn a fee."

"Are you saying this person is like a slave to you?"

"Wouldn't quite use that term, but I would say that he is obligated to fulfill certain requests without question. I could never be the owner of a slave since my heritage is African American, and we are all descendants of slaves in this country. In this particular case I saved him, his parents, and their house. He was about to be kicked out of the Academy for non-payment. I knew he was smart and that one day he would be playing in the billionaires' playground. Therefore, I invested in him with certain requirements; never ask about a task, never ask the risk, and always say I will."

"Damn, Vincent, you are a slave owner," Helga state.

Vincent looked sternly at Helga and said, "Please don't equate me with that act."

Helga said, "I'm sorry. I didn't mean to offend you."

"You didn't offend me, you were on the verge of crossing a line in the sand, that would have created a negative discourse between us, short-lived hopefully but one that would have to be addressed. Listen, we are on a new path. We don't know shit about each other, and we will only learn from what issues come up. I told you I love you and I got your back. I am the man who respects you and your mission and that is why I am here," Vincent replied.

Helga began to cry and admitted that no one has ever cared about her, just as long as she was able to give them what they wanted. She said, "You show me kindness when there is the possibility that I have crossed an unannounced artificial line in the sand. You keep me grounded, you keep me interested, you keep me loved and I pray to heaven and hell that you never stop being who you are with me and that you find a way to keep me in your heart."

Vincent stated, "You give me too much credit. I am still trying to figure out how to actively keep you as my one and only mi amante. Anyway, where should we head to? I mean should we go across country and stay in cities where there are lots of people. Do you happen to have a functional passport?"

Helga replied, "I have several, how about you?" I have one that works well for me. I think if we can get to Switzerland, we can get lost there."

Vincent immediately said, "Anywhere but that cold-ass place. Isn't there somewhere warm that we can go and learn to be natives and move around the islands like Bora Bora?"

Helga said, "Whatever we do, we have to do it alone and kind of hook up and play that game. Perhaps we should take a long cruise."

"Now, I like that idea. I have never been on a cruise, and this might be a good time to begin exploring you and the world. I have nothing waiting for me in Annapolis. I'll send my landlord a year's rent fee and I'm sure he'll keep my stuff intact, mainly my stereo equipment and albums. Nothing sacred or fluffy like a dog or a cat. I'm up for this adventure. However, I'm in need of some basic clothing items that can be acquired at Walmart or Target."

Suddenly, Vincent seemed sad, and Helga asked, "What's wrong? You seem to fall upon sadness all of a sudden. Is there something you're not telling me?"

Vincent smiled and replied, "The only thing that I hope for is that this works out for both of us because I truly don't want to be away from you for more than a minute."

Helga's eyes became watery, and she suggested, "Let's not head north. Let's head south, dump the vehicle in a garage in Miami and see if we can get passage on a ship heading to Spain. That is approximately a fourteen-day trip. By then, we should know if the world is our oyster or if the fling of all flings, wasn't worth the heartache."

Vincent glanced at Helga and said, "I need to transfer funds from a functional account to one of my variable accounts and then wait for it to hit on my debit card. I'm going to move half a million into that account and that will give us breathing funds until we can figure out our grand plan. By the way, this guy you were searching for in Annapolis to determine if he was alive or dead, did you get any information on him?"

Helga responded, "Not really. He was last photographed with significant scars on his face as if someone tried to carve a "V" for victory on his face. All indications lead to him having suffered a terrible demise. We were using one of his friends and probably someone who participated in his last hurrah to secure DNA evidence from the local morgue. The information was forthcoming but then we had to do the dash and get the hell out of Annapolis. Listen, so far, you have made me the happiest woman on earth. I'm not used to being treated royally, with expressions of love that focus on me attaining a zenith in what we do. No, I was more about making the ex-Holy Father complete by cleansing his body of un-godly considerations through means of catharsis. I was his negotiator, terminator, whore, bitch, and everything else that he needed. His trust was only in me until he started to develop a need for more experimental relationships with neophytes that entered the Vatican and who wanted to serve the Holy Father. Some came with exceptional skills. I watched a newcomer secure the Holy Father's entire member in her mouth while providing him stimulus from his nipples with her fingers. It provided him with the desire for greater creativity, a thing that an older woman like me was not interested in helping him achieve."

Vincent looked at Helga and stated, "You're not that old and even if you are, your package is magnificent and I'm proud to be your wanna be lover!" They both laughed.

Around Richmond, Virginia, Vincent began to yawn and decided to stop at a rest stop to get a cup of coffee. He put on a hat and dark glasses and retrieved a fold-up walking cane to accentuate his disguise. Helga, who was no stranger to camouflaging, got out of the car, put on a baseball cap and glasses, and walked ahead of Vincent into the store. Vincent found his way into the men's room and Helga playfully walked in and shouted, "OMG, this here ain't the babe's room" and walked out.

Once back in the car, Vincent announced, "You're one crazy lady. Are you on meds?"

Helga replied, "I am on a drug, and it's called you, my love. Listen, I'm good at driving straight, just not comfortable at parallel parking and small streets. Pus I want to tell you a few new things at a time about me. Driving will help me do that."

As Helga slowly reentered 95 South, Vincent said, "This is a high-speed merge, so step on it." Helga stubbornly refused to acquiesce to his request. Vincent looked out of the rear window, and exclaimed, "If you don't do as I say, you're going to get us killed!" Helga looked in the mirror and saw a truck barreling down on them and slammed on the brakes. Helga pulled off the road and once the car was completely stopped, Vincent faced her, without words got out of the car, walked to the other side, offered his hand to Helga who accepted it and he said, "That was close, my love. Please, if I ask you to do something in the tone that I did, don't hesitate." He held her and kissed her until she stopped shaking. He then quietly escorted her to the passenger's side.

Sixty miles later, Vincent said, "If we're going to make this great escape a reality, we must trust and believe in each other. After all there is no one but you and I, and we have to be smart, calculating and determined in our objectives. No more hesitations. If I ask you to respond, then please do so. It's as simple as that if we're going to survive."

Helga asked, "Did I tell you I am a nun?"

Vincent looked at her, and replied, "So am I."

Helga retorted, "No fooling, I am a nun, who was corrupted and abused her entire life. I am also a mother."

Vincent once again countered, "So am I."

Helga proclaimed, "I am a nun and a mother. As a matter of fact, my youngest child is being raised by that handsome brigand who impregnated me and who is a member of the Beckmire clan. Zanthius Beckmire DeLombardo is the father of my child. He and his dad, Ben Beckmire, stole my child from a bunch of money-hungry nuns in Valencia, Spain who ran an orphanage. I thought I told you this, but anyway, I had them defrocked and sold into slavery."

Vincent, who was nearly pissing his pants after hearing the information, realized that he and this lady were more than lovers. He said to himself, "Zanthius is my half-brother, little Ben is my nephew, Ben and Courtney Beckmire are the parents I tried to terminate to assume all that they have. How fucked up is this, and how despicable am I?"

For the next hour, Helga told Vincent about all of the things that she was assigned to do in the name of the Holy Father. At first Vincent began to think that he had connected with a real nutcase but after fifteen or so minutes things began to fall in place. Vincent tried to change the subject and at each turn, the story became more and more bizarre. Unfortunately, he asked about her family and Helga cried a river of tears for over five minutes.

When she finally composed herself, she said, "My father tied me to a bed, and from a window I could see him stomping on something and then brutally beating it with a stick. At that point I thought it was my first-born who was created with a mixed parent. So, I have an older child and a younger one.

Vincent asked, "Who was the father of your oldest child?"

Helga once again broke into tears and quietly announced, "He was a Priest, who became a Bishop, who turned into an Archbishop, then became a Cardinal and finally the Holy Father."

Vincent sighed and stated, "None of that matters to me. All I know is that I'm committed to you without any reservations."

The true confessions went on and on as Vincent fought to keep his eyes open while driving. Helga suggested, "There are lots of reputable overnight places along the way. Why don't we stop and get a room for the night? I'm tired as well and you're fighting Mr. Sleepy." Helga undid her seatbelt and eased over to Vincent, and kissed his earlobe. Vincent remarked, "That is a solid idea."

# # #

Vincent knew that eventually he would have to level with Helga, for many reasons. Every encounter with Helga presented a new set of sensations for Vincent. He was accustomed to "wham-bam and thank-you-mam" encounters. However, each kiss with Helga became more sincere and filled with passion and desire. Vincent found himself murmuring the words, "I love everything about you. I love your smell, your touch, your kisses and when I am in your body I become overanxious, and I fight having a shattering orgasm before you do. I try to last longer in our lovemaking, but the sheer joy of our interactions, overwhelm all of my senses. The fact that you are drop dead gorgeous doesn't help me any. Once again, I never sought love, I only wanted satisfaction. With you, there is a magical flute playing that tells me that you are the only thing that matters at this moment in time. I have only one question; will you show me how to be effective and the absolute best lover that you've ever experienced? I want to be king of kings of that place. I want to know how to rule it with love and not domination."

Helga laughing hard, announced, "This is yours and will be yours for as long as you treat it like the queendom that you enjoy ruling. Listen, most of my life was spent, excuse the expression, just fucking those in charge of the church. I don't ever remember enjoying a man's touch, his tongue, or his member. I was the slut of the Holy Father, and I was hated by most, poisoned twice, deadly spiders were put in my shoes, and an occasional snake would appear. You, my friend, come along and perform like this queendom has been yours forever. You touch it right, you kiss it beyond belief and when you enter her, it welcomes you fully because it has never experienced the emotional aspect of copulation. No, Vincent and you have made love to that universe as if it has been yours and only you can command how it performs."

#

Vincent knew he was exhausted from driving and their sexual interactions. He yawned first, turned to his right second, and third he found the warm lips of Helga who was waiting to provide him with additional pleasure that would cause his exhaustion to dissipate and his might once again to jump to attention in order to invade that palace that had been given to him. During this event things became soft but were easily raised to the competition level by a marvelous set of lips.

Vincent, while assisting Helga to another apex, once again announced, "I love you Helga and never before have I experienced the sensations that you provide me. I forever want to be with you, not just for the love making, but for the ability to love you unconditionally despite not knowing you very well but learning who you are and the challenges that you have faced."

A panting Helga asked, "Would you like to experience and swirl that product I'm holding in the back of mouth?" Without further ado, Vincent kissed Helga, and they swirled the remnants of their lovemaking around in each other's mouths.

An exhausted Vincent said, "All of this has been phenomenal and I'm wondering when the real Helga is going to show up."

Helga looked at Vincent and said, "Ditto. I'm wondering the same damn thing." They both laughed, had a sip of their drinks, cuddled for a moment and were off to sleepy land within minutes.

CHAPTER THIRTEEN

On the other side of the water, an attempted takeover of Jong's nephew's business was being attempted by the *Benauijuu, the Young Guns*. They appeared to be an association of uneducated, indentured, and ruthless people. The organizational chart mirrored that of a strong corporation, president, vice president, chief operating officer, human resources, fund development, strategic alliances, legislative liaison, tactical and security relations. Their international headquarters was located in Macau, the only Portuguese speaking colony located off the southeast coast of Mainland China. It is a Special Administrative Region (SAR) of China and maintains a separate governing and economic system from that of mainland China. Macau is by far the largest site of gaming activities in that part of the world. As such, with large sums of money are transferred each day, corruption and legitimate off shoots of different business models are attempted with extraordinarily little interference from the government.

The cousin of a banker in Macau who was on holiday spoke to a relative about how certain traditions and transactions in America followed the old the country's ways without a lot of oversight. He spoke freely of how an associate of his has access to billions of dollars from a single client. He told him that his associate operates in a rented room in one of the old country's banks and how ripe the conglomeration is for old country ways in the barbarian land of America. After several more drinks of Scotch on the rocks, he began to give names and locations.

The banker in Macau made calls to his people in America to assess whether there was an opportunity to make some off-the-books money. He was told how the established banks on the ground level do everything by the book and how the real people's banks exists in the basement. He was told that the lower you descend into the bowels of some of the buildings the greater the risk/reward becomes. He was also informed about a young banker who does business from the ground level to basement level four and how although he appears poor, he is actually rich and the people he represents are considered legitimate crooks, if there is such a thing. After hanging up the phone from his associates, he called a ranking member of the *Benauijuu* and asked, "What's the going price for new acquisitions, eventual control, and administrative costs?"

The person on the other end asked, "How many divisions will have to be involved? Is it a strong walk in and take over, or are there tactical and security types needed?"

"I don't have empirical information, but I want to investigate the possible acquisition of more than a *choudoru*."

There was quiet on the other end of the line for a few moments and then a sudden exhale. The other party asked, "How much on top can you guarantee, and who is the *hakase*?"

"At this point, it is purely investigative. Once an analysis has been conducted, I will answer your questions."

#

It was a Monday morning when three men entered the normal bank that some people used to do their real banking. They descended to the second level and one of the men said to a banker, "We want to buy into your business at a reasonable cost, and we won't take no for an answer."

Jong's cousin responded, "That is not how this bank works. It does not allow or encourage takeovers."

The man doing the talking, repeated, "I now want to buy into your business at a discounted price, and I don't suggest that you give me the fundamentals of banking. Just open your books and we will tell you what accounts we want to acquire. Now, if that's a problem then I can assure you that our employer won't like us coming back to him empty-handed. Tell you what, my employer is a reasonable person. You go home and play with your wife and two sons and let me know the value of sanctity in your home or better yet, that you still have a healthy family. Listen, we will be back at the same time tomorrow. See you then and do sleep well."

As the men were about to leave, Jong's nephew humbly asked, "Which accounts are of interest to you?"

The man talking asked, "Do we look like paupers? No, sir, we are only interested in working with accounts, let's say, over a *choudoru*. Take care of that family of yours and we'll see you tomorrow."

Jong's nephew knew exactly what was happening and decided to text his uncle and simply say, "There is an immediate and aggressive bid to assume your accounts, please advise."

When Jong received the text, he was with Beckmire and Chakes. He said, "Mr. Beckmire, I think we may have a problem."

"What's with this Mr. Beckmire, shit?"

"Sarge, I just received a text from my nephew, you know the one who manages a significant amount of our assets. He states that an immediate and aggressive bid for our accounts is in play. In other words, someone is trying to take over his operation, thus having a fractional control over our funds without our input, using his family as bargaining chips."

"What the hell does that mean in English?"

"Simply put for simple minds, if they take over his business, they take over our funds."

The Sarge looked at Jong, rubbed his left ear, and asked, "Did you just call me simple?"

"Mr. Sarge, if that's your interpretation, it certainly isn't mine. I would never call my leader simple, maybe a few other things, but simple, never," Jong stated.

The Sarge said, "As usual, you're full of shit. Have you given a response any consideration?"

"Indeed, I have. I want to send Dempsey, Hood, and their ladies to do an assessment. I propose we position them with $2 million and let that be their entry into my nephew's bank, with a note from me recommending his institution. If you like, we can send Brown and Bernstein or Jilkes and John Lee with them. However, I think they are enough on their own, but I don't know what snake pit they might enter."

The Sarge saw Courtney playing with Marcelus and said, "It's time to visit our home in the country. Let's take the group for an extended time in the States, with strong rules for touring."

Jong looked at the Sarge and asked, "May I feel your forehead? I think you have fever or something positive."

The Sarge said, "Make it happen. What's our timetable for interacting with your nephew?"

Jong paused and said, "My only concern is that my nephew thinks these people are members of the *Benauijuu*, an international group of opportunistic thieves that prey on older institutions that don't have modern-day guardrails protecting them."

The Sarge asked, "He's like a broker, he can't act without our permission, is that correct?"

"Mr. Sarge, we gave my nephew considerable decision-making authority concerning our accounts. In essence, he could liquidate 30 percent of our portfolio without our permission. The people who are trying to gain administrative oversight are probably aware of that consideration as well as the fact that our combined portfolios border near the trillion-dollar mark. I agree with you on this one, we need to go in force, but we need an assessment to make sure we won't have an international team of crooks coming after us," Jong stated.

The Sarge said, "Let's make this seem like the women want to go back stateside and enjoy the luxuries of sitting on toilets, running water from a faucet, opening a refrigerator door, and answering a doorbell. Why should we blame our exploits and assaults strictly on us? Let's spread the blame."

# # #

That evening, after an earlier consultation with Wajickee, the menu was going to be John Dory. Everyone was excited about the selection, knowing that it was a coastal fish, definitely hard to acquire in the Outback.

As the clan gathered for dinner, Ayesha casually signed to Mary Alice, "Each time we have John Dory, a mission is required between bites and bullshit is served for dessert."

Mary Alice initially seemed confused and just stared at Ayesha. After several minutes had passed, Mary Alice comprehended the message from Ayesha and said to Hyshime, "I hope you're not involved in an unsanctioned mission. That fish spells a plea from the leader to get us involved in horseshit. Don't lie to me, or you'll be sleeping with the children for the next year."

Jong lowered his head and said, "Bad people are trying to take over our accounts from my nephew, with the subtle threat that his family is in danger."

Mary Alice asked, "Why when there is a problem, you men have to suck your thumbs before announcing the urgency to us women? Listen, you expose it before our leader soft-pedals it, or the next time you feel that mountain rise between your legs, it will be many moons from now before you'll have me. Do what I ask, Hyshime, don't play around with this one. I want to go and sit on a real toilet and soon."

Jong saw the Sarge with Mallory and Marcelus and hastily walked up to him and said, "Don't fall into the pit of bullshit when you speak tonight. The women are aware that there is an issue and by providing John Dory through Wajickee won't work this night. Go straight to the problem and all will be well. Play the surround sound noise and you'll be on a plane by yourself."

The Sarge immediately asked, "Did your whimpering ass expose our issue to your wife?"

"No, Mr. Sarge. That smart-ass Ayesha signed to my wife that when we offer John Dory, look out for the bullshit that comes for dessert."

"Did Ayesha really sign that?" the Sarge asked.

"That is exactly what my wife stated," Jong replied.

The Sarge thought, "How intuitive of her. I need to remind myself to watch what I say around her."

# # #

Later at dinner, as the Sarge was setting the stage for his goals, Courtney took the mike and said, "I've been appointed to tell all those who look like me that when the men serve John Dory as the main course, be on the lookout for the bullshit for dessert." Everyone began to laugh and agree on the perception and perspective.

Monica rose and asked, "So, my fearless and awesome leader, what have your minions talked you into doing? Are they tired of not terminating and maiming people and, therefore, they've concocted some kind of emergency that requires the entire clan to board our covered-up plane and fly across the waters?"

The Sarge stood there with a broad smile and yelled without the microphone, "People do you like being rich?" The boisterous sounds began to diminish until there was absolutely no one talking. Casually, the Sarge reached for his drink and said, "I will present a situation to all of you after we have enjoyed the John Dory, and then it's bullshit time." He proceeded to his table and acted as if nothing had been said except the smart and real understanding of Ayesha. He laughed a little and looked at Courtney playing with Marcelus. Courtney asked, "What's up, Doc?"

After dinner, the Sarge began his comments by thanking Ayesha for teaching everyone in the village to use sign language. He said, "I guess there are a lot of other things being said that I need to make sure that I get. Therefore, my entire crew and I going to faithfully learn how to sign."

Courtney interrupted the Sarge and said, "Honey, there is no need for you to learn signing now. We rarely use it except when we're talking to Ayesha."

The Sarge continued and said, "As I said, we're going to learn to sign so that we can keep up with the extremely talented and smart female members of our clan."

"On a serious note, without our permission, a group called the *Benauijuu*—are trying to take over the numerous accounts that we have with Jong's nephew. In other words, they're trying to rob us of our money, but, more importantly, they have threatened Jong's nephew's family, with special emphasis on his wife and children. I first considered sending a surveillance team to check it out, but this group may not wait for that and may act to the detriment of our friend's family members. I am thinking that we can spend time in Virgina at the farm until we have handled this matter. Also, I have a question for all of you to consider; is it time to utilize more controlled institutions as money managers, thus avoiding situations like this one?"

McArthur stood and asked, "Do you have any idea who these people are?"

The Sarge responded, "They're a wing of an international terrorist group that achieves its goals and objectives through pure violence. Listen, I asked the institutional question because the less aggressive behaviors we face, the better off we are. I mean I don't think any of us can do a push-up without having a damn heart attack."

There was laughter until John Lee rose from his seat and said, "That there might be the reason that we try to live better and longer." There was only silence after he spoke.

After a short period of reflection, the Sarge said, "If some of you want to remain here, then that's okay because I think this is the most secure place on earth for us. At 0800 hours, I am heading to our plane to make the long journey across the pond to make sure that no one takes what is rightfully ours and that they for damn sure don't hold our friend's family as hostages."

# # #

The following morning, a steady line of people entered the old school bus to head to the airport. Wajickee said to the group, "Use caution at every turn, do not underestimate these people and watch each other's backs. Also, be sure to listen to your pilot, he is one smart cookie."

# # #

A call had been made to the pilots to make ready the plane for an overseas mission. When the group arrived at the airport, Captain Harris suggested that they delay departure for approximately 2 hours because of a weather front that didn't appear friendly. The Sarge said, "Listen, you don't have to ask me about safety and comfort. I rely on you and your crew to do whatever is necessary to make sure that we travel safely and with a modicum of comfort."

Captain Harris said, "Then sir, I would like to delay this flight until tomorrow because it looks like bad weather from here to the west coast of America and all across the States. The plane can handle it, but some of the weather fronts look like funnels and they are not pleasant for planes or passengers."

The Sarge asked, "How about we fly to Sydney, spend the night there and proceed in the morning to America?"

Captain Harris replied, "Excellent consideration and one that is most doable."

CHAPTER FOURTEEN

In the morning, Helga woke up first and entered the shower. Vincent, hearing the noise awakened with a woody. He walked to the bathroom door, making noises to alert Helga he was near and asked, "Do you mind if we save some water and I shower with you?"

Helga, with a smile on her face said, "If you don't, then I'm going to be a pissed-off passenger all day long."

Vincent entered the bathroom, with his member at attention and said, "Permission to enter your space, my queen?"

Helga fell to her knees and said, "Permission granted, provided you give me first taste of that wonderful-looking thing pointing at me."

Twenty-eight minutes later, Vincent and Helga emerged from the bathroom, clean, satisfied and committed to each other. Her stride indicated that this man covered all of her bases and made sure there was no sand lingering around.

After checking out of the hotel, the two began their drive south and Vincent asked Helga, "Have you ever had a *Fully Loaded*?"

Helga responded, "I thought that was what you gave me in the shower."

"No, silly girl. I mean a sandwich that has ham, bacon, sausage, egg, and cheese on a croissant?"

Helga responded, "That sounds like an invitation to a heart attack. However, I am hungry and if that's what you want to eat, then I'll try it also."

Vincent pulled off at an exit that advertised fast food establishments and pulled into the Burger King lot that offered a meal known as the *Fully Loaded*. He ordered two sandwiches and orange juices.

Helga asked, "Is the orange juice needed to cure whatever it is we're about to eat?"

Vincent laughed and said, "No my love, it's for your daily dose of Vitamin C."

Helga looked at the sandwich and said, "If ever there was something that would drive me to become a vegan, then this is it. I don't really think I can eat this."

Vincent bit into his sandwich and said, "Sometimes, people need to forget their stints in high cotton and remember where they came from. While at the Academy my associates and I thrived on this concoction."

Helga looked at it again and said, "I'm hungry, I guess one bite won't hurt me." Within three minutes, she was folding up the empty wrapper and wiping her lips. She mused, "Ugly, but oh so good."

#

The upcoming sign read, "Welcome to North Carolina." Vincent said to Helga, "I hope you haven't turned that phone of yours on since we've headed down this road."

Helga looked at him as if he were stupid and replied, "That phone of mine is resting in a storm drain in Annapolis. This isn't my first rodeo, my friend and believe me I appreciate your thinking forward because the people who will be looking for us won't relent. Also, before leaving Annapolis, I changed the passwords to all of the accounts that hold $300 million or more. I also left a laptop that is bugged and can be tracked for my ex-employer. Listen, knowing how money hungry he is, this allows us time to methodically plan our disappearance without a trace. He won't come after me once he realizes that the passwords for the accounts have been changed and even he, the owner, can't withdraw from them. I once loved this man until he became the pope. He trusted me to no end and rightfully because I was dedicated to his every whim and desire. I can transfer every dime out of his accounts because I am the designated caretaker."

Vincent asked, "If you mean that much to him, why does he have you out looking for someone who more than likely is dead?"

Helga smiled and replied, "I am good at that kind of work. Plus, I like the challenge and the capture of those I am hunting."

Vincent quickly shot back, "It doesn't seem like the task I would give to the person who also can make substantial withdrawals from my account. That person would be kept close by at all times."

Helga maintained her silence for over a minute and then asked, "Why did you bring up that Beckmire kid? If not for him, there would not be this long drive to points unknown for the two us together. Plus, he is sitting on trillions of dollars and doesn't have a damn clue. His desire to kill his parents, their clan, his brother, and his nephew, indicated to me that he was a heartless son-of-a-bitch. Not many sane people would plan to kill their parents even for billions and when and if he looks at their last will and testament, he'll see that the quadrant of land roped off for him is worth more than a lot of countries' GDP. And besides, my ex-lover Zanthius is the father of my child, and my child was on his hit list. I'm not sure I can stand by and let this nut kill my child."

Vincent stated, "There seems to be a lot of nuts in that equation you just spoke of. Does that kid, what's his name again?"

"It's Beckmire," Helga stated.

"Right, does he know about that partial of land that's worth trillions to him?" Vincent asked.

"I'm not sure and really don't give a hoot. My concern is that in the clan there is a young girl, Ms. Beatrice by name, who is a powerful bruja, if you believe in such things," Helga stated.

"A bruja is another name for witch, right?" Vincent inquired, knowing the answer but wanted to appear to be unsure of it.

Helga laughed and said, "Everyone knows what a witch is, but few know that a bruja is another name for a witch."

Vincent asked, "So is your mission to protect the girl and your son, or what?"

"Listen, a coup on the entire clan would net the Beckmire boy over a trillion in assets and also, he would gain another trillion from that land that is exclusively his. My job is to make sure that he turns it all over to my ex-employer before I cut him into little pieces. That is why the job was delegated to me, anyone knowing this information might develop a new set of objectives that would complicate the smooth transition that he and I imagined."

Vincent, pretending to be paying attention to his driving, is literally fighting back tears because of the picture that Helga painted of the Beckmire boy. He asked, "Was this kid spurned by Lucifer himself? I mean, he would kill his parents, friends, and other family members to gain wealth that he couldn't spend in a hundred lifetimes. What is wrong with people?"

Helga noticed that Vincent's eyes were tearing and asked, "Why the tears?"

"Because I can't believe any human being would kill their parents for the sake of money."

Helga laughed and said, "My friend, that is not what you would call money. That is pure wealth, the ability to do, buy and own pretty much anything that enters your mind."

Vincent responded, "Naw, that's evil and I don't like this person on any level." Vincent saw a rest stop sign and said, "I need to use the loo."

The two entered the rest stop and went to their respective facilities. After locking the door to the stall, Vincent began to cry hysterically. For the first time in this ordeal, he thought about his mother and father. He said aloud, "I am better than that. I'm going to prove that I am better than that."

As he met Helga in the lobby of the rest stop, she asked, "Have you been crying? Your eyes are bloodred."

He continued walking and said, "We are heading south where my allergies are going to be forever present. As a matter of fact, check out that vending machine and see if it dispenses any allergy medicines."

Helga checked out the machine and announced, "We need to find a pharmacy and get something for you, like Benadryl or one of those other allergy medicines."

In the car, Vincent went on the offensive and said, "You know some really terrible people, individuals who would terminate their own families for money. How can you be involved in a mess like this?"

Helga, surprised by the notion of a continuation of the conversation, thought for a moment, and responded, "I was someone's slave. I was told that my godly place and purpose was to make sure that the Holy Father never needed anything that was potentially available through me. I was his slave, his whore, his bitch, and he did whatever he wanted to me. Okay, momentarily, love walks in the room from a stranger who has remained by my side so far. I felt the love, the sincerity, the appreciation, and the kindness. Vincent, no one has ever treated me like you do. No one has ever touched and loved my body like you do. And Vincent, I felt every impulse and urge within me to reciprocate. I have never known or felt this way and so far, if love is what I'm feeling towards you, then it is a first."

# # #

The sign read "Entering South Carolina." Vincent asked, "What should we do, keep on pushing? Shall I keep on driving, and you keep on talking?"

Helga laughed and replied, "Keep driving, James. Are you hungry again? I certainly could use a snack and a go in the loo."

After another forty-five minutes of driving, the two pulled off at an exit that offered fast food and lodging. As they drove down the road, the best-looking place of potential residency was a Hilton property. They both agreed that if there was space in the inn, then they would rest there and leave early in the morning to stay on an unwritten schedule. Vincent said, "I had some real valuable stuff in my apartment that I'm going to miss."

Helga asked, "Like what? Pictures of Marilyn Monroe or someone as stimulating as her?"

Vincent looked at her inquisitively and asked, "Where have you been? The 21st century women are much more beautiful than that relic. I mean, oh my goodness, just walk down 5th Avenue in New York or Connecticut Avenue in DC, or show up at the Four Seasons on International Drive, in Baltimore, or just go for crabs at one of the local dives and you'll see beauties and bodies that make your suggestion look like worn tires on a rusted truck. Today's women are more fit, intelligent, uninhibited, independent, decisive and they are exponentially sexier than those of that era. Have you ever watched an Academy Awards program or any of the other shows when they dress to the nines and show as much flesh as the law will allow and by the way, they don't need a fan to blow up their dress because the dresses they wear are permeable."

Helga frowned and said, "I don't see much character in 21st-century women. They seem easy to lay, hard to get rid of and money hungry. Everything is about them and what you can offer. How about down where we're heading, they have a dating fee. Don't look at me like I'm an alien. I'm telling you that if you want to have a date with one of those mindless bodies, then you have to pay a fee for the initial date."

Vincent paused and then continued, "Some of what you say I agree with, but the whole world is about money and the notion of "me first." I'm glad that you're not after my money or you're not an older lady looking for a young stud to keep that fire going."

Helga began to fume and said, "Stop this fucking car right now. Are you saying that I'm too old for you? Why didn't you say that in Annapolis? Why are you saying that shit now?"

Vincent was momentarily lost for words, but then yelled, "Your interpretation is all wrong. I'm with you because I happen to feel as though I'm in love with you. I'm leaving my life behind because I want to be with you. Don't pull that old lady shit on me ever again, or I will walk the fuck back to Annapolis without your crazy ass. I'm a sucker for you. Oh, and by the fucking way, I don't know how old you are, and I don't give a rat's ass about that. All I know is that you have electrified all of my senses and I don't ever want to experience this bullshit again unless you want out."

As Helga began to cry, Vincent arrogantly said, "You should cry all the way to Florida, because I've walked away from my life to be with you. Don't play that age bullshit with me. I'm with who I want to be with and who I want to die with, of course in due time and who makes my heart flutter at the very sight and thought of her."

# # #

The sign read, "Welcome to Georgia, The Peach State."
Vincent occasionally glanced at Helga snoring up a storm and
slightly drooling from her mouth. She was snoring so loud
that she woke herself up and asked, "What's all that noise I
keep hearing?"

A polite Vincent replied, "It's the brakes on this thing.
We should change vehicles soon just to try and stay ahead of
those looking for us."

Helga stated, "Vincent no one is looking for you, so why
did you say us?"

Vincent smiled and announced, "Not sure you're aware of
this, but I am on the run with you, just in case you forgot.
Look, another rest stop. Let's stretch our legs and use the
facilities. Is that okay with you?"

Thirty minutes later, the two resumed their drive heading
south, with the final destination unknown. Vincent asked,
"Was money the only reason that kid tried to kill his parents
and their friends?"

Helga thought about it for a moment and responded, "I
really don't know the answer to that one. However, the ex-
pope thought highly of him because of his determination and
desperately wanted to include him in his next reign of power."

Vincent asked, "Why, because he was unopposed to
killing his family?"

Helga fired back, "No because he was committed to
killing them and he tried several times to out-flank them and
slaughter them on their farm, ranch, and in the Outback. He
was dedicated to that premise."

Vincent asked, "Again, besides the money was there any other reason he wanted them dead?"

"Oh, yeah! According to the rumor mill, he felt that his parents were sub-par and were not the kind of people that he wanted to introduce to his friends and their families. He detested the fact that his dad was a cop, and his mom was just a doctor. Somehow, he left the planet on that reasoning, and they probably could have saved each other some aggravation if they had aborted his dumb ass."

Vincent snapped, "Why do you call him a dumb ass?"

Helga stated, "Vincent, that guy had everything going for him and he didn't appreciate or understand what he had. First of all, I hear the Beckmire woman is forever scarred by his reactions but sends him money whenever he needed it. His father and mother afforded him every benefit of that prestigious institution called the Naval Academy. I hear he left there without owing a single dime."

Vincent asked, "Where did he go?"

Helga continued, "I think he went straight to hell, and I do believe that his associates fed his ass to the fish."

"What a tragic story. Anyway, I'm thinking that we can make it to Florida before the sun sets. What are your druthers?" Vincent inquired.

"Um, I don't care as long as I'm with you. I feel as though I've known you all my life and everything that happens between us is second nature. Being with you is spiritual and meaningful and it never feels new or uncomfortable. I hope you're the real deal and you're not hiding any issues such as you're bi-sexual, purely gay, hedonistic, or you just like killing people for sport or for money much like that Beckmire kid," Helga announced.

Vincent laughed, reached over and gently massaged her hand, pulled her hand to his lips and with eyes looking intently at her, he tongue-kissed her hand."

Helga smiled and said, "I have a very special place that you can do weird things to with that tongue of yours, so don't over exercise it until I make sure it fulfills a chore that so desperately needs attending too."

Vincent grabbed her hand again and began to suck her fingers, while bringing Helga almost to the point of enjoying another orgasm. She said, "I prefer you keep your eyes on the road and save this sucking you're doing for later."

CHAPTER FIFTEEN

The group's plane landed at their airport in Maryland. After going through customs in San Diego, there were no additional bureaucratic obstacles facing them. In Maryland they were met by people loyal to the group who were aware of the impending action against the clan. The lead driver of the ancient-looking mini-vans said to Jong, "I don't speak for your nephew, but I do know that he and his family are in danger. Those attempting to take over his accounts are from an international group and I consider them terrorists. Their record is clear, final and they never leave witnesses. I now drive and no more talk. Welcome back. All at the farm is well, some of the horses have gone to horse heaven and a few new members have joined."

Once in Virginia and as the mini vans navigated the roads to the ranch, Jilkes whispered to John Lee, "There are a lot of memories on both sides of this road."

John Lee responded, "A lot of them memories almost be fatal situations that I don't care to think about. You, me, and this group have been spared by the Almighty to do his bidding in a very strange way, and I won't question why. I mean, just remember when at bootcamp them fellas had to pull me off you because I was giving you one hell of an ass whuppin, but after that we became the bestest of friends. Who would have ever thought that could happen after that severe beating I gave you."

Jilkes smiled and said, "I am simply happy you beat some sense into me. Otherwise, who knows what might have happened to this group."

At the ranch, Asiram said to Zanthius, "I think we should sell this place because we don't use it much."

Zanthius looked at the bales of hay and said, "Sometimes people are blessed with more than they need or can handle. In our case we are in need of this farm, and we can handle it. Honey, I know it makes you sad that we spend a lot of time in the Outback, little time here at the farm and even less time in middle America. If you think about it, we also spend less time in the islands. I suggest that at dinner I talk to the group about our different assets and the need to use them systematically. I will say we should either use the farm or sell it. I will also say the same thing about the ranch. However, we know that the group can't dictate to us to sell or to keep anything, those decisions are clearly ours and ours alone. We're just trying to be diplomatic, inclusive, and making sure that the group has a say in the maintaining or dispensing of assets."

Later at dinner, before the Sarge jumped into his sermon, Zanthius opened the meeting by saying, "People we're under attack once again. It has been over a year since someone has attempted to assault us. I am preempting my dad, because my wife thinks that we should sell our properties in middle America and this farm. I totally disagree with her however, in essence both properties are hers. In her defense, it's true that we have not used the farm or the ranch much and the memories that she has of all of our places, as well as mine, are filled with death. Every place that we have been in or owned is saturated with scenes of murder and mayhem. However, there are other memories that surpass the negatives, such as Hood and Dempsey marrying the two beautiful sisters in the fields amongst the horses and Larry insisting upon continued excavation and finding all of us alive and well. Listen, although Asiram is the sole owner of the properties and the final decision rests with her, she gladly admits that this has not been the way of the group—that is making individual decisions without the input of the group. Therefore, I ask with my wife's permission of course, should we sell this property and the one in middle America?"

John Lee stood and asked, "Why on earth would we be wanting to sell those paradises? We be done learned a lot about farming and ranching. I be saying for me, my misses and them there youngins of mine, and I know my minority friend feels the same way and we responds with a resounding, no. Ain't that right Mr. Jilkes?"

Everyone was waiting on Jilkes to respond negatively, but his reply was stoic. "Whenever my brother believes in an act or our mission, then he speaks for me."

A "wow" sound resonated throughout the dining room and the Sarge said to Jilkes, "That is a mighty huge power of attorney you just gave him. Are you certain about your declarations?"

Jilkes smiled at John Lee, looked at the Sarge, and said, "Absodamnlutely!"

# # #

After the affairs of the state were attended to, the Sarge asked for questions or concerns about the impending issues with Jong's nephew. Jong murmured, "I received a text from my nephew that people are patrolling and sitting outside of his house, on a 24/7 basis. I just want to get him safely out of his home and swiftly send an uncurable message to the *Benauijuu* that they are now on our hitlist. I don't mean to speak for the leadership, but people can't take what is not theirs and use any means to make it happen. No, Mr. Sarge, I want to place my foot into their asses and watch it exit from their mouths."

The Sarge felt the intense nature of Jong's resolve and replied, "I agree with Hyshime, we got to take these mother, 'you know what's' on, and hopefully eradicate them.

# # #

In China Town, around 7th & H Streets NW, Hood, Angel, Anel, and Dempsey strolled through the streets acting like normal tourists. They came upon a place that   advertised original old Cantonese recipes. Hood said, "I doubt if this place serves up dog, cat, duck and rat."

Anel said, "Who on earth eats that?" Hood responded, "In the former Canton province, now called Guangzhou China, people would line up to buy fresh versions of those items. Seriously, duck, cat, dog and rat sell out first thing in the morning."

Angel asked, "Have you ever tried any of those items?"

"Naw, I was never that adventuresome when it came to food. I stayed with the traditional items and rarely tried stuff that didn't make sense to me such as cats, dogs and especially rats."

As the group walked past the bank on the other side of the street, they saw people hanging out front, smoking, and playing Mahjong but were aware of the strangers looking at them. Dempsey uttered, "Those guys are the new bank guards. Look at the bulge in the back of the one in that 76er's jersey. That's a big weapon. Let's keep walking."

Midway down the block, people began to approach them from the front and rear, while others began to cross the street. Hood said, "No matter what, we don't want a confrontation with these people, yet."

One of the men asked, "Why you in this neighborhood?"

Anel looked at him and said, "This is America, a free country." The man aggressively approached her. Hood threw his hands in the air as if he were surrendering and said, "Friend, we don't want a problem. We're just touring."

The man screamed, "Tell your bitch never to address me. She's a low-life dog and had better never talk directly to me."

Hood replied, "We don't want any problems, but I suggest that you not address my wife in that manner, or I will have this place raided by my agency. You really don't want this problem, but if you insist on confronting us for walking down the fucking street, then I'll have 100 agents down here to harass your asses every single day. Now that I have made it clear, I suggest you apologize to my wife and if you don't, in less than two hours, this place will become a war zone. Don't fuck with me!" Hood pulled out a badge that they had used before that was a perfect replica of the real thing.

A non-descript guy moved forward and said, "My friend he drinks too much Sake early in day. No harm, no foul, man.

No harm, no foul." He turned to the guy who called Anel the names and screamed in a foreign tongue at the abuser. He essentially ordered the man to kowtow to the low-life ugly bitch.

Hood said, "Sayonara!" He also uttered several complete sentences in Japanese which got everyone's attention. Hood then said, "We're out of here." As they began to walk away, an SUV pulled up in front of the bank and men got out on both sides to evaluate the landscape. This caught Angel's attention as well as Dempsey's.

The Sarge saw the activity as well and said to Jilkes, "I hope they ignore that vehicle."

No one gave it any attention, and they walked away, a little frazzled, but they avoided any confrontation. Several blocks away, the Sarge who listened intently at the exchange and was prepared to send people in from the east and west to do what they do best—wreak havoc. As he and Jong looked through binoculars, they saw that after the men checked out the environment, they didn't move until a signal was sent from a window across the street from the bank. As the men ushered four people out of the SUV, Jong yelled, "That's my nephew and his family."

The Sarge said, "We can't go in there with blazing guns. We need a strategy to get into the building and then we take control of the vermin."

Jong asked, "Did you see how my family was walking? It looks like they have weights around their ankles."

The Sarge replied, "I wasn't looking at how they walked, I was more focused on the fact that they are still alive and wondering how to keep them that way."

Jilkes said, "I recorded their movements. Let me take a look and see if I can discern any abnormalities in the way that they were walking."

After zooming in on their ankles, Jilkes discovered that each had a bracelet attached, like the one's the courts uses to keep up with criminals who are under house arrest. He said to the Sarge and Jong, "You're correct, they have bracelets around their ankles." He looked at the street once again and said, "Sarge, this reminds me of that time in Hong Kong when we were fighting that triad gang. Look at all of the windows where people can open them and make us a part of a shooting gallery. I don't like this one bit. I would rather get my country friend and walk down that street and start some shit and even shoot a couple of assholes. Us marching in there like boy scouts will leave a lot of people dead. There is no cover."

As the Sarge considered his concerns and as he focused his binoculars on a rooftop, he could see that someone was smoking. He said to Jilkes, "Fifth building on the left side. Is that smoke I'm seeing or what?"

As Jilkes focused, he said, "That's exactly what I'm talking about. Look five rooftops down on the same side." There were two men stretching and doing make-believe martial arts exercises.

The Sarge announced, "Good catch, my friend. I can only assume that the other side of the street is covered as well. If we walked into that mess, we would be unceremoniously executed.

After lowering his binoculars, the Sarge blurted out, "Where is my daughter and her brother?"

CHAPTER SIXTEEN

The sign read, "Welcome to Florida, the Sunshine State." Helga smiled and said, "You drove all this way without my help. Vincent, I really appreciate you. I really hope you're into me as much as I am into you."

Vincent replied, "Helga, I'm not really into you. I just like driving Ms. Daisy from danger and hopefully to a place and time where she doesn't have to look over her shoulder. Two things before you get crazy about what I just said. I think you should consider changing your hairstyle and color. In addition, I suggest that you get rid of those two rings that you continuously wear. Also, you always seem to be dressed to the nines. How about some jeans, tennis shoes, T-shirts and even the bra-less look? Now, I don't know how far we would get while I'm staring at those perfectly round breasts."

Vincent paused for a moment and then stated, "Changing the subject, there has been one thing that has been on my mind since we talked about the person you were looking for and that is what is the connection between the ex-pope, the little girl and the Batmire guy?"

"The name is Beckmire, not Batmire. That is a long story and one I'm not sure I want to talk about at this moment. I would rather save that for an evening when we are at sea, sitting on our balcony and watching the waves crest. Listen, I'm not sure of your belief system, but there are things that exist in the world we live in that will make you a believer and give you the motivation to try to penetrate the veil that would make you pure and whole. Trust me Vincent, as a nun and in the catacombs of the Vatican, there are things that exist that have no answers to them. There are life-forms from another time and place that will scare you for the rest of eternity. Let us save the conversation for a time when we are on the water and hopefully secure with each other." Helga stated.

Vincent looked at her and said, "Two can play that game."

"What the hell does that mean?" Helga asked.

"That means that two can play in the same sandbox with information and secrets that are mind-blowing," Vincent retorted. Vincent then said, "I want to watch the waves crest and sit on our balcony as we travel to lands unknown to each of us and tell you things that you don't know about me. My situation is not as complex as yours, you know, people are apparently looking to exterminate you. And by the way now that you drafted me into your mess, I just want to say that this is thrilling, adventuresome and romantic. I keep telling you that I have had sex before, but I have never made love where my mission is to please, not like my previous goal which was to be pleased and completed without any regard for the other person."

Vincent pulled safely off the road and once again tried to stop Helga from crying. She said, "One day, I hope to never cry around you about anything except how happy you make me. I love you, Vincent." Vincent reached over and kissed her tenderly on her lips and suggested that they stop soon at a hotel and enjoy each other to the maximum.

At a Hilton property, Helga and Vincent checked in, showered and dressed casually for dinner. Helga said to Vincent, "I hope we can do both versions of dining."

Vincent asked, "What does both versions of dining mean?"

"Silly boy, it means both formal dining and casual. I want to dress-up and look good for you."

Vincent looked at her, and his eyes began to fill with tears because he had never really been in a relationship where emotions and honesty were at the top of the menu. He reached for her hand and said, "I am all that you will ever need in life, and I feel that you are everything that will make me reverse the way I have lived. I can't wait to get further lost with you, soon. That brings me to another point. I have untraceable credit cards, how about you? I know we spoke of this before but now is the put-up or shut-up time."

Helga laughed and said, "I can shut down my ex-employer's operation at any time. His people are trying desperately to get around my firewall that demands three security identifications. Personally, I have access to more than $300 million of ungodly funds, taken from dictators, drug dealers, crypto currency pirates, and other nefarious individuals. I also have complete access to another $232."

Vincent asked, "Is that $232 thousand or what?

Helga emitted a long laugh and said, "Silly boy, I don't deal in thousands. That is $232 million, a gift to my sons if something were to happen to me. They're already rich, but another hundred or so million won't hurt, because they are righteous and will hopefully use every dime to help people help themselves. This I honestly believe because my youngest child's father, grandfather, great grandfathers and beyond, believed in that notion, that people need help and if I had caught that Beckmire boy that would have been another pot of money. In a way I am happy you showed up and the expedition to find that boy was unfruitful. I think it might have been complicated for me to do bodily harm to the uncle of my child. I guess I'm getting soft in my old age." Vincent smiled at her but didn't elaborate.

As they continued down 95 South, Vincent asked, "Why are you interested in me? I am poverty stricken and unable to help anyone except on random occasions when I help people with small financial problems.

With teary eyes and a sincere straight on look at Vincent, Helga announced, "No one has ever extended me the emotions, respect, passions, feelings, and sincerity that you my friend have offered me. I was just a symbol of limited pleasure for a select few, not for emotions, just 'please me and be on call when I want or need you.' No one has ever taken me for a long ride to nowhere without the expectation that after I finish doing my work for them, that they would drop me off and be gone. It's not too late for you to escape my future expectations. Oh, stop at that cellular store over there. I need to lock down our security."

Vincent asked, "What does that mean?"

Helga replied, "That means I'm going to lock my ex-employer out of his accounts *ad infinitum.*"

The duo stopped at a local Verizon store and were very much aware of the cameras. Vincent stayed in the atrium of the store while Helga, completely disguised, purchased a throwaway telephone. During the connection process, Vincent stepped outside and got back in the rental vehicle. As he sat in the car, he watched two men smoking weed. Vincent thought they were going to go into the store next door, however, the two pot-heads entered the Verizon store. He saw the bulge in the back pocket of one of the men and watched the other expose a weapon once inside. Vincent immediately got out of the car and entered the store to secure his new paramour. As he entered the store, he knew that the two potheads were trying to rob it. Vincent announced, "Oh, I'm sorry, I think I'm in the wrong place."

One of the crooks who was terribly high instructed, "Put your money on that fucking counter or I will blow your head off!"

Vincent began to plead with the guy, while the other weed head entered the storage area where all the equipment was, leaving the totally inebriated one trying to keep his balance and his eyes open. The crook looked at Helga and stated, "When we finish here, I think I'm going to make you my bitch!" There was a hard thud, as the recipient of the right hook fell to the floor. Helga grabbed his weapon and threw it to Vincent. Vincent jumped across the counter in front of the door to the storage room and waited patiently for the other crook to return from the storage area. When the door opened, Vincent hit the crook in the forehead with the other crook's weapon and knocked him unconscious. He reversed the role and demanded to know where the camera storage locker was.

The scared clerk said, "It is out of order, and the service people should be here any minute."

Vincent said, "I perhaps saved your life. Are you telling me the truth?"

"Mister, I swear to you."

Vincent looked at him and said, "Call 911. I am going to secure these assholes with those instrument locks. Give me five minutes to get the hell out of here. I don't need no heat. Is that a deal?" In the background he saw Helga leaving the building.

"Sir, just go! We ain't got nothing to say to anybody because these two could have hurt us. Just go!"

Vincent left the building but didn't see the car. He started to walk to his right and there in a breezeway was Helga behind the wheel. She moved over and Vincent asked, "Suppose I would have turned to my left?"

Helga smiled and said, "Then your dumbass would've been walking towards the police department. I know you saw that big-ass billboard pointing to the station."

Vincent asked, "Did you happen to confiscate the weapon that terrible crook had?"

"Did you?" Helga inquired. Vincent laughed and pulled out the .9mm from the back of his pants. Helga smiled and showed him the .40 caliber weapon that she confiscated.

They both laughed and Vincent announced, "Those two weed heads will get off lightly. No weapon, no robbery, and no foul!"

# # #

Later, Vincent gently nudged a sleeping Helga and indicated that they were in Miami. Helga woke up and saw rows of cruise ships preparing to depart the pier for ports unknown. She asked, "Did I sleep all through Florida?"

"My dear, I'm afraid you did. However, it gave me time to study you, your expressions, your drooling, and your inadvertent occasional smile. On several occasions I wanted to pull over to touch and kiss every part of your body. I am so addicted to you. I love the stimulation I get from just watching you sleep. I just enjoy every aspect of you. I am committed to this thing for as long as I live. I love you!"

Helga replied, "Let's take this thing one day at a time. I am so afraid that you're going to hurt me. I just feel it in my bones because I am giving you all that is me and when you get tired of that, you'll probably find a reason to leave me on some island, alone and in tears. However, I want to make sure I take every opportunity that I have to be happy and to make you happy, until we end."

Vincent said, "I still feel as if I'm in love with you, no matter how short of an existence together it has been. Let me try this on you. I had no real relationship with my mother and every woman that I've been with was expressly for carnal engagement. I mean, I've kissed a few, had a few dinners with others and I've had some great sex in that my completions were powerful. Now, as I compare every interlude with you, my completions are not powerful, they are nuclear, and my entire mission is to make sure that your resolution is as explosive as mine. I have never given a shit about whether my partners enjoyed sex with me or not. I couldn't have cared less. With you, I want more and more, I want your touch, your kiss, your love, and your body on me and around me at all times. If that isn't the feelings of being in love, then I don't think I will ever know what true love is." Helga reached over and began to lightly rub Vincent's leg, and he said, "I wish you would turn your attention to those big and scary ships lined up and see how we can get on one of them at the last moment."

As they drove by the docks, Helga saw a sign that read, "Our last-minute ticket prices are absolutely insane." She directed Vincent to pull the vehicle over so that she could see where the ships were heading and how much the tickets were.

Inside of a little office, there was a beehive of activity going on as people were coming and going with smiles on their faces. She asked one couple, "May I ask where you're sailing to?"

The man replied, "We're going to cross the Atlantic and spend some time in Europe. We were able to get an outside suite with a double balcony for the cost of an inside room with no view, no balcony and near the propellers."

Helga asked, "When did you decide on taking this trip?"

The man replied, "Yesterday afternoon at lunch."

Helga eagerly asked, "Suppose I wanted to take a trip like that suddenly, what would I need?"

The woman jealously stated, "Money! Come on honey, I'm hungry."

Back at the car, Helga asked, "Do I look intimidating to you? Or better still if you were with a woman, would I make her jealous?"

After an exceedingly long laughing session, Vincent replied, "Have you looked in the mirror lately? I mean have you really viewed the body that you present, with an unintended amount of sexuality and those lips that were designed by Holly Croft and built by the gods? Oh yes, you're a very intimidating and hedonistic- looking beautiful woman that I absolutely adore and admire."

Helga exclaimed, "Damn! Is that more bullshit or is that how you really feel?"

Once again, Vincent laughed and when he finished, he announced, "I left Annapolis with a woman that I don't know because I wanted to be an Uber driver all my life. Please, get a life. I still can't believe that you are still with me and haven't tried to ditch me at any point. In real time I'm feeling blessed and honored. The more we talk and express our feelings, the better decision-making considerations we make."

Helga stared at Vincent in a way he had never witnessed and said, "That was an exponentially delightful announcement."

"My love, I said all of that to state that each moment I spend with you, my life turns closer to good rather than the evil I've pursued. I will say this over and over again until you believe me—with you I feel as though I have found love and what love should be," Vincent stated.

Helga, feeling bad about her comment, said, "Vincent, I have given up everything so that I can be with you. Bad people are going to be seeking me out because I have halted the ex-pope's ability to access millions of dollars. He is pissed at me and is an expert at retribution and retaliation. He will hurt me in so many ways, but he can kiss that $300 million goodbye. I might buy time in terms of giving false information about accessing the accounts, but my final statement to him will be 'kiss my ass you pompous, selected by an all-male group of other pretenders who like entertaining each other.' At that point, the money will be sent to the Beckmire group. I know, you want to ask how do I know that? I can only say that I swallowed a capsule some time ago like the one Zanthius swallowed that held the formula to the Carbon Factor. His was information; mine activates an electronic signal that connects to the Beckmire group's China Town Bank that when my heart beats no more it sends every single penny to them."

Vincent yelled, "Damn, I'm about trying to live and keep you alive. Can we get on one of those magnificent and scary vessels and let fate play its game?

After moments of complete silence, Helga said, "I saw a fourteen-day cruise to Spain."

Vincent looked suspiciously at Helga and asked, "Is that where the ride ends for me?"

Helga forcefully reached over the console, grabbed Vincent by the back of his head, and thrust her tongue so far down his throat that his member jumped beyond attention with a new intention.

She responded, "Please, please, let this fantasy last as long as possible without any predetermined expiration dates. Vincent, I have never felt these emotions before in my life. Again, please enjoy what is happening now and hopefully we can look forward to tomorrow, the next day and week and the next month. This is all so sudden. Everything in my life has been scripted by others. I've made the decision to cut off a person who was once the most powerful person on earth. In doing so, I have corrupted his cash flow and locked his money away so tight that he couldn't find it even if he spent an eternity looking for it. I did all of that because a stranger driving an Uber picked me up for transportation and looked at me, talked to me, laughed with me, and never asked or demanded anything in return. Oh, then I made the decision to abandon the few principles that I have left and engage in a reckless affair with a perfect stranger. Please let's just enjoy the moment and worry about the bullshit later."

Vincent smiled and asked, "Alaska or Spain? He then announced, "It matters not to me, as long as I am with you, my love."

CHAPTER SEVENTEEN

When Larry approached his father, the Sarge said, "I need my guy, Larry the Wanderer. Has anyone seen him? I know he knows that this is Chinese New Year's, and people do crazy things."

Larry said, "That guy is so old, he can barely walk straight."

"Yeah, and that's why I want him. I need him to sashay down a street and distract some of the residents and even perhaps kick a few asses in the process while his sister covers his ass with drones from the van."

# # #

An hour or so later, in the bank, Jong's cousin and his family were being terrorized by members of the *Benauijuu*. They thought that he was in total control of the passwords for the accounts and that he could arbitrarily access any account with a primary password. The apparent leader of the group uttered a few words and decided to make a call for clarification of the procedures.

Accompanied by one of his henchmen, he made a call to a number and asked about account accessibility. He was informed that without the password an account was sealed and that after three failed attempts, it was locked and could only be opened after answering a series of questions and responding to emails and text messages, to authenticate the owners.

As Larry was approaching the entrance to the bank, he heard the apparent leader say, "No witnesses. All die!" Hearing that, Larry panicked and decided to go rogue and do his own thing. He staggered towards the two men and asked for a lite. The apparent leader told his henchman, "Get rid of that dog." As the guy approached Larry, Larry raised his hands in the air and then opened his pen knife and stabbed one of the men under his arm pit repeatedly. Before the guy hit the ground, Larry grabbed his pistol, gathered up the stunned leader, placed the weapon to his head, circled behind him, and entered the building.

The Sarge yelled, "Something critical must be going down for Larry to break protocol and go rogue. Everybody on the streets with your eyes focused on windows and rooftops."

In the building Larry fired a round into the ceiling and yelled, "I want everyone out of this place and now." Larry knew that the Sarge was listening to his transmission. That's when Anel, Angel, Dempsey, and Hood began without consideration to execute anyone that looked like a lookout or a member of the gang. The men on the rooftops were sitting ducks. As soon as the action started, .9mm rounds were fired from the makeshift weapons on each drone. There were eight pre-targeted individuals and eight simultaneous kill shots.

At the end of the chaos, Larry's prisoner asked, "Do you know who you're fucking with? Do you know that I will rape your children, fuck your wife in front of you before slitting her throat?" Larry took the confiscated weapon, smacked the man across the forehead, and then took his right hand and slapped the man in his ear with all his might. This gave the man a ringing sensation, one that would last for a while because Larry fractured the man's eardrum.

Larry whispered in his other ear, "Do you have any additional idle threats that you would like to issue?"

The guy said, "I am a *Benauijuu* and I will have my vengeance."

Larry smiled and said, "See you in hell, "young gun!" The guy sat and stared at Larry until the Sarge walked in.

The Sarge asked, "What makes you think that you can waltz in here and take what is ours? I know how ruthless you people are when you're in your packs, but individually you're just another street punk wreaking havoc on those who can't and won't fight back. Let me announce to you right now. We don't fall in either one of those groups.   Mister, we are seasoned warriors and there must be several thousand souls waiting for us in Hades. The only question I have right now is whether we're going to let your thieving ass live."

Larry said, "Dad, he said he was going to rape my children, screw my wife in front of me prior to slitting her throat. I didn't want to brutalize him, but he wouldn't shut up while I was trying to communicate with you. I know you have a rule concerning the treatment of prisoners, but his guy is just an asshole who can only operate with his pack of other terrorists."

The Sarge asked, "First of all, why are you focusing on our holdings with this institution? I know it's alleged that you're a *young gun* member, but you're probably a ranking member. Am I right? Okay, I don't expect you to answer, because you have this macho code of no ethics policy that you subscribe to. I am still trying to decide about your future. Now, I have people who can make you talk and who can change your sex. I'll let you consider my words as we drive you to a place of no return where you can scream until your lungs burst and no one will hear you."

The Sarge looked at Larry and said, "Give him a shot and blindfold his ass."

# # #

Jong asked his nephew, "How did these people find you?"

His nephew responded, "I do not have any idea, Uncle. They come to the bank, they get invited to sub banks and the next thing I know, they show me pictures of their associates in my house."

"Is your house a mansion or something?"

"No, honorable Uncle. It is a three-bedroom rancher in a middle-class area where people go to work every day to provide for their families. We're not flashy, my car is old, I cut my own grass to save money and we don't have lavish parties or celebration events. We live a slow and moderate life, nothing out of the ordinary and nothing that would indicate that I manage and invest a lot of money. People at the bank know it's bad karma to discuss other people's business practices, be they good or bad. It is a place where privacy is of the utmost importance."

Jong continued, "Somehow, someone knows that you are in charge of a lot of money and that is not good for you and not good for us. We have to relocate you if you want to continue to do our bidding. This place is compromised, not safe for you, not safe for us, not safe for family members. Is there anything in your office that is important that you need to continue to do our business?"

"Honorable Uncle, there is nothing there of importance. No footprints, no records, just old newspapers, and cheap artifacts. I bring a computer that is voice, hand, eye, password, key coded and a picture of honorable uncle that is a QR code. All business is sent through five layers of security before any actions are processed."

"I hear these people are international and there will probably be repercussions for our attack on their people. You will go home, pack only essentials and leave that place. No information should be left that gives a hint as to where you may be. Am I clear?"

"Honorable Uncle, you are truly clear."

"I will send people to watch your back while you pack essentials. Is your house Americanized or a picture of pure living like in Japan?"

His nephew bowed, and replied, "Honorable Uncle, we are simple people who follow tradition and are always prepared to leave in a hurry."

The Sarge approached and reconfirmed Jong's beliefs that his family was no longer safe doing business at this bank. He suggested that he could do the same kind of thing with their Native American friends and families that live in Minnesota. Jong's nephew bowed and stated, "Wherever I can make a difference and help people help themselves, that is where my family and I will go if so directed."

The Sarge looked at Jong and asked, "What are your thoughts on this matter?"

Jong smiled and said, "He can help in the Outback. There he can teach money, grow money, and make money from using his vast network to move our precious stones and gold. What be your thinking on that proposition?"

The Sarge gave a huge grin and exclaimed, "That's a brilliant idea! My only question is, how do we allow him to do business without people being able to track him?"

His nephew asked Jong if he could reply and Jong gave him a nod. His nephew went on to tell the Sarge how to be in more than one place at the same time but never the same place twice.

The Sarge looked at Jong's nephew's family and realized that they did not have input into the proposition. He asked the man's wife, "Do you know much about the Outback?"

The woman bowed and replied, "It is a place where I believe my husband can help many people and keep us safe. I and my children will go where my husband feels that we can do good and be safe."

The Sarge bowed slowly and low and when he was upright, he said, "You are both gracious and beautiful and your husband is a very lucky man."

Jong jumped in, "Enough of this cheek kissing." He turned to the Sarge and requested that he send Anel, Angel, Dempsey, and Hood, along with Jilkes, John Lee, and himself.

The Sarge said, "That's an enormous show of power."

Jong replied, "Better to show strength early than pretend it is available later."

The Sarge replied, "What on earth does that mean?"

"I don't know!" Jong exclaimed. "It just sounded strong in my mind."

The Sarge said, "What should we do with the leader of this gang? We just can't let him regroup to come at us another day. I was thinking we should just go earthly on his ass and bury him where no one will ever find him. Otherwise, he will come at us strong and lethal."

Jong's nephew interrupted the conversation and requested that he be assigned to provide justice and vengeance to the man who humiliated his wife, threatened his children, and slapped him around as if he was his whore. Everyone was amazed that the mild-mannered, quiet financial genius could speak in such terms.

His wife said, "He placed his hands in places that are sanctioned only for my husband. I want to be a part of his agony. I want to place my hands roughly in unsanctioned places until he screams for mercy."

Jong looked at the Sarge and asked, "Can we have a sidebar?"

The two men walked a short distance away and began to discuss the emotions that were in existence. Jong said, "If that was Mrs. Beckmire proclaiming her disgust for invasion of her private zones that were reserved for you only, what would you do about that?"

"You know exactly what I would do. Have Anel and Angel back the van up to the back of the building."

The Sarge looked at Jong's nephew and his wife and said, "Once you head down that alley, there is no returning."

The wife immediately exclaimed, "When without invitation you touch my husband's golden pond, then the hands that converged will congregate no more!"

The Sarge looked at the woman and decided that there was nothing else to be said. He said to Jong, "Put the people in play and let's get the hell out of here before the sun sets. That's when the real Chinese New Years occurs and it'll be hard to distinguish between fireworks and gunfire."

Jong replied, "I'm on it, Sarge. We should be rolling in fifteen."

CHAPTER EIGHTEEN

At the motel they were staying in, Helga researched the potential trips and decided after getting input from Vincent that the approximately 14-day trip from Miami to Valencia was an excellent get-lost-at-sea excursion. Even more impressive was the fact that the vessel was leaving in thirty-six hours. Vincent said, "I hear those ships are never sold out and if you wait until the last moment, you can get a great deal on an outside cabin. My friend Arnold Nickleson told me that. He and his wife cruise a couple of times a year."

Helga smiled and asked, "In all seriousness, can you handle being with me that long?" Vincent rushed to her side, embraced her, and proclaimed, "I have never been this happy with a woman. I guess that's because I only wanted one thing from them and I never considered a relationship of any kind with anyone. You my love, come along, sweep me off my feet, throw me into a chapter of an espionage novel and here we are planning our escape from the villain by taking a 14-day cruise across the Atlantic. How romantic, how special, how forever joining!"

Helga replied, "How I hope those notions are sincere, because I'm beginning to feel special, wanted, protected and in love."

Vincent began to do what he had learned to do better and that was to make this woman shiver with orgasms and have her reciprocate by loving every inch of his body. Helga murmured, "We should go shopping. We can do this thing for 16 straight days uninterrupted."

Vincent continued to kiss her lips, suck her ear lobes, and make love to the nape of her neck. He uttered, "I want to do this for 17 straight days, my love."

After 45 minutes of heaving, hauling, sighing, and moaning, the two had joint conclusions that were epic, thunderous, and exhaustive. As they lay on the bed, Vincent asked, "Are you satisfied with the way I make love to you?"

Helga responded, "I am never going to be satisfied, because I know you will make me feel better each time we make love. Oh, Vincent please don't turn out to be a dud."

He laughed and suggested, "If you think I'm a dud after 8 days, then I'll get another cabin and let the experience be just what it was, a magnificent journey about appreciating you and learning to love one another."

The two drifted off into that nocturnal world where the mind goes wherever it wants to. In Helga's case, she focused on being needed, appreciated, and loved. Vincent, on the other hand, considered the consequences of admitting that he was the Beckmire person that she had hit orders for.

Later that evening after dinner, Helga said, "The mall is still open. Do you want to go and shop a little?"

Vincent looked at the vivacious body in front of him and replied, "I am already at the mall and everything that I need, I'm looking at."

Helga laughed embarrassingly and said, "Man, put some clothes on and let's go shopping. Not together but within shouting distance of each other. I don't want some young blonde looking at my man and me having to sign her death certificate. No, I want to watch my man from afar."

Vincent laughed and said, "I'll be ready in fifteen minutes."

# # #

At the mall, the twosome acted as if they weren't a couple. Vincent went into the men's section and within thirty minutes picked out four jackets, five pairs of pants, eight dress shirts, six Polo sport shirts, three pairs of jeans, five pairs of shorts, and three bathing suits. Helga, on the other hand—well, women are a little more self-indulgent when it comes to shopping. An hour and a half later, she signaled Vincent that she was almost done. Vincent looked across the corridor and saw a store that sold suitcases. As he started towards the door, he noticed two young men apparently trying to figure out some sort of action plan. Vincent continued toward the store that sold bags, but said to himself, "*I know that look. I have to make sure that Helga is not in any danger.*"

Vincent turned around and headed back to the store. He didn't see Helga, but he saw the red light on over a dressing room. One of the guys was standing outside of it looking around nervously, while the other had apparently entered it. Vincent nonchalantly walked by the dressing room and coldcocked the guy on the outside. He caught him before he hit the floor and gently laid him out. He then forcefully grabbed the handle to the dressing room, pulled open the door, and threw a straight right-hand punch to the other guy's throat, damn near killing him but knocking him out.

Helga laughed and asked, "What took you so long? I was never in danger. I had his every move calculated, especially since he kept looking outside of the room for his henchman."

"Nevertheless, we don't need any heat. Let's get out of here. You can pay for those things at another counter. No one saw who was in that room, so play the part and avoid looking up at the cameras. I'll catch you outside. Please don't dally," Vincent advised.

# # #

Later at the motel, Helga began to inquire about the cruise, the ship's age, safety concerns and finally the discounted cost since the ship was not sold out. She settled on The Virgin Lattigo, a new ship that was commissioned three years earlier. She explained to Vincent that the literature indicated that the best cabins were mid-ship and that they were the most sought after. Helga also indicated that size seemed important when selecting a cruise and a ship, especially when you would be at sea for fourteen days.

Vincent asked, "Do you think it might be better if we cruised down to one of the islands and just tried to blend in?"

Helga considered the thought but announced, "I allegedly was executed in St. Thomas at the Four Seasons a while back. Also in Puerto Rico, I am the prime suspect in a murder for hire arrangement. Oh, and in Casa de Campo in the

Dominican Republic, I am accused of orchestrating the annihilation of several wanna to be dictators and it's also alleged that I succeeded in getting the communists out of the country. It was stated that I tried to kill Charles, the chairman of Gulf and Western at the time, who also was in charge of the sugar plantation, several hotels, the cattle farms, and a host of other activities that allowed G & W to smuggle large amounts of cash out of the country. No, lover-boy, nowhere in that part of the world do I want to show up with my new man. It would be suicidal for both of us."

Vincent stared blankly at her and finally inquired, "Is there anywhere on this planet that you are not sought after?" He paused again and remembered that she is the mother of his half-brother Zanthius's child. *Oh shit, this is going to get messy once I start telling her the tales of how all this shit is intertwined.*

Helga asked, "Are you alright? You seem to have retreated to another world."

Vincent moved closer to her, kissed her lips tenderly and said, "I'm just hoping that all is well between us and the rest of the world if we make this journey across the Atlantic. I've never been on water for that long and I'm hoping I don't become a sickly puppy that you have to care for. I must admit, I used to get car sickness from riding in it for long periods of time. I'm just going to tough it out and make you proud of me my love."

Helga smiled and said, "I would love to take care of you for a change. You're always there for me and I need to show you that I'm no little punk when it comes to caring for my man."

"Anyway, back to the proposed trip, are you sure this is what you want to do?" Vincent asked.

"I am not sure of anything. All I know is that my ex-employer will spare no expense or time trying to find me once he realizes that I have complete control over all of his ill-gotten funds. If we're caught, he will probably dismember you in order to make me give him access to his funds," Helga replied.

Vincent vehemently stated, "Wait a minute. You mean you will let him mutilate me and then you'll give him what he wants?"

Helga laughed and said, If he or his cronies lay one finger on you, he can forget that money for the balance of eternity, because the passwords will recycle every ten hours from the day I give him the number until the world is no more. That way I know that you are no more, and neither am I. I won't blame you if you want to bail out right now. I will be hurt but I will remember the most memorable time of my life and that is finding love in an Uber and wanting so very much to have the driver in my life for the rest of my days."

Helga began to cry and that is when Vincent announced, "I wish you would make the fucking arrangements so that I can see Valencia. I've always wanted to go there."

Helga happily ran into his arms and said, "I never want to ever deceive you about anything, and I wish for the same consideration from you."

Vincent once again stared blankly at Helga and responded, "If we take this trip, we will have fourteen days to get to know each other and tell all there is to tell about ourselves. I look forward to sharing all that there is to know about me including my previous inability to fall in love, but to enjoy only lust. Listen, if we're going to do this thing, then you had better make it happen before I lose my nerve. Those ships look like massive buildings that should be anchored in concrete somewhere rather than on water."

Helga changed the subject and said, "I want to go back into town. I need more underwear and from what I saw in your bag, so do you—but not as luxurious or attractive as what I have in mind for myself."

Vincent shot back, "Oh, now you're monitoring my bag. Just so that you know you can operate without stealth, you're permitted to open anything that I have, my love."

"Wow, I'm liking that 'my love thing' you keep saying."

Vincent replied, "If we're going back to town, then let's plan on having a quiet dinner and maybe a martini and then a glass of wine with our food. Seems like all we've been doing is watching our backs, escaping from mayhem and more importantly, making fantastic love over and over again."

Helga said, "I sense you're getting chilly about fourteen days on the ocean with me. Am I correct?"

Vincent smirked and replied, "Make the damn reservations, right now."

"Are you sure?" Helga asked.

"Make the damn reservations, right now!" Vincent exclaimed.

# # #

After booking a penthouse on the ship, Helga said to Vincent at dinner, "We've got to get that name thing together, in order to minimize suspicion. I'll simply say that I want to keep my maiden name because I am the last member of the Winter family. Also, how long have we been married, where do we live, do we have children and if so, what are their names? Do we have a dog or a cat? Do we go to many plays, what's our favorite TV show and what is our steady alcoholic drink? You see where I'm going with this. We can't stay couped up in our cabin for fourteen days. We will have to be seen eating at appointed times, using the gym, the sauna, and getting joint massages as often as possible."

Vincent, looking a little worried said, "I have got to find a way to pay for my place and make sure my record collection and equipment remain safe. Damn good thing that I don't have a cat or a dog, because what I'm doing would be considered animal cruelty. Anyway, no one is looking for me who I would want to find me and therefore, I just have to secure my place."

Helga responded, "You have a cellphone. Unless it's the government looking for you, I doubt if anyone can hack the system and know exactly where you are. Anyway, are we going shopping and to dinner or what?"

Later at the Capitol Grill, Helga and Vincent toasted each other with slightly dirty vodka martinis. Vincent recalled, "This is really the first time that we've had a real sit-down dinner and a great-tasting martini. Here's to the woman that has changed my mind and reactions to the female gender. I typically used women before meeting you and now I am witnessing all of the value and potential meaningful relationships I could have enjoyed, had I known or taken time to consider someone other than myself."

Helga smiled and said, "I sure as hell hope you mean everything that you've been espousing."

Vincent shook his head and replied, "I am here and I am about to board a building that glides across water. Don't get no more meaningful than that for me. I'm praying that in fourteen days or less, all that is me and all that is you, is discussed and analyzed and that it will clear the air insofar as any uncomfortable conversations we might have especially since you're being hunted and in some eyes, I am a fugitive as well."

Helga perked up and asked, "What does that last statement mean?" Are you on the lam from the law?" Are you a pervert or murderer or something? Come on Vincent, I need to know what that statement means."

Vincent dropped his head and murmured, "Some really bad people are looking for me for collection purposes on a bet that I made, lost and wouldn't cover. Nothing I've done amounts to perversion or murder. No, mine is more about abandonment than anything else. This is a recent issue, and I surely don't want to discuss it on the eve of us taking a cross-Atlantic trip. Listen, we will have plenty of time to air our dirty laundry and to see if anything that is mentioned is worth separating us from this extremely fast and wonderful body-and mind excursion that we've been on."

CHAPTER NINETEEN

On the drive to the farm, Jong's nephew's wife pulled out her Cultivatew and slapped the young gangster right across the bridge of his nose. The young gangster moaned. The wife quickly hit him again in the same spot, at which point he began to choke on his own blood. Jong commanded, "Enough! No more hits with that weapon. We're almost at our destination and there you can cut off that thing he proposed to use on you."

She responded, "I want him to watch me slowly decapitate his penis."

As the vehicle traveled down the long and bumpy road, blood could be seen oozing through the makeshift bandana. Jong said to Brown, who was driving, "Go straight to the barn, this guy is bleeding all over the place."

At the barn, he was helped out of the vehicle and led into the first stall for the horses. His hood was removed and it was obvious that he had lost a lot of blood from the two whacks across the nose.

Jong's nephew's wife walked in front of the man initially but decided to cover his mouth and nose to keep him from spitting his blood on her. She then put on a pair of gloves and a mask. She had huge shears in her left hand. She then said,

"You and your gang think that because you are many, you can take and do what you want to people."

At this point, the guy's eyes were opened as big as apples, and he was struggling to say something. Jong's nephew's wife pretended that she didn't care what he was trying to say. Her husband whispered to her, "You no like him, listen to him beg for mercy or for death."

His wife bowed to her husband and removed the prisoner's mask. She stated, "My husband asked me to be merciful but deliberate and to listen to what you have to say."

The Sarge entered the barn and said, "I didn't sanction any harm to our prisoner. Who is now taking my place as the un-elected leader of this clan?"

Jong fell to his knees and said, "Boss, I wanted to avenge the threats to my nephew's wife's honor and thought that you would allow me to move on this guy without a hearing."

The Sarge bellowed, "We are not barbarians. However, the wife has every right to dictate the punishment of one who invades another man's property. I don't like this type of revenge, but I will yield to her and allow her to dispose of this vermin in any manner that she sees fit."

The wife said to the captive, "You were trying to say something before the bossman came in. Please be brief because I intend on cutting that thing of yours off at the base. So, speak up and let me get on with my mission."

Blood was running down his face, so the wife grabbed a towel used to dry the horses off and blotted the man's face with it. He then asked, "Is there anything that I can do to prove to you that I am sorry for touching another man's property? As the leader, I require that certain privileges be given to my men, or they will lose respect for my leadership. By disrespecting you, I gave a clear and unapproachable mandate that you were to be mine and mine only. Had I not, all of my men would have violated you in the worse possible manner. Yes, I did touch what was not mine, but in doing so, I made it clear that no one else was to even consider such a challenge to my authority."

Jong said, "We need to talk this through. All actions are suspended until I have consulted with my leader.

The two men walked out of the barn and as the man continued to plead his case, the Sarge walked back in and said, "No conversations without my being a part of them."

The Sarge walked out of the barn and said to Jong, Brown, Bernstein, Jilkes and John Lee, "We need to find out how this motherfucker found out about our funds. He's just a minion. His group is international and has a savage reputation that precedes its arrival. Any ideas as to how we should play this one?"

John Lee said, "We play him like he's going to die regardless of any plea and how him wants to die becomes the question. I mean, we let that lady in there torture him—and damn, she be scary—or we place a bullet in his head and be done with it."

Jilkes said, "I have to concur with my friend. We have to find out where the weak link is before we do any concluding. I mean our shit is randomly placed out on the internet. Now, someone has eyes on us."

The Sarge looked around, and the rest of the guys agreed with Jilkes and John Lee. He said, "Let's play hardball and see what he's willing to give up."

Back in the barn, the Sarge vehemently stated, "If it were one of our women that was violated to any degree, we would want to cut his penis off at the root. However, I appreciate him giving your wife sanctuary status because we know how this thing can turn out." The Sarge looked at the captive and asked, "Why did you give her sanctuary?"

"Because I don't subscribe to violating women through strength and force. I watched my mother provide services to fourteen men before her blood from all of her orifices turned them off. The last guy shot her in the head. They drafted me and told me to never think of her and that she was not a good woman. She offered herself to men. Anyway, that's why," the guy said.

The Sarge asked, "What is your name and how did you people identify our accounts as takeover options?"

"My name is Kenzo and the information was sold to our leaders. I get orders, I don't do the buying or the selling my job is to do the collecting."

"And apparently, you collect no matter what. So, tell me, should we be on the lookout for more collectors like you?" the Sarge inquired.

Kenzo replied, "Absolutely! You have something they want and they will stop at nothing to get it. Sir, you should prepare for war because they will continue to come for you until they have achieved their goals."

"How many are in this group?"

"Sir, internationally there are probably four to five thousand people in the group. It's a conglomerate that does not accept 'NO' for an answer." Mr. Beckmire—oh yeah, I know who you are and everyone else here. I would like to begin a bargaining session, if possible. I mean, I have strategic and management information that might ease the conflict. I first would like to have the wife of the accountant stand down from cutting my penis off. After that, I'll be a free willy because I failed and failure equals death in the Benauijuu."

The Sarge said, "Hold on a minute Mr. Kenzo." He looked at Jong's nephew's wife and asked, "Did you believe what he said about granting you sanctuary?"

She looked at her husband, bowed and asked permission to truthfully answer. He slightly bowed and she said to the Sarge, "I accept what he has said and in an offhand manner I thank him for not allowing his crew to violate me. Also, I think that I may be the cause of this event."

Everyone came to attention upon hearing this information and the Sarge asked, "Please elaborate." He looked at Jong's nephew and asked, "May I inquire as to your wife's given name, as well as yours?"

"My name is Lang and my wife's name is Daika."

The Sarge bowed to both and asked Daika, "Please elaborate on how you feel that you may be the cause of this new event." In the meantime, the Sarge ordered the release of Kenzo and offered him a hose to wash the blood off of his face.

Kenzo said, "Thanks for your intervention. I was forced into this life after they accused my mother of stealing. She was then raped and shot in the head. I had nowhere to go, no one to look after me and they became the only family that I had, yes, Benauijuu. They accused my mother of stealing thousands of dollars from her street work and assigned her alleged theft and debt to me for repayment. I was sixteen when I started this line of work and now, I am twenty-five years of age and I still owe my overlord thousands of dollars. In essence, I and a lot of other people are slaves."

The Sarge shook his head and said, "I need to hear from Ms. Daika how she may be the cause of the attack."

Daika lowered her head and announced, "When talking to my sister in Hong Kong, I bragged about my husband's job and told her that he has clients from all over the world and that he handles billions of dollars on a daily basis." She looked at her husband and said, "Please forgive me, honorable husband and provider, but she tried to make you look small."

Lang looked at her and shook his head. He said, "Your sister is a seller of information. She exists to make money on other people's misery. How could you have such a conversation about my work and put all of my clients in jeopardy? I must take a walk and try to figure out how to further protect my clients and forever disappear. My clients are in danger, we are in danger, our children are in danger." Daika, crying her eyes out, said nothing.

In the interim, Jong placed a weapon and clip in the shitter. Ten or so minutes later, Kenzo asked, "Is it possible that I can visit the loo?" The Sarge nodded affirmatively and off he went. He opened the door, saw the weapon, and announced, "There is a weapon in here."

Jong replied, "My bad. Knowing your circumstances, why didn't you take the weapon?"

Kenzo replied, "It was probably a setup and wouldn't fire anyway." Jong placed a silencer on the weapon, slid round into the chamber, and fired into a post.

Kenzo stated, "Nothing is going in my favor this day. No sense in rushing my death."

The Sarge looked at Jong and asked, "Why did you leave your weapon in the damn loo?"

"Sorry, boss, I had to blow the top off the shitter."

"Please be more mindful of your weapon especially since we have an enemy in the camp that could have hurt one of us had he gotten hold of the weapon."

Jong replied, "I don't think he is an enemy any longer. However, that is up to him to prove." He looked at Daika and asked, "Please indulge me. I know he touched what is not his, but my question is, was it in a manner to totally disrespect you or save you from his men?"

Daika, looked at Jong and then at Kenzo and stated, "He placed his hands up my dress but did not go under my panties."

Jong added, "Do you believe the story he told about him selecting you for himself and saving you from his men?"

Daika lowered her head and said, "If there is a polite way to touch another's property, then I would admit that he made noises, but he did not touch my husband's garden."

Jong quickly asked, "Then do you believe he was protecting you?"

Daika slowly replied, "I sincerely believe that he was trying to do right by me. His men were fondling themselves and pointing fingers down their throats. He told them to focus and not to even consider touching me. He stated that I was his first, and then available to whoever wanted sloppy seconds."

The Sarge asked, "Ms. Daika, could you ever trust a man who violated you?"

Daika replied, "He did not violate me, he aggressively went under my dress but intentionally missed the target that he told his men was ripe and waiting for him. That's when he instructed that no one was to touch me."

The Sarge asked, "Did he at any point after that encounter suggest or attempt to violate you?"

Daika replied, "Mr. Sarge, he did nothing of the sorts. He never looked at me and when he did, he gave a respectful bow. He never attempted anything with me. He protected me from his gang, I guess."

Jong asked, "Can we parley outside for a minute?"

Once outside of the barn, the Sarge asked, "What's up with you and that weapon?"

Jong replied, "Sarge, the weapon couldn't fire because it requires my signature finger. I don't want to kill this guy and Daika is beginning to soften as she considers his advances and the rogue nature of his gang and what they would have conceivably done to her. If his story is correct, then we should find a way to do a Dempsey, Hood, Anel, and Angel kind of thing with him. Not to mention Michael, and the list goes on and on. Listen, death is what we have dealt for years. How about a little rehabilitation and try to make people whole and Bonafide."

The Sarge smiled and said, "As long as I live, I will always believe that we are good people who try our best to help people help themselves. I know we have been burnt a few times but, in reality, this is the best job that we've been able to do. That Hood, Dempsey and the two sisters, Michael and others, well, hell, they were sanctioned by God himself. We must never stop trying to rehabilitate people. Okay, but what is the premise as to why we try to save this guy?"

Jong quickly stated, "Why must there be a premise? Why not give him shit jobs, make him our stooge for a while, and hopefully get good intel on the potential shitstorm that is heading our way? Perhaps he can lead us to the head of the snake, and we can do a surgical strike and place that group in disarray. Let's give the guy a chance while acknowledging he has intel that we need. We want to know if he will fire on his former compatriots."

Back in the barn, the Sarge said, "Mr. Kenzo, it is clear that you protected Ms. Daika from the animalistic desires of those lesser in your command. Although you entered a sacred part of her anatomy, you apparently did it with respect and concern for her. You also gave a convincing story about the issues surrounding your mother and the final outcome. I don't want to put a bullet in your head, because I look for the good in people. I need you to convince my compatriots why we shouldn't kill you, knowing full well that you came to take what is rightfully ours, at any cost. Tell me why I shouldn't blow your head off right now?"

There was a silence in the barn that was eerie. Kenzo thought about the notion of dying for a cause that was built upon deception, slavery, and never-ending interest payments. He said, "My mother taught me to respect people and their belongings. *The Benauijuu* are evil people who hire the scourge of the earth to make their royal fat asses fatter. It has been over ten years, and I am still working for minimum wages. They catch people like me, kill their parents, and announce that we have inherited our relative's debt. And, as I check around the group, they all are on the same penitence—they owe for someone else's debt. I have no allegiance to them and strategically, I am willing to share all that I know about them and their approaches to battle. I will not try to deceive you. I studied your group once the information was sold to the group by Ms. Daika's sister. I mean no disrespect, but your sister is known as an influencer. She does not realize what happens to the information that she randomly acquires from her Tik Tok, Instagram and other on-line platforms. The

Beckmire fortune is not the first one that she has indirectly sold to the group. As a matter of fact, five different families have been destroyed by her casual conversations on her platform about making people rich. What I'm sure she doesn't realize is that when she makes a sale, she also participates in the death of as many people as necessary so that the group can maximize its intent. Your sister is responsible for over one hundred and fifty people being murdered."

Kenzo continued, "That's' not the question asked or the full answer that should have been given. I hate these people. I watched one of their henchmen smile as he fired a bullet into my mother's head. I made a promise to my dead mother that I would avenge her death. While being indoctrinated and taught to seize opportunities for the good of the group, the person that fired that fatal round into my mother's head said, "Your mother was a street whore, a wretched bitch, not worthy of consideration." I want to place his dried tongue on a monument that was built in her honor in a secret place."

Jong quietly replied, "You weave a convincing tale, my friend. I can recommend that you are to be set free and be given funds to travel anywhere, but I don't know if we'll have to face you in the future. If we allow you to stay with us and there is a hint of deception, then I'm sorry, but you'll be turned over to our butcher and his apprentice."

"Listen, I need another chance. I'll tell you things that you won't believe about this group and their power base. I'll show you how to take what they have taken. My only concern with that idea is that the residuals may not get to the people who need help. Also, I'm like a high-ranking slave, working off my mother's alleged debt. She had to do unspeakable things to earn a living, but a thief she was not."

Jong announced, "Oh my, here comes the brothers from another mother. Kenzo, please be thoughtful about what you say. These two guys are like prophets; they see and hear things that most of us can't figure out."

John Lee walked into the barn with Jilkes and said, "I thought this here fellow was a prisoner and in need of some sort of exorcism. He seems to be done placed you people under his spell and has provided you with a bunch of horseshit. What be your take on this here matter, Mr. Jilkes?"

"As usual, my brother is once again perceptive of a ruse. He rarely judges the book incorrectly. My questions are amazingly simple. Is this the same guy who kidnapped your nephew? Wait a minute before you respond. Is this the same guy who fondled your nephew's wife and forbade anyone from touching her except himself? Lastly, is this the same asshole who threatened your nephew's children?"

Jong waited a few seconds and sarcastically asked, "Are you finished?"

Jilkes looked at him and inquired, "Do you hear me asking any more questions? Of course you don't. So, Mr. Smarty-pants please oblige us and let us know why this guy still has his head on his shoulders."

Jong replied, "Since you were assigned the role of judge and executioner, you should have been here earlier and you might have surmised the value of his continued existence. Had you and your anomaly been here when we started the inquiry, you two would clearly agree that there is value in this person that we need to explore."

John Lee exclaimed, "You know my minority friend be jousting with you. We know you asked the right questions and therefore, him still has his head on them there shoulders of his."

Jong responded, "We're at the point of trying to decide his fate and it seems like there are things that we can learn from him about his former compatriots. I mean, to them, he is dead, but he doesn't know that."

The Sarge, after listening to all sides, asked if he could ask a question.

Jong shot back, "Dictators don't ask, they just do whatever they want. Why you playing nice now?"

The Sarge gave Jong one of his serious looks and Jong knew to cancel his comedian act. The Sarge stepped in front of Kenzo and commented, "Your gang members are bad hombres. We've dusted off our security systems and have activated most of them. My burning question is a simple one and that is given the opportunity to hurt one of us, will you execute?"

Kenzo replied, "I watched a man place his pistol to the head of my mother and pull the trigger. I watched the perpetrator laugh after sticking his finger into the hole in my mother's skull. I finally got the opportunity after a few years of working my way up the latter, to execute his ass. He was a ranking member of the *Benauijuu,* totally illiterate, but gained favor because of the macabre manner in which he murdered people. That was the only goal that I had in life—to kill the man that murdered my mother in front of me. I'm not interested in becoming rich, famous, or any bullshit like that. I only wanted that person in front of me so that I could see if he found his own impending death as funny as he made my mother's demise seem."

The Sarge stepped a few paces back, turned around and asked, "Why didn't you live up to your gang's code of conduct? You know kill as many as you can before you're killed."

"Sir, I've been working off the alleged money that my mother supposedly stole from them. I've been doing this kind of work with oversight for many years. It has been said that I have five more years before her debt is canceled."

The Sarge repeated, "My question remains, will you at some point try to hurt me or one of my family members? There was an active weapon left in the shitter. Why didn't you come out with it blazing away at us?"

"First I thought it was a trick, but even then that wouldn't have helped me reach my goal. I thought that the lady would eventually vouch for my actions, in that my entry under her dress was in no way trying to violate her. I knew that if I hadn't done that, those men would have raped her repeatedly until her only choice would be to ask for death. I've seen this happen before and many times at that. Sir, members of that gang have no scruples or respect for anyone. When they finish, they do all kinds of hideous things to their victims. Their victims, essentially become toilets for the gang members, with an 'anything goes' attitude," Kenzo commented.

"I don't know you, but your calling card is an evil one. I am going to have you bound with movement capabilities. You have access to the toilet, and those horse blankets will keep you warm. We will decide your fate in the morning. Good night, Mr. Kenzo."

Chapter Twenty

After settling in their penthouse on the ship, Helga and Vincent popped the top on a bottle of champagne and toasted to a long and profound voyage. Helga kissed Vincent lightly and murmured, "Please be as kind as you can possibly be with me. I've told you my history of lack of emotions, love, caring and consideration. I want to enjoy my first ever honeymoon-like adventure. Can you promise me that you'll be ever attending and considerate of me and my feelings?"

Vincent set his glass down and reached for hers. He leaned her up against the cabin double doors and stuck his tongue so far down her throat, she began to choke. They both laughed and she asked, "Where in the hell has that thing been? I mean, is that the same tongue that gave me thunderous orgasms over and over again. I mean, I need that guy down and in the middle and right now."

Vincent backed her into the cabin and began to undress the already minimally attired Helga. He eased her ever so gently onto the bed, while continuing to kiss her and unstrap garments. He removed her panties and began to kiss her inner thighs. He came up for air and kissed the nape of her neck, her ear lobes and began to whisper after each kiss, "I love you more than life." Vincent slowly made his way back to the center of her universe and from there Nirvana was opened up to Helga. She moaned and rubbed his head as he gave her explosive and body-shaking orgasms, one after the other until she was exhausted and unable to move.

# # #

The four loud blasts of the ship's warning system jarred her as she awoke to a smiling Vincent sitting in a corner on the balcony watching the ship maneuver. Vincent announced, "Helga, you snore as loud as the ship's horns. He laughed but Helga began to cry. Vincent asked, "My laughing at you causes you to cry?"

"No, silly man. I've never felt passion, commitment, desire, love, and unadulterated pleasure designed especially for me. I have never in all my years been treated like a goddess. I'm used to being a slave to the demands of others."

Vincent gathered her up and began to kiss her so passionately that she yelled, "Stop! I can't move. I feel as though I've been drugged."

Vincent vociferously stated, "No, my love, what you feel is the result of being loved and admired. Helga, I am in this thing with you until I am no more."

With tears flowing down her face, Helga whispered, "I'm unable to attend to your needs and your desires. I feel as though I can't stand."

Vincent smiled and replied, "I'm so happy for you. Just remember there are fourteen days of euphoria waiting for us, my love. That's right, fourteen days of bliss and all of the love that we can throw each other's way."

# # #

The ship set sail but Helga missed a lot of the beginning of the voyage. For the first 24 hours, she was either throwing up or asleep in their cabin. Vincent said, "I thought it would be me in that miserable place. Hahaha, it's the love of my life feeling terrible."

As he sat on the balcony and watched the water ebb and flow, he decided to tell Helga that he was her mark. Just as he was confirming his intentions, the door to the balcony opened and there she was in her birthday suit, covered only by a full-length see through gown. She said, "I've been sick as a dog for the past day or so. Is there anything that I can do that you desire?"

Vincent stood up and replied, "Yes, can you please take a shower so that we can go and eat?"

Helga laughed and said, "I'm going to enjoy this adventure. You're so easy, never demanding, just requesting and partnering with me. Vincent, I know it's too early, but you my friend, I love so freely and I will not stop saying it. I love you, Vincent. I have never been made to feel special, wanted and loved. No, I was just an elevated street whore, who happened to be a good nun and pretty enough to service the Holy Father. My entire life has been a series of failures; an unexpected pregnancy with my ex-employee and another with a person whose life I saved and whom to this day, I hate because he and his father stole my child from a monastery that was inhabited by crooked and money-hungry nuns. Shame on them and may their souls rot prior to entering hell."

Vincent pulled her closer to him and announced, "This trip is not about looking back, but looking at how we can survive the kind of people who will certainly be on the lookout for us. Listen, I'll say once again, I've never provided the kind of pleasure to a woman as I do for you. It seems natural, not learned, as I react when your body shifts. I can assure you that I have never investigated a woman's anatomy as closely as I have surveyed yours. It was all organic, honest, and not pretentious. I knew that I had to share an ultimate experience with you to convince you that this was not just a moment in time, but a movement towards pure love and understanding."

Because she was still shaking from the over-abundance of orgasms, Vincent helped Helga out onto the balcony. After securing her against the balcony door, he fetched two oversized blankets and led Helga to a chaise lounge. There he covered every inch of her body before joining her. As he was starting to relax, Helga asked, "Do you think we could have a little Grande Marnier to take the chill off?" Vincent went into the cabin and prepared one full goblet of the fine liquor.

He handed it to Helga and she inquired, "Where is yours?"

"I assumed that we would share."

Helga smiled and took a huge swig of the drink. She was very much aware of the fact that Vincent helped her to achieve countless orgasms, but she felt that she had not satisfied him. Helga began to kiss his neck and rub his breasts ever so slightly. Once she reached his mouth with her tongue, she could feel the rise and wetness of his member against her leg. She reached down and began to stroke it while providing him with tongue treatment. Helga then began to work her way down to where the other brain was standing at attention and waiting for assistance. She began to enjoy the reactions and was amazed at the amount of liquids being provided. She inserted his member into her mouth and watched him lurch, moan, and sigh at each insertion. She stared deeply at Vincent and provided him with cataclysmic body reactions until he had an atomic resolution. All that was provided was savored by Helga.

# # #

In the morning at breakfast, the two sat at a table and were joined by two fellow travelers. Helga and Vincent provided little information about who they were, where they were from, how many children or any of the other conversations that people have to get to know someone. Helga politely stated that they were mourning the loss of a family member. "Please forgive us if we seem unfriendly, but our loss was very recent. After that comment, the other couple stopped asking questions and enjoyed their breakfast.

Later, when they were back in their room, Vincent said, "We should at least develop a marketable strategy for providing bullshit to people that we meet on this cruise." Helga grabbed a notepad and headed out onto the balcony. When Vincent joined her, they began to develop a snapshot of who they were, where they were from, how long they'd been married, number of children, professions, and that they were between homes.

That afternoon in the gym, as luck would have it, they ran into the same people that they had shared breakfast with. As Helga looked at the lady, she whispered to Vincent, "Look at the body on that lady and why is she providing you with a perpetual smile?" Vincent looked at the lady and nodded his head. Helga said, "I hope this is not the beginning of an issue."

Vincent shot back, "I think the woman is checking *you* out, not me. So, my love, don't try to convince me of a menage a trois, because I am a devout husband." They both smiled and began to do their things in the gym.

Vincent later acknowledged, "Oh, and by the way, her body looks manufactured, whereas your body was designed by the gods. Moving forward I don't want to deal with bullshit, so let's make it about you and me and not about superficial nonsense. Remember, if all that you say is true, then the ex-man himself is going to be looking for your ass. Now, I am here for the long run so keep the idea of jealousy in the closet. Think it, but unless you have perfect information, don't bring it to me. You will learn, hopefully during this voyage, that I am a one woman's toy and I don't need extras."

Helga began to cry and said, "You can't imagine how much I need you, your wisdom, your kindness, and your love. Vincent, I would be lost without you. You keep me grounded and focused. I can't stop worrying that you'll find pleasure elsewhere and leave me vulnerable to making mistakes."

Vincent grabbed her hand and kissed it. He exclaimed, so that all could hear, "I love you more than life!"

#

As the afternoon was concluding and the evening began, in a lounge in a corner, away from the crowds, Helga spoke of her many episodes of doing what was requested of her. Vincent paused the conversation and said, "I prefer to have this conversation in our cabin. Let's grab a snack and head back."

Back in the cabin, Vincent immediately started fooling around with Helga. He said, "Honey, can we make a deal that we won't start conversations about our past until tomorrow the third day of this cruise? I just need to be about enjoying you physically and mentally rather than hearing about and sharing our pasts. What say you?"

Helga threw both hands in the air as if she were frustrated, but when she lowered them, they landed in the middle part of his body. She began to massage Vincent ever so slowly and deliberately until he was ready for that member of his to come out of its hiding place. To her knees she descended and helped Vincent with exposing her late evening snack and pleasure syndrome. Vincent gently stroked her hair and finally dropped to his knees where he found a pair of voluptuous lips waiting for his. They kissed like teenagers and made out like them as well.

Once out on the balcony with throw blankets, Helga felt the urge to continue the discussion that they were having in the lounge. She said, "I need to tell you a few things right now Vincent, or otherwise I won't sleep tonight."

He kissed her and said, "Helga, I'm all ears."

She replied, "Can you fix one of those big drinks for us to share?"

Once he had returned and they both had took a swig of the drink, Helga said, "I won't bore you with all of the minutiae, but I became a nun for so many different reasons only to find out that there was as much disgusting behavior and treachery among the leaders of the church as there was in the world I was trying to escape. I was seduced by a priest, who later became a bishop, who graduated to become a cardinal and finally he became the Holy Father, of the Roman Catholic

Church and I was impregnated by him. He sent me away to protect his image and to ensure his chances to ascend to the head of the church. During my absence, we talked often about his needs, expectations, my absolute silence, obedience, and my loyalty. He even told me that our child would be welcomed in the church community once he was of age, but under no circumstances was the child to know that he was the father. Anyway, that child is 25 years old now. The politics of the church are cutthroat. I was given missions where people were terminated, held for ransom and other unimaginable things. I once found the illicit daughter of one of my ex-employer's enemies and was given instructions to terminate her and to make it horrific. I still dream about that incident and many others. If you went against this man, nothing was sacred and his ability to demand macabre results was incredible as if he himself was performing the execution. Can you fix us another drink?"

When Vincent returned, he saw that Helga was crying. He sat the drink down, kissed away her tears and murmured, "I love you so much. Stay with me. I know we can get through this thing together. I want to know that I can trust you no matter what the past entailed and that you will not consider or do anything rash such as trying to leave me alone on this ship. If you go, I'll come looking for you and you can take that to the bank. Let's save part two of this information-gathering session for another day."

"No Vincent, I need to get through this now. Let me at least tell you about my being a spy for the church."

Helga continued, "I had two names, Sister Mary when I was on official church business and Helga Spengatsenburg when I was working as a spy. A few years back, a new dirty bomb called the Carbon Factor was developed. Well, the Holy Father wanted to gain control of it. I was the lead investigator and this is when my world got messy. I met a guy who I was supposed to terminate once I obtained critical information about the Carbon Factor in Switzerland. As a spy, you sometimes find yourself doing disgusting things to get the results that you want. However, I liked this guy. He was a neophyte, almost a virgin, handsome and quite manly. The fascinating thing about him was that I made him swallow a capsule that had critical information about the dirty bomb so that no one would kill him until the deciphering process was available. Well, I had a few go-rounds with this dude, he melted my heart and he reminds me a lot of you. He was a good person who I could love, I thought. Anyway, the sex was sex, but not nuclear like our interactions are and he too impregnated me."

Helga took a big swig of the drink and continued, "Twelve months later, I left my child at a monastery in Spain, off the grid, away from humanity, with a group of nuns who swore to me that they would care for my child no matter what. Well, no matter what lasted until the baby's father and his father showed up with enough money to buy all of Spain. In a matter of days, my child was on his way to America with citizenship papers and a State-issued birth certificate. Okay, that's not the bad part, everyone thought this guy was a loner and had no support systems. How fucking wrong were they. This guy and my so-called friend Asiram were on a plane that was descending to an airport, when suddenly they were being jerked around by a dude on the ground with a joystick. The idea was to scare this guy into submission. No sir, his father, whom he didn't know, had been contacted by his mother who had disappeared on his father during her pregnancy. She told him that his son, their son, was "the idiot spy" and that people were trying to kill him. He earned that title in Switzerland because he didn't know anything or even the reason he was there. He thought that he was there for an energy conference. Baby, I have to do some whizzing, be right back."

When Helga returned to the balcony, Vincent pretended to be asleep. She exclaimed, "Not funny, Vincent, I'm exposing my soul to you and I need you to be attentive as I attempt to humiliate myself in public to a man that I just met and whom I absolutely love. Not funny!"

Vincent stood up, pulled Helga sinfully close and said, "I was only pretending. I'm here with you now and forever if you will have me."

Helga explained, "I did not know that this guy was surrounded by a small battalion of former Vietnam vets. His people were considered an elite, badass group of killers. I totally ignored it and with the assistance of a few spies who played for money and who were connected to mercs, I and a few other agencies and papal groups challenged them. Well, the score card was as absolute and final as can be—them no fatalities—our gangs completely annihilated. Listen, this is the guy I saved and didn't know that he jettisoned enough sperm into me to create a new country. This is the guy who I endowed with the Carbon Factor in order to save his life. The church had a version of it, but its version and the one the Russians had continued to detonate in their labs. This guy had the real deal, and this is the guy who took my son from the monastery. Wait before you interrupt me. My mother and her sister convinced my other son to join up with the Beckmire group." Vincent choked on hearing that name—his real name.

Vincent asked, "Honey, would you like to take a walk around the ship or maybe go to the casino for a little bit and play those mindless slot machines?"

Helga looked at Vincent and replied, "Babe, do I look and sound like a fucking slot machine type of lady tonight? No, I don't think so. I am not finished with my catharsis, and you want to go and play games."

Vincent interjected, "Helga, you seemed so bothered by the events that I'm trying to find a way to ease your mind so that we can soothe each other's bodies later on."

Helga smiled and said, "Come here, man. I just want to kiss those beautiful round lips of yours. If you want to go and gamble, then so be it. I can finish my stories later."

Vincent replied, "Not at all. You can talk until you're blue in the face, but this guy is going to sit here and listen and analyze everything you say. Do you think we can share another drink before you proceed?"

Helga began to tell Vincent about the time that the Beckmire boy and his crew were at the Vatican and were guests of the Holy Father. She said although she was never face to face with the Beckmire boy, she saw him from afar and began to remember their interludes.

Realizing that she may be insulting Vincent's manhood, Helga stated, "After seeing him sober, respectful and with his family, I thought he was a nerd. He looked the part, wore funny pants and shoes, but was very attentive to one of my former contemporaries, Asiram. I also saved her because I helped them escape from a chalet in St. Moritz and on that plane controlled by a joystick on the ground."

Asiram was such a bitch, always following up behind me. Oh, and as a matter of fact, Mr. Beckmire and his group were in the Vatican when the former Holy Father went missing. He didn't really go missing, we planned every second of that event. What was alleged to be between \$2 or so billion in bearer-bonds, was actually closer to a trillion dollars that the crooked leadership in Venezuela stole from the people by selling much of its oil products on the black market to China and North Korea and pocketing hefty profits. That's the real reason he went missing. It was that trillion, plus the trillion or so that the Beckmire group had amassed and the trillion that the diamond mine that the Beckmire wayward son, was owner. My ex-employer felt that he himself had to oversee those acquisitions and therefore, planned his disappearance."

Helga swallowed a huge amount of their drink and continued, "Anyway, in order for me to remain in an active capacity with my ex-employer, I had to fake my own death.

In Mexico City, I found this remarkable look-a-like. I convinced her to meet my ex-lover and play a role that was inherently me. When shit goes wrong it sure as hell has no limits. Anyhow, she was in St. Thomas, in a restaurant, at the Four Seasons Hotel, in a corner in the dark with sunglasses on. Mr. Beckmire and his son entered the place with their makeshift security and my look-a-like did exactly as we had planned. She was tutored to say, "I want to be made whole and I want to be righteous and the only way for me to achieve those feelings is by you returning my child to me. That's right, my child will make me righteous and I will feel whole."

At that moment, an elite squad of papal security entered the restaurant and placed two fake rounds into her body, and one to her head. The rounds were constructed as splatter bullets that did not hurt the person but they would feel the impact. At that point, they were supposed to scour the place and leave without any additional casualties. It all seemed so real and final, until my ex-lover, Zanthius Beckmire DeLombardo grabbed a pillow, placed it over my look-a-like's head, and fired real rounds into her head and another into her heart. His father, it was alleged, looked at him in amazement, and do you know what my ex-partner said? Of course you don't. That motherfucker said, "Dad, she has a habit of coming back from the dead, and I just wanted to make sure that this time her ticket to hell was punched, accepted and she was on her way where she belonged."

Helga began to cry uncontrollably and Vincent gathered her up in his arms and assured her that all would be rectified. He said, "Honey, we will get through this and everything else that confronts us and we will do it together."

It would be a long night, and Helga would repent for so many different and nefarious events that she was responsible for, until she cried herself to sleep.

In the meantime, Vincent was trying to calculate how to avoid telling Helga that he is the Beckmire that she was searching for in Annapolis. As he considered options, one scenario kept entering his head and that was that he didn't have to admit to anything because they were on a journey to nowhere. Reality drove him back to earth when he realized that his lady friend had locked down hundreds of millions of dollars of her ex-employer and that he wasn't going to stop looking for access to his money at any point in time. Out of nowhere, he thought about how two of her offsprings could land in the same camp. He hesitated for a minute and recalled all that she had acknowledged and how painful that must have been for her. He thought that his only problem was that he had to be sure that her search for the Beckmire person was over and that if he acknowledged who he was, perhaps there would be disharmony, but in the end perhaps perfect bliss would be the outcome.

Vincent watched Helga sleep and realized that this was the only woman that he ever truly had some lasting emotions for. He said to himself, "She gives me balance, she gives me her soul, she gives me all that I need and she states that she loves me. I have never heard anyone say that they love me other than the woman who birthed me, but even with her I didn't want to be involved. It's probably natural for people to love their parents, but I don't remember a time when I could actually say that I loved them. They gave me everything that I wanted, sent me to that military school, which only exacerbated my disgust for them as human beings, but not the assets that they controlled. Perhaps we can hide on some secluded island, and I can hire people to excavate, control, manage and monitor the fortune that my mother, who I never acknowledged, has purchased for me. I don't know if I should send her a note thanking her or what. I guess that's a bad idea since it's been reported that I'm *dead*."

CHAPTER TWENTY-ONE

Mr. Kenzo kept a vigil after seeing two cats, each perched in a window of the barn, staring at him as if they were his prison guards. Mice and rats stirred all night long and kept him from sleeping. Around six in the morning when the sun began to crest over the mountain-top, he finally fell asleep. Mr. Kenzo slept for approximately an hour before the cats in the window disappeared and were replaced by two horses staring at a thing in their blankets. When he woke up and saw the two horses, he screamed and asked, "What kind of devil worshiping goes on here? Last night two cats watched me all night long and now they have turned into horses. That's not even logical but I know what I saw."

Around 6:45 a.m., James the caretaker, rode his all-wheel drive vehicle into the barn. He saw the horses in the window. When he turned around, he saw Mr. Kenzo clutching blankets and the chain extending from his leg. James said, "Morning, looks like you be in a shitload of trouble. If they chained you last night and said they would determine your fate in the morning, then mister, your ass is grass. You be pushing up some daisies in a few months or so on that there ridge over yonder. At least I can offer you a cup of coffee. I don't have no fancy sugar or that artificial shit, but I do have some plain old black coffee."

James fetched his thermos and poured Mr. Kenzo some coffee in the thermos's top. He said, "This be all I got. You can finish it up. By the way, what in the hell did you do to these fellas?"

Kenzo looked at James and said, "I thought I saved the accountant's woman from being abused by eight of my guys. I ran my hand up her dress, trying to avoid touching that particular area and then I laid out the edict that this woman was mine and only mine, and that if any man even looked at her, I would have his dick cut off. I protected the woman, but the fact remains, I acted savagely when I went under her dress, but I acted respectfully by trying not to touch anything. The woman told them that I abused her and touched her husband's property and that she wanted to castrate me."

"Damn boy!" James exclaimed. "You had better tell the Sarge that shit right off, or he'll turn you over to the devil in disguise and his disciple and that's a thing that you don't want to happen. Them two guys find new ways to torture and kill people at every turn. No sir, you don't want to be left alone with them two."

No sooner than said, Jilkes and John Lee walked into the barn and spoke to James. Jilkes looked at Kenzo and said, "I hope you like ham and scrambled eggs. That's what's available for breakfast."

Kenzo dropped his head and whispered, "I guess that's my last meal?"

John Lee asked, "Why you say that? You planning on committing suicide or something?"

Kenzo said, "James told me about you two, the devil and his disciple and that you find new ways to torture and kill people."

Jilkes laughed and said, "That James be telling a lot of shit out of school. You know John Lee, we might have to experiment on his ass."

James replied, "You do that and that wife of mine will kill the entire State of Virginia. How you boys be doing. I gave him the plays just as you called them. I think he saved that lady by going up her skirt. He didn't act like he did it with lust and I just think he might be another one of your converts. Those be my three cents and I stick by them."

Kenzo raised his hand as if he were in school. Jilkes asked, "What's your question?"

"Last night a black cat was perched in the window on the right. In the window on the left, a white cat and they watched me all night long. When I woke up this morning, there was a black horse head in the window on the right, and a white horse head in the window on the left."

Jilkes asked, "Do you believe in witches and goblins?" Do you believe in spirits and that there are people who are hundreds of years old? If you don't and you're closed-minded, then if this group spares your life, the things that you'll be subjected to for approval will either shape your humanity or drive you horribly insane. In all fairness we are not a part of the judging group. We like to feed our potential victims so that if and when they are judged negatively, we can watch how their body responds to our demonic behaviors."

After Jilkes said that, the Sarge walked into the barn with Mallory, Dempsey, Hood, Anel, and Angel and said good morning to everyone. He then said, "Let's get this over and done with. I saw some huge fish jumping in the pond. I want to go fishing with my son, his uncle, and his brother."

He looked at Kenzo, and said, "Unfortunately, not everyone believes your story of how your violation of Jong's nephew's wife was a sign to your comrades that she was off-limits. I've heard a lot of shit in my life, but I've never met a man who has invaded a female's body and claimed that he did it in her-defense. I say horseshit to all you say and may God give you a different direction in your next life. Sentenced passed. You people know what to do!" the Sarge exclaimed.

As the Sarge turned to exit the barn, James said, "Mr. Beckmire, I don't agree with your sentence. I believe him."

The Sarge walked over to James and whispered in his ear, "I appreciate your voting yourself into our group without a ballot or support from us, however, some sentences are perfunctory and without resolution. Wait for the final card to be played. Thanks James."

Jilkes unlocked the bracelet on Kenzo's ankle and whispered, "I could make it fair and give you a 15-minute advantage."

Kenzo replied, "I think that I've had my run of things. I mean I got the guy who killed my mother and saved a woman from being savagely violated. I only ask you make my demise quick. Not really down with that torturing thing."

John Lee asked, "Do you think you can handle going into town with me and Jilkes for some provisions?"

Kenzo replied, "What, are you're going to put me on an abandon road and chase me down and run me over?"

John Lee smiled and said, "No, crazy man. We're going to buy you some clothes so that you can begin your penitence. Ain't nobody here going to kill your ass. Jong's nephew's wife begged for your life. She said that although your hand was deep under her dress, your fist was balled up. Doesn't sound like a man who's about to sexually assault someone. So, listen, here's the deal *The Benauijuu*, is probably going to come for us as well as you, which means we probably should align ourselves to make sure we get them before they get us. What's be your thoughts on that?"

"Please indulge me. So, you're not going to kill me and you're not going to maim me or anything close to that?" Kenzo asked

Jilkes responded, "No, dude. We're going to take you shopping and get you some clothes that don't smell like horseshit."

Half-way up the highway, John Lee told Jilkes to pull the van over. Jilkes asked why and he replied, "Because I have to take a leak."

Kenzo who was sitting in the back, stated, "I guess I should take a leak as well."

John Lee looked at him and said, "If you be having to take a leak, you wait until I come back and then you can go. I don't know you well enough to be taking a piss with you. We ain't all that yet."

John Lee got out of the car and walked by some roadside bushes. After finishing his business, he returned to the car. He looked back at Kenzo and said, "Well if you got to go, then go. We ain't going to be hanging around here all day waiting on your ass."

Kenzo replied, "I can wait until I find a proper facility."

In town at the Walmart, John Lee told Kenzo to pick out some staples and a nice pair of pants and shirt for special occasions. Jilkes looked at him and asked, "Old country, what special occasions are you talking about?"

John Lee replied, "Everyone should have a nice shirt and pair of pants in case of an emergency or a special dinner or something. You never know someone could invite us back to that there Vatican again."

Once they were back in the van and heading towards the farm, Kenzo asked, "Are you guys hungry? Do you think we can stop at that Chick-fil-A over there?"

After ordering food and drinks, Kenzo asked, "May I speak frankly and freely, and with impunity?"

Jilkes looked at John Lee, arched his shoulders, and announced, "This here be a free country. You don't have to ask my minority friend for permission to speak."

Kenzo asked, "Do you guys know why you're being targeted?"

John Lee replied, "Everybody wants us dead until they need us alive. We be done sent a whole lot of souls to hell and they be waiting on our arrival. I mean, collectively, we're talking several thousand people."

Kenzo replied, "That's not the reason you're being targeted. In addition to your personal fortunes, it is alleged that you were given several billion dollars in bearer bonds to hold until a more people friendly person oversaw a certain country."

Jilkes and John Lee were all ears and Jilkes asked Kenzo to continue. Kenzo asked, "Did anyone ever go through those bonds and authenticate the amounts?" Again, Jilkes looked at John Lee who once again shrugged his shoulders.

Jilkes replied, "We were never concerned about the amount of the bonds, just that they belonged to the people. It was initially stated to us that they were worth approximately $2 billion."

Kenzo smiled and asked his question again, "Did anyone ever evaluate the bonds?"

John Lee fired back, "What is this cat and mouse game that you be playing. We didn't sit there and count each one to make sure they totaled $2 billion." Kenzo said no more and began to devour his sandwich.

After he finished eating his sandwich, Jilkes said, "I deduce that there is something you're not telling us about those bonds. Is that correct?"

Kenzo murmured, "There is a lot of misinformation about those bonds that is now saturating the dark web. I prefer to have a single opportunity to share my information with leadership, rather than telling you guys and then having to go over it again with those in charge."

John Lee exclaimed, "Pull this here van over. We gonna have one less rider."

Jilkes made a quick path to the side of the road and Kenzo yelled, "Okay, I got your message. If you're going to kill me, then do it. Stop jerking my chain."

At that point, he could hear John Lee send a round into the chamber of his weapon. Kenzo loudly responded, "Okay, guys, listen up. I'm going to enlighten you about the true facts surrounding what you're holding allegedly for the people. Can I first give you a history of the *Benauijuu?* The *Benauijuu or young guns* were created by the most powerful institution on earth, the church. It was a localized situation at first until it proved how effective it could be. There was never any direct relationship with the institutions and definitely no in-person meetings. Large institutions of every denomination would make members of their flocks who were on the other side of the legal system do their dirty work and essentially blackmail others. I mean from murder, blackmail, extortion, and the threat of death for all who are a part of the family. We have made those mega-church deacons pay millions upon millions and if they ever thought that they could break away from their tithing, then family members would begin to have freak and fatal accidents. Listen, religion at one point in time controlled the world. It's now losing its grip as a result of COVID, but it has found other ways to make sure that the flock is diligent in activating their schemes that enrich them and their institutions."

Kenzo paused, took a swig of his soda, and said, "Listen guys, I was in servitude. I was working off an amount of money that my mother allegedly stole from those crooks. It was once stated in a meeting that I attended in London that the funds stolen from the people and turned into bearer bonds, totaled 2 billion dollars. It was then announced that the real value of those bonds on the open market is worth shy of a trillion dollars. The price of the bootlegged oil sold to other dictators may be worth $2 billion, but the rest is a function of stolen artifacts worth billions of dollars including missing paintings confiscated by the Germans after the Second World War and of billions of dollars seized from banks that did work with the Germans. Oh, it was also noted that the gold taken from the teeth of the dead, and sold to faithful Germans at a depreciated price was included in the real price of the bearer bonds. These were not open conversations witnessed by honest people or the press, no sir. These were back door negotiations to escape murder, save loved ones, or any number of things that could fatten the inter-faith coalition's pockets and control."

Kenzo continued, "Mr. Jong's nephew's wife's sister spoke of the issue on her podcast and I did the investigation in order to knock years off my sentence. I followed the dictator's offshore businesses with the North Koreans, the Chinese and the reciprocal charges between the dictator and the Russians. They would charge each other for the product and bill each other with percentages depressed to falsely depict the value of each transaction. Each of those bonds have a multiplier on them, meaning that they aren't truly bearer bonds but are negotiable by only a select few institutions. If your people had read the fine print on the bonds, they would have seen the calculated amounts on each one. That dictator was told to buy from a particular bank in Switzerland and to transfer to banks under the registry of the church itself. Listen, there are literally trillions of dollars in stolen artifacts, bullion, diamonds, and everything else of value in the coffers of the church. So, in plain English, the bonds you have are not worth a couple of billion but on the contrary, they approach an existential value of plus or minus a trillion dollars.

Jilkes looked at John Lee and asked, "Do you believe that horseshit that guy just gave us?"

John Lee clicked the safety button on his Smith & Wesson .9 millimeter and said, "I can better show you my answer than talk about it." He turned around in his seat and said, "Mister, how dumb do you think my minority friend is? Do you think he's stupid enough to buy the bullshit that you just tried to sell him? Listen, this ain't personal. I don't want you to think it is when you find yourself in hell." He pointed the weapon at Kenzo and asked, "Any last words?"

Kenzo took a deep breath and said, "Yes there are. Fuck you and your minority friend and both of youse can kiss my shiny ass!" He then closed his eyes and waited for the paralyzing effect of being shot in the head at point-blank range.

Thirty seconds went by and John Lee had returned to a normal sitting position in the front seat of the car and neither man said a word.

Kenzo asked, "Is it possible to ask a question without being threatened?"

Both men in unison shouted, "No!

After five or so minutes of listening to bad music playing, Kenzo said, "I must finish my story. You have to hear me out."

A few seconds later, John Lee lowered the volume and asked, "What else is it that you want to say?"

Kenzo smiled and said, "I want to prepare you for an onslaught of violence that is going to be heading your way. Listen, the person that assigned you to the role of caretaker of the bonds, knew that you had an upcoming expiration date and that you would offer little resistance to those who would be coming for you."

Jilkes looked at John Lee and they both broke into laughter. After a hearty laugh, Jilkes looked in the rear-view-mirror and asked, "Do you think that we're going to just lie down and let people come into our homes and take advantage of us? Is that what you think?"

Kenzo exclaimed, "Then stop threatening me and query me on their approach and timetable! I have a lot to offer.

Listen, you can kill me or let them motherfuckers do their dastardly trip on me. At this point in time, it don't fucking matter. I got the son-of-a-bitch that executed my mother and the rest is bullshit."

John Lee retorted, "Save some of this nonsense for leadership. No more talking. Just enjoy the scenery and be thankful that you're still alive."

CHAPTER TWENTY-TWO

Around 3:30 in the morning, lightening could be seen on the horizon by those who were still awake. The boat began to sway gently, but gradually it turned into a hold-on-and-stay-in-your-cabin kind of night. Helga woke up for a visit to the head and found Vincent kneeling near the toilet with a cold compress over his neck. Helga said, "Honey, why didn't you wake me up?"

"Babe, I didn't want you to see me like this and more importantly, to have to deal with this mess." Helga ran water on another towel and placed it over Vincent's head and asked, "Is it the food or the motion?" Vincent made the hand motion of a boat going up and down. Helga smiled and said, "I want a real man who I can share my issues with and he can share his regurgitated products on our first voyage. I love you so much, and thanks for listening to me. I'll be right outside of the door if you need me."

Vincent grabbed her hand and stated, "This whole event is an incredible invitation to love. I love you Helga."

Ten or so minutes later, Vincent emerged from the head and said, "I need to step out on the balcony for some fresh air."

Helga immediately advised him that it was against the ship's rules and added furthermore, once you see those big waves, you're going to empty everything that's left in your stomach, please don't go out there or open the door. I think the sound of the waves as well as the sight of them are going to lay you down for weeks. Why don't you stretch out on the floor, where there is no multiplier effect you know the boat rocks, the room rocks, and the bed rocks. On the floor, you just have a limited amount of rocking."

Vincent laughed and inquired, "Where will you be?"

"I'll be right beside you as usual. Now just lie down and I'll get us some pillows and blankets," Helga stated.

# # #

In the late morning, Vincent stirred first and stared at a sleeping Helga. He smiled and murmured, "I've got to come clean with her. I swear, this woman haunts me with pleasure, understanding, meaning and love. I've never felt this way before about a person of the opposite sex." Vincent looked outside and saw that the boat had finished that up-and-down motion and appeared to be moving along smoothly.

Helga moved and reached over to see where Vincent was. After not feeling any parts of him, she turned over and saw him smiling like a little boy at her. She asked, "What is that big Cheshire cat grin about? By the way, how are you feeling?"

Vincent replied, "I feel as though I have nothing in my stomach other than pain. I need to eat something light and then drink a lot of fluids. I know I cleaned out my stomach last night. I want to go and have something to eat. Do you want to join me? I mean in the next five-to-ten minutes. I'm feeling weak, and I know I need to eat something."

Helga responded, "I'll be ready in five."

Helga essentially pulled a Pamela Anderson skit and was without any make-up. After washing her face, she put on a little moisturizer and was ready to go. When she entered the cabin, Vincent asked, "Did you put make-up on?"

Helga responded, "No silly man. Look at me. Do I look like I have make-up on?"

Vincent replied in a boyish style, "You are the most beautiful woman that I have ever had the pleasure of saying I love you to. I am honored and I will begin our next leg of this journey by telling you exactly everything there is to know about me. I only hope and pray that you accept my honesty and that you will decide that we should stay on this journey."

Helga looked curiously at him and asked, "Vincent, what could be more challenging than who I am? Who are you running away from? Tell me."

At breakfast, Vincent asked, "Can we just eat first and talk later? Just like I was attentive to what you were portraying when you had your catharsis. I want to be able to do the same thing without passing out from a lack of nutrients and vitamins in my system. I am shaking because I'm so hungry. Please extend me the same considerations as I did to you."

Helga replied, "Silly man, I don't care what or who you are. All I know is that I love you and that you're the only person I feel who cares about me and loves me."

Vincent with tears in his eyes, said, "I'll just get something to go and then we can clear the air about what I have to say. Listen, I'm no villain, I'm no murderer, yet I have had people murdered. I am not a rapist or anything remotely close to that and more significantly, I am in love with you—lock stock and barrel."

The two had Bloody Mary cocktails and carried two back to their cabin for consumption. Vincent was in a funk but decided that he was going to be forthright with Helga.

On their balcony, Vincent stared at Helga long and hard. He finally admitted, "I know the person that you were seeking in Annapolis."

Helga stirred in her chair but said nothing. Vincent took a swig of his drink and was grateful for the fact that this morning was a lot calmer than last night on the water. He then said, "The Beckmire kid was an anomaly in that he was brilliant, possessed and focused on a single objective and that was the demise of his parents and their friends and the assumption of their wealth."

Helga once again stirred in her chair. Vincent said, "I know this because I was a staunch friend of his. One night after having crabs and beers, things that he didn't handle very well, I gave him a ride back to the Academy and he told me the long story of his parents, their friends, and their wealth. I initially found it too hard to believe, but after a while, I began to enjoy his tales, his recorded conversations with his mother and her ability to send him funds whenever he needed or wanted them."

Helga interrupted him and asked, "Did he ever talk about the Carbon Factor?"

Vincent looked at her and asked, "Is that the new age bomb or something like that?"

Cautiously, Helga replied, "Absolutely."

Vincent wanted to continue with the fabrication but looked at Helga and felt guilty about what he had said and began to cry. She asked, "Vincent, what is going on? Why are you crying?" At this point, Vincent was uncontrollably crying, wheezing for breaths of air and totally out of control. At every attempt of telling Helga the truth, his inner rage for himself would propel him into a crying and wheezing outburst.

Vincent began to dry heave and that's when Helga knew that he was in a bad way. Vincent violently began to regurgitate the food he had eaten and even when he thought he had reached emptiness, he continued to dispel any and everything that was left in him. He fell to the floor of the balcony. The neighbor on their right heard all the commotion and called the emergency number for assistance. Luckily for Vincent because he had nothing else to give to the sea. He had thrown up all that there was in his stomach.

Four minutes later, there was a large noise from outside the cabin and the steward yelled, "Medical personnel are in attendance. We are responding to a call from a neighbor that a cabin member was violently regurgitating. "We are entering your cabin, please do not impede our mission."

When the medical team reached Vincent, he was almost in a comatose condition. The chief medical attendant immediately searched for a vein in Vincent's arm and inserted a needle to begin the provision of fluids to reduce dehydration. He also said, "We have to get him to sick bay immediately to provide further medical treatment. Miss, you might want to thank the person next door who heard the commotion and who was familiar with that sound and immediately called us. Your mate is in a bad way and he is in need of immediate medical attention."

CHAPTER TWENTY-THREE

At the ranch, Jilkes saw the Sarge and suggested that he listen to what the new captive had to say about the group he used to belong to. The Sarge asked, "Can it wait until we are certain about who we're dealing with?"

John Lee butted in and said, "I don't think so. If that there fellow is telling the truth, then we need to make sure our outlying systems are up and ready to be used. I personally believe him, not like my minority friend."

The Sarge asked, "Can you guys get Mallory, Chakes, Berstein, Brown, Montomie, McArthur and Jong and his nephew together and meet me in the barn in half an hour?" Both men nodded and proceeded to argue about who was going to tell whom.

When Kenzo was escorted into the barn, he saw a lot of people who were staring at him with skeptical—looking eyes. Jong scanned Kenzo and found that he had been injected with a locator device. He showed the Sarge the reading, which was scant because of the limited internet connections at the farm. The Sarge asked, "So, Kenzo, when were you going to tell us that you had a location device implanted in your back?"

Kenzo looked at the Sarge and stated, "I don't have any devices implanted in my back and if I do, I can assure you that I don't remember accepting them."

The Sarge said, "Let's move on. First of all, succinctly tell me about the bearer bonds that we were entrusted with that you seem to know so much about."

"Sir, I only know what I overheard. You were told and you think that they are worth two billion dollars, and I say the word on the street has them priced at just shy of a trillion dollars. In small print, visible under a magnifying glass, you will see the intrinsic value of each bond with a multiplier next to it. As an example, if a bond is worth $100,000, then at the bottom, the kicker is noted along with the security number of each bond. Yes, on face value, the bonds are worth $2 billion. When you add the kicker and the authorization number to each one, again, it's almost a trillion."

There was quiet in the room. Jong's nephew was fumbling with his phone until he found a photo in his apps of one of the bonds. He enlarged it and yelled, "I'll be a blind mouse. I'm looking at one of the bonds that I took a photo of when we first got them and he is correct. There is a multiplier number, a security code, and the actual value of each security." Everyone gathered around to see what he was talking about, but no one understood what any of this conversation meant.

The Sarge asked Kenzo, "How do I know that you're not setting us up?"

Kenzo replied, "Frankly you don't, but I know that I am a dead man on both sides of this equation. I don't know how to prove to you that I am telling the truth, and that I know that they're going to be coming for you in strength in a matter of days. If what you say is true about the internet, then they'll start canvasing at the last strong signal. Then they will reach out to their members and be knocking on your door. I've participated in many events such as this one and I was successful on every occasion, because I wanted to be ruthless and show them that I can be trusted to leave a calling card of significance. I have butchered a lot of people, which allowed me to get closer to the man that killed my mother. I have no fight with you and I knew that if I didn't address the lady in an aggressive manner, then they would have desecrated her in ways that you can't imagine."

There was a quiet in the room and John Lee blurted out, "What be the ways that your people violate people?"

The Sarge looked at him and suggested, "John Lee, use your imagination. We aren't interested in the degrees in which people hurt others. Notwithstanding the amount of hurt and torture we have been a part of, my friend, let it go."

Kenzo asked, "May I give him an example of how the *Benauijuu* torture people?" The Sarge looked around the room and from the looks on the faces of his people, he determined that it was necessary. He then thought "*When I make arbitrary decisions, they will further see me as a dictator.*" He asked, "By a show of hands, how many want to know what the young guns do to torture people?" Every hand in the barn was raised.

The Sarge looked at Kenzo and said, "Give us a medium picture and not the most sordid."

Kenzo looked at Jong's nephew's wife and said, "After each man would have had his go with you, at the end, they would have straddle your legs and inject HCL into you. They then would take bets on the timetable and the outcome."

John Lee asked, "What be that HCL?"

The Sarge yelled, "Enough! That is as sick as sick can be. Tell me about what we can expect from them if they happen to find their way here?"

Kenzo shook his head and said, "I am embarrassed to tell you about the things that I and my former group have done, and let me be completely transparent. I have sanctioned and participated in activities to get the necessary information. We would use children to the max to gain immediate information. There are no limits to what they will do to get what they want. I can only suggest what I would do if I were a member of your group. Mr. Sarge, when they come here, I would kill every one of them and brutally. I mean if they are wounded, I would put six more rounds into their bodies. I would then get on a plane and begin to purge them from the top to the bottom, realizing that they are a function of the church community. I would then make sure to send a message to their leaders stating that there is no sanctuary between heaven and hell that they can exist in. I would end each communication with one message, and that is, "if you think you've seen evil and torture, wait until you're at our party."

The Sarge said, "Well, that's nothing new to our group. We are good at terminating evil people."

He looked at Kenzo and asked, "Did anyone give you a PD session on us?"

"Mr. Sarge, there was some noise about when you guys were in Vietnam and that many of you had moved on to the other side. Our intel was that you people are old, decrepit, and using walkers and other items to move from point A to B," Kenzo stated.

The Sarge asked, "As you see us now, what are your thoughts?"

"If accepted, I selected the right side," Kenzo announced.

The Sarge responded, "You made a lifesaving decision, my friend. We don't bow down to anyone except each other. You come here for aggression, and you don't get to leave."

# # #

In the morning, everyone was curious about the new guy and what he had to offer. The Sarge asked Mallory to handle his orientation and his due diligence.

Mallory suggested, "To catch a thief, let's use a few. I want him detailed to Dempsey, Hood, Anel, and Angel. If they smell that he's dirty, then he's dead on the spot."

The Sarge looked at Mallory and gave him a half-smile, but interjected, "The stakes are a lot higher now. If Kenzo is correct about the booster factor on the bearer bonds, then I'm wondering if I can trust your ass."

Mallory laughed and said, "Yeah, I know. When it comes to the greed factor, it's usually the leader who wants everyone dead except himself so that he doesn't have to share. Just remember *Treasure Island*."

Courtney eased up beside them with Marcelus, who asked, "Pops, can I feed the horses today?"

The Sarge smiled and was about to respond when he saw several flashes from the hillside. He held back his fear, threw Marcclus in the air, caught him, and proceeded into the barn. He said to Courtney, "Girl, walk slowly as possible to me. Someone is scoping us out." Courtney walked into the barn, as the Sarge was giving an alert signal to Rashida. Rashida told Juan that they were being scoped and to gather the children and give them the code word.

Juan walked to the front door and yelled, "Hey guys, it's time for school." This was a sign that all was not well and that they were to act as normal as possible.

In the meantime, Jilkes, John Lee, Chakes and Brown, were racing through a tunnel that hadn't been used in over a year. As they grabbed weapons, they recognized that they were oiled and ready to fire. Jong, Montomie, McArthur and Bernstein raced through an adjacent tunnel. When the group with Jilkes reached the end of the tunnel, he activated the solar camera that scanned the area 180 degrees. When Jong and his group reached the end of their tunnel, he engaged the camera system and received the opposite 180 degrees view. As they viewed the monitor, they saw teenagers scouring the area with binoculars. As they were about to call off the alert, Bernstein said, "I see you motherfucker."

Everyone looked but didn't see what he was talking about. Jong focused for a minute and after seeing something move, he said, "These people are earth focused. They blend right in and are using those kids while they take pictures of our layout."

McArthur said, "If that's what they're doing, then they are not too bright because you can Google where we are and get topographical images of everything within a fifteen-mile radius."

Jong looked at the legs of two of the alleged children through binoculars and saw that they had matching tattoos of a spear through the head of a dragon. He said, "Those teenagers, must be a part of the surveillance team." He called the Sarge. When he answered, he said, "The enemy is here. Prepare our response."

The Sarge replied, "Do not engage. I repeat, do not engage unless there are no other options."

As Jilkes and his crew watched the monitors, a keen-eyed John Lee demanded, "Back that there picture up. That guy must think we be blind or something. Look at him trying to see the farm."

Jilkes said, "Listen you country asshole, I don't see anything. Do any of you guys see anything?" Everyone shook their head and confirmed that they didn't see a thing.

John Lee said, "When we get back, I'm taking all of you people to the damn doctor that looks into your eyes." He turned around and pointed to two well camouflaged predators.

Bernstein said, "I am definitely going to go peacefully to the doctor to have my eyes examined. Look at that butthead. He looks as if he's an animal blending into the fall environment."

# # #

Rashida called the caretaker and said, "We got here late last night. What did sign in your yard say?"

James slowly and reluctantly replied, "My place is up for Sherriff's sale in a couple of days."

Rashida yelled, "What the fuck is going on? We left you with an open bank account to handle all taxes and other expenses for the farm and your place. What happened to the money?"

After a slow start, James replied, "I don't know nothing about debit cards, plus I couldn't remember that damn password. I was afraid to ask for help because that would have given the key to the vault to somebody else. I just couldn't bring myself to do that."

Rashida shot back, "Why in the hell didn't you call me?"

James replied, "I called you from a phone booth in town. I didn't want anyone listening in on my conversation."

Rashida responded, "James, it probably went to my spam list. Get a pen and a piece of paper. I am going to give you access to my personal account. Whatever you do, do not let your property be stolen from you. If someone bids $10 million, then you bid $15 million. You will spend as much as it takes and I mean up to $100 million and then we'll be there in force to make sure that place is not sold. Listen James, we're under attack again, we need your eyes, security and help with this one. By the way, what time is the auction?"

James responded, "It jumps off in two days at 9:30 a.m. Ms. Rashida, can you please show up or get someone to do this thing for me?"

Rashida paused for a second and then said, "I might have the right person who can do this for us. I'll call you back. In the meantime, accept no offers and don't answer that phone of yours unless it's me."

An hour later, Rashida informed the Sarge that Jame's property was up for Sherriff's sale in two days. She asked, "Is there anyone we can call to get it delayed for 48 hours?"

The Sarge responded, "We can't let that happen." He looked at Monica who was talking to Larry in the next room and beckoned them over. He said, "Larry, we have eyes on us, but our caretaker's property is going up for Sherriff's sale in two days. I need you to figure out a plan to be at that auction and make sure Jame's property remains his, even if you are forced to buy it and sign it over to James on the spot."

Larry asked, "How much does he owe on it?"

The Sarge responded, "I don't know. Ask your sister, she's in contact with him. Whatever it is, make it happen seamlessly and correct. As a matter of fact, take Kenzo on as your mentee, but keep a sharp eye on his ass." The Sarge then said to Larry, "Give Clyde a call and see if he and the gang are available for some work. Also, make the call to our friends in Minnesota."

Later in the afternoon, Larry said to Kenzo, "I've been assigned as your mentor. I need to know everything there is to know about you. Before you start, let me be fully transparent. There are few people at the farm who believe your story. I haven't heard it so you can begin there. And please, spare no details. I want you to start when and where you could put together a sentence, call your mother by her name and the exact address where you lived. I want that kind of detail. Do you have a problem baring your soul to me, a complete stranger but potentially someone who can vouch for you and make people feel at ease around you? We're going to do that here because we believe some of your former compatriots are spying on us and I guess with the hope of getting a glimpse of you."

Kenzo exclaimed, "If that's true, then you probably have two or three days from now before they come at you in force."

Larry asked, "Tell me what that means, your comment about coming at us in force? Oh, and since you're being trusted, I'm going to trust you to wear this bracelet. If at any time you get the notion to bolt and join your friends, then this little GPS device will recognize that you are out of range and it will leave you minus an arm. And then, the potion takes hold of your body and offers you the most horrid death that you can imagine. This is just a safety device for me since I don't know you from Adam. Are we good to go?"

# # #

Late in the afternoon Kenzo was still telling Larry about who he was, his family, especially his mother, and how he was sentenced to work off some alleged amount of money that his mother purportedly stole from the group. He also told Larry that he had avenged his mother by killing the person who murdered her in front of him. Larry felt a lot of pain for Kenzo as he thought about how he was wayward until the Sarge took a chance on him.

Kenzo said, "I'm confused about something, but I don't know if it's appropriate to inquire about it."

Larry smiled and said, "Hey go for it."

"You have a vicious group of individuals preparing to swoop down on you like locust and you people move about as if there is no impending storm. If your people saw them, then you can rest assure that they will be here to hurt as many of you as they want until they can find out the passwords for those bonds. I just don't get it. No one seems to be alarmed," Kenzo remarked.

Larry exclaimed, "We have been here and done that before! When you look around, what do you see?"

Kenzo replied, "A pool, a main house, a guest house, horses, hay, and lots of land to just dream about. I've never been on a farm and I've never seen horses up close. My first night here, before I finally fell to sleep, there were two cats perched on two separate window ledges. When I woke up in the morning, there were two horses peering at me. At first I thought I was dreaming, but then I thought, these people are devils; they turn cats into horses and horses into cats. Okay, I must admit, I was a little dehydrated and hungry but that was my first impression."

Kenzo continued "The lady who initially accused me of going up her dress, even she recanted and realized that I was providing a safety net over her. Trust me, I've seen those men do dastardly things to women before executing them. I thought I saved her life, her dignity and she finally realized that my invasion was without sexual meaning. Anyway, I got off track from my initial inquiry and that is, why aren't you people getting ready for a fight?"

Larry turned, stared at him straight on and said, "If you come here to bring a fight, then I suggest you also bring your own body bag. Not sure what you may have heard about us, but we've had thousands of people to come at us only to find themselves entering the gates of hell. Those old guys are warriors. As a group, they probably have many thousands of souls waiting for their arrival into Hades. This is our domain and here, you enter at your own risk."

Kenzo said, "I hear what you're saying Larry, but might I confirm that these guys and girls who will be coming for you are animals? They will play cannibals on your wounded to make a statement. They will stake out and barbeque one or two of your young, if they have time. I can only recommend that you play an even more aggressive game than they will. I mean you got to be prepared to decapitate, gouge eyes out, cut bodies in half and every other thing that you can think of. Show no weakness and torment them with the heads, arms, and anything else of their brethren."

Larry looked at Kenzo and asked, "That bad, eh?"

Chapter Twenty-Four

Approximately a day and a half later, Vincent began to stir in the infirmary, and wondered why he was being restrained. Although the restraints were easy to break, he still considered the issue concerning. After looking at the ceiling, he finally focused on a corner in sick bay and saw Helga sleeping. He stared at her and once again began to sniffle. That's when Helga woke up and said, "Don't you dare start crying again. You almost cried yourself to death if there is such a thing. How are you feeling? Are you hungry?"

Vincent smiled and announced, "I love you so much, Ms. Helga. You are more than I deserve, but I'm going to settle for your love, kindness, attentiveness, and more importantly your honesty. As soon as they let me out of here, I am going to start showing you my unadulterated method of returning love to you. I have never been so happy about being with someone as I have been with you. You are a blessing in disguise my princess and I will always love and cherish the moments that we have and will share in the future. Do you think I could have a little kiss on the cheek? Oh, and by the way, why am I being restrained to the bed?"

Helga smiled and said, "The medical team thought it was best since you kept trying to go to our cabin to be with me?"

A little embarrassed, Vincent asked, "Is that on the level?"

Helga replied, "Ask those who tied you up why you were restrained."

#

Later in the cabin, Vincent asked, "What is that box on the table over there?"

Helga replied, "Just a little something that I thought you could use since I have never seen you with one?"

"One what?" Vincent asked.

Helga replied, "One of those things in the box."

Vincent asked, "May I open it now or is it like my birthday present?"

Helga replied, "It ain't all that. It's just a little inexpensive thought that I wanted to buy for you so that you'll always remember me."

Vincent chuckled, "I don't think I'll need a trinket to remind me of you. You are indelibly etched in my mind, my body, and my soul."

"Vincent, open the damn gift," Helga requested.

Vincent fumbled around with the box by first holding it in the air, then bouncing it up and down, then smelling it and finally placing his ear to it. He then exclaimed, "Well, I don't think it's a damn bomb!"

Helga said, "If it were, I wouldn't be in here with your crazy butt. Can you please open the package? Tell you what, it's one of those new age bracelets that you get to decide what it means. Just a keepsake for the man I love."

Vincent walked over to her, sat the package down and began to kiss her. Helga announced, "You were told to take it easy—no stress, no gym, no you know what, or anything else that will drain your body of more fluids. Dude, open the damn package before I toss it out of the door."

Vincent sat down, undid the ribbon, took the box out of its cloth cover, and flipped open the lid. To his amazement, sitting in the box was a stainless-steel Rolex Submariner. He asked, "Is it real?"

Helga frowned and asked, "What do you think? Are you real is my only question?"

Realizing he had hurt her feelings with the slight, he said, "I didn't mean it like that. I meant, I don't know what I meant, but I do know that I've never received anything like this from a woman and especially one as beautiful you. Listen, I'm just overwhelmed by the gift. I appreciate it, but more importantly I love you." They began to kiss and the rest is history.

At dinner Vincent couldn't keep his eyes off his magnificent gift. He asked Helga, "What on earth drove you to honor me with such a gift?"

She looked at him for a minute or so and then said, "I am honored to have you as my lover and I hope this is the beginning of an incredible journey through time and space. Just be my hero and not my pimp."

Vincent's eyes filled with tears and Helga decreed, "No Vincent, not now, and not here. You just got out of the infirmary for that. Let's grab a to-go bag, watch the sunset, and discuss anything that concerns you. But not here, my love."

In the cabin, Helga said, "I'm tired of those old martinis. Can we have a real drink?"

Vincent asked, "What would you consider a real drink?"

"Cruzan Rum and Coke," Helga responded.

Vincent said, "I know a lot of people who drink that and my love that is a perfect segway into a discussion that I would like to have with you. I'll be right back. How strong do you want your drink?"

Helga murmured, "Depends on what you're about to tell me. Just kidding, make it mostly rum and two dashes of coke."

Vincent turned and said, "That's exactly how I like mine."

When he returned, he said, "Once again, I am just bewildered by the gift and I thank you with all my heart." He leaned over to where she was sitting and gave her a salacious kiss and gently rubbed her right leg down to her knee. He sat down and smiled at his new toy.

Vincent continued by saying, "What I'm about to tell you is the God's honest truth. I can't believe how this matter happened and how we met. I cried myself into dehydration after thinking about how much you mean to me."

Vincent took a swig of his drink and said, "When I picked you up in my Uber, all I could do was just stare at you. I felt strangely close to you as you sat in the back seat and looked out of the window. Now, I am enjoying a cabin with you in the open ocean and pretending that you and I are married. I'm loving every moment of this event. I'm going to cut to the chase and give you some startling information. However, I will preface everything with one fact, and that is I am deeply in love with you."

Helga said, "Wait a minute. Are you going to tell me that you like guys better than you like women?"

Vincent laughed and asked, "Girl, do I make love to you like you're another man? Absolutely not. I love you for who you are and who my heart feels is good for me in the long run. No, dear, I am not gay. However, I am a Beckmire."

Helga's eyes opened wide and she replied, "Not funny."

Vincent asked, "Would you like another drink? I need one before I tell you the real deal about me."

Vincent returned with the drinks, toasted Helga, and asked, "Where was I?"

Helga immediately replied, "You were at the point of assuming someone's identity that I was supposed to dispose of after gaining knowledge of his fortune. And, Vincent, everything I told you was the truth. I really didn't like the fact that you used a target or nemesis to make a joke about."

Vincent sighed and said, "Helga, I apologize for minimizing the information you gave me and in a sense, making fun of it. However, what I said before is the absolute truth. Zanthius Beckmire DeLombardo is my half-brother. Your oldest son is Jelani Latinmire, the child that you and my half-brother gave life to is young Ben Jr., named after my father."

Helga sat with her eyes wide open and listened to this unbelievable story summing up a part of her life.

Vincent slowly attempted to move closer to Helga and she hauled off and slapped him as hard as she could. She then exclaimed, "I should have known that this was too good to be true. I trusted you, Vincent. I gave you everything that I have as a woman. You lied to me. You led me on. You knew that this venture was going to end with someone going overboard. I'm going to go and get my own cabin and hope that I never in life see you again."

Vincent yelled, "Wait a minute. Are you the same woman who was going to find me, torture me and find out how to access the diamond mine that I allegedly own? I'm sorry, is this the same woman who, after obtaining that information, was going to dispose of me like a piece of rotten meat? Listen Helga, I'm all in this relationship. I know that ex-pope and his people are going to eventually find us and save us the trouble of killing each other. I'm all in. I want to either live loving you, or die trying. I've never met Zanthius, your son's father and my half-brother, and I certainly didn't know about Jelani until I hired people to kick his FBI ass. Now, I'm here with you on a cruise in the middle of the fucking Atlantic Ocean and telling you with all my heart and soul, that I love you, I never want to be apart from you and if that's not good enough, I'll jump into the fucking ocean and I assure you, you'll miss the one thing that you have never experienced in your life."

Helga asked, "What in the hell might that be?"

"True love, Helga. True love, for if my death is a testament to my love for you, then so be it." Vincent opened the clasp on his brand-new watch, took it off, and sat it on the table. He then said, "Helga, I thought we could work this out, especially since you and I both tried to kill my parents. How sick is that? I thought I could convince you how much you mean to me and how much I love you. However, even I must admit that this is the most bizarre situation that one could ever imagine, and that is also quite unbelievable. I only ask one thing of you and that is to tell me that you love me, or watch me go for a final swim."

## CHAPTER TWENTY-FIVE

Prior to dinner, Larry saw the Sarge working Courtney with moves that would suggest a late-night rendezvous. He said, "You people are the spirit of this group. I mean you're always trying to get into each other. I consider that an admirable trait and one that parents should try to model for their children. Dear Dad, when you have a moment, I would like to discuss the arrival, in small numbers, of people who are interested in taking over all that we have accomplished and assumed. Their movement is targeted on our master as well as our individual systems. So far, they're just gathering information, smoking weed that can be smelled a mile away and acting as if we don't have a clue that they are near. I spoke with my sister earlier, and she said that the mechanized systems are online but haven't been tested."

Larry continued, "So far we're winning this battle because they're in place and they haven't made any aggressive movements. Their snipers are in view and we have two weapons targeting them as we speak. What's disheartening is my conversation with Kenzo. He suggests that we become barbarians and do a lot of decapitations and severing of bodies. Sorry Mom, but we're about to be attacked by people who like abusing women, barbequing children and doing whatever else that is sordid to their victims."

Courtney suggested, "Well, big guy, since they're going to disturb your only encounter of the week with me, I suggest that you play their game and be as contentious and malicious as possible. You know, no holds barred."

The Sarge looked at his beloved and said, "Why Doctor Beckmire, I thought your objective was to save as many lives as possible."

Courtney chambered a round into her weapon and said, "On the night that my husband is supposed to do some dastardly but pleasurable things to my body, well, anyone who interrupts that opportunity will receive no hall passes from me."

Later, the Sarge asked, "Has anyone seen my daughter? As long as those people are in place staring at us, at any time we can send a hail of bullets their way. I want to check in with her and see if she invited our friends from mid-America."

Larry indicated that he had not seen her but had asked their extended family to come visit. He stepped away from the group and called Rashida's cell. Juan answered it and asked, "Who dares to call my beautiful, beloved mother of my children and wife to the king of my castle?"

Larry said, "I suggest that you leave those drugs alone, my friend. Where is my sister?"

Juan replied, "She is where every good married woman should be, in the arms of her beloved husband."

"Please, prince clown, let me have a moment with your wonderful wife and mother of those brilliant children of yours."

Rashida came to the phone and asked, "What's up, bro?"

"I made contact with our mid-America families. I was wondering if you heard from them?" Larry asked.

"I had people picked them up and they should be at the post office outfitting themselves. Why don't you check with Clyde and see if they're there?" Rashida requested.

Larry responded, "Who is watching the operations center?"

"Bernstein and Brown should be in there. Why don't you take a walk over there and make sure those two are watching the perimeters and not playing with the Formula racing game?"

# # #

After arriving at the turnoff, Clyde called ahead to Larry and indicated that he and his group would be outfitting in the post office parking lot. Larry acknowledged and indicated that the intruders were slowly making their way towards houses. Clyde asked, "How do you want to position us? We can drive down to the first turnoff at the other property and continue for a few minutes and then off road the vehicles. Oh, and if Rashida is listening, tell her the wife has some high-flying drones with space age lighting. I know it's not my call, but are we going to give them fellas an opportunity to take their wares and try and sell them somewhere else, or are we going to be downright devilish?"

# # #

After handing off the information to the Sarge, Larry said to Kenzo, "Come on let's take a walk over to control."

Kenzo responded, "I smell curry being cooked, do you?"

Larry sniffed the air and admitted that he didn't. Kenzo announced, "Before my old gang would make a mess of the enemy, they would cook curry to gain their strength, determination, and agility. I think by mid-night, you're going to have a shitload of drugged and deluded people trying to sneak up on you and cause a problem."

Larry responded, "Stay right here until I come back."

Larry reported the information to the Sarge, who saw John Lee and asked, "Do you smell anything strange in the air?"

John Lee looked at the Sarge and asked, "You don't be smelling that curry cooking over yonder?"

The Sarge said, "Give the silent signal for people to prepare for an incursion. Kenzo indicated that before they did their work, they feasted on curry for supper."

Not simultaneously, but every 60 seconds, everyone received a text message indicating that this is not a drill. Cover your appointed areas with calm. Meaning, don't alert the enemy that we know they're out there but to go about business on a as usual basis, everyone must carry a pistol.

When returning to Kenzo, Larry asked, "Do I have to restrain you for fear you might want to join your brothers?"

Kenzo looked at Larry straight on and replied, "They are not my brothers, my friends or even my acquaintances. They were my opportunity to avenge my mother's death. I fight with you and this group. No one knew the meaning of the smell of curry or how they fight and what they would do to the weak and defenseless. I've seen these people go to work and when they finish, it is clearly a bloodbath."

Larry responded, "I'm going to have a quick discussion with my father. He reads people like a spirit. If you're on a mission against us, I can only wish you a speedy demise. Hopefully, one day, you'll be able to visit a place where time is of no essence, spirits walk amongst us and live to tell stories of the olden days. I personally like you and believe in you, but before I give you a weapon, I need approval."

Five minutes later, the Sarge, Ms. Beatrice and Larry approached Kenzo. The Sarge said, "Mr. Kenzo, this is Ms. Bearice."

Ms. Beatrice reached out and shook his hand and felt the warmth and sincerity in the man's heart. She said, "Nice to meet you and I look forward to speaking with you soon." Ms. Beatrice turned and walked away without saying another word.

Larry chambered a round in his weapon and handed it to Kenzo. Larry requested, "Don't hurt yourself with this thing."

Kenzo smiled and said, "I'll try not to. So, who was the little lady that shook my hand? Her hand was hot and dry."

Larry smiled and said, "If you're lucky to do the right thing then I'm sure you'll meet one of the most fascinating people you'll ever have the opportunity to greet. She is as pure as the driven snow and as wise they come. Yes, Ms. Beatrice is quite an anomaly."

# # #

The Sarge ordered everyone to put their ID badges on. He called Rashida and told her to reach out to Clyde and the others to make sure that they didn't enter the property without IDs. In the meantime, he summoned Larry and instructed him to outfit Kenzo and to add him to his barn-and-beyond-detail.

Larry handed Kenzo a medallion and said, "Son, if you lose this, then I want you to do only one thing and that is to keep your ass as still as possible and play dead and I do mean play dead. What you're about to witness is without soul, heart, love, or consideration and it will leave you dead. Don't try to guess what I'm talking about. Just do as I ask and that is to play dead and stay motionless until I find you."

As the members of the team pretended that the evening was coming to an end, they entered their units, turned on the lights, and turned on their TV sets. In reality, they armed themselves with the requisite weapons and proceeded to their assigned points of coverage. The children were in the tunnel, and all personnel were waiting on the word to engage.

John Lee said to Jilkes, "I feel rusty at this here thing. We ain't done nothing like this in a long time. How you be feeling?"

Jilkes announced, "I've never heard hesitation in your voice before, is there something going on in that empty head of yours that you need to tell me about?"

John Lee replied, "You be such a butthead at times. I don't know how I've been tolerant enough to keep you around me. You be pushing that pencil, and I advise you to be a little more beholden to me."

Jilkes replied, "Pushing the envelope not pencil."

John Lee with a huff asked, "Why you got to be right all the time. You ain't no Einstein. You just be Jilkes and you ain't all that smart. People just like to say that you're smart because they don't like to be hurting your minority ass's feelings."

A transmission came across the lines and it was a *Benauijuu* announcement on an open channel that the prey was turning in for the night.

Jilkes said, "Now that's a cousin of yours, announcing over an unsecure channel that we're shutting down for the night. Are any of your relatives smarter than you?"

Anel interrupted the two men and asked, "Do you two people love each other?" There was a sudden quiet and then a turn towards what was relevant.

Jilkes, said, "We usually don't allow people to get involved with our discourse, but I must admit—and I'm sure John Lee will agree as well—he is me and I am him, and I suggest that you never again try to interpret what's going on between us."

Quiet continued in the tunnel when Rashida's voice came over each earpiece and stated, "Staging is beginning. They're looking in Jame's barn and house. On the western front, there are 25 dots on the horizon and on our most vulnerable eastern front, there are 33 identifiable objects. From the road and at James's place heading down the road, it appears to be their main force. They seem to be abandoning their vehicles and are making the trip by foot. Clyde, are you and my other family members in place and what is your strength?"

"Roger that!" Clyde exclaimed. "We're in place and our Minnesota family members are placed high over the eastern front and my other people are covering the western front. Your soft point is where the horses hang out. There be 26."

"Roger that, is my girl with you?" Rashida asked.

"Can't leave home without her," Clyde announced.

"Do all those boxes have labels on them?" Rashida inquired.

"We ain't crazy.   We packed that first before we considered underwear."

"Listen, you all know the sounds change random. Keep an ear open and thanks for coming to assist your fellow church members."

# # #

In the barn, the bales of hay were stacked six feet facing the front door and off to the side. Behind each bale of hay was two thick metal plates, portholes, and 180-degree firing option. In other words, it was a sweep of both automatically operated weapons and individually fired options.

From the road, the main forces of the *Benauijuu* could see the lights from the main house and the guest house illuminated. One of the leaders of the group kept flashing a closed fist every 20 to 40 yards, requiring his forces to freeze. His men began to ask each other, "What's the big deal?"

He summoned his other commanders and said, "This smells like an open invitation to hell. Are we sure we did enough reconnaissance on this place and these people? How can they act so carefree knowing that they are highly valued targets? I don't like the smell of this thing. I'm calling it off until more reconnaissance can be conducted. This seems like a bad fucking idea. Look at that place. No one is stirring about and all we see are lights, TVs playing, but no people."

A subordinate asked, "Perhaps we should send a couple of our people to scout the place out further. We're here on their land and in position to do what we do best."

The commander looked at him and asked, "Are you attempting to assume control of my command?"

The guy lowered his head, but then another person spoke up and said, "He's not, but I am." The next sounds that anyone could hear were puff, puff, puff!

The next transmission made to the group was, "Red Six is down. Blue Nine is in custody. Proceed to your positions but do not engage unless absolutely critical. We will take a position inventory in ten, until then lie with the sheep and remain quiet."

Twelve minutes later, the new commander stated, "This is Blue Nine, is there any activity that seems suspicious? Report by groups?" First to report was sniper group SN2, and the senior in that group said, "We've been here 1.5 days, no concerns here."

Commander section EB1 (eastern corridors), reported, "Deer walking, not spooked." WB2 (western hill range), commander stated, "No concerns here—we're right below SN2."

The new self-appointed commander arrogantly responded, "At my mark, set time to 10:30. Mark!"

The new commander then ordered the snipers to eliminate anyone who was an obvious target that wouldn't set off an alarm. He told the forces in the east and west to get within thirty yards of the houses. He indicated that his group was approximately one mile away from target facilities and at the half-mile mark, he would hold position, recon resources and set an advancement time.

Larry paused and recalled what Kenzo had told him and on the open channel said, "These people will hurt our children and our women. Their deeds have been defined and demonstrated and therefore, no quarter is to be given to anyone who is on this farm. No acknowledgement of the white flag, no parlay, and no surrenders. This is a final mission for either us, or them. Now, I say this without the sanctions of the Sarge, but unless he over-rides my edicts, then our plan is mortal, terminal, and unforgiving."

Without hesitation, the Sarge chimed in, "I agree with the field commander who just gave us our marching orders. According to a former member of the attacking group, they abuse women to death and they stake out children and barbeque them. They practice cannibalism. Just to add yeast to what Larry has stated as our marching orders, I also want to add this tidbit to what has been decried by our field commander. If you run across a wounded invader, do not hesitate to conclude their existence. Their dying wish is to take as many of us with them as they possibly can. Watch out for grenades and other explosive devices. Oh, and Clyde, station a couple of people in the barn at Jame's place. I'm expecting an official government cleaner to assist us in the removal of the garbage."

## CHAPTER TWENTY-SIX

On the balcony there was abject quiet. Forget the roar of the waves, the churning of the engines, or anything else for that matter. Helga sat intensely quiet, as Vincent toyed with the guardrails on their balcony. He broke the tomb-like silence by saying, "I can find a steward and request a separate cabin if you so desire. Listen, how was I to know that you were hunting me when I first picked you up? I must admit I heard a rumor that a woman and two associates were looking for someone named Beckmire. It just so happened that I was there when you picked Frank up. I took pictures of you and your associates and sent them to the dark web. It stated that you were killed in the Four Seasons Hotel on an island some years back. As I studied the pictures of you from then and now, I became fascinated by the fact that you were reported dead, but yet here you are. Your two cronies were easy to discern, they had long rap sheets for everything that is dumb. Anyway, I decided to abduct you and really make sure that your ass was dead. However, when you opened the door to my Uber and placed one leg in, I knew that I had to watch you because you were apparently trained in self-defense and I was suddenly defenseless. What really got my dander up was when you innocently smiled at me. It was at that point that my entire game plan changed. If this is too much information and you want me to leave, I will, without incident. Shall I continue with my story, and if so, do you mind if I fix myself a small drink to calm my nerves? Would you like one as well?" Helga violently shook her head in the no position.

A few minutes later, Vincent came back with a healthy drink and continued by saying, "You came looking to kill me. I came playing a game to capture you to find out why I was of interest to you and then perhaps kill you. Aren't we a loving couple? I didn't know anything about the alleged diamond mine located in a certain quadrant that my mother had purchased for me in the Outback and frankly don't believe that it's true. So, as I see it, our meeting was not based upon false premises or nefarious intentions. It was based upon chance. Since then, I have moved away from the history that will destroy us. You made a decision to retire from being your master's lap dog and to go on this adventure to escape his tentacles. I decided to go with you because I found the invitation to be with you too compelling to turn down. As I was trying to say earlier, when you entered my Uber, you captured your sought-after victim, but it was his heart. When you gave me that natural smile of yours, I knew that I needed to find a way to be with and within you. I found myself being as silly as I could be because I just admired everything about you. I love the way you love me physically, I admire how we play with each other's hands and I feel oh so secure when I am asleep with you, because my mind and my heart are at rest. Lady, I love you and even though it didn't start off on the right foot, at least there is a window for it to continue with you having my back and me having yours."

Meanwhile, Helga was silently weeping and recalling all of her failed relationships where she was just a thing for exploitation and fulfillment. She reconciled the fact that with Vincent, even though she really wanted to kill him because of his treachery, she knew that this was the first time in her life that she felt as though she was a partner. She loved Vincent for loving her but was so afraid that whatever he was running away from could eventually impact the relationship as well as her feelings. How ironic, she noted that the very person that has been exceptionally good to her, is the same individual she was assigned to corrupt and eliminate.

Helga whispered, "I would appreciate an extraordinarily strong drink if you don't mind. I have a lot of soul searching and purging to do at the same time. However, I am requesting that you stay near the railing."

Vincent returned with two strong drinks. Helga asked, "So you're a Beckmire, the brother of Zanthius Beckmire DeLombardo, the uncle to Ben Jr. who happens to be my child and stepbrother to Jelani, my other son? So, tell me Mr. Wizard, how the fuck does this play out? I want my baby Ben, I love my son Jelani, and I'm just wondering, how does this all turn out?"

Vincent took a huge swig of his drink and said, "In biological terms, you had sex with my half-brother and that union bore a child. Sometime, way before you had sex with my half-brother, you met and excited someone else and that, too, resulted a child. You were a Catholic nun, but your resolve was to give birth to both. Now, you're in the middle of the Atlantic Ocean and it is agreed that you had sex with another Beckmire, although, conception is uncertain at this time. Listen, Helga, here's the deal. If you pledge not to kill me during this voyage, then I assure you that I will love you as long as you will allow me to. This I can emotionally agree to because in my heart and soul I've never cared for or enjoyed a person of the opposite sex as immensely even though you were tasked to conclude my very existence."

Helga immediately responded, "My goal was purely business. Your objectives were deception, captivation, chicanery, information gathering, and termination."

Vincent approached Helga and she urged him to back away. She stated, "If you come to me with games, then come to me on your knees and engage me until I scream I can't stand anymore. That, my friend will be your punishment for deceiving me and encouraging me to take this long ocean voyage so that you could neutralize my animosity towards you and every other Beckmire, except that fucking Zanthius."

The two toasted, hugged, kissed and Vincent went precisely to where he was directed to go to seal the deal. After salaciously kissing Helga's lips, he dropped to his knees and began to provide heavenly orgasms under the glow of the full moon. No words were spoken, she felt loved, he felt exonerated and they felt the full force of love as partners.

# # #

After a full night of making love, swearing that they loved each other and acting as if they did, Helga woke up and said to Vincent, "In order for us to live without looking over our shoulders, we're going to have to make some tough decisions and I think the sooner the better. Listen, lover boy, there is a tremendous bounty out on your ass and the entire church community is probably going to issue a capture order on me.

If they kill me on sight, close to $300 million gets locked up for what will initially seem like an eternity, providing revenue for the bank and banker in charge of the accounts, but ultimately and indirectly, becoming a part of my children's portfolio. No, they won't kill me, but they certainly will do some dastardly things to that magnificent body of yours to convince me that I should spare you pain and dismemberment, by giving them the codes to the accounts that I changed. Now, that's current and foremost on my side of the equation. You know you have something that they want and they will stop at nothing to obtain ownership of those quadrants in the Outback. Overtime from the analysis, that mine should bring in excess of a trillion dollars over its lifetime. The mine that the Aborigines own is probably worth half trillion. Now that's a lot of potential money to fund various nefarious activities. In summary, they will execute you and attempt to terminate your family as they have tried in the past. This time it will be an all-out effort and every single person—men, women, and children—will be slaughtered. Since they had me searching for you, I know by now they've probably commenced actions against your people. Ironically, I have two children in that camp and for a moment I thought that they didn't matter to me because I didn't matter to them. That was my excuse in order to accept the consequences."

Helga continued, "I would at least like to try to save my children. Meeting you and falling madly in love with you has sparked a better vision for all who matter to me. At one time everyone was expendable, but now, after feeling and witnessing the power of love, I don't want anything to happen to them." Helga began to cry.

Vincent gathered her up in his arms and whispered, "I'm having the same kind of thoughts about my parents and their friends. I used to hate them because they were not representative of who I thought they should be and therefore, I placed them in a subservient role of making sure that my education was paid for on time at that prestigious institution I attended. I developed schemes to kill them and to assume all that their clan had amassed. I was not concerned about anything other than the outcome and women, men and children would have to be terminated if I were to achieve my objectives. How sick was that? Anyway, our time together has made me realize the value of life and that the only permanent riches are those stored in the bank of 'Family First and Love.' If that rumor about the mine in the Outback, its value and my ownership is real, I would gladly give it to those chasing you to gain our freedom to love freely and eternally without having to look over our shoulders. I know it has only been a millisecond in the scheme of life, but you and our relationship, have created a different Vincent."

Vincent paused for a moment and then announced, "I would like to one day look in my mother and father's eyes and beg their forgiveness. I would like to hold my mother in my arms and tell her that I was not a good person and that I beg for clemency. My heart and soul ache knowing that I tried on many occasions to connect with many disreputable groups to achieve my objectives only to now realize that my father and his people are the ultimate messengers of death. However, what makes me smile and want to live life to the fullest is you, my love. We have shared our dark, dark secrets and seemingly want to move on with each other throughout what time remains for us."

Helga asked, "What is this seemingly mess? Dude, I'm in this 100 + percent."

Vincent smiled and replied, "I going to love every minute of being your mate. Do you think we should get married?"

CHAPTER TWENTY-SEVEN

Clyde called the Sarge and asked, "Are you guys cooking curry? There is a strong smell of curry up here near the road."

The Sarge responded, "Can't smell it down here, but would immensely appreciate it if some of your people would investigate, evaluate but not terminate."

Clyde responded, "Roger that."

Clyde pointed to three senior citizens and four agile young men from Minnesota. He whispered, "I smell curry cooking and we ain't been invited. Check it out, but don't engage unless all and I do mean all targets are sighted and a guaranteed quiet demise is possible. I don't want a gunfight before people try to surprise our family down there and create havoc in response. If it ain't a clean and silent termination, then back away. Remember, we ain't supposed to be here."

Gilda with her hands on her hips, exclaimed, "Clyde, do you want to sleep with the horses when we get back? Boyfriend, I have a drone that can determine how many there are and where they are positioned."

"Honey, I'm trying to impress you with my on-the-ground-skill set. Okay, baby, can you fly that high-flying drone over that area northeast of here?"

Gilda sucked air between her teeth and said, "Clyde, do we have to have a long conversation after this night is over?"

Clyde quickly responded, "Not at all dear. I just made a tactical error. Don't worry it won't happen again."

Gilda called Rashida and told her that she was going to launch a highflyer with a lens that can read the license plate on a car. She stated, "If you lock your systems into the coordinates that I will text you, then you'll be able to view where those cockroaches are hiding on the farm."

Rashida replied, "We're hot over here. Send your scope high up and we'll be tracking heat waves from both sides of our electronic defense system."

Gilda replied, "I'll be hot in 45 seconds."

After both systems were ready, Rashida cautioned Larry with the following message, "Hey, bro, at the back entrance to the barn and less than a quarter of mile away, there are a significant number of heat signals. I'm guessing 30 to 40. I ain't got time to dissect the number but heads up. Do you think you'll need some additional support?"

Larry considered both outside and inside support and replied, "If the automated system doesn't clear them out, then I'm sure we can handle what's left."

In the curry cooking area, 50 to 60 dots appeared on the screens. Other heat waves were reflected throughout other parts of the farm.

The Sarge walked into the control center and asked, "How's my favorite daughter?"

Rashida smiled and said, "You only have one daughter of record. Should we be investigating your time off in other parts of the world?"

The Sarge replied, "Just like your mother. Anyway, where are our weak points and are all systems ready to deploy?"

Rashida whispered, "I didn't have time to sight the automatic weapons in with live ammo and I didn't personally inspect each tranche. In lieu of that, my assignments are strategic and will cover the area the systems are responsible for."

The Sarge commented, "I never liked that automated mess, but it has saved us on many occasions. How about the barn? Do we have enough coverage there?"

Rashida replied, "I spoke to Larry and told him that they have about 30 to 40 bandits hiding within a quarter mile of his position."

The Sarge paused for a moment, and said to Rashida, "I'm investing a lot of humanity in a person that I don't have a clue about. Don't we have two automated systems in the barn?"

Rashida smiled and said, "I am truly your daughter and Larry is your other son. I gave him a tracking medallion. You know one that has two beams and two weapons pointing at the person using it at all times. Any disconcerting movements towards a medallion-carrying person and the weapons will not fire. It is completely reliant upon AI. I know, that's a lot of faith in an entity that is all numbers and symbols. However, Dad, I'm not going to make my brother an easy target."

The Sarge hugged her and said, "You and Larry make so much sense to me and your mom. I love you and your brother so very much and you guys are such a blessing to me and Courtney. Let's get prepared to send these assholes back to hell!"

# # #

On a secure line, the Sarge said, "You know who this is, and it's been a long time since we've had to relate to this theatre. In this play, here are the following guardrails. The devil is in the house and he has decided that since we are a believing people then we should be easily compromised. Therefore, there will be no parleys and no sympathy equations. Instead, there will be complete mayhem, automatic and manual, total annihilation, and total disrespect for the dead. There will be systematic decapitations and all other evil thoughts that come to your mind. I know, you're saying and trying to decide if you will follow this new edict. The people who are lurking in and around our farm have decided to do what they want with our women, violate our children, hang our heads on sticks and most savagely, barbeque children on rotisseries while they are still alive. Now, people that is beyond and below what Lucifer himself would do. We are Christians, but I am asking you to momentarily place your faith in a basket and inflict vile and demonic pain and death onto our enemies. Tonight, I ask you to play in blood!"

Clyde looked at Gilda and the members of his group and asked, "Is it possible that we can join in prayer? Our leader has asked us, for good reasons, to abandon our normal beliefs, our deities, and our souls. He has asked us to engage our enemies without discretion or humanity, but instead with total damnation. That means he's requesting that we do to them what they would do to us, without any considerations or discounts for age. Listen, a while ago I watched the devil blow the ranch into oblivion with my family members inside. There was nothing left but rubble. Larry insisted that we dig until we discovered bodies and thank God he had the foresight to demand that. Anyway, a long story made short, we are being asked to set an example of what happens when you come for us. Frankly, I've asked the Lord for forgiveness every day since these people showed up and rid us of carpetbaggers that fleeced and had some of us murdered. If we didn't cooperate, our bodies would be involved in some contrived accident. People, I'm a man of God. I practice, pray, preach, and believe in our Father the Lord Jesus Christ. Having said all of that, this is my plan of action; I'm going to ask the Lord to forgive me for my sins, but I'm also going to desecrate the enemy beyond anything that I've ever done. I have killed for this family and this family has terminated for me and my community. I'm going to wreak havoc on any and everybody that has come here to this farm to hurt my family members. If the ask is too heavy for some of you, then at least make sure that our backs are protected."

# # #

Larry asked, Kenzo, "How do you turn people into animals?"

Kenzo replied, "You corrupt or accuse a family member of stealing and then you enslave their children and husbands into a work-off situation. In the interim, you feed them, give them the opportunity to violate people and surprisingly, over time, you've just developed a small army that is international in scope."

Larry proclaimed, "Wow! The people who are planning to attack us—is it fair to say that some are your friends?"

Kenzo looked at Larry and replied, "Not fair at all. I was determined to achieve one goal in that gang and that was to execute the man who shot my mother. They are like wild dogs, they feed off each other's hideous acts. You know, to see who can do something worse and better. Larry, you gave me a weapon. I hope it functions because these people need to be eliminated totally and then actions against their international group have to occur. This activity tonight will determine how they respond in the future. If you don't massacre every individual on this farm then you're going to face double the number the next time around. Mr. Sarge was correct when he said that there should be no parlay, no sympathy, because the people coming for us will do the most unthinkable things to survivors."

Rashida announced that there was coordinated movement from the east, west and north. The barn contingency had held fast. She also said, "Please make sure that your ID badge is on you.

After hearing that, Kenzo asked, "Why the emphasis on ID badges?"

Larry looking through night glasses, responded, "In about ten or so minutes, I'll explain what is going down. In the meantime, check to make sure those weapons you have are ready."

Kenzo looked at Larry and asked, "Are you telling me these are live weapons?" Larry smiled and said, "Just don't miss the incoming targets."

Rashida called out the positions of the groups, and was continually told by the Sarge to "Hold." She replied, "Dad, are you inviting them into the farmhouse?"

He chuckled and replied, "Hold."

Clyde and his group fanned out to make it virtually impossible for anyone to flee through their position. Before his people began to spread out, he said, "This is an ungodly group of people and we have to make sure this cancer is operated on until it's all gone."

The Sarge said calmly to Rashida, "Please clean both east and west positions on my mark. Fifteen seconds later, the Sarge calmly announced the word, "Mark." Puffing sounds filled the air as men and women were felled by the unseen enemy, *Mechanized Mayhem*. Target after target received terminal rounds that tore through their false armor.

As the sounds began to cease, Rashida said to the Sarge, "People are beginning to move towards the barn." She called Larry and told him to expect company in a matter of minutes.

John Lee said to Jilkes, "Now when them there people be running up in and near the barn, you make sure you keep your minority ass behind the bales of hay. Last time we be here, your ass got shot. I don't think I can carry your big butt anymore."

Jilkes looked at him, and asked, "Did you take your meds today? You seem to be a bit cranky."

The incursion by the *Benauijuu* members lasted a little more than fifteen minutes. After Rashida engaged the mechanized systems by the barn, 57 people were put out of their misery. Kenzo proved to be an experienced warrior and executed many of the people who he once commanded. He said to Larry, "I have mixed emotions and feel as though I'm a traitor or something along those lines. I have vivid pictures in my head of these guys and girls butchering kids, cooking them, and then eating them. I have cried many nights and I'm feeling a purification of sorts, because there is no room in the world for people like them. I'm so sad to have been a part of it, but I had to work off my mother's so-called theft. Anyway, are we going to canvass the area?"

Larry responded, "Never at night. We had a situation like this one in the mid-West, went searching for the enemy in the dark and three of our people ended up in the hospital. Naw, never at night."

Clyde called Rashida and indicated that three huge trucks were flashing their blinkers on the main road. She called the Sarge who in turn told her to have Clyde's people check the vehicles and have someone escort them down the road. The Sarge said, "Our friends on the hill are lending us those units. I hear they're incredibly special and efficient in that once in, everything is decomposed to its essence—nothingness."

Near daybreak, non-barking dogs led the recovery team to those who needed packaging. It was swift and efficient when the dogs made a discovery, they would sit until it was acknowledged and tagged and then they would move on. If there were many victims in the same vicinity, the dogs would stay until all were tagged.

Rashida called Clyde and told him that images were moving his way. Gilda at the same time stated, "We have non-friendly people moving in our direction." Clyde alerted his team, and everyone was locked and loaded.

Ten minutes later, four face-painted or tattooed individuals walked into an area where 12 weapons being pointed at them. Clyde proclaimed, "Drop your weapons now or die a horrible death!" The individuals complied with his demand. He then told them to back up two paces, turn around, get on the ground, and lock their fingers behind their heads. One of the individuals decided he would turn around and ask a question and he was shot six times by the group. Clyde then remarked, "That is an indication of our resolve. You will follow our commands to the letter or you will be shot dead like the vermin you are."

Clyde called Rashida and informed her that they had captured 3 prisoners— what should he do with them?"

Rashida saw her dad and said, "Clyde has three prisoners, what should he do with them?"

He thought about what Kenzo had said and knew that there were a lot of deceased individuals on the property. He said, "Bind them tightly, blindfold their eyes, turn them around and around and have three of your people march them towards the farm. I'll have people waiting to receive them in about ten minutes."

Once in the barn, John Lee, Jilkes, McArthur and Montomie waited in long rubber aprons, boots, and gloves for the individuals to be delivered to them by Anel, Angel, Jong, and Chakes. When they arrived, Chakes said, "Hey, people, the Sarge will be here shortly and if you want to practice your skill sets, by all means go right ahead."

When the Sarge arrived, he looked at the prisoners and asked, "Is there anything I can get you? Would you like some water?" Everyone in the barn looked at him as if he had lost his mind. The prisoners cocked their heads as if they couldn't believe what they hearing.

One of the prisoners asked, "May I have some water?"

The Sarge replied, "Absolutely!" He went over to one of the stalls, picked up the hose, ran it for a few minutes, crimped the hose in the middle to slow the flow, and placed it on the side of the man's mouth. The woman next to him asked for water as well as the third man and they were all given water.

After the drinking session, the Sarge asked, "Are you guys and gal hungry?" There was no reply and that's when the Sarge said, "I'm going to ask you some questions and I would appreciate a truthful reply. Now, what was the purpose of this attack? I mean, what did you expect to gain by killing and torturing my people?"

The woman replied, "I know you know that you're holding damn near a trillion dollars in bearer bonds."

The Sarge asked, "What is your rank in the *Benauijuu*?"

Surprised that he could pronounce the name, the woman said, "Like most here, we are foot soldiers. Our leadership was decimated by a machine gun over on that hill. However, I am senior amongst us. I know that you have the bearer bonds because the ex-pope brags about your dutifulness and your faith. We are also interested in a mine in Australia that your wife purchased for your departed son. We have a lot of information about you and we now know that we must prepare much better for our next assault on your clan."

The Sarge asked, "You do see these people in aprons, boots, masks, and gloves don't you? They're not here to bathe you. No, no. My dear, they are going to butcher you people into small pieces. So, I don't think you'll be a part of any future events against us."

She smiled and replied, "I didn't mean to insinuate that we would be in the next wave, silly man. We already know that you're going to kill us."

The Sarge continued by asking, "What is so unique about the mine in Australia? We are a part of lots of mines there. Why the emphasis on something my wife bought our son, who is no longer of this earth?"

The woman smiled at the Sarge and said, "One of our disciples, who builds electric cars and rockets, saw an interesting phenomenon from space on one of his trips. After magnifying and doing some other stuff that I don't understand, it was predicted that within those coordinates that your wife purchased for your son, there are stones that are bigger than baseballs and a motherload that can't be calculated. Don't worry, our people are staging that area as we speak. However, this event, sir, boils down to bearer bonds. I am only repeating fourth-and-fifth hand rumors that I've heard."

The Sarge asked, "How can you be so certain that your associates are going to be successful in Australia in their attempt to steal something that is recorded all over the world?"

The man sitting beside the woman, whispered, "Shizukani Shiro," in Japanese which means "shut up!" The once talkative woman no longer had a word to say.

From outside the stall window, Jong yelled, "He told her to shut up. He must be the leader."

The Sarge told John Lee and Jilkes, "Take his ass outside and cut his fucking legs off at the knees." He turned to the woman and said, "I can set you free and give you enough money to hide out for a lifetime—all you need to do is make me smarter about the *Benauijuu* and tell me where I can find the head of this snake."

The woman lowered her head and murmured, "I must obey my husband as long as he is of this world."

The Sarge retorted, "I can fix that. Be right back."

The Sarge called Larry and told him to come to the barn with Kenzo, straightaway. Five or so minutes later, everyone in the barn heard people shouting in Japanese. Kenzo screamed at the man who was furthest away from the woman.

His words were clear, "You killed the man who tried to save all those people and you took control to move up the ladder."

The man replied, "Yeah, I killed that piece-of-shit who shot my father."

When the Sarge walked outside, he said, "I need that woman's husband dead, now."

Kenzo announced, "He is not her husband. He's her lover three days a week. This one is the husband."

The Sarge replied, "What a fucked-up situation."

Kenzo asked, "Do you want them dead and if so, do you want me to attend to it?"

The Sarge, as he started to walk away, said, "This is so dysfunctional. Take care of this mess."

Kenzo chambered a round in his weapon and said, "I hate wasting two bullets on you rapists, child molesters, and sadistic assholes. He lined them up, fired a round into the first man's heart that entered the second and then quickly placed a shot to the head of the first man, that entered the second man's head. Before hitting the ground, they were both dead.

## CHAPTER TWENTY-EIGHT

"Chapel of Love." That was the song that was playing when Helga and Vincent entered the balloon-filled chapel and swore their love and allegiance to each other. They purchased gold rings from the ship's store and presented each other with a symbol of their commitment. Prior to the service, Helga said to Vincent, "I've done a lot of despicable things and I'm not happy about them. I just want you to know that I will give you my life and all that I have in the hope that we will share a marriage that is meaningful and with purpose. This is all so sudden."

Helga continued, "I, Helga Spengatsenburg, will love you until the day I die. All I ask is that you make a similar commitment to me. I've never been genuinely happy until now. Vincent, if there is an ounce of doubt in your head as we proceed to legally tie the knot, then please let me know. I know that I will never be able to find and love a person like the way I love you."

Vincent knew where she was going with her comments and announced, "I've never loved anyone in my life like I love you, including my own parents. I am telling you that when you entered my Uber and gave me that smile, my entire life changed. I ran away with you because I was lost, without meaning, sick in the mind for trying to do dastardly things. That day in my Uber, my world, my thinking, my realizing what love is, became obvious and immediate. I never had doubts about what I felt for you. I had concerns about how to tell you who I am. In the scheme of things, when I placed that gift that you gave me on the table, I was moments away from being lost at sea. Helga, I've never considered marrying. I have never considered the notion of love and I sure as hell have never thought that I would be a captive and a student of honesty, emotions, and love. You are all that I need and want in this life and the only eyes I want to see before I die are yours, my love. Please love me as much as I love you."

They embraced for a long time before Helga announced, "I'm older than you. Are you sure about this?"

Vincent shook his head and stated, "If I were marrying an age, then I would be in my old mindset. I'm marrying the only person that has ever prompted me to show feelings, commitment, and love. Helga, don't go with the artificial, stay with me and help me expel my demons as I intend to help you with yours. Artificial numbers are just what they are."

The captain, asked, "Is this a matrimony of convenience and idealism, or a marriage of the hearts?"

Helga looked at Vincent and he responded, "This marriage is the real deal, based upon truth, admiration, and love. No, sir, no hidden doors, and no unintended results, in this union."

In the meantime, Helga was shedding tears of joy, appreciation, and love. She whispered to Vincent, "I was so happy to become a mother, but my feelings about this moment and you, are on par with motherhood. I'm so happy and I pray that we find our center, enjoy being individuals and love for eternity. You've made me the happiest woman on the planet."

Vincent lowered his head to hide the tears flowing from his eyes and replied, "This is the best moment in my life. Nothing comes near the joy that I'm feeling. To be with someone I can care for and love, and who I'm simply mad about, now that's heaven. I love you babe!"

# # #

Later in their cabin, after sharing some champagne, Vincent reached behind the lounge chair and handed Helga a medium-sized box. Excited, she asked, "What is it? It's rather large, what is it?"

Vincent responded, "Helga, open the box and see for yourself." After opening the first box, Helga found another box that she demolished in a flash and then she saw that there was still another box. She looked at Vincent, and said, "I hope I don't have to terminate you on our wedding night." Inside the next box, there was yet another box. Helga began to laugh and then cry and that was when Vincent went into his pocket and gave her the lady's version of the watch she had given him.

She fondled the watch and exclaimed, "I didn't know I meant that much to you."

Vincent laughed and said, "Now, that we're married, you mean that plus one trillion more." Vincent excused himself and said, "I'll be right back, my love."

Vincent entered the cabin and secured his toiletry bag. In the bag, his blue pills were well wrapped and secured. He gathered a full-sized blue pill, swallowed it, and flushed it down with water.

Back on the balcony, Helga was setting her watch and silently praying for a never-ending marriage, hoping that Vincent would soon take her and make wicked love to her.

When he returned to the balcony, he had two moderate size glasses of Cruzan and Coke. The newlyweds toasted each other and made humanly possible commitments, not flighty ones. Vincent said, "When I went into the cabin, I made us drinks, and I took a little blue pill, because I want to make love to you until I can't move."

Helga asked, "So, do those things really work?"

Vincent replied, "I think they are more for people with ED and those who are just fucking."

Helga asked, "Which one are you?" Vincent laughed and responded, "None of the above. We had an intense union last night and I want to travel to the moon with you tonight. Honey, make no issue of this, because I am telling you what I did. I will not start my marriage off by lying to my wife. I'm just making sure that I keep it real with you and I hope that you do the same."

A few minutes later, Helga announced, "It's been such a stressful day, I think that I'm going to call it a night and look forward to being with my husband, not my lover in the morning. This is incredible and a thing that I have never known. Good night, my love." She started to walk away but turned around and said, "Vincent, I want you so bad, just hold me, fondle my body as I play with yours and then I want you and that little blue pill to act like you're at work on Sunday when they pay triple for overtime."

# # #

In two days, the ship was initially due to dock in Valencia, but it made a wide turn to port to avoid a massive storm that was rolling ships around. On the second night of their marriage, Vincent and Helga talked about the things that they wanted to change in their lives moving forward.

Helga said to Vincent, "I would like you to promise me one thing and one thing only."

Vincent replied, "Anything, my love."

With tears of joy and sorrow in her eyes, Helga announced, "I would like to kiss and caress my two boys before I die."

Vincent stared long and hard at Helga and replied, "As long as you promise—Helga aggressively interrupted him and announced, "This isn't a quid pro quo request. This is something that I desperately want to do before I die. Let's not start off with if you do, then I must do."

Vincent cut her off and asked, "Helga, are you through?"

She smiled and replied, "It's tough to piss you off, isn't it?"

Vincent shot back, "Not really, but as much as I love you, I doubt if you'll ever have the opportunity. May I finish what I was about to say?" Helga nodded yes and took another swig of her drink. Vincent acknowledged, "Your boys are an integral parts of my parent's clan." He paused and Helga could see his eyes begin to fill with tears and immediately Vincent went into the wheezing, sniffing, and unable to catch his breath mode that she had witnessed before. She jumped up, ran inside, and hit the emergency button on the wall to summon help.

Four minutes later, the emergency team entered the cabin and found Vincent on the floor in a bad way. They placed a mask over his face and the flow of oxygen followed. They place Vincent on a gurney, strapped him in, and proceeded to take him to sick bay.

# # #

Twelve hours later, Vincent began to stir and cough, and he asked the same question as the last time—"Why am I in restraints?"

Helga replied, "Honey, please don't think about anything that may cause you to cry. When you start crying, it becomes a violent battle from within."

Vincent asked, "How many days have I been here?"

Helga smiled and said, "Baby, it's only been 12 hours. Not like the last time, because when you started coughing. I knew right then and there that I needed assistance. I ran into the cabin, hit the emergency button and your loyal associates were here in record time to assist. Before we leave, we'll have to give those people significant appreciation gifts."

Vincent turned slightly in the bed and began to cry again. Helga said, "I beg of you to stop crying. I love you so much and it hurts me to see you in such turmoil from trying to say that you're sorry. Listen, I get it. Just tell me what it is you want to do before you die?"

Vincent jerked around to ascertain the nature of the last statement and Helga said, "I cut you off after telling you that before I die, I want to embrace my two children."

Vincent took several deep breaths and slowly exhaled each one. He then said, "I just want to state the facts. I have been a part of groups and I have even led some of them to kill my parents. Think about it. I tried to have my parents killed so that I could consume all of their earthly treasures. How about this as a kicker? You and your masters come along later and try to accomplish the same damn thing. And, as a nuclear kicker, you have two kids living in their domain and one is by my stepbrother. Now, how fucked up is that? I say that to say this, I want to see my parents, beg for their forgiveness, hug them both and disappear from their lives forever. I need closure as well as you do. Helga, no matter how convoluted the associations and the by-products are, you're now my wife and my life."

After a moment of silence, Vincent suggested, "Heck, perhaps we can have our own family or at least adopt a ton of kids and give them a great and caring life."

Helga crying her eyes out, sitting next to the gurney, whispered, "Vincent, I love you so very much. If you mean what you just said, I would like to try to have another child and if that's not in the cards, we can adopt a few. However, we need to make a settlement with my ex-employer and believe me, he will agree to anything to get those codes, but as soon as he does, he will wipe our DNA off the planet. I don't trust him and I've seen him make promises to obtain his goals and then turn around and terminate entire families. He is a monster. However, his brilliance or lack thereof, can be his downfall. We just have to be strategic in planning how we turn over his illicit fortune to him, if at all."

Vincent, who looked as if he were in another world, announced, "Honey, you can give him the codes with the proviso that each withdrawal has to use another code that only you have. That's an easy fix and one that even I can instruct you on how to create it using binary calculations. This is something that I can construct and require an active security code for as long as our DNA naturally lives. We could even hold a percentage out or a limit and state that it's insurance money. I know of a group that has been in existence since the beginning of time and they will collect on policies issued, no matter who the insured is. They will collect on any human being living, no matter their status."

Helga looked at Vincent and replied, "You have so many talents, but the only one I'm interested in is the one where you just make me your everlasting priority."

# # #

Back in their cabin, Vincent asked, "Do you think we can ever be forgiven for our sins?"

Helga smiled and said, "Even the Anti-Christ was forgiven. Why would it be any different for us? We played the game, failed, joined forces, and saved each other. Love and discovery are two powerful things, my husband. I came looking for you to torture you and to take what was yours through force and here we are months later married, talking about children and wondering how to ask for forgiveness for those bad deeds that we both executed. I think that we'll get through this together, maybe not as we might want it to be, but in the end, we'll be together under the same tree and hopefully with some little ones running around. Oh, and Vincent, that would make me the happiest person on earth if we could have children naturally or adopted. What do you think, at minimum, a boy for you, and a girl for me?"

Vincent hugged her and said, "Sounds homey to me, my love."

CHAPTER TWENTY-NINE

A crony of the ex-pope, placed a generic message on the dark web that asked, "Has anyone seen my disturbed son who keeps trying to kill me? He's a very bright person, a graduate of the Naval Academy and is known for his disdain towards his parents and their friends. When I use the word disdain, I'm sure there must be another term for children who try to kill their parents. People think he's dead, but I'm not sure. This message is from those who seek the truth."

Kenzo saw Larry at breakfast and humbly asked him to meet him outside once he finished his meal. Kenzo made a protein shake and hurriedly left the dining area.

After Larry finished his meal and attended to his wife and children, he said, "I'll be right back." Once outside, Larry asked, "Why are you acting like there is a bomb in the dining room?"

Kenzo responded, "I know those people in there are suspicious of me and I guess I'm a little paranoid as a result of defecting from the *Benauijuu*. I keep looking on the dark web searching for information about my treachery."

Larry asked, "Do you feel like a traitor for saving a woman from being raped repeatedly and then violated even further? I mean, listen, everyone is cautious of newcomers. Chill out and let them gravitate to you. Don't go and try to make friends and the only person who should feel indebted to you is afraid to completely acknowledge your efforts to save her from humiliation and perhaps death."

Kenzo asked, "Can I have an honest conversation with you about that? I mean, I got an assist from her."

Larry asked, "What does that mean?"

Kenzo said, "Please, can we take a ride around the property and make sure that my former comrades are no more?"

Ten minutes later, Larry handed Kenzo a vest and said, "I'm not sure if the place has been cleaned thoroughly. So, just in case there are sleepers out there, put the vest on, and grab two AR-15s for you and me with four sleeves.

As the two made their way up the road, Kenzo said, "Can you pull over there, by that big oak tree?"

Larry asked, "Did you happen to bring your ID badge with you?"

Kenzo replied I did not. Are we in danger?"

Larry laughed and asked, "What's that we shit, Tonto? I got my badge on."

Kenzo asked, "Should we go back and get my badge?"

Larry hit his walkie talkie and yelled to Rashida, "Hey, Sis, I'm out here with Kenzo and he's without his badge. Send a drone high into the heavens to keep us safe."

Rashida responded, "Larry, I put a drone in the air the moment you left the dining room and by the way do remind Kenzo that there are at least five weapon stations targeting his ass and do tell him not to breathe too hard because two stations are AI controlled and work on heart rates and sudden changes in composure."

Larry responded, "Rashida I love you, but I trust him with my life."

Rashida blurted out, "I don't trust nobody with my brother's life."

Kenzo asked again, "Larry am I safe?"

Larry responded, "As safe as I am at the moment. Tell me about that assist that you received from the lady that you were protecting."

Kenzo stated, "This may all be conjecture or my imagination getting the best of me, but when I announced to my comrades that she was not to be touched and demonstrated that she was mine to be, I carefully ran my hand up her dress with my fist closed and tried to only touch the surface. She then locked her legs on my hand as if to suggest that she desired my touch and whatever came next. She then looked at me in a salacious manner before unclenching my hand from under her dress. One of my lieutenants slyly winked at her. I thought it was a sign of disrespect to my edict that she was mine but then it all started to become clear to me. There perhaps were two signals being given—a scandalous desire for attention and the other was that her husband was in cahoots with a member of my team. It just seemed too easy to walk into an underground bank without resistance, gather the bank president, escort him home to gather his apparently waiting family and then return to the bank to attempt to transfer sensitive codes for certain accounts. This whole fucking thing seems contrived and orchestrated to me."

Larry thought about what was said and asked, "So wait, who the hell are you accusing of being the loose light bulb? Is it the wife or the husband?"

Kenzo looked hard at Larry and without hesitation said, "The wife is warm, sensuous and in need of love instead of manipulation. I think the meek and mild-acting husband is deep in the bowels of this deception. That's my take, but let me also color it with honest human information. Larry, I like the woman and I saw in her eyes a gleam that I hadn't seen since my mother was alive. That woman is in a world of hurt and I think her responses are tailored with the knowledge that her husband would kill her and his own children if she didn't play this game. Listen, Larry, we're talking about close to three trillion in bonds, collective assets, and land in the Outback that is loaded with the alleged mother lode of diamonds. Okay, Larry, according to my rough math and without using an abacus that's $3 trillion in potential assets that are up for grabs after the demise of your clan. Let me be truly clear, I don't give a shit about money, I got what I wanted when I killed that asshole who shot my mother in the head in front of me, who laughed and said, "She was a thief and not a good person."

Larry after suggesting that they take a walk, asked, "What is this nonsense about my brother being the owner of a diamond mine? Zanthius has never mentioned anything about a diamond mine."

Kenzo replied, "I wasn't referring to Zanthius. I am talking about your other brother, the Sarge and Courtney's blood child, the one who went to the Naval Academy and who audaciously attempted to kill his entire blood line to inherit all that there is."

Larry fired back, "Last I heard he was very dead."

Kenzo responded, "If that is for certain then why did the ex-pope send people around the world to locate and secure codes from him? I'm not sure that what is announced and accepted is correct and/or accurate. I've seen my ex-associates create stories, multiply the results and not back down from affirming the accuracy. That other Beckmire may still be alive and the likelihood of his existing is greater than 70 percent. That means no DNA, no confirmation of body, ashes and descriptive information is available. You see how the bad shop the untrue and win elections? That new guy lied his way back into the White House through the use of negative stories, misinformation, forecasted disasters and false statements about horrid acts by immigrants. I don't have empirical evidence, but I do know that there is a strong surge in activity to find out whether or not your other brother is deceased. We're talking about trillions of dollars, that's a lot of moolah."

As they sat behind trees with drones monitoring their every move, Larry asked, "Are we talking about the same Beckmire that tried to kill everyone in this clan?"

Kenzo announced, "That's exactly who is at the epicenter of one of the trillion-dollar buckets. You know that Beckmire had his eyes on a single prize and didn't know of the fact that he was the sole owner of land in the Outback that would net him more money than he could use in a hundred lifetimes and that is so perplexing to me. If your mom secretly purchased land that is allegedly where the mother lode is, then why would he want to kill his people?"

Larry responded, "I believe you just answered your own question. People are unstable, greedy and if you think about it, how sick are you to hire people to kill your parents so that you can gain another trillion in assets, if in fact what you say is true. I'll have to ask my mom about that."

Kenzo asked, "Do you think we can head back? I really don't like all these woods and trees. I damn sure don't like all the different noises that I'm hearing but I ain't seeing a damn thing."

Larry laughed and said, "Okay, scaredy cat. Here you are used to doing despicable things to people, but you're afraid of being in the woods. Let's head back and not a word to anyone until I speak to my dad and query my mom."

Later back in camp, Larry saw both parents sitting on a bale of hay on the front porch. He asked, "Are you people okay?"

His dad responded, "Your mom is feeling sad about your other brother. She has been having dreams of him almost every night."

Larry grabbed her hand and kissed it. He said, "Without your love and guidance, I don't know where Rashida and I would be. However, I need to ask you a very pointed question."

Larry paused for a second and then inquired, "So, Mom, did you buy land in the Outback for your other child?"

Courtney jerked around as if she had seen a ghost and exclaimed, "Oh, my Lord! Larry, only your father knows about that. How on earth did you find out about that?"

Larry asked, "Guys can we talk in your room and perhaps have a drink?"

The Sarge asked, "When did you start drinking?"

Larry said, "I'm going to have a drink tonight because a lot has been spoken about in general but without closure."

The Sarge said, "I need to hear what you've been able to find out from your new best friend."

Later in his mom and dad's room, Larry announced, "This world is too small. The new White House guy's best friend, you know the one who owns that electric car company and records anomalies from his spaceship, is also in to much more than he acknowledges. One of his discoveries allegedly turned out to be, he and others think, the mine you purchased for your other son. After doing analysis after analysis, it looks as if there might be in excess of a trillion dollars' worth of diamonds in the quadrant. Here's the scary thing, Kenzo said, that the ex-pope's people are scouring the earth looking for leads to determine if my brother is dead or alive. This loss of life on the farm was a function of trying to turn you people into scarecrows or something. I know, apparently, they didn't do their homework. People are looking for my brother to take that mine from him and they will come at us full strength next time to conquer all that we have accomplished. Dad, I know you always say keep your enemies close to you, but it seems to me that Kenzo is like your Dempsey, Hood, Anel, Angel, and Michael. I trust him, but I've trusted before and got my feelings hurt."

Courtney sighed and said, "I dream that he is alive and he is calling out to me. I feel it in my bones and I pray that I get to see him before I die. You and Rashida have been more than you'll ever know to us. The big guy worries about you and even had Rashida fly a drone while you were walking with Kenzo with him in its sight. We live a precarious existence and if something happened to you and your sister, I would simply not want to live any longer. You've given us meaning, family, love, and trust. I still recall our formative days when you and the Sarge took out the garbage in Philly. I owe you two a lot, more than you'll ever know."

Larry said, "Mom, you and Dad pulled us out of chaos and placed us in a family, but Dad likes mayhem and here we are."

The Sarge said, "Larry don't be going there."

Larry said, "Guys, I think you need to hear this from Kenzo and make up your own minds about the validity of what I may have embellished."

Courtney looked at the Sarge and asked, "Do you want to go back in that mindset, Honey?"

The Sarge said, "Honey, I want you to have as much information about what terrible parents like us, who tried to raise a brat who was influenced by people who didn't pay a nickel for his education, are."

Courtney responded, "Obviously, you're still pissed at the way he treated us."

The Sarge murmured, "That's stating it mildly. However, Honey, this might be cathartic for you. Let's hear what that pirate has to say."

Minutes later, Larry found Kenzo and told him that his parents wanted to speak to him.

Kenzo asked, "Why do they want to talk to me?"

Larry responded, "Because you may be able to bring closure to them in terms of their son."

Kenzo responded, "He tried to liquidate them. That seems like enough closure to me. My only goal in life was to kill that guy who shot my mother and made me watch. Knowing that your child tried to kill you on multiple occasions seems like continuous bad dream."

Larry said, "I caution you about upsetting my mother. You handle the information truthfully and direct and leave his actions and your interpretations out of the equation. If you put my mom on the edge, that would be a deal-breaker and probably your death sentence. Listen, don't fuck this up."

When Larry and Kenzo appeared on the front porch, the Sarge had some beers in a cooler waiting for them. The Sarge asked, Kenzo if he would like a beer and he replied, "I'm still on duty, sir."

Larry looked at him and asked, "What's that supposed to mean?"

Kenzo, in a military manner, responded, "You've not given me permission to drink, Larry. I was assigned to you and you're my overlord."

Larry uncapped a beer and handed it to Kenzo who stared at Larry. Larry unfamiliar with this behavior said, "Kenzo, have a beer." Kenzo continued to stare at Larry. Larry finally said, "Drink the damn beer man."

Kenzo guzzled the beer completely down, belched, apologized, and said, "That was amazing. Mr. Sarge and Mrs. Sarge, do I have your permission to speak freely? Larry told me the outcome if I blow this."

The Sarge asked, "What did he say to you?"

Kenzo looked at Larry, who responded, "I didn't ask you the question, my father did."

Kenzo asked, "Do I have your permission to respond to any inquiry asked of me?"

Larry said, "Absolutely."

Kenzo began by stating, "This is all about Trillions of dollars." Kenzo expressed the nature of the bank situation and the appearance of an orchestrated arrangement. He spoke of how the wife of Jong's nephew clinched his hand under her dress as he demonstrated to his men that she was not to be touched. "One of my people winked at her as if he were aware of the scam. Kenzo stated, "I don't have empirical information, but it seemed too easy to conquer the bank president, escort him home and apparently gather his waiting family for the ride back to the bank. It all seemed contrived."

He then said, "It is alleged that the bonds that you took from a certain dictator are supposed to be worth billions, but they are actually worth just south of a trillion, if not more. As I indicated before, each bond had a kicker, an exponent acceptable on the open market at face + value. That's the first trillion-dollar scenario. The second occurred here on this farm just yesterday. Collectively, previous leadership valued your individual and group assets of a trillion. The third trillion is the mine that you purchased for your other son, Mrs. Sarge. Ex-leadership is full of knowledge about these things and the value of properties, directly and indirectly owned."

Courtney asked, "How do you know so much about what leadership wants and knows?"

Kenzo calmly responded, "I was allowed in regional meetings that discussed the various assets boxes that your group and others have. What is more important about this conversation is that, as we speak, there are people scouring points on the map looking for DNA and any other confirming data that would tell the truth about the status of your son. I'm sorry Mrs. Sarge, but some think he's still alive."

Courtney began to cry harder and the Sarge stated, "That'll be all for now. Larry, catch up with me later. Thanks."

As the two men started to walk away, Courtney asked, "So, Kenzo, are you a true friend or a chameleon?"

Kenzo dropped to his knees and responded, "I watched a man shoot my mother. I avenged her death. I'm ready to die for my sins, but I assure you, that there are no schemes, untruths, or games being played by me. I heard things and all I did was repeat what was said. I am no Judas—I'm Kenzo, loyal and honest."

# # #

Near the pool, Larry and Kenzo enjoyed telling tall tales to each other. Larry brought it back home and said, "I hope you weren't bullshitting my mother. That would really strain our relationship and it would check in as a zero or non-existent. I can, without harm, let you leave now and the next time we meet on the battlefield, it will be you or me that lives to see another day."

Kenzo looked at Larry and recounted, "I've only lived with vile people who were recruited as a result of some alleged crime committed by a parent or a spouse. Listen, Larry, I'm happy at both ends of the spectrum, dead or alive. However, if alive, then I want to live a righteous life, not the one I just left where I killed people at the behest of other people who were without character or values. I was taught that the only thing that I needed to know was that I owed the bank and until it was paid off through blood and sweat, I owed my being to the *Benauijuu*. If you'll completely accept me, then I'll do all of your front-line work with pride and joy. What I said to Mrs. Sarge is true, I'm not a Judas, I am loyal, honest, no games, no schemes, no dual masters, just you and the group, Larry."

After a few minutes, Larry asked, "How do we discreetly investigate your hunch about the wink and the clasping of legs around your hand?"

Kenzo replied, "Larry, I prefer not to be the one to try to determine that. As my former men lusted over her, she looked at me for salvation. I never took my eyes off hers until she released my hand. I kinda jerked my hand away because I felt strange from that interaction."

Larry cut him off and asked, "What does that mean?"

Kenzo replied, "I think it means that I care for her. I've been with many women of the night, but I've never felt a closeness like I did when I marked her as my property. I know that's not a good way of expressing it, but I felt—I mean, I don't know what I felt, but I just felt weak from looking at her. Larry, my men would have violated every aspect of her being, over and over again. I've seen them in action."

Larry shot back, "Are you saying that you've never joined in the fray?"

Kenzo smiled and responded, "Not once, never considered it and I used to cry for the victims, because they were going to be passed around like cards."

Larry said, "Okay, back to Jong's nephew's wife. Do you think she's the culprit that led your group to us?"

Kenzo quickly responded, "No, I don't. I think her sister is the link. I think the woman was telling on her husband without telling if that makes sense. She had hurt, need and love in her eyes Larry. I don't want you to think me a fool, but I saw what I believe was love for me in her eyes. It was magical, but my problem is that I've never known love before, just completion and dismissal. In those nanoseconds of my hand being under her dress and purposely trying to avoid all aspects of her anatomy and my eyes never blinking away from hers, I felt something that I've never felt before. I don't have a damn clue, but I know I felt something for this woman."

After a brief pause to take a drink, Larry said, "I think we should circle back to that question. What is intriguing is your use of the language and your seemingly considerable knowledge of finance and values. You've been living with heathens according to the way you describe them and yet you seem knowledgeable about a lot of issues that common pirates wouldn't know about. Are you an educated man?"

Kenzo thought about the question and then asked, "What do you mean by educated? Do you mean institutionally trained and learned? If it's that one, then the answer is absolutely no. While my people were raping and pillaging, I spent my time learning to read and I started with coloring books and then anything that I could find that had words in it. I then started listening to audiobooks, music and following along with the words. Once I finished with an audio book, I found a year-old copy of *The Economist*. From that magazine, I learned finance, interest rates and the GNPs and other financial matters of every economy in the world. My ex-leadership were pretty much thugs, they could read, but they couldn't discern financial things that they read and therefore, I was invited into meetings about global issues and the caretakers of bonds from a dictator that were miscalculated. Anyway, I became a *Benauijuu* Rhodes Scholar of sorts. No awarded degrees, but a plethora of knowledge that common thugs couldn't understand. They needed me and I needed them to get near the man that shot my mother in her head in front of me and accused her of stealing."

Larry asked, "Would you like something a little stronger than beer?"

Kenzo responded, "If you're going to have a drink, then I would like to have one as well and to continue this understanding session."

Larry shrugged his shoulders and stated, "Understanding session, ha. Nicely framed. Let's go and get the real stuff."

Later, after having two drinks each, Larry announced, "My wife is going to come looking for me any minute. It's been informative and clarifying and tomorrow I'll get you a room in the guest house, but for now, take your ass to the barn. In the saddle room there is a pull-down bed. Put on the heater and sleep well my friend."

Kenzo dropped his head and stated, "You called me your friend. I will make sure that you know that I am who I am and worthy of being considered a friend by you, Larry. Appreciate you. Good night."

CHAPTER THIRTY

It was announced over the ship's broadcasting system that the vessel was approximately 36 hours away from docking in Valencia, Spain. All the requirements for disembarking were explained along with a ton of other issues.

After hearing the announcement, Vincent stated, "Honey, it does not feel like we've been at sea for over 14 days. All of a sudden, we have to head back into the stealth mode that we haven't discussed. Any ideas as to how we should proceed once we have to leave the ship?"

Helga laughed and said, "Don't worry, love, I've been attending to things while you were in sick bay, and/or otherwise, under the weather. I found us a nice Air B&B, facing the water in a historic part of town. You just enjoy the ride, baby, I got this matter under control."

Vincent asked, "Do you think we can have an out-of-cabin dinner tonight or do you think it's too risky?"

Helga paused for a moment and then replied, "We've crossed the Atlantic Ocean and more, and with the new facial recognition systems, I'm sure my ex-employer is searching the world for me. No, baby, I would rather have dinner in the cabin, with a nice bottle of champagne and then make love to you until you're comatose. What about that?"

Vincent asked, "Do you think that you'll ever get tired of me?"

Suddenly the mood changed and Helga inquired, "Are you getting tired of me already? Is our lovemaking beginning to bore you? What can I do to solidify our marriage and our lovemaking?"

Vincent gathered her up in his arms and said, "I'm only going to say this once. Without you, I don't want to live. With you, I want to live until I can live no longer. I love you more than life itself. Helga, I will repeat this over and over again. When you entered my Uber, I became dizzy and discombobulated. I was used to just having sex with women. I never saw a woman that created havoc in my mind and body until I met you. Baby, I will love you until the day I die, because you are the most important person to me on earth. I will admit that I'm now feeling terribly guilty about my plots to murder my parents and that is why I need to beg for their forgiveness before I die. Don't get shaky on me now, I'm with you and our marriage until death do us part."

# # #

That night, Vincent and Helga shared a piece of prime rib that was big enough for three, with garlic mashed potatoes, asparagus, clam chowder soup, a Caesar salad without croutons and two bottles of champagne.

Afterwards, Vincent said, "That was some meal and it was with the most beautiful woman that I have ever known and loved."

Helga kissed him and said, "I have to use the loo, be right back."

Vincent slouched in the chair and began to feel the results of those three glasses of champagne. As he dozed off, Helga opened the sliding doors and stated, "My husband, I don't care what you need to do for this session, but I need you to take care of your new wife and I want it to be up against that railing, until I yell for Jesus. After I conclude, I'm going to drop down low and hopefully give you the best head that you've ever had."

Vincent half asleep, jumped up and said, "Baby, I'm yours, do what you want to me."

Helga revealed what was under her negligee and said "Husband, enjoy the taste of your dessert."

After the two completed their desserts, supported by the railing of the balcony, they ventured inside for a night of restful sleep. Vincent, unbeknownst to Helga, swallowed a little blue pill and was almost ready for another session. He said, "Helga, I love you so much." He rolled over on top of her, they started to kiss and the magic began again.

The next morning, they both decided to go to the gym and enjoy stretching sessions with CADI C, a woman who was accused of being the best stretcher on the high seas, and easy on the eyes. They each had a 30-minute session with her and they were amazed and convinced that this activity should follow them for the rest of their lives. After the stretching sessions with CADI C, they had massages, sat in the sauna and steam rooms, and then decided to go to the pool. It was their first time entering the pool, when Vincent announced, "Honey, I don't like this idea. Too many eyes looking. Let's get a couple of Bloody Mary's, head back to the cabin and talk about our next steps. I mean where are we going to stay, how long are we going to be here, and everything else in between those decisions. I sincerely want to get on my knees, beg my mother and father for forgiveness, hug each one, and then disappear forever."

The mood changed considerably from relaxing to one of having to discuss options, timing, living arrangements, disappointments and other essential matters that were necessary to consider when the entire world is looking for you. Helga flopped down on the bed, sighed, and said, "I guess it's the real test of everything that we feel and honor. We both have tried to murder your parents and as a true test of my loyalty to the ex-pope, I was to sacrifice my children, unbeknownst to them. I think the first thing we should consider doing is making our way to them when they're in the Outback. The ex-pope told me how magical and spiritual it is there. I'm thinking that perhaps that is the place we make our apologies, say our farewells, and disappear into the night."

Vincent replied, "That sounds like the ideal place, but we can't disappear into the night unless we're going to give up the land that my mother purchased in my name that just so happens may be worth a trillion dollars, last I heard."

Helga responded, "That's not such a bad idea. It would show good faith on your part, but I don't think they want to be involved in the mining business beyond what I hear they already do, which brings me to another question in terms of assets, and just because you own a business doesn't mean you have to operate it."

Helga asked, "How much disposable income do you have, Vincent?"

Vincent shrugged his shoulders and said, "Like I said before, I have about nine million and some change. What about you?"

Helga immediately replied, "As I indicated before, that's a tough question and one that we'll decide once we figure out our next move, but as I told you when we first started thinking serious about a relationship, I know I have a good $80 million, and I believe in other secure accounts, I have $15 million, and the keys to another $300 million."

Helga paused and said, "If we're ever caught, they'll use you as leverage to get the codes from me. How much pain can you tolerate?" She laughed and said, "Just kidding hubby, just kidding."

Vincent stated, "Well, that doesn't seem like something I want you to joke about. That too is a matter that we should plan for in the event that it becomes a reality. We can devise systems that give temporary access and changes the codes in 120 seconds, and then you have to enter a secondary set of numbers or codes. In the final analysis, 24 hours later we can expect another set of codes before the transfer is completed. Anyway, we can set rotary, digital, and specific entrees to the process. So as an example, the bad guys slap me around and decide that they're going to eliminate my happy guy and then you yell, "I'll tell you everything, but I need a guarantee we won't be bothered beyond that day, or some shit like that. We need to put some basic protocols in place for these potential unforeseen contingencies, including announcing our insurance policies with a specific group in Northern Africa."

For the next eight hours, Vincent and Helga strategized about every conceivable situation that they would more than likely encounter in the future. They embraced and feared the worst based upon the propensity for violence of the people that they were up against.

Out of the blue, Vincent said, "I can't believe that you were going to fuck Frank."

Helga asked, "Have you lost your mind? If you ever see him again, ask him what my people did to his lame ass."

After a long silence, Vincent said, "I'm learning the role of being a husband and sometimes what is past is not necessarily prologue and I apologize for jumping over the curb in the middle of a strategic discussion. Helga, you'll have to humor me on occasion, because I've never been this close to any woman where I'm giving up my machismo and deciding things jointly. I would normally say, 'this is what we're going to do.' Babe, when I laid my watch on that table, my next move was jumping into the fucking ocean. I am that crazy for you, but believe me, I'll get better as I understand that we're a team, and I'm not the captain."

Helga replied, "I told you how I was used and abused, and never loved until you came along. Vincent, unless you're looking for sordid details, I was like a whore to the ex-pope. I'm not embarrassed, because now his ass can't access the stolen fucking money that he took from people. Speaking of poor people, we should consider a scheme where we give the $300 million back to the people. When we're caught, there will be no mercy, so, we might as well plan for a horrible demise, but with the knowledge that I love you and you love me."

Helga continued, "How and why does a single so-called religious person have access to that kind of money? He's a crook and so was I. We can take him to the cleaners and then figure out a scheme to give it back to the people. I mean that would clear some of the points against us as we enter Hades. What do you think? But wait, new hubby, I gave you the 911 and the 411 on me. Please believe me that after that ride in your Uber and watching you watch me, I lost my all to you and felt a sense of security that I've never imagined and from a complete stranger. You're all that I have Vincent, beyond my children who probably would hate me on sight."

Vincent gathered Helga up in his arms and whispered, "Please be patient with me. I'm learning how to love, a thing that I've never done before, including loving my parents. You're all that I have. I will leave stupid alone and move harmoniously with you into our golden years. I'm sorry, baby, for that outburst, but that too is a learning experience for me."

Between tears and apologies, the two managed to ruffle the sheets on the bed one more time. After an incredible interlude, Vincent suggested, "Why don't we prepare for capture as our first priority and develop signals for survival, such as codes that digitally change on the hour."

Helga said, "Baby, after making love for an hour, I don't want to do anything but go to sleep and think about the amazing man I met in an Uber, who was the man that I was hunting and who I fell head over heels for. My God is a good God, even for those who have violated all his commandments."

Two hours later, there was a hard knock on their cabin door. Vincent stirred first and looked for a defensive weapon. He remembered he had his Swiss Army knife. He opened the dresser drawer, grabbed the weapon, and placed a finger over Helga's mouth, indicating for her to be quiet. He went to the door and stated, "We indicated that we were not to be disturbed unless there was an emergency.

The cabin steward said, "I need you to open the door and accept these towels that I have in my hands and listen to what I have to say. I'm on camera and this is live. Open the damn door."

Vincent opened the door and the steward said, "We will be in port in approximately two hours. There is a lot of chatter about the people in the cabin next to you. I'll probably not have a job after this cruise, but you people have been extremely generous to me and I appreciate it. In exactly one hour from now, this wing of the ship will lose power for a little under three minutes. At that point you should gather all that is important to you, leave everything else, exit your cabin, turn left, and walk quietly toward the watertight doors that are approximately fifty yards from here. That door will be open. Proceed for 25 yards, turn left, and proceed for another 20 yards where a person in a server's outfit will give you further instructions. Make sure you have your passports and other identification documents?"

Vincent responded, "Of course, why do you ask and what is going on?"

The steward replied, "The people next door to you have been identified as being wanted on an international basis. It is rumored that they are left-wing European bomb makers who plan on blowing this ship to pieces once we're at port. You may not have noticed it, but we were boarded by the Spanish Coast Guard, two bomb squads and lots of police types. This is way too much information that I'm providing you, but I request that you remain calm and follow the instructions of the steward that's going to meet you."

As Helga was throwing things in her bag, the steward said, "You can only bring satchels, no heavy luggage, or other noise-making bags. This is supposed to be a stealth operation. In addition to being your steward, I am also part of the ship's security system. We've been watching them since the ship left port in Miami."

Helga, having been trained as a spy in addition to taking vows of celibacy with the church, put on her snoop hat and looked at Vincent in disbelief. Vincent asked, "Is this a drill, or is this real?"

The steward replied, "As real as real can be. Once you're escorted to the where the gangplank is usually placed, you'll see more people board this ship with uniforms and weapons. Yes sir, this is as real as you and I are."

The horn started blowing and the steward said, "It's time to go. Be careful and hopefully we'll see each other when this is over." Helga once again looked at Vincent and whispered, "This may be all about us. If so, remember our tentative plans about what we should do if captured. You never answered me about your pain threshold."

Vincent said, "I will die first before telling anything about you, my love. You can take that to the treasury."

# # #

After making the convoluted trip, Vincent and Helga were met by a steward in a white jacket who led them to a stairway, where other passengers were making their way. Helga announced, "I'm feeling a little better about the potential outcome of this event. However, the jury is still out."

As they watched the ship begin its docking maneuvers, they noticed six food trucks parked near where supplies are loaded onto the boat. Helga and Vincent's room was on the starboard side of the ship, and it was being docked to the port side. Vincent murmured to Helga, "I think we've been discovered. No matter the outcome, I've lived a lifetime in this short time that we've been together, and I will remember every moment until I can't."

Helga began to cry and whispered, "Ditto, my husband. So much life I lived and enjoyed immensely during this short time."

As they sat waiting for someone to flash credentials, they held hands and kissed. Vincent said, "In all my years of being around females, you're the first and only woman that I have even looked back at. I love you baby."

In the interim, six trucks were emptied of people in uniforms, including bomb squad members and other gun-toting personnel. As they entered the room where Helga, Vincent, and a lot of other people were being housed, Vincent attempted to stand up but was pulled back down in his seat as the person in charge said to everyone, "Folks, we'll have you out of here in a jiffy. Please be patient as we do our job."

Helga smiled, looked at Vincent, and said, "I'm going to have to school you about certain situations that when they are inevitable, sit back and relax."

A shaking Vincent responded, "There is so much to learn from you, my love. I was planning to go out as your protector and had set my mind on being the aggressor. OMG, what a disaster that would have been."

## CHAPTER THIRTY-ONE

The following morning, Larry grabbed his badge and a small caliber weapon and decided to go for a run up the road and back. Kenzo had already run slowly around the farm fearing drop-off points in the landscape.

When Larry came out of the farmhouse, he saw Kenzo washing out the horse's drinking tub. Larry approached him and asked, "What are you doing?"

Kenzo responded, "I'm cleaning out the horses drinking tub, it was full of algae and moss." Larry began to help and saw the caretaker coming up the hill in his four-wheel drive unit.

James said, "I was on my way up here to clean that thing out. I had a cold for the past few days and didn't get around to doing it."

Kenzo spoke to him and said, "If you don't mind, I'd like to finish what I started."

James said, "By all means but I do have one question. You didn't use any kind of cleaning solution to clean out the tub, did you?"

Kenzo smiled and said, "An idiot I have never been accused of being. No sir, I used fresh water, and that bristled brush I found in my sleeping quarters."

James said, "Oh, so is this some kind of penitence for you?"

Larry jumped in and announced, "Kenzo was the newest member of their group." The two men officially introduced themselves and James thanked him for lending him a hand.

Larry said, "I'm going to make a run up to the road. I'll catch you later."

Kenzo asked, "Is this some kind of mind-bending thing you're about to do, or is it possible that I can accompany you?"

Larry stated, "I was told that you ran around the farm earlier. Are you sure you can make it?"

Kenzo stated, "I see you have a small caliber weapon and your badge, let me get my badge and my .9 millimeter. It is awkward to run with, but I'll manage."

Larry laughed and said, "When we return, I'll get you an everyday piece to carry." Kenzo dropped his head and started to walk away.

Larry asked, "What's up dude?"

Kenzo responded, "I'm not used to freedom, choices, and gifts. This is all new to me, Larry."

As they started their run up the hill, Jilkes and John Lee were slowly running back from the road. John Lee yelled, "Hey Larry, who that there person you be with? Him be your new best friend?"

Jilkes joined in and yelled, "Me and my boy like him."

Larry slowed his pace and exclaimed, "Congratulations!"

Kenzo asked, "What did I do?"

Larry asked, "Did you have a chance to meet those two guys?"

Kenzo replied, "I did briefly, the devil and his disciple."

Larry said, "When we get back, I'll make sure that you officially meet them. Now, before and when you meet them, they'll probably be arguing about something or another. Whatever you do, don't jump in and don't take sides. They are like husband and wife until you penetrate their veil and try to offer solutions. They'll eat you alive and forever not trust or want to be near you."

Breathing moderately hard from running up hill, Kenzo replied, "There are a lot of dynamics in this group."

Larry responded, "There are not that many dynamics, but with those two, the drama can be huge. Just don't get involved even if they ask for your opinion."

At the top of the hill, they saw James, who said, "I could have given you guys a ride up the hill. All that exercise ain't good for you. You got to get you a good ole chair and watch more Fox News." Both men smiled, turned around, and started their run back to the farmhouse. As they talked on the mostly downhill run, Kenzo was on the west side of the road, and Larry was on the east side of the road. Out of the corner of his eye, Kenzo saw a flash and instinctively knocked Larry off the road and into a ditch. Larry yelled, "Have you lost your fucking mind?"

Kenzo replied, "Perhaps, but I thought I saw a flash out the corner of my eye."

Larry called Rashida and said, "Sis, I was knocked into a ditch by Kenzo. Can you scour the west side of the farm, preferably where those trees are?"

Rashida responded, "Stay down. There may be a few hostiles in the area. Did you trip and fall into the ditch?"

Larry hesitated but finally said, "I was knocked into it by Kenzo."

Rashida closed her eyes, took a deep breath, and said, "Larry, on the ridge on the west side of the farm, people are hunting on private property. Are you hurt?"

Larry looked at Kenzo and replied, "No, Sis, I'm in good hands. Send a vehicle up here for us, until we can make sure, that the hunters are not hunting the hunted."

Back at the farmhouse, after McArthur, Montomie, Anel, Angel, and Chakes, had secured the area and made sure that the farm was safe. Larry asked Kenzo, "Do you think you could have just pushed me aside, rather than tackling me full force?"

Kenzo whose head was already low, murmured, "I thought at the sign of the flash, the round was already on its way and I was sheltering you with my body. Sorry to be so aggressive, but it was instinctive and intentional!"

Larry asked, "Why don't you look directly at me and other people when you talk to them?"

Kenzo replied, "I have been working off an alleged crime of my mother's and I was taught to never look at the bosses straight on."

Larry replied, "I'm not used to people talking to me with their heads down as if they're talking to their master. I am your friend, so please don't ever do that again. However, if an opportunity to save my ass arises, me, my wife, my father, mother, my children, and the clan, will always be appreciative of your efforts."

Brown and Bernstein appeared up the road with two vests, two AR-15s, and four clips. Bernstein said, "Ladies, your chariot is here." He threw them two vests, and said, "Let's roll."

No sooner had he said that the sound of a weapon being fired echoed over the farm. The round hit Brown under the left arm in a place where the vest is reinforced from the double clasping of the Velcro adhesive. Brown slouched over in the vehicle and Bernstein began to scream. Larry called Rashida and told her that they were under fire and that Brown had been hit. Rashida tracked the vapor trail of the round and sent a drone to the area with a small explosive device, that acted more like a huge firecracker than a bomb, but with a stunning and paralyzing effect. Rashida wanted this person alive. She sent Dempsey and Hood to secure the assassin.

As Bernstein and Larry attended to Brown, their emotions overwhelmed their ability to provide life saving measures. Kenzo yelled, "Both of you move, stop hugging him and let me find the wound to see how bad it is."

Kenzo removed the vest, saw no blood, and realized that Brown was one lucky son-of-a-gun. Where the round had hit, there were two layers of Kevlar, but the impact probably broke a rib or two and knocked him unconscious. Kenzo directed Larry to inquire if it was safe to head back to the farmhouse with an injured Brown. Larry called Rasida, and she told him to get the wounded and head back to the farmhouse.

At the farmhouse there was a beehive of activity going on because Courtney was ready to operate on the fly. She had her emergency room ready for an intermediary response to the issues facing the wounded until he was able to be transported down the road to the main hospital. Smartly, Bernstein, Larry, and mainly Kenzo, provided the chest compressions to Brown that were essential to his survival. When they arrived at the farmhouse, Kenzo yelled, "He's unconscious but he has a pulse and there is no entry or exit wound. I repeat, no entry and no exit."

Courtney yelled, "I need him placed in that van, I need oxygen, an IV, and three essentials to provide support and protection."

Kenzo faded into the crowd and Courtney yelled, "Kenzo, get your ass in that vehicle and continue the compressions until I can take over." Dempsey headed for the driver's seat, and John Lee directed him to get into the passenger's seat. Jilkes looked lost, until Hood pulled up in another vehicle fully loaded with armaments and followed the lead van to the hospital.

# # #

After cautiously approaching the site from where the assassin made his shot, McArthur sent Anel and Angel to the right, Chakes and Montomie to the left and he would be the spoiler and head straight on, making as much noise as possible. When the group converged on the scene, the spotter was still knocked out, but the apparent shooter had escaped. The shooter was disoriented and began to make his way towards the pool and guest house. Rashida tracked a non-badge wearing person and fired rounds from the automated system to his left and to his right. The drone gave him precise instructions from above. When the group encountered him, he incoherently kept saying, "Kill the algae."

The spotter and the assassin were taken to the barn and placed in the first stall, hanging slightly off the ground, in an uncomfortable position. Mallory and Michael were in position to receive the intruders. As the men were stripped to the skivvies and doused with cold water at a relatively cold point in the day, Mallory said, "I know it's no use asking you guys any questions, so we're just going to torture you until there is corroborating information offered by both of you."

Michael opened the closet and cogitated about which weapon he was going to use. He kept pointing to one unit and then another, but finally decided on a Viking-looking relic, that when someone was hit with it, there were multiple wounds, and when it was pulled away, it would take a lot of flesh with it as well—much like an oversized fishhook, with three sides, to snatch flesh with.

Michael flipped a coin high into the air and pointed to the spotter. He said to the man, "I know you're a warrior and that you would probably rather die a horrible death than tell us what we want to know, so I'm going to hit you with all of my force, and see what body parts come back when I yank this thing out of you." Michael had a discussion with Mallory and flipped a coin high in the air again.

Michael handed the weapon to Mallory, who was smiling and murmuring, "I'm going to show you how to make a grown man scream until he is dead." He put on a long apron, placed a mask around his face, and then put on gloves. He said to Michael, "I suggest you put on a mask and an apron or watch from the saddle room, because this is going to be one messy ordeal."

He turned to the spotter and said, "God forgive me for what I'm about to do to this person." As if he was swinging a bat, he took a few warmup swings and without warning, cocked up to deliver a blow. The man screamed, "Wait, I didn't shoot anyone, I just spotted."

Mallory screamed, "That makes you a co-conspirator and you might as well had pulled the trigger. I'm going to rip flesh off your body."

He cocked up again, and the man yelled, "I'll tell you everything that I know. He's in charge of this mission and he can call 40 men to raid this farm. He is in charge."

Mallory said, "I don't give a shit about who's in charge. I want to know your goals and objectives, or my first blow is going to hopefully pull your body apart."

The shooter opened his mouth and said, "You're talking to a moron. He has no knowledge of anything that is going on. Hell, he doesn't even know why we're here or what's at stake. Listen, is there a chance that there might be a quid pro quo discussion? I don't want to be disfigured by that crude weapon. Tell me, are there any possible deals to be made?"

Michael approached him and asked, "What kind of information are we talking about being shared?"

The shooter smiled and said, "How about bearer bonds, diamond mines, and the entire assets of your group."

Mallory said to Michael, "Call the Sarge and request his presence."

#

At the hospital, Brown underwent a full body scan that failed to show any internal wounds. It showed a massive bruise under his left arm and rib cage. One hour later, the attending doctor realizing that bullet wounds required police investigation, stated, "Listen, you showed up to trauma care, we don't do bruises from hitting your side on a railing after consuming too many beers. Therefore, I don't see any reason to keep you here, unless you're in some pain that I haven't discovered the cause of."

Courtney looked at the doctor and said, "We appreciate your concern, and the services you and your team provided and as soon as we have a meeting, we'll contact you and see what the hospital needs that we can hopefully provide. I thank you, doctor and this inebriated individual will wake up tomorrow wondering what happened. We'll be on our way."

Back at the farm, Brown, who was on his way to his room asked, "Did we catch the s-o-b who shot me?"

Monica replied, "I hear they have some people in the barn for interrogation."

Brown started back towards the barn, and said, "I want to see the asshole that shot me."

# # #

Later in the barn, as the shooter was telling Mallory and Michael about the overall objectives and goals of his mission, Brown walked in with Bernstein, his stalwart friend. He walked over to the shooter and said, "I'm glad you're not a good shot."

The shooter looked stoically at him and replied, "I'm an excellent shot. I never miss and I never leave a target alive. In your case I knew that the vest you were wearing came together with double clasps that secured the front and the back. I didn't want to kill you, I wanted to put everyone on the farm under duress. I didn't think that you people were sophisticated enough to use a vapor-trailing unit to pinpoint the explosion."

Brown responded, "Two things I want to say. One, I'm glad your mission was not to kill me and two, when they finish with you, I going to show you what an old-fashion ass whooping feels like. I'm going to make it fair, and you probably got some skills, but even with my left arm under stress, I'm going to show you how we kicked ass in the Nam."

The man replied, "I don't want to fight you or anyone else, I'm trying to finish my sentence that was imputed to me by my father's crimes against the group, much like that traitor, Kenzo."

Brown replied, "I'll take that into consideration as I try to beat the living shit out of you."

The Sarge appeared and asked Brown, "If he had a chance to kill you and only injured you, don't you think you should reconsider some of that violence you want to deliver to him? I mean, the man said that he is an excellent shot and for that reason alone, I'm thanking him for not killing one of my brothers. I'm not trying to persuade you from your mission of kicking his ass but just remember, he could have shot you in the head and then one of us would have to take care of those mixed-race children and that wonderful, smart, and beautiful wife of yours. Just saying, man!"

Brown looked at the Sarge and then at Bernstein, who threw his hands in the air and said, "You know the Sarge is right. I would rather be a good friend than to have some stranger come along and petition for the job of new dad and husband. That would be terrible. Let's just call this one a draw. He had you in his sights, he shot you in the strongest part of your vest and from where he was and the distance of that shot, it was pretty strategic. I suggest you forget that ass-whooping mission and silently thank him for not doing a head shot. Let it go, my brother, let it go!" Bernstein exclaimed.

The spotter announced, "He had orders to injure underlings, but at first sight of you Mr. Sarge, your wife, John Lee, Jilkes and Zanthius, he was to do headshots to disrupt the organization."

The shooter looked at him and suggested that he only answer questions that were asked and not be so bitchy. The Sarge looked at the shooter and asked, "Is that true?"

The shooter replied, "Mr. Sarge, I had you in my sights 8 times, your wife 12 times, Jilkes 4 and John Lee 4 times."

The Sarge asked, "Then why did you shoot Brown instead of one of the others? By the way, what is your name?"

Dusimon smiled and said, "My name is Dusimon. I'm like someone's slave. Sometimes during the night, I would pull out a book and learn to read, knowing full well that if the master caught me, he was going to punish me really bad. The pain is not what I fear, Mr. Sarge. I know I'm going to hell because of horrific things that I've done to women, men, and children. We are the damned, we kill for others and there is no pay involved, just some pretended ledger that has the amount of time I have to do before I'm released. Funny thing, in all the years that I've been marauding and killing people, that ledger has only been X'd offed three times and I don't know of anyone who has ever made full payment and was released from the mental, physical, and emotional hell that we're indoctrinated into. They turn the weak into boy toys, for the strong."

The Sarge remorsefully responded, "Your world is for the dead. It has no resolution, no forgiveness, no love and

humility and no truth. It resembles a Hollywood horror show.
Your world is the preamble to Armageddon; it is lifeless."
With tears in his eyes, the Sarge decreed, "Take them to the
post office and set them free." He looked at the spotter and
the shooter and said, "If I ever encounter you again, I will
personally remove the skin from your entire body. Your
master may be mean, but we have been known to be demonic
in the application of pain."

As the Sarge started to walk away, Dusimon, the shooter,
said, "Mr. Sarge, my life is without meaning, so can you just
execute me where I stand or give me a weapon with a single
round in it?"

The Sarge bellowed out, "You're not going to get out of
life with my help, or that easily."

Mallory after listening to the discourse, asked the Sarge if
he could have a word with him. The Sarge replied, "I know
exactly what you're thinking, and the concern is how do you
think Brown would feel. After all, that guy shot him, although
I must admit strategically, but the fact remains, he shot him."

Mallory said, "I'll discuss this with Brown and let his
decision be the guiding light."

Mallory went directly to Brown's room and after playing
with the kids and telling Okema how lucky her husband was,
he asked, "What are you feeling right now towards the guy
who shot you? He asked the Sarge to execute him. What are
your thoughts relative to rehabilitating him?"

Brown looked at Okema and asked, "Honey, can you give
me a minute with the Corporal?"

After Okema left the room, Brown asked, "May I speak
frankly, Corporal Mallory?"

Mallory realized that he was being addressed formally, acknowledged the question, and replied, "Absolutely."

Brown then asked, "Corporal Mallory, have you lost your fucking mind? That motherfucker shot me."

Mallory paused for a few seconds and asked, "Do you think that was a lucky shot or was the shooter just a bad shot?"

Brown looked at Mallory hard and responded, "Anywhere but here Mallory. Anywhere but here. My wife asked me 20 times, why would he shoot you where he knew that it was double Kevlar? Anyway, my decision would be to send his ass to the Outback where I know he'll be tested and I can, when I'm there, taunt his ass. He could have taken me out and I know that. Send his ass away from here, Mallory."

As Mallory was heading towards the barn, he saw the Sarge and said, "Brown wants him in the Outback where he knows he'll be tested."

The Sarge replied, "I could have saved you a trip, I know our people."

## CHAPTER THIRTY-TWO

After all of the suspense and drama, Helga and Vincent were allowed back in their cabin to finish packing. Helga said, "The first thing customs officials are going to ask us, is where are we staying. So, my dear, I took the liberty of booking an Airbnb near the water, isolated and hopefully lives up to its pictures. Just make sure while we're in customs you don't get too far away from me lover-boy."

"When did you do that and why didn't you tell me?"

Helga replied, "Oh honey do you remember when you had that first hissing fit? Anyway, while you snored, I continued the planning of this adventure even though you were out like a light. I'm sorry I forgot to bring it up again. Just prior to that knock on the door, I was going to inform you of that and other things. Honey, did I do something wrong?"

Vincent smiled and said, "I can't imagine you doing anything that was not for our benefit. I trust you impeccably and I do remember something about your planning. I didn't mean for it to sound like an inquisition."

The two continued to pack and check behind each other. The cabin they occupied was located near the gangplank that would be placed, and they would be some of the first to disembark from the vessel.

# # #

Once in customs, they were served individually. As Helga predicted, the official working with Vincent asked the question about residency while in Valencia and in Spain in general. Vincent more worried about his passport, replied, "I don't know. My wife made the accommodations."

The customs official asked, "Your wife booked the accommodations but you're here with me and I don't see a wifey."

Vincent looked for Helga who had been checked and admitted quickly. Helga loudly called out Vincent's name and he turned around. Vincent said, "That's my wife."

The customs official realizing that Helga was admitted, said to Vincent, "Sir, in the future, know as much as your wife does, just in case she decides to dump you and disappear. After all, she's easy on the eyes."

Helga said, "Honey, you look guilty. You're sweating, moving anxiously and you're shaking. Are you alright?"

Vincent responded, "That woman scared me by the way she looked at me. I suddenly forgot that I'm a Naval Academy graduate. I was afraid to be conciliatory because I wasn't sure which passport I gave her."

Helga said, "Honey, we're in Valencia now. We'll work on your customs officials-skill set."

On the ride to their temporary housing, Helga remarked, "It is so beautiful here. Honey, just look at that water, the houses near it and look how people are smiling and not growling at each other."

Vincent asked, "Are we staying near the water?"

Helga replied, "Ah, close enough to see it from one of the bedrooms in the house."

The driver jerked his head and looked at her suspiciously. He knew the area and felt certain that he knew where the house was located and that it had a spectacular view of the Mediterranean Sea.

When they arrived at the address, Vincent exclaimed "OMG! Oh Honey, this is spectacular, can we afford it?"

Helga laughed, gave the driver a $100 tip, and asked, "If we want to tour, go out to dinner, out for drinks, or just to the museums, are you a person who can stop what he's doing and take care of us?"

The driver responded slowly in English, "I am here to service you. My card has my number and I am Alfredo. I will take good care of you and show you my city and the local places to eat where the food is fresh and not overpriced."

Helga responded, "I am Helga and this is my husband, Vincent. We're probably going to need some provisions—is that something that you can do for us?"

Alfredo replied, "I can do one better. I can send my wife over, and she can at least set you up on a temporary basis. I'll call her now and tell her to shop for basics, water, wine, bread, fruits, more wine and anything else that you can think of or need. While you are here, think of the services that you would like me to accomplish, check your budget, and give me a call with a reasonable offer. Thank you and if you want my wife to set you up with the basics, tell me and I'll call her pronto."

# # #

FOUR MONTHS LATER!

Vincent asked Helga, "Why are you so contrary in both actions and statements? Did I do something to unplug all of that love and passion that we shared? Please tell me love. What did I do? Among all of our other external issues, nothing between us should be beyond repair. You act as though I'm a bother and like you wish I would disappear. I love you so much, Helga. Please tell me what I need to do to restore all that we used to share."

Helga replied, "See, it's just that kind of 'what did I do' bullshit that bothers me. Can't I have a moment to myself without you pawing all over me and demanding sex? You act as if I'm a machine or something and my only function is to do what you need to get your rocks off. Listen, Vincent, I've been there and done that. It was a requirement of my last position—you know, when the ex-pope needed to relieve his stress, it was my job to make it happen. I feel as though I've moved from one dictator to another."

Vincent shot back, "I'm no fucking dictator. I'm your husband who is trying to figure out what is going on with the woman he loves."

Helga replied, "Please, I'm tired. Can we talk about this tomorrow?" Vincent walked outside and dove into the pool without responding to Helga's request. Helga made that sucking sound with her teeth, went into their bedroom and closed and locked the door.

Later that day, Alfredo dropped his wife off with more provisions and asked Vincent how his wife was doing.

Vincent replied, "We've seemed to have hit a rough patch in the road at the moment. She's always tired, stays cooped up in our bedroom watching endless news programs and is not eating well."

Alfredo said, "Those periods don't last long, but they seem like an eternity when you're dealing with them. Have patience, my friend, hopefully things will get better, or they will become exponentially worse and at that point you will know that something is wrong physically or mentally. Don't make any assumptions about anything. Let her come to you and share what is troubling her."

Vincent looked at Alfredo and said, "I have another issue that I want to bring to your attention, but I'm afraid it's too early in our relationship to begin to ask you for all that I think I need. Anyway, one of my concerns is that I saw people scoping out the place on two separate occasions and if they decided to come into the house while we're here, I have no way of defending us."

Alfredo responded, "There are cameras all over this neighborhood. It's unlikely that you'll have a problem, but if you find that those earlier visits are discomforting and create a problem for you when it comes to sleeping, then I might have another solution, but it can be tricky and expensive."

Vincent asked, "How much is your security and your wife's worth to you?"

Alfredo smiled and stated, "I know a guy who may have a tool that provides extra security. However, Mother Spain has extremely strict weapon's ownership policies. If you have an illegal intent and commit an illegal crime with a weapon, your sentence will be extreme. Are we talking about the same thing at this point?"

Vincent looked at Alfredo and said, "Loyalty and trustworthiness are the key to a long and trouble-free life."

Alfredo, responded, "That is a two-way street, if I'm not mistaken."

Vincent asked, "Are you free at noon tomorrow?"

Alfredo stated, "I am free tomorrow, but I am only the connection, I don't know what people do and who they do it with. Are we clear?"

Vincent responded, "We are crystal clear and I appreciate you, my friend."

Later, Vincent knocked on the bedroom door and asked, "What's your pleasure for dinner tonight?"

Helga responded, "I'm not feeling well. You go and have dinner and I'll see you later."

Instead of asking any questions, Vincent replied, "Okay love, catch you later."

Walking down the road, Vincent saw a flashing pizzeria sign. He went to the window, looked in, and thought the place seemed clean from the outside. He went in, saw the menu posted behind the cashier and said to her, "I would like a small pizza with pepperoni, mushrooms, prosciutto, ground beef and artichokes."

The cashier said, "Obviously you're not from here. May I make a suggestion?"

Vincent looked at the young lady, smiled, and said, "I'm open to suggestions, by all means go for it."

She said, "Let go the ground beef because it's going to take up the entire flavor of the pie, unless that is your intent."

Vincent said, "How about a little and we'll see what flavor wins the pie."

Vincent sat at a table waiting on his pie and caught the flirtatious winks of a woman sitting at a table with another woman. Vincent tried desperately to avoid eye contact and decided to keep his eyes fixed on the menu on the table.

When his pie was completed, the cashier brought it to his table with a note attached to it. The note read, "undercover Policia looking for solicitation.' Don't buy unless you're desperate and want to land in jail."

Vincent ignored the note, took a bite of the pizza, and exclaimed, "This is the best pizza that I have ever had. What's your secret?"

The cashier/delivery person said, "If we told you, we might have to bury you."

Vincent smiled and asked, "Can you recommend an extremely light beer, similar to Coors light that I can try out?"

The cashier responded, "How about a Mahou, that is rated as one of the top beers in our country."

Vincent knew this, but said, "I'm game, let's try it."

The cashier brought the beer over to Vincent, he took a sip and acted as if he was just admitted into heaven. He then said, "This is a little heavy for me, but it has an excellent taste."

The door flung open and in walked Alfredo. He said, "Vincent my friend, what are you doing so far away from home and where is that beautiful wife of yours?"

Vincent replied, "She's not doing so well, and I wanted to have a beer and pizza for dinner and she didn't. What brings you here?"

Alfredo responded, "Vincent, this is the best pizzeria in all of Mother Spain, and it's owned and operated by my beautiful daughter."

Vincent asked, "Is that her coming out of the kitchen?"

Alfredo responded, "Oh, yes, that's Inma, short for her real name that her mother insisted upon, Immaculata."

Vincent said, "If you're not on duty, would you like to have a beer with me?"

Alfredo replied, "No, my friend, this is my night to help my daughter run the pizzeria, it's one of the busiest nights for her."

Vincent looked around and said, "I can at least help. I mean I can take a pizza to the table and collect the cost."

Alfredo laughed and asked, "Why on earth would you want to work in a pizzeria?"

Vincent replied, "Because I can and I want to help you and your daughter. Besides, I don't have anything else to do tonight. My wife wanted me gone, so here I am."

Alfredo replied, "My friend, that happens to the best of us. Come, wash your hands, get an apron and let's get ready for the crowd coming from the football game."

Thirty or so minutes later, people began to slowly trickle in and place their orders for beer, wine, and pizzas. Everything was working smoothly until two hours later, when a group of four individuals walked into the pizzeria and the whole place acted as if Lucifer himself had walked in. Everything shut down in terms of conversation and enjoyment. Vincent, who was delivering a pizza, recognized that the volume had been turned down and wondered what had just happened. He turned around and saw the four individuals who came in, and one walked over to Alfredo's daughter, grabbing her by the neck and forced a kiss upon her. Vincent assessed what was happening and decided that these guys were local thugs. He slowly made his way to a table and asked if the pizza was good and then he walked toward the counter. As he approached, the man who forced a kiss upon Alfredo's daughter, asked, "Who the fuck are you?"

Vincent looked around as if he were trying to discern who the man was talking to but never acknowledged the person. Vincent ordered two Mahou's and two Greek pizzas. He turned to walk away, and the man grabbed him by the arm. Alfredo responded, "Please, he's a guest and a friend helping out."

The man looked at him and asked, "Did I ask you a fucking question?" Alfredo dropped his head in a subservient manner and did not respond.

Vincent decided to walk away, but the man said, "Did I give you permission to walk away?"

Vincent responded, "I didn't know that I needed to ask permission to do my job for a customer."

The man said, "I'm an indirect owner of this place."

Vincent said, "Oh, then I'm sorry, I quit. I don't like how you treat people." He took off his apron and headed for the door.

One of the man's henchmen said, "My boss is talking to you, and you need to ask him if you can leave."

Vincent looked at the positioning of the four individuals and decided that they were too close together for him to do the nasty on the boss. He then said, "Listen, I don't want any trouble, but I'm not going to work for someone who treats his people poorly. I'm out of here. Good night."

The man thought about how disrespectful Vincent was and yelled, "You don't go nowhere until I say so."

Vincent replied, "Dude, fuck you. I'm out of here."

One of the men in the group hit Vincent hard in the stomach and he buckled over as if he were hurt. The boss said, "Bring that little bitch to me." As the three men got Vincent closer to the man in charge, he asked, "Do you know who I am, bitch?"

Vincent acting as if he was winded, didn't reply. The man yelled so that all could hear, "This bitch disrespected me and I'm going to publicly show you assholes what happens when I'm disrespected." He told two guys to hold him upright. He cranked his head from left to right and threw a punch at Vincent's head. Vincent slipped the punch, pulled the man on his right under his arm, side kicked the man on the left, head butted the person in charge and faced the fourth guy who was brandishing a knife.

Vincent said, "Drop it, or I'll make you eat that fucking thing." The guy smiled and swung the blade at Vincent, who kicked him in his groan and then side kicked the person in charge and threw two violent punches to the person who was holding him, knocking everyone into another dimension, and ending up with the person in charge's throat under his right foot. He then exclaimed, "Any further aggressions towards me or this pizzeria will end in your deaths."

From under his foot, the person in charge asked, "Do you know who I am?" Vincent looked down at him and said, "No, I don't know who you are and from this moment forward, you'll have to look over your shoulder because I don't give a shit about who you are and if anything happens to the people who hired me, then your entire DNA will be erased by the CIA." He then stomped the man's head, rendering him unconscious. He motioned for Alfredo to meet him in the kitchen.

Once they found a secure place, Vincent asked, "Who was that little crook?"

Alfredo shakingly stated, "He's the son of the local mobster that runs this area."

Vincent proclaimed, "Oh!" Where can I find his father?"

Alfredo responded, "I know where he lives but he'll be here before you get to where he is."

Vincent responded, "Alfredo, I just entered another dimension and if anything were to happen to me in this area, the results will be a shitstorm of agents, mercs, and independents looking for the source of my demise. Therefore, I need to be aggressive. Give me the address of the people who I will allow to live or that I will conclude tonight."

Alfredo responded, "But you're only one person."

Vincent replied, "Yeah, I know. I hear that all the time after I've done my work and Alfredo, I usually leave a cemetery full of bodies. I came for pizza and they came to shake you down for money. I'm in an evolutionary stage of my life where when I'm finished, shakedown artists are no more. This is war and I'm the perfect weapon. Just one thing—please don't mention this to my wife."

# # #

An hour away from the pizzeria, Vincent found himself standing at a gate talking to the gatekeeper. He asked, "Can you tell your employer that a member of the CIA is at his gate wishing to have an audience with him?"

Five or so minutes later, the gate buzzed open and two armed men escorted Vincent up the driveway to what appeared to be a front porch. A few minutes later, a middle-aged man came out and asked, "Why is the American CIA knocking on my door?"

Vincent responded, "I was at a pizzeria and your son, I guess, came in ordering people around, calling me out of my name and scaring the occupants. I was a guest server and didn't know that he came from substance. He tried to beat me up in front of the other guests to show his power as well as his stupidity. I defended myself and beat the shit out of him and his three comrades. Listen, I'm really not here, neither are my other agents. If I have any further problems from your son or you, then I suggest you make a reservation and call the mortician to bury everyone here. That's all I have to say, good day, sir."

The man asked, "Do I get to ask you any questions?" Vincent smiled and said, "Only in the presence of your attorney."

# # #

Back at his rented home, Vincent quietly opened the front door and there she sat with a demonic look on her face. Helga asked, "Where the fuck have you been?"

Vincent replied, "Can I at least use the bathroom before you interrogate me?"

Helga saw his knuckles and asked, "Did you get into a fight? What happened to your hands?"

Vincent replied, "Again, can I wash up first?"

When he returned after cleaning himself up, he asked, "Do you mind if I fix a drink and would you like one as well?"

Helga replied, "Since when do I control when you want a drink? Since you're fixing yourself one, then I'll have one as well, just don't poison it?"

Vincent looked at Helga and asked, "What have I done that could spur such nefarious and deadly thoughts in your mind? Is it because I went out for a pizza and a beer? Anyway, I went several streets south, entered a pizzeria and ordered a beer and a pizza. Ten minutes later, Alfredo walked in, introduced me to his daughter, and told me that it was her place and that it was going to be a busy night, so he was there to help her. I explained that I didn't have anything to do and no one to love me, so, I was available to offer my serving skills for free. I helped them serve pizza and beer until these four young thugs came in and the vibrant sounds of people having fun turned into what seemed like a funeral. I didn't know who anyone was. I sure as hell didn't know that this guy was the son of a local mobster. They threw the first punch and from there I gave them a lesson in getting your ass whipped in mass. I went to his father's place and literally threatened him. I told him that I was with the CIA and that me and other agents were in the area and that if there was any further contact with him or his son, then they should make reservations with the undertaker."

Helga remained silent, waiting on Vincent to tell the truth. She asked, "Okay, now that I've heard the bullshit, give me the real story."

Vincent looked at Helga and asked, "What's going on with you? You've been acting as if I have rabies or something. What in the hell did I do wrong?"

Just as Helga was about to say something, the doorbell rang repeatedly. When he looked at the ring camera, he saw

Alfredo, his daughter, and the little thug. He demanded of Helga, "Go to the kitchen and get us two knives." Helga was about to ask what was happening, when Vincent emphatically stated, "Do as I ask."

They went to the front door and Vincent slowly opened it and said, "We weren't expecting company this late Alfredo. Is there a problem?"

Alfredo responded, "I'm with my daughter and Piero— you know, the guy you met earlier. He wants to have a word with you."

Vincent asked, "Is his word peaceful?"

Alfredo responded, "Oh, you can bet his life on it."

Vincent invited everyone into the kitchen and started the conversation off by saying, "My wife has some strange idea that I was somewhere fooling around. If nothing else, you guys can confirm that I was working diligently until Piero and his crew showed up."

Piero replied, "I am sorry for the misunderstanding, and I would like to ask you how I can make up for my terrible display of character?"

Vincent responded, "The only thing that will make me happy is if you and your father find a more legitimate business enterprise, one that does not prey upon your neighbors. That's all I want."

Piero replied, "We will not do business with the pizzeria. Will that satisfy you?"

Vincent vehemently announced, "Hell no! You'll let them do business without your claws in their tills, but then you'll rape other neighbors as well. No sir, that is not a solution, save one and tax everyone else."

Helga asked, "Honey, may I see you in the other room for a minute?"

Helga said, "Listen I know I've been a real bitch for the past few months, but I am not well, Vincent. I will tell you everything after we deal with that pirate, just follow my lead."

Vincent requested, "Screw that bullshit. What's wrong with you?"

Helga replied, "I need your undivided attention on my issue, please, let's deal with the crook and then we'll talk."

When Helga and Vincent returned to the kitchen, it was noticeable that Vincent was with concern. Helga said, "My husband told me about the little skirmish he had at the pizzeria, and I thought that he was full of it. Anyway, we are totally against what you and your family are doing here Piero. I guess my husband told you that he works for the CIA. I work for an agency that makes the CIA look like boy scouts. You will stop stealing from your neighbors and you will make monthly payments to them to clear up all that you owe them. You will begin to work for one of our agencies, doing good and helping people to help themselves. In turn you will set up a meeting between your father and us immediately to discuss other ventures that bright people can be involved in that will keep the law off their backs. Do you realize what would happen if my husband reported the fact that he was accosted by you? Probably not, but let me just say, your entire DNA would be eradicated. Are we on the same page so far Piero?"

Piero stated, "I think so. I have to take this back to my father."

Vincent said, "Tell your father this is a non-negotiable conversation. However, be sure to tell him that we will fucking blow his ass all the way into hell if he threatens our friends again."

Helga said, "Vincent, don't be so dramatic, I think Piero, by the fact that he is here understands the detriments of this situation. Am I correct Piero?"

Piero quickly stated, "We are going to begin the retribution process immediately."

Helga paused and reminded people that she was not feeling well, but asked, "What are the business opportunities that are needed in this area? Listen, that means all of us and your father will discuss strategies where you all can grow, prosper, and expand. Thanks for coming by. Call us in the morning when you have a time, say 11:30. We're free and Alfredo could you and your lovely daughter pick us up?"

# # #

After the uninvited company left, Vincent fixed himself and Helga a glass of Grand Marnier heated in two crystal goblets. With tears in his eyes, he asked, "Do you feel that you made a mistake marrying me?" Helga sat her glass down and broke into a crying fit. Vincent approached her, but she raised her hands motioning for him to back off. After she had cried for two minutes, Vincent retrieved a bottle of water and cold towel and began to try to calm her down. He said, "I know I'm not the best person on earth for you, but in terms of loving someone, no one's feelings will ever surpass my love for you, Helga."

Vincent continued, "I, at the end of your command, will conclude my life. I've tried to kill my parents, I've had a lot of people killed and if I'm not the right apple off the tree, then let me leave and forever be distraught with the results of my first attempt of being in love."

Helga responded, "I'm happy and I'm sad because I have never felt love before. I've always been a pleasure provider for men. Then here you come along, driving a fucking Uber and never taking your eyes off me while you were driving. I was so turned on by your eyes staring inquisitively about what they were seeing. The first time we made love to each other, I wanted to tell you then that I loved you, but that would have seemed a little mentally imbalanced. Instead, you run away with me, we get married, you make me happy and I hope I make you happy. Listen, the evilest people on earth are going to be searching for us and I think after tonight, it's going to be fairly easy to find us. I'm sad because I put you in danger. Listen, my husband, I only want to live long enough to have this child that I think I'm pregnant with."

Vincent after taking a swig of his drink said, "Helga, I agree, that ride in the Uber was so intense. I couldn't take my eyes off you and knew right then and there, that if you would give me—wait did you say you are pregnant? What does that mean?"

Helga responded, "Sometimes I think you're daft. Dude, I think I'm pregnant!"

Vincent stared long and hard at Helga until it registered what she was saying. He asked, "Helga did you announce to me that you're pregnant?"

Helga with her head lowered, responded, "I'm no doctor but for the past few months I've been having symptoms that remind me of being pregnant."

Vincent began to cry again and Helga stated, "Vincent, I think I'm pregnant, not you. Don't do that crying thing and end up in the hospital. I need you to stop, and to stop now! And besides, I'm too damn old to be having a child." Vincent cocked his head to the side and asked, "How old are you?"

Helga replied, "Vincent if I told you my age, then I would have to murder you." He laughed and said, "We need to make a doctor's appointment. Let me call Alfredo and have him recommend someone we can see. Baby, that would be 'efinn' incredible. Do you remember we talked not long ago about having some little feet under our roof."

Helga began to cry and Vincent demanded that she only cry for giving him a life, a wife and now perhaps a child. I should be the one crying, not you."

Helga gasped for air and said, "Vincent, there are some really bad people looking for us and they would kill our child in front of us to get what they wanted."

After several minutes of silence and introspection, Vincent asked, "Honey, could it be something else?"

Helga responded, "If it is, then I'm in trouble. I mean, I silently want to be the mother of your child, because I have never felt the kind of love that you give me. I worry about growing old before your eyes and you walking away and leaving me in a terrible funk. I worry about being fat and you not finding me attractive anymore and then you start to wander. I worry about so many silly things because I love you more than life. I just want to rid myself of my past and move on with our lives, but my past and maybe yours will make it impossible and hard to overcome."

Vincent didn't respond immediately, but when he did, it was prophetic. He said, "We need an intermediary. The best and only one that I know, I tried to eradicate on several occasions directly and a few times indirectly."

He looked at Helga and continued, "If there is any way possible for us to survive this new epidemic, then I'm going to have to call my mother and father and ask them for forgiveness, and claim some kind of mental illness that led me to those past behaviors."

Helga said, "If I know your father and your brother from another mother, they'll shoot us on sight. You must be crazy and I must be a simpleton for listening to you. I have two children in that encampment and an ex-sexual partner. You want to return home like nothing has happened? What would you say to your brother, "Oh, hi, Zanthius, nice to meet you. You know my wife, Helga, also known as Sister Mary, the mother of little Ben, and you know the lady that you thought you murdered after putting two bullets into her head while she was in St. Thomas. And, oh, hi, Mom, hi, Dad, so good to see you people alive. Sorry about the numerous hits I placed on you and your friends, but I'm home now and will you take us in? There are some really bad and connected people looking for us because my wife has changed the access codes to $300 million in cash. What's for dinner?"

Vincent stared blankly into the room and then announced, "I believe that I too may have a child there. I think my mom and my dad are the people who adopted my child after the mother concluded her life. It's so sad and for a while, I have been wishing that it were all a dream. I'm not sure, but I know that my mom would do whatever she had to do to acquire that child. I went back in hopes of trying to find out what happened to him, but it appeared that everyone who saw me wanted me dead. Yeah, I messed up royally by taking complete advantage of that woman, but I never once thought that she would terminate her own life. That's the main reason I ran away with you. You make me focus only on you and there is no time to consider anyone else. That's the amount of love I have for you, Helga. So, that going to Australia idea is not a good one or a practical solution for our issues. However, I was also thinking, who would look for us in Australia?"

Helga looked at him, half smiled and replied, "That might be a great strategy to explore, I mean your parents think you're dead, my children probably have forgotten about me, and your brother will drop dead just from seeing me, after putting two final bullets into my minion's head.

## CHAPTER THIRTY-THREE

Courtney said to the Sarge, "Honey, you know I still dream of holding him in my arms and rubbing my face on his belly and sending him into hysterics. I know it's been many years and I know we have Marcelus but every time I look at him, I think of our son."

The Sarge, eased next to Courtney, hugged her, and said, "Even though the little fucker tried to kill us, I too think of him and wonder what drove him to the dark side. I mean, you remember when someone made innuendos that the Beckmires were trying to take it all. By the strength of my ten guys and the one non-commissioned officer, a lot of that noise was dispensed with. Nevertheless, when a son has strategic information about certain functions of the group, you have to admit it seems suspicious. Our problem with our son was that we introduced him to the world, gave it to him, and told him that it was his to command. I guess he took that information literally."

They both laughed. Courtney replied, "Even during war, Ben, the parents of a fallen soldier at least got a flag and the condolences of a grateful nation. Is it true that he was cut into little pieces and fed to the fish?"

Ben Beckmire dropped his head and replied, "Honey, I don't know what is fact or fiction. All I know is that there is credible information that solidifies the notion that he is probably in heaven or hell, most likely the latter."

Courtney asked, "Ben, did you ever love our son?"

Ben shot back, "Honey, did you? We both thought that he was a demanding little guy and that he sucked up all of our time together because of his demands and needs. I mean, think about it. When he finished high school and said, "I want to be a Naval Academy graduate, well we both said hallelujah because it was his first admission of a desired goal. We also tried to persuade him to choose a less costly institution after we found out that the Naval Academy would charge us an arm, three legs, our pensions, our properties and at one point, I thought our marriage."

Marcelus came into the room and exclaimed, "I had a bad dream."

Ben found his way to his knees and asked, "Was it scary?"

Marcelus replied, "The white horse wouldn't move, and Mr. James picked him up with the tractor."

Ben asked, "Marcelus, would you like to sit here with mommy and me and watch the moon disappear over the mountains? It's way past your bedtime but we'll let you stay up a little longer."

Marcelus replied, "Okay." Fifteen minutes later, he was out like a light.

In the morning, James appeared in the dining room and asked Ms. Asiram if he could have a word with her privately.

Zanthius never far away, asked, "What's going on James?"

James asked, "Can you excuse yourselves for a minute or two?"

On the porch, James said, "I had to scoop Whitey up last night. I've already taken him down the hill to the fire pit. I just didn't want to say this while you people be eating breakfast."

Asiram fell to her knees and began to cry. Zanthius and James comforted her because Whitey was her first and most treasured horse. Asiram cried like a baby until Dr. Beckmire approached and saw the three people on their knees. She asked, "Who has upset my favorite daughter-in-law?"

James rose from his knees and announced, "Doc, Whitey has transitioned." Courtney stated, "Yes, I know, Marcelus told us last night. She then asked Zanthius and Asiram to walk with her. As they started to walk, she turned around and asked, "Well, James, are you just going to stand there, or are you going to join us?"

As they walked towards the barn, Courtney asked, "James, did you scoop Whitey up with the tractor?"

James looked at her strangely and replied, "Yes Ma'am, I did."

Courtney then asked, "What time did you gather Whitey?"

James replied, "Doc, I didn't want anyone to see the way I had to load the horse, so I did it after midnight."

Courtney demanded, "James, please be sure about the timetable."

James replied, "Doc, them funny people who joke all the time, their shows had just ended. Why the inquiry Doc?"

Courtney replied, "Thanks, James, I know I'm not crazy. I need to talk to my family in private."

James made his way back to the dining room, gathered some grub and walked towards his four-wheel vehicle.

Courtney said, "Oh, there she is." She yelled, "Monica, I need you over here girl. I need you now!"

Zanthius said, "Mom, you're acting terribly strange. What's going on?"

Courtney said, "Baby, give me a moment and I'll tell you what's happening."

Monica showed up and Courtney said, "Hey girl, wait to you hear the latest." She then said to the group, "Marcelus woke up crying and told me and Ben that he had a dream and in it, he saw James scoop up Whitey with the tractor."

Asiram said, "Mom, that's exactly what James said."

Courtney replied, "James said he did that after midnight. Marcelus told us that at 8 p.m." A sudden quiet came over the group and Monica asked, "My dearest friend in the entire world, are you sure you heard him correctly? Someone's clock is off. I mean 8 p.m. to midnight is four whole hours."

Courtney said, "Girl listen—no, all of you listen. I asked James the question twice and he confirmed that he didn't remove the horse until after the late-night shows went off and that ain't at 8 p.m."

Zanthius asked, "So, Mom, you're the doctor in the house, what's your take on this matter?"

Courtney replied, "I'm going to talk to your father and see what he has to say and speaking of him, there he is looking for me."

Courtney called out to Ben, and he waved and headed her way. When Ben arrived, he said, "This looks like an auspicious group ready to attack all of the issues in the world. Just kidding. What's up with you people?"

Courtney asked, "Did you talk to James about the removal of Whitey?"

"Honey, you know I don't get in his way. This is his domain and he takes care of it dutifully. Sorry to hear about Whitey. Anyway, why all the concern?"

Courtney responded, "I talked to James and he told me that he removed Whitey after midnight. You do remember that Marcelus had his dream around 8 pm."

Ben said, "There must be a mistake. Someone is obviously mistaken about the time. I mean Marcelus told us around 8 p.m. Had James been drinking when you spoke to him?"

Courtney responded, "He was as sober as you are."

# # #

The following morning at breakfast when Ms. Beatrice and her little brother entered the dining room and he asked for shredded wheat and warm milk. Ms. Beatrice went over to where the Sarge and Marcelus were having breakfast and said, "Good morning Mr. Sarge, how are you doing?"

After a brief discussion, Ms. Beatrice asked, "Marcelus, do you want to go fishing with us after breakfast?"

Marcelus responded, "No thanks. I'm sad because Whitey is dead." Ms. Beatrice reached out, touched his shoulder, but quickly withdrew her hand back.

The Sarge witnessing the event, asked, "After breakfast and before you go fishing Ms. Beatrice, do you think that the two of us plus Mrs. Beckmire could have a conversation?" Ms. Beatrice responded, "It is important that we do, Mr. Sarge, it's important that we do!"

When Marcelus saw Courtney walk into the dining room with Monica, he bolted from the table and ran towards her as if he hadn't seen her in years. He jumped into her arms and she said, "My son, you are getting too heavy for me to catch on the fly. How about you jump into your dad's arms and I'll drop to my knees and give you a magnificent hug and kiss. How about that?"

Marcelus replied, "Mommy, I don't want to hurt you. I'll do what you say." Marcelus grabbed her hand and walked her to the table where his dad's was sitting. He said, "Mommy can't catch me anymore and I don't want to hurt her. Will you catch me and throw me into the air?"

Ben Beckmire looked at his son and said, "I'll throw you so high in the air, you'll say to me not so high daddy."

Marcelus then replied, "Daddy, I don't want to fly away. I love you and mommy, don't throw me away." Ben Beckmire gathered Marcelus in his arms and said, "Son, I will only throw you as high as I can reach out and make sure that you can't get away from me."

Courtney acknowledged the amount of love in the air and said, "I want to say a prayer right here and now for all of us. God has been extremely good to us and continues to be. I love everyone here. I love my son, my husband and more than ever as we reach ripe old age, we must be there for each other. I just feel the love, the commitment, the fellowship and the, I got your back until the end, and we help people help themselves.' Oh God almighty, continue to bless us and watch over us in these uncertain times and lead our youth into leadership roles so that they may continue the good work of this unsanctioned clan. In your name we pray, Amen!"

There was an immediate quiet until John Lee and Jilkes walked in, and John Lee stated, "I be feeling that spiritual conversation Doc. We need to be doing that more often and as a matter of fact, me and my minority friend were thinking about joining the church down the road near the post office. I be thinking that be a good thing for us and the community when we be here."

Jilkes said, "If I may make a comment. We need a place of worship in all of our residency locations. We are all children of God, we have all committed sins and we need his blessings, as we think about transitioning leadership roles to some of the younger whipper snappers that are a part of this crew."

Kenzo walked in and approached the Sarge in what appeared to be an aggressive manner. Jilkes stopped him in his tracks and said, "Whoa dude. What's on your mind and why are you looking like you're about to hurt someone?"

Kenzo backed off and said, "I report to Larry and Mr. Sarge, that's my orientation. I have to speak to Mr. Sarge. It's important."

Jilkes said, "Okay, soldier, but first I'm going to search you. Is that okay with you?"

Kenzo replied, "Please, get it over with. I think we're about to be attacked." The Sarge bellowed out, "Let him through."

When Kenzo arrived directly in front of him, the Sarge asked, "Why the aggressive look?"

Kenzo replied, "I see signs of deployment on the western front. I see movement, I see flashes and I saw the birds take to the air as if something has spooked them. I know the signs,

I have led the groups and what I see is an impending shit storm directed at the farm."

The Sarge called Rashida, who was busy being a wife to Juan in the control room.

The Sarge asked, "Why do you sound out of breath?"

Rashida responded, "I was exercising.   Is that not allowed?"

The Sarge asked, "Baby girl, do we have a problem?"

Rashida took in a deep breath of air and said, "Dad, I'm sorry but the rabbit is in here with me."

The Sarge said, "Kenzo informed me that he saw signs of an impending firefight.   Can you scan the western area and then use heat signatures for confirmation."

Rashida responded, "I'm on it, dad."

In the interim, Juan noticed where the ambient temperature was consistent but in spots, there were spikes.   He said to Rashida, "Honey, look at this area and tell me what you make of it.   There are a lot of spikes but no movement."

Rashida, called her dad and proclaimed, "Full alert!" She directed group A to the western tunnels, Group B to the tunnels that lead to the guest house, Group C to the barn, and group D to the gun ports in the main house.   Ms. Beatrice, her mother, and Maryann were assigned to secure the room where the children report to.

Kenzo began to walk away, when the Sarge bellowed out, "Kenzo, get my vest and one for you.   Dude, if this is accurate, then you'll be assigned to my daughter for surveillance."

Kenzo bowed his head and the Sarge said, "The next time you pull that slave mentality on me, I'm going to personally place your ass on a bus.   That's not how we operate here, my friend."

Kenzo jerked his head, looked at the Sarge, and stated, "Mr. Sarge, you called me friend. Was that just a conversation piece with you or what?"

The Sarge looked at him and responded, "Dude, get with the vibes. Look people straight on, keep us safe and you'll be able to live normally, richly and with a family to support any decisions you want to personally make. Yes, I called you friend because I trust and believe in you. Is that a problem or are you so entrenched in being someone's slave that you don't recognize honesty and sincerity? Get with the program and you'll receive benefits beyond your wildest imagination, my friend. Just don't turn out to be a turncoat."

# # #

Larry asked Kenzo, "Where did you leave my dad?"

Kenzo replied, "I got his vest and one for me and we walked to the control room. He directed me to find you and follow your lead, so here I am."

Larry replied, "Okay, you and I are going to take a tunnel that leads into the woods but gives us a low-to-high firing scenario. We're going to become snipers tonight. Are you up for the tasks?"

Kenzo paused for a few seconds and announced, "Mr. Sarge called me friend. Did he mean it or is that his normal way of addressing people?"

Larry responded, "Kenzo, my dad is an incredibly special man whose family comes from an incredibly special place. He is the most honest person that I have ever met, and his word is his bond. He doesn't engage in idle dialogue, he says what he means."

As the two men made their way into the tunnel, Larry asked, "Do you remember when your comrade who shot Brown asked the Sarge to execute him because his life was without meaning? Well, that was one of the most opportune decrees he could have made. The Sarge told him that he wasn't going to help him end his life and therefore, ordered the guys to the bus stop. Corporal Mallory pulled him aside and suggested another course of action. My dad told him that he had already measured the man and decided that if he were truthful, then we would welcome him with open arms, after his stent in the mines. Yes, my dad forgives people whenever possible."

# # #

At one of the exits, Larry placed a finger to his mouth to indicate to Kenzo to cease talking. He then opened a panel on the wall of the tunnel, keyed in a set of numbers and watched the outside of the tunnel come to life. He checked for heat signatures and movement but found none. Larry then entered another set of numbers and a panel slowly and quietly slid back. Inside of the panel were 4-Ruger Precision Rifles. He handed one to Kenzo with two clips and gathered another for himself. He then entered the original numbers that gave him a view and caution lights to see if there were people within 30 feet of the exit.

The two men scaled the ladder leading out of the tunnel and set up a firing scenario. Larry gave Kenzo an earpiece and the two men tested them. They placed 20 yards between them. Larry set up a retro system at ten yards to disguise where shots would be fired from. Larry out of nowhere asked, "Kenzo, do you have a passport?"

Kenzo responded, "I do, but they have it as well as my birth certificate, social security card and everything else that they needed to control me."

Larry shook his head and said, "This too we can fix my friend, this too."

Kenzo whispered, "Check out two o'clock. The dude is smoking while trying to be camouflaged. Give it a moment he will exhale." Within a matter of seconds Larry saw the trail of smoke.

Kenzo said, "There is movement at 11:o'clock as well. Shit, that dude has a rocket launcher. Shall I take him out?"

Larry paused for a moment and then said, "If you suspect that I'm checking you out, why would you send someone with a rocket launcher first knowing full well that he is a major target? Kenzo, I think they're trying to assess our strength. Keep a beam on his ass. I'll scan the area and have my sister send a large candle over there. That'll get the attention of everyone over there. If that guy takes aim at any structure, you blow his fucking head off. Am I clear?"

Kenzo responded, "Larry, he has his finger on the firing mechanism. I know this nut he'll kill his own mother if they ask him to."

Larry said, "End this discussion."

Kenzo fired a round that destroyed the weapon and entered the guy's neck. Larry asked, "Why didn't you shoot him in the head?"

Kenzo responded, "Larry, I destroyed the weapon and the shooter. Both are incapacitated. Had I shot him in the head, one of his crew could assume his firing position."

Larry said, "Okay, got you. They are now looking for where the shot came from."

Larry signaled Rashida to light up the area and for the dance to begin. He and Kenzo executed the camouflaged snipers. The automated system did the rest. Invaders were being systematically concluded. There would be no parley at this event, just 42 men and women terminated on land that was familiar with blood baths.

# # #

At the crack of dawn, the new cleaners were at the top of the hill. They began to remove the remains of individuals who were trying to make a fast dollar at someone else's cost.

Later in the morning, the Sarge took a vote on their next stop, and it was clearly articulated that the Outback should be where they should head. Kenzo said to Larry, "I have heard that you people have an impenetrable environment in the Outback. What makes it so special?"

Larry responded, "The Great Saltie."

Kenzo asked, "What is the Great Saltie? I have heard it mentioned before."

Larry replied, "Definitions are unlikely to convince you of the magic of the Outback so, I'll just say that once you get there, you'll understand and witness a world where it seems like things are magical, but in essence, it's spiritual and non-believers don't fare well."

Kenzo said, "Okay, Larry, level with me. What is so special about the Outback besides the people are different, the water is sky blue and I hear the seafood is spectacular."

Larry said, "Dude, we have to figure out a way to make you legal. You have no paperwork, but my brother-in-law is working with our lawyers to fix that issue. We have your DNA and other identifying information about you and we're hoping that will work. You are twenty-five years old and you were born in the Dominican Republic, is that correct?"

Kenzo looked at Larry and asked, "How do you know that?" Larry replied, "We know a lot about you my friend, just do as you're asked and everything will be okay."

## CHAPTER THIRTY-FOUR

Vincent and Helga moved to a less conspicuous area of Valencia and kept Alfredo as their point man for information and special services. Alfredo arranged for an evaluation of Helga, who continued to feel terrible and experience massive mood swings. Vincent, being the man who loved her, tolerated her ups and downs, and who tried to calm her with music and conversation. The music worked well, but it was his conversations that would create anxiety for Helga. She noted, "It's that smooth talk and big smile that got my ass into this mess. I'm too old to be pregnant and every indication suggests that I'm either menopausing or I'm three months or better pregnant or more. Look at me, where is my body? I don't know this person I'm looking at."

Vincent replied, "I see the beautiful woman I picked up in my Uber."

Helga said, "Bullshit. How in the hell did I get mixed up with an Uber driver? I, who have access to millions if not billions, fell for an Uber driver. I don't blame you, it must be the drugs that you slipped into my drinks."

Realizing that she had just crucified the only person that she could trust and who loves her, Helga placed her hands on her hips and said, "If I'm still the woman you met and fell in love with, why has it been almost a month since you've made love to me?"

Vincent shot back, "Well, you ungrateful fiftyish person, each time that I have made an advance, you shunned me with an evil look or the words, 'I'm tired.' I understood that, but when you turned your back to me, I really felt like I'm in the wrong place at the wrong time."

Helga screamed, "I hate you, you fucking Uber driver. I hate you." Helga went into the bedroom, locked the door, and commenced to cry an ocean. She eventually cried herself to sleep.

Later in the day, Alfredo came by and asked Vincent, "Where is that mother-to-be?"

Vincent smiled, made the sign of the cross and said, "She's in the room blaming me for everything that she perceives is wrong."

Alfredo replied, "That is what they do my friend. That is what they do. Anyway, I have to be at the pizzeria soon to help out my daughter. By the way, Piero is volunteering there and making eyes at my daughter. I'm not sure he is the kind of man I want for my child. He is a crook and a thief, but I've never heard him disrespect a woman. Your visit seemingly has caused the father to make payments to everyone that he has extorted. What did you say to him?"

Vincent replied, "I promised him life after tomorrow and a profitable new beginning. He paused for a few seconds and then proudly announced, "I believe we are going to invest in a few businesses that I think he and his son can manage, grow, and become casually rich."

Alfredo asked, "Is there room in that plan for me?"

Vincent replied, "You're going to be the president."

Alfredo laughed and asked, "Where is the funding coming from?"

Vincent smiled and replied, "My friend it will happen, in a matter of weeks. We'll draw up some operational papers, you know roles, responsibilities, financial transparency, and fees. By the way, do you know a good lawyer that we can engage?"

Alfredo replied, "My brother-in-law, but that's not what I consider an arm's length relationship. I do know of a young woman who's a waitress and graduated law school a few months ago but won't accept the jobs that are being offered to her, or the tenets of employment."

Vincent quickly asked, "What does tenets of employment mean?"

Alfredo responded, "It's alleged that in one of her interviews, a high-powered attorney touched her thigh and told her that he was testing her ability to work in different domains."

Vincent stated, "I would at least like to speak to her. Can you make that happen without giving her any knowledge of what we might want her to do?"

# # #

Helga, still in shock that she was pregnant, had considered correcting the issue but realized with all of the other commandments that she had broken, the rules of being a nun and the continued negative behavior even after confessions, she could not think of that as an alternative. She had seen the doctor every week for three straight weeks, and the same information was given to her—you're pregnant, so, now let's make sure you do everything that is necessary to birth a healthy human being.

#

Helga and Vincent talked about investing in businesses in Valencia and using the wannabe mob guy and his son Piero, Alfredo, and his daughter, Inma.

When Helga met Gabriella, she whispered to Vincent, "Don't make me kill you and that young girl."

After the introductions, Gabriella stated, "Alfredo invited me here to meet you guys but didn't give me a clue as to why."

Helga requested, "Can you come with me into the kitchen?"

In the kitchen, Helga said, "I'm going to ask you some very personal questions and I would like you to be completely honest with me. Is that something you can do?"

Gabriella responded, "Absolutely."

Helga stated, "Forgive my manners may I offer you something to drink?"

Gabriella responded, "Water would be terrific."

A few seconds later Helga said, "So, let's get right at it. Have you ever talked with or seen my husband before?"

Gabriella responded, "Today is the first time I have met your husband. Alfredo spoke of you two but that is the extent of my knowledge of both of you. Why do you ask?"

Helga asked, "Have you looked in the mirror lately?"

Gabriella gave her a strange look and said, "Not sure of the relevancy of that question or for that matter any questions that you've asked me so far. Is there some notion that I know your husband and perhaps he and I have had a liaison? Is that what you are inquiring about?"

Helga stared at Gabriella and finally retorted, "I'm pregnant and I don't want to knowingly hire a beautiful young woman to steal my husband."

Gabriella asked, "Have you looked in the mirror lately? Anyway, I'm not that clever or dishonest to attempt to take anyone's husband. Not looking for a relationship and certainly not with a man whose wife is with child. This interview seems a little strange and I think that I'm going to thank you for the water and your time and be on my way."

As Gabriella stood up, Helga said, "Please sit down for just a minute longer." Gabriella paused, but sat down and Helga took a swig of water, and asked, "In your country, do you have a vetting process before you take a job of trust and responsibility?"

Gabriella responded, "Oh, yes. There are forms that you have to complete and licenses that you must obtain that demonstrate that you have not been convicted of a crime and as a lawyer, the qualifying documentations are much more stringent.

Helga replied, "I'm not worried about you doing anything stupid other than perhaps getting too close to my husband."

Gabriella, proclaimed, "Please stop! I don't know the man and I respect you enough not to play where I work if I were hired. Good day!"

On her way out, Gabriella said farewell to Alfredo and thanked Vincent for the interview. Vincent said, "I don't know what happened, but I respect my wife's judgement. Thank you for your time."

As Gabriella stepped through the front door, Helga yelled, "I have one more question that I would like to ask you. You got here by way of Alfredo. "Please respect the current relationships that are in place."

Gabriella paused, took in a deep breath of air, turned around, and replied, "Listen, lady, I don't know your husband, I don't want your husband and you need to seek help to get rid of that jealousy gene that will ruin your marriage in the long run. I'm not interested in working for you guys and I thank Alfredo for thinking of me, but this scene appears to be too toxic for me. Thanks, and good day."

Alfredo followed Gabriella to the car and asked, "What was that all about?"

Gabriella replied, "I think that woman thinks that I know or want to get to know her husband. She's pregnant and probably concerned that good-looking guy would chase someone like me. Even if he did, I can't respect a man that would cheat on his wife who is pregnant. Listen, Alfredo, I appreciate your trying to get me out of the business that I'm in, but they seem too dysfunctional for me to want to work for."

Alfredo patted Gabriella's hand and said, "I don't know who they really are, but I do know that they work to help people. Vincent kicked Piero's *culo* the other night as he volunteered to serve pizza. Piero and his crew came in demanding things and threatening people and that's when Vincent went to work. They are weird people, but they care about small people. Give her another chance. If she pisses you off again, we'll both leave. Can you at least give it one more go?"

Gabriella walked back in and said, "Ms. Helga, I am only interested in representing you and your husband with any business-related or legal matter that may come up. I have no other interest in anyone or any matter that isn't concerning my legal opinion."

Helga replied, "You're a little fire brand, aren't you?"

Gabriella responded, "If you mean that I don't take shit from no one then you're correct. I'm all about starting my legal profession and nothing more."

There was a lull in the conversation when Vincent decided to venture into the kitchen. Helga asked, "Honey, do you foresee any issues with hiring Gabriella as our legal counsel to handle our future businesses and partnerships?"

Vincent replied, "Helga, she comes highly recommended by our new confidant Alfredo. I see the relationship operating from afar and on secure portals. We need to begin focusing on where we're going to have the baby. I think the first thing we should do is open an account here under the guise of a trust and have Gabriella and Alfredo be the guardians of it. Alfredo has a keen sense of what he would be in charge of and the requirements of transparency on everyone's part. Yes, baby, I think we have found two people who we can endow, trust and who will always have our business objectives as their motivating direction."

Helga asked Gabriella, "Would you prefer to work on a retainer, or be salaried?"

Gabriella, responded, "I really hadn't thought about that aspect of my career. I was just busy trying to find someone to believe in my abilities as an attorney. What would you guys suggest as a fair way to proceed?"

Helga smiled and said, "I realize that this is your first rodeo and therefore, I want to give you an opportunity to evaluate the benefits and costs of each direction. Also, I want you to obtain an overseer firm, one that you would consult with on any matters that may seem legally complicated to you. In other words, I need you to act as if you're cramming for an exam and come back to us with your thoughts and needs. You'll have Alfredo as the president, you will be the legal person and the two of you should find a young and hungry person to be your CFO, to account for our funds and to manage our investments."

Gabriella announced, "Guys, I think this might be over my head. This is *like,* starting a business."

Vincent smiled and said, "It's not *like* starting a new business, it is in fact starting a new business."

Helga announced, "Gabriella, you handled me with ease and grace. You're new and new is what we want. Listen, you'll make mistakes and people will try to handle you, but between the CFO you choose and Alfredo, you'll do simply fine. This is going to be an on-the-job training venture. Think of this as a small plant that you want to grow. Find out everything that will sustain it, you know, water, sunlight and what other ingredients you can use to nurture it and make it grow. At some point in time, we'll ask you to be our partners. That in itself should be one of your goals and objectives, I think. I, rather we, only demand loyalty, fidelity, and transparency."

Vincent said to Alfredo and Gabriella, "There are many banks here in Valencia. Is there a small community bank that attempts to help the people and charges fair rates?"

Gabriella remarked, "Banco De Valencia."

Alfredo responded, "I agree. It helped my little girl open her shop with reasonable rates and assistance from their bankers. Very thoughtful people."

Helga asked, "Is it possible for us to convene again tomorrow afternoon? We need to discuss exactly what and who we want to invest in, how much we want to start off with and develop the infrastructure to manage, monitor, and grow the businesses, if you're so interested."

# # #

The following afternoon, Alfredo and Gabriella arrived at Vincent and Helga's house and were greeted warmly by Helga. She hugged Alfredo and kissed both of his cheeks and surprisingly, she did the same thing to Gabriella. Helga announced, "I've come to grips with my pregnancy and I will stop tormenting my husband who loves me so dearly. Listen, guys, you need to know a little about me and Vincent."

After obtaining some water, Helga continued, "I am a former nun who was the concubine of the Holy Father, leader of the Roman Catholic Church. I have probably violated every commandment there is and some that have yet to be written. I met my husband in Annapolis, Maryland as I hailed an Uber. Needless to say, his charming smile and quiet demeanor captivated every cell in my body. I did not know at the time, that he was the man I was seeking to torture in order to discover information about a diamond mine in Australia, alleged to hold a trillion in product. In the interim, he had been a part of several unsuccessful attempts to terminate his parents and their clan in order to secure a trillion in bearer bonds. In addition, it is estimated that his parents and their clan have amassed assets in excess of a trillion dollars. Wait a minute, I know you have a ton of questions but let me finish my catharsis."

Helga paused, consumed some water, and said, "So, in essence we're talking about a total of 3 trillion that we've tried to fetch. In addition, I am the only individual in the world who has access to my former employer's fortune that's in excess of $300 million. If he attempts to withdraw or transfer funds from the accounts that he has, a secondary code is needed and that's where I come in and the new code is forwarded to a restricted number that I alone have. Okay, one last thing, I bring an estimated $85 million to the table and Vincent adds another $9 million. *It's all about the trillions!* Now, the floor is open for questions and I'm sure that because you people are very smart, we're going to be here all afternoon and into the evening.

Gabriella went right for the jugular and asked, "Am I to assume that in street language, you two are crooks who are on the lam? Am I correct?"

Helga replied, "That's a little harsh but warranted. I obtained my money by essentially syphoning off the top of my ex-employer's ill-gotten funds. He sold his soul to mobsters, crooked business owners and I took from him. What I didn't know was that he had two other accounts totaling $425 million that the mob paid him for information and absolution. We're coming clean because we want you to know who we are, but we definitely don't want you involved in our personal affairs. The people hunting us will stop at nothing to find out where we are and I'm sure there is a massive reward for information leading to our capture. I mean, I'm thinking at least $15 million. The only problem is that when we do business, we also contract with the most ruthless hit men in the world."

After a moment of silence, Vincent remarked, "The one thing that I learned from the parents that I tried to assassinate, is that you have to help people help themselves. Alfredo has been dedicated and transparent in our dealings. I learned a lot about the man when I volunteered to help out at his daughter's pizzeria. I saw a struggling business with a lot of heart and soul involved. Now don't get me wrong, the pie I had was excellent. I mean not many places can accommodate my toppings. I mean, I had artichokes, pepperoni, mushrooms, ground beef, anchovies, chicken, salami, sausage, bacon, and it was all fresh. Unfortunately, I smell my food before I bite into it, after a couple of food-poisoning episodes, that's the first thing I do. Anyway, we can help you people expand, hire more locals, create more pizzerias, and put that crooked ass Piero and his father on a path of the straight and narrow. Now, that's where we should begin our conversation, if in fact you can get past the fact that people all over the world are looking for us. All we're going to do is invest in people, good people and some who pretend to be bad people who can be redirected to a new path."

Helga from left field asked, "Gabriella, what's your annual salary?"

Caught off guard, Gabriella replied, "In dollars, I make about $35k per year."

Helga looked at Alfredo and asked, "Alfredo, what's your take home salary at the end of the year?"

Alfredo replied, "I make a little over $50k. It's enough to take care of my family and live a simple life."

Helga smiled, after running numbers through her head she said, "Gabriella, with that law degree of yours I assume you know a little bit about business, is that correct?"

Gabriella replied, "My undergraduate work was in Business Administration, so I have a theoretical framework to guide me."

Helga said, "That's exactly what you have is a set of guiding principles that require you to mix your knowledge base with all of your life's experiences. Okay, I don't want to drag this thing out, we'll pay $125k to you Alfredo and $110k to you Gariella, of course in US dollars to put everything in place, non-profit status, for-profit angles, create an office, hire a financial advisor on a retainer, and begin to develop the corporations. Alfredo will be the president, and you will report to him. He is our guy. Vincent and I will be silent partners, only brought in to discuss complicated arrangements or relate to people who are not living up to their commitment to help people help themselves."

Gabriella inquired, "Where did that help people help themselves notion come from?"

Vincent replied, "There was this 6'8" Black Baptist preacher by the name of Leon H. Sullivan who started a worldwide movement to provide job training, education, and a thing he called the feeder program. My parents believed in his message because he lived what he preached. Anyway, when you have time, google Leon Howard Sullivan."

Helga announced, "Guys, we're not going to be resident here. After we set you up, we're out of here, without your knowledge thus diminishing your complicity and awareness of our whereabouts. By the way, we will contact our associates in Northern Africa and set up an account to deal with any individual or group that insists on you telling them where we are."

Vincent said, "So, Gabriella and Alfredo your first chore tomorrow is to open a bank account in your name as the signatory for the H & V Corporation, that you will set up according to Spanish law."

Vincent smiled and asked, "What do you think baby?"

Helga replied, "I like it, honey." Helga broke out into laughter and exclaimed, "I love it! Helga walked over to Vincent and whispered, "Let's drop $2 million and see if they go crazy and buy luxurious shit that means nothing." Vincent kissed her dearly and replied, "Excellent idea."

Helga announced, "This relationship is being constructed based upon two over-arching principles and they are trust and fidelity. No games, no hustles, no fancy cars, and/or other ostentatious trappings. Keep on the down low and we'll continue to watch you convert crooks into law abiding citizens and make the city of Valencia the capital of new innovations. Think big my friends, invest in little people with ideas, watch them grow, and help people help themselves."

CHAPTER THIRTY-FIVE

At their airport in Maryland, the group with their fanny packs boarded their plane. Larry and the clan's external associates had developed identification models for Kenzo that included a state ID, birth certificate, passport, social security number, a savings account, debit card, and credit card. From what they had discerned about his history, everything was in play except his signature. Larry felt that it had to be original. He said to Kenzo, "You're going to sign your name on the signature line on this computer screen and like magic, you're going to have a credit card, debit car, social security number, savings account, birth certificate, and a state ID."

Kenzo asked, "How can that be? I've only been in banks to rob them, and I don't have my social security card or any of those other documents. Those people have all of my papers."

Larry laughed and said, "Welcome to the new way of doing business in the world. This is all legal and the only hold up for your creating documents digitally, as well as allowing our pilots to take off, is your signing the screen."

Kenzo asked, "Is there a special pen or something that I have to use?"

Larry replied, "On second thought, let's practice your signature."

Kenzo wrote his name as if he were writing a paragraph or something. Larry casually asked, "Have you ever signed your name on a document before?"

Kenzo replied, "I don't think so."

Larry gently asked, "Do you know how to write in a cursive format?"

Kenzo asked, "What is that. What you see is my signature."

Larry responded, "No, what I see is the spelling of your name that could be written by anyone. Your signature needs to be indicative of you; bold, aggressive or whatever."

Kenzo looked at his name, studied it for a few seconds, and then made a capitol "K" tied to a small "k" slanting.

He asked, "Will this do?"

Larry examined it and asked, "Are you happy with it and can you repeat it every time you sign something?"

Kenzo signed his name ten times until Larry said, "Okay, I believe this is what you want your signature to look like. Now, here is the hard part. When you get to customs, they will probably ask you a series of questions. Just tell the truth, which is that this is your first time traveling to Australia and that you're with the Beckmire clan. Don't become creative, just answer the questions truthfully and if there is a problem, yell loud for Mr. Beckmire."

As Kenzo approached the exit door of the lounge, an alarm went off and he was moved to the side. As the local staff scanned him, a definite spot on his back called for attention. Larry asked, "Are you wearing a bug?"

Kenzo replied, "Why would I wear a bug, I don't even like them."

Larry shook his head and asked Kenzo to remove his jacket and shirt. As everyone else entered the plane, Rashida returned to the lounge after hearing the alarm and asked, "When you were in that other camp, did they like, vaccinate you?"

Kenzo replied, "Every year they said we needed new shots.

Rashida smiled, scanned his back, and announced, "This is like a vaccination, it's going to burn a little, but you'll never need another one again. Rashida turned the knob on her contraption to maximum and scanned it across Kenzo's back. She massaged the area of the implant, cut her unit on again and scanned his back again. A green light started flashing, indicating that the implant was incapacitated.

Kenzo after seeing the plane, asked Larry, "Is this like a Delta or United airplane?"

Larry replied, "No, Kenzo, this is our private plane, piloted by our own crew, and this airport belongs to us.

Kenzo remarked, "Wow!"

As a result of the alarm going off, Larry stated, "I must warn you that once this plane takes off and lands safely in the Outback you should tell the truth because there are spirits there that will read you like a book and if there is a problem, you will be fed to the Great Saltie."

Kenzo stated, "That's the fourth time that you've mentioned that name. What or who is the Great Saltie?"

Larry laughed loudly and responded, "I can better show you if the powers that be will allow me, rather than try to explain that anomaly. Listen, all will be known if you're pure, in good time. Where we're heading is as special as one of your wildest dreams. All things are possible."

# # #

Kenzo, halfway through the flight, woke Larry up and asked if there would be food provided. Larry got out of his seat and walked Kenzo back to the galley. He showed him how to use it and at that very moment, Ms. Beatrice entered the galley and introduced herself again to Kenzo. She offered her hand and he reluctantly accepted it. This would be the second time that he would shake a woman's hand. Holding his hand for a few seconds, Ms. Beatrice announced, "You're going to love your new world." She turned and walked away.

Kenzo stated, "I met her at the farm?"

Larry responded, "That's Mr. Chake's daughter. You'll see and learn more about her once we land. Okay, you understand how to work these machines now?"

Kenzo stated, "I think so. Sorry to wake you, boss."

Larry cautioned him and said, "I'm not your boss. We are a group. Learn to work with everyone and not be stuck on who you think controls your actions. In the Outback, it's you and nature, my friend. You'll learn and it will recondition that slave mentality of yours. If you have any other questions, just wake me up."

# # #

As usual, the captain planned to refuel the plane in Sydney. Kenzo looking out of the window, said aloud, "Oh my goodness. Look out the window." Everyone had seen the sight before, but some joined in with him realizing that some moments, although old, are not guaranteed.

In the gift shop, Kenzo said to Larry, "If you spot me $40, I'll give you an extra 10 hours of work."

Larry looked at him and said, "I'm going to lend you $100 and you'll not owe me a single hour. When we sign you up for work in the mines, you will earn your pay and then you can pay me back."

Kenzo responded, "You keep talking about working in the mines. What exactly are you referring to?"

Larry responded, "Just like I told you about the Great Saltie, I'm referring to the mines, because you'll have to do a stint in them until we are sure you're on the right side of the road."

Kenzo asked, "What's on the left side?"

After boarding the plane, Marcelus walked up to Kenzo and asked, "Are you a bad guy who wants to be a good guy?"

Courtney chided, "Young man, that is not how you greet people. You should have said, "Hi, I'm Marcelus, who are you?" Kenzo smiled and kept walking to his seat. Feeling a bit more at ease, he began to touch the various buttons and watch as his seat moved to a full-length bed position. He kept saying wow, at every new adventure he was having with his seat.

When they arrived in the Outback, Kenzo asked Larry if they were staying in a hotel and Larry told him that they lived in huts while here. Kenzo asked, "Now, that's why you need vaccinations to keep the bugs away."

Larry laughed and said, "In time my friend, all will be made known to you."

Driving the bus was the almighty and old spirit himself. He welcomed everyone with a smile and a kind word until Kenzo appeared before him. He asked, "Where did they rescue you from?"

Kenzo, not knowing who Wajickee was stepped back to respond but thankfully, Larry interceded by replying, "Wajickee, as you are aware, we believe in giving people a second and a third chance. Please welcome Kenzo to your village and we will immediately have him do sweat equity in the mines, if that is approved by you."

Wajickee looked hard at Kenzo and said, "You're going to do well here my son. You have a lot to learn, and I will make sure you are exposed to the wonders of the Outback."

Ben Beckmire and family appeared and Ben said, "My dear friend, it has been a long time since we've seen each other. I would like to meet you soon by the billabong that houses my ancestors. Marcelus, say high to Uncle Wajickee."

Marcelus looked at him and shyly uttered the word "hi" and walked away.

Wajickee remarked, "All is well here. Your nephew and his crew have that mining thing down to a science, including shipping, accounting, security, and management. However, many eyes have appeared on that property that Ms. Doctor purchased for your other son. As you know, she randomly selected that property in hopes that your family would be reconciled and he would have a place to grow old."

Once in the village, Courtney appeared with Marcelus and Wajickee descended to his knees as the child viewed him from behind his mother. Courtney said, "Marcelus, I want you to meet once again, your father's oldest friend in the world. He is special, friendly, kind and he loves children. Please go and shake his hand like your dad showed you."

Marcelus slowly came from behind his mother and said, "Hi, I am Marcelus, what's your name?"

Wajickee smiled and replied, "I am called Wajickee. Nice to meet and see you again."

Marcelus asked, "Is this your home?"

Wajickee responded, "No, this is everyone's home including yours. I have been waiting to see you again and now, if you would like to take a walk around the village with me, I'll show you some amazing animals, plants, natives, and mountain ranges."

Marcelus asked, "What is a native?"

Everyone laughed and Wajickee responded, "They are the people who look and dress like me."

Marcelus smiled and asked, "When can we take a walk?"

# # #

At dinner, Wajickee appeared and asked Ben Beckmire to accompany him to the billabong that housed the Great Saltie. At this point in time, it was more like a cocktail party prior to dinner. Ben kissed Marcelus on the head and started to walk toward Wajickee. Marcelus said, "Dad, I want to go with you!" Ben Beckmire motioned for him to come. As the threesome started their journey towards the billabong, Kenzo was standing in hearing distance and Wajickee stated, "I will talk with you soon. Do not try to follow."

Kenzo went directly to Larry and asked, "Why is that guy held in high regards? I mean, he tells Mr. Beckmire to come with him, and Mr. Beckmire complies without missing a beat. Who is that guy?"

Larry asked, "Did he tell you that he would talk to you soon? Okay, then wait until the moment happens and then you'll have another two hundred questions. I told you this place was special and that you would have a lot of questions, my friend. Just wait until you're summoned."

At the billabong, Marcelus said, "Dad, look at all those lights in the water."

Wajickee spoke up, "Marcelus, those aren't lights my friend, those are the eyes of your dad's relatives."

Marcelus looked at Wajickee with an incredulous expression on his face and asked, "Are you trying to fool me?"

Ben Beckmire said, "Son, your uncle Wajickee will explain all that there is to know since he told you that they were relatives and you know most of your relatives, your uncles, your aunts, and cousins. Those eyes in the water are another kind of relative that you have that over time you will come to understand, appreciate, respect, and know that their domain is a sacred one—one that should not be breached, unless you're invited."

Marcelus inquired, "Dad, what does that word mean? Uncle Wajickee, can you help me understand what Dad means?"

Wajickee began to fumble with his words until there was a significant roar from the billabong and all of the lights or eyes began to disappear. Ben and Wajickee knew that it was the Great Saltie about to make an appearance.

At the water's edge the world's largest and oldest saltwater crocodile appeared. As if in a trance Marcelus made his way to where the Great Saltie rested and asked, "Are you a relative of mine?" Within a millisecond, a giant snake-like tongue exited the crocs mouth and gently slapped the back of Marcelus's leg and disappeared back into the billabong. Marcelus began to cry and said, "My relative didn't like me."

Ben Beckmire made his way to his son and began to comfort him. He said, "Son, that was the Great Saltie, your great-great-great-great-great, grandfather. It's a long story, but over time, I'll explain everything to you."

The Great Saltie appeared once again but this time it flung a pouch onto the shore. Wajickee picked it up, opened it, and said to Marcelus, "Your relative has just presented you with a gift of love and friendship." In the pouch there was a rare stone that would signify Marcelus's importance in carrying on the work of the clan.

Back in the village, Marcelus approached his mom and said, "Look what my relative in the water gave me."

He showed Courtney the stone and she replied, "That uncle must love you a lot to give you such a gift."

Marcelus replied, "You and Dad love me a lot because you always give me gifts." Courtney hugged him and began to cry.

# # #

Ms. Beatrice sat quietly around the fire until she saw the Sarge, Wajickee and Marcelus. She said to the Sarge, "When I was in the dining room in Virginia, as you recall, I touched Marcelus on the shoulder and quickly withdrew my hand. As my friend Wajickee will attest, Marcelus is with entitlement. We will discuss soon, but until we confirm his sway, let us keep this between the three of us."

Wajickee replied, "I knew from day one, but like you Ms. Beatrice, your direction had to be self-decided."

The Sarge said, "People, I need my son to be left out of that world of mystics and kept in the realm of just a child."

Wajickee responded, "If it were up to me, then so be it. However, Ms. Beatrice will become his mentor and therefore, all will be good within the Beckmire village.

## CHAPTER THIRTY-SIX

The one thing that seemed to work in Vincent and Helga's favor was the banking system. Vincent and Helga easily transferred $1 million each to the new entity. After filling out all of the necessary forms and as the two were exiting the bank, Gabriella asked Alfredo, "Did we just open bank accounts and deposit $2 million US, and we are the sole signatories on the account?"

Alfredo laughed and replied, "Indeed we did and more importantly, we aligned ourselves with people of questionable character, who are apparently looking for absolution for all of the hurtful things that they have done in the past. The question becomes, did we just sell ourselves to the devil?"

As Alfredo and Gabriella drove towards his daughter's pizzeria, "He asked, "What's our first order of business as you see it?"

Gabriella smiled and replied, "I am as lost as you are. However, we need to find a place to set up shop, install phones, copiers, internet and define our business model. As I see it there are two arms to this arrangement. The first is that our benefactors want to invest in social programs that strengthens communities and families. To me that means, below market-rate loans to people who the banks completely ignore, unless there is property involved as collateral, affordable health care, senior projects, and security for all. The second arm will be dedicated to growing, expanding, and securing neighborhood businesses. To manage both of these activities, we will need qualified local staff who can learn and grow while taking on the role of advisors for our companies. In order to begin to think strategically about what's next, we have to finish incorporating both entities under separate accounts. I mean the laws governing non-profits are totally different from those that govern limited liability companies. Now, those are two things that I can do ASAP. However, we need to elect officers for both organizations. You will be President of both entities, and I'll be the Chief Executive Officer."

Alfredo quickly stated, "I don't know how to be a president of a company."

Gabriella replied, "You'll have to start reading what successful businessmen and women do to achieve their goals. Remember, this is our first rodeo and Vincent and Helga expect us to learn on the job, make mistakes, but always be able to know what we did incorrectly and not repeat stupid."

Alfredo after considering the tasks, announced, "I don't think I'm qualified for this opportunity. I think there are other aspects of developing both divisions that I might be helpful in but as president I don't think so."

Gabriella looked hard at him and asked, "Did you develop the implementation and operational plans for your daughter's pizzeria? It is no different my friend and plus, all we want to do is to make sure that we make smart decisions about finances, characters, likelihood of a payback and to develop a board of directors for each corporation. I mean, it's not hard to tell Ms. Agamond that we can't fund her plans to launch a rocket ship to Mars. It's common sense and what we don't know, we hire the right help to help us to make informed business-based decisions. She laughed and said, "The last time I looked, I was making less than $40k per year. How about you Alfredo?"

Alfredo smiled and said, "This is huge and we got to do this right or not at all. After laughing loud and long, he muttered, "I think we have hit the jackpot, but we have to stay conscious and cautious of who our benefactors are and what potential direct or indirect liability this relationship may warrant for us."

Gabriella responded, "We should discuss those matters further with them and see if they foresee any short-term issues. They don't seem like people who have done some of the things that they confess to, but you never know. It would be smart to begin board development for help with some of the things that we don't know. Our board may have an opinion or know how to accomplish some of the tasks. I think we should stipend the board a fixed amount just to assist in transportation and other expenses."

# # #

A few days later, Gabriella and Alfredo made their way to the flat that Vincent and Helga leased. When they entered, they saw that they had packed their few belongings and were preparing to leave. Helga asked, "So, people, tell me what have you completed in your list of things to do?"

Alfredo smiled and said, "Me and the CEO opened bank accounts, with the intent of splitting the endowment into a not-for-profit arm and a for profit one. I must admit, I wasn't too enthused about becoming the president until my young friend here reminded me of exactly what we're supposed to do and that is to help people help themselves. In doing that, we're supposed to seek out assistance and help in areas that we are not familiar with and surround ourselves with people who can make a difference in the lives of the people we can touch."

Vincent exclaimed, "Whew!"

Helga announced, "My friends most of what you say is ambiguous and is in concert with what our expectations are. We want you to try to figure out how to help people help themselves and there is no written script for that. Honey, what do you think?"

Vincent replied, "I think all of you are out of your minds and that is what is needed to achieve an ambiguous goal."

Helga paused for a few seconds and said, "I think we should have quarterly progress meetings. What are your feelings about that?"

Alfredo looked at Gabriella who nodded in the affirmative and replied, "I think that is a good timetable. However, I would like to have the ability to contact you if in fact we are challenged in any manner whatsoever."

Vincent responded, "That is exactly what we would want you to do. And remember, this is a test situation because we want you guys to try to improve the existence of everyone in Spain. I know your next question is, what about the funding? The answer to that is we will work through the Valencia equation first and then we will meet to discuss strategic expansion."

Gabriella noted, "It looks as if you people are moving on. Is that a correct observation?"

Helga responded, "How perceptive you are. We should plan scheduled zoom meetings as well as talk by telephone. However, back to the quarterly meetings, we just expect to hear what you have accomplished, your wish list, what are the projections for the return on capital, are the problems with existing investments, problematic investments and frankly, your failures. Quite different in perspective and in response. Listen, don't do stupid, get a third and unfamiliar opinion when relating to family, and just be honest and truthful and we'll have fun helping people help themselves."

Vincent asked Alfredo, "Do you think you can give us a ride to the airport in about an hour?"

Alfredo responded, "Absolutely and I won't ask where you're going because I don't want to know in case someone comes trying to pry information out of me that I don't have."

Helga laughed and asked, "Perhaps little Ms. Gabriella can accompany us as well. Is that possible?"

Gabriella responded, "I'll be in the car with Alfredo."

# # #

As the group was heading for the airport, Vincent remarked, "You guys know that you can pocket that money and perhaps no one will ever challenge you. Just saying."

A serious looking Gabriella responded, "In life nothing is easy and most of us have to work hard to achieve a modicum of success. I see this opportunity as a gift from God and as such, it will be respected and managed in an acceptable manner. No personal gain is in play here; we're just trying to make sure that we don't disappoint you guys in any manner. Therefore, as I see it, the only failure that may happen is in our management of the funds and our being either overly ambitious or too cautious, in failing to execute in a manner that you would expect."

Helga replied, "Once you have your parameters established—I mean the fundamentals of what you're trying to accomplish—in my estimation, you're a bank competing with other banks to give the community the best possible and reasonable rate. Again, you're not going to invest in some hare-brained scheme to land on Venus or Jupiter. No, you're going to help rebuild your community and add value to the existing homes and businesses, which will in turn create a desirable place to live, and courts outside funding for more projects and expansion. Listen, you're going to find situations where there is no payback and that is when you should show your strength by providing cost-free support to those who can't pay for repairs or remodeling. For this first year, tell us what we should be doing, show us how we can do better with perhaps more financing and how we can assure the community that their homes will remain in their families hopefully forever. We want to help people help themselves and not have them find themselves in a position where the banks are smelling repossession. Also, those funds should be used to attract local monies to spur growth in Valencia and our organization. Partnering is key to success, in my opinion. Hopefully, you'll force the banks to partner with you and our project."

Gabriella asked, "Why are you doing this, and why here and now?"

Helga replied, "Why not here and now? Listen our first gift will be followed by others as soon as we find a safe place to be and to try to live life to the fullest. We both know that there are some bad hombres seeking us to unlock money that was stolen from the people or earned on the people's souls as a result of addictions and drug dealings. However, that's our problem. The funds you have received are ours and ours alone. Now, there is something that is swirling around in my head that I haven't talked to Vincent about yet. Vincent, do you mind if I propose another critical role for our two new trusted friends and allies?"

Vincent replied, "Helga we have 40 or so minutes and the more information we present in person the better our friends will feel about proceeding down this road."

Helga looked at Gabriella and announced, "This is extremely personal. As you know, I am pregnant at this ripe old age and if something were to happen to me and Vincent, I would like to know that there are some guardian angels who are looking out for our child. Therefore, I'm going to need you to open up another account that is restricted in nature and set aside for the express use of my child's development, education, well-being, security, and future. Now, one relationship is not dependent upon the other and therefore, you have the right to reject this request."

Gabriella responded, "Helga, you're a trip and one that I can learn a lot from. Of course, we will accept that responsibility and put into place future clauses so that the entitlements are without question. I will begin seeking the necessary help to set up an impenetrable will and trust for your child."

Helga began to cry and announced, "I like you, lady, please stay true to all the commitments you have signed on to and Alfredo, I need you to help guide her in all of the legal vaults she's going to have to open. By the time Vincent and I get to our next destination, we will have an opening amount for our child's account. We will have a second installment to act as an endowment for the other two accounts so that the interest payments earned will help guide the ship and that will also support the various business models that we're trying to influence that don't necessarily fall into the helping people help themselves category, but will give us an alternate source of financing. Once again, you guys have to use what you have to leverage funds to help offset all of your expenses.

Vincent stated, "Hey guys, we have to go. However, at some point we will have a percentage that will directly benefit our child from the various business ventures that you engage in the profit side. We'll be in touch and I will send you an emergency number if you need to reach us. Don't try to do us a favor and get hurt if the wrong people show up asking questions. Tell them the truth and the truth is, you don't know where we're off to."

Vincent pulled his hoodie over his head and placed his sunglasses on. He instructed Alfredo and Gabriella to remain in the vehicle. Helga gave each a pretended long-distance kiss and exited the vehicle.

# # #

After watching Alfredo and Gabriella drive off, the two walked out of the terminal and caught a cab to the international lounge. Once in the terminal, they proceeded to Qantas Airlines gate. Prior to heading to the desk, Helga said, "Here is the deal. I have us booked in business class traveling to Sydney, Australia. I didn't tell you because I didn't want a soul to know that we're heading to the place where you may

have a child and where I have an old lover who happens to be
your stepbrother and two children. Who on earth would look
for us there, knowing the web of deceit that represents the
past?"

Vincent looked at her and asked, "Why do you say I may
have a child there as well?"

Helga paused for a few moments and then asked, "Do you
think that your parents would let any blood relative live in an
orphanage or even worse, be adopted by some strangers? No,
sir! Those folks of yours are as dedicated to your fuckups as
they are probably to wishing that you aren't supposed to be
dead. Think about it. Your mom sent you money even though
your dad knew that you were trying to kill them. How fucked
up is that? Don't answer, all I'm saying is that somewhere on
that vast continent, there is a haven for us and our child. Let's
hope we never run into them or need their help if the wrong
people come looking for us."

Vincent responded, "Helga, the only thing I know and
care about is you and our child. I'm happy that you have that
devious mind that considers all correlations and decides upon
the least probable place for us to be looked for. Oh, and by the
way, we have the deed to a diamond mine in the Northern
Territory. Perhaps we should consider having Alfredo and
Gabriella come here as our agents to make sure that the
paperwork is in fact in place and that there is no one visiting it
in the night and enjoying our profits."

Vincent recalling a message from his mother that stated
that the mine had to be excavated to the probable depths of 50
to a 100 yards, looked at Helga and noted, "I don't think we
have to worry about people digging on the property because
what I was once told was that it needed deep excavating."

Helga replied, "Honey, let's be sure we're on the same page. I don't plan on living in a desolate area where animals roam freely and there are no emergency services such as banking, shopping, grocery stores, hair and nail salons or indoor restaurants. Honey, we ain't going to do no Australian version of *Alaska, 'Zero Below'*."

Vincent began to laugh and responded, "Although you're on the right path, consider the benefits of low-country living, where you don't have all of those luxuries and people tend to live in isolation. Not a bad idea, but one that I'm not interested in either."

Helga continued, "Vincent, let's get to Australia first and then see what life unfolds for us. I've left breadcrumbs all over the world, in hopes that people will spend an enormous amount of time trying to find my shadow in some place that has reported a sighting of me. I do hope you've not made any calls of significance to people indicating where you are and what you're doing."

Vincent responded, "At the Academy, getting lost was a two-semester course. I didn't leave crumbs, a scent, or anything. I just drove to Florida with a woman who I fell immediately in love with, and I've never looked in the rear-view mirror since."

## CHAPTER THIRTY-SEVEN

Wajickee asked Ben Beckmire if he could have a moment with, he and Dr. Courtney, and he responded, "Of course."

Wajickee thought about his request and then modified it and asked, "Could all of the Beckmire's join him at the billabong?"

Once at the billabong, Wajickee looked at Courtney, Asiram, Ben, Zanthius, Larry, Rashida, and all of their children. He asked the locals to take the children for a small walk, but in eyesight of their parents.

Ben Beckmire asked, "So, my mysterious friend, you have us all here, now might be the time to tell us what has been troubling you."

Zanthius said, "Dad, you're not supposed to ask a mystic a question until he tells you a story. By doing so, he may decide to hold this event on another day."

Wajickee who was running his hands through the water announced, "Thank you Zanthius, and you're right, I can delay this meeting until the moon is full again, according to customs. However, I won't."

Wajickee looked deep into the billabong, turned around slowly, and said, "My dearest friends and family, I've been having a series of conflicting reveries and manifestations of late. They are all concerned about a member of the Beckmire clan. In some, I see a woman, not you Asiram holding little Ben Jr., and cuddling him. I also see this same woman hugging Jelani in my dreams. Courtney, I also see a man gather up Marcelus and give him unconditional love and affection, the kind a child receives from a parent after a long separation. Each day, these visions become more distinct, visually clear, and emotionally discombobulating. Some, Zanthius, say you executed Helga Spengatsenburg aka. Sister Mary. Some, Mr. & Mrs. Sarge, say your distracted child was fed to the fish. Some say a lot of things, but I'm saying I'm having accelerated visions of people who are supposed to be dead!"

the end

also in the 'idiot spy' series

Available at Amazon and BarnesandNoble.com

www.ingramcontent.com/pod-product-compliance
Lightning Source LLC
Chambersburg PA
CBHW030803260626
47169CB00001B/168